Mr. Jack and the Greenstalks

A Novel by GENE HOROWITZ

Mr. Jack
and the Greenstalks

W · W · NORTON & COMPANY · INC · New York

for Carol Houck Smith, editor, friend

Contents

Part One

The Last of the Solid Gold Eggs

Chapter One

"If I didn't tell you before, Phil, now you'll know once and for all. My whole life it's by one motto. Everyone should only live and be well. Live and let live. To me, it's the only way."

"What way, Morris?" Philip Hanssler had, until that moment, been on his way up front, to the showroom. He stopped because Morris Trebnitz held his arm. These days Morris was always holding on to someone or something.

"What do you mean 'what way'? I just said it. Everyone should live and be well. Like a son I look on you, Philly. Like a son I love you. So I'm telling you you shouldn't go up front to A.F. and complain. Promise me that one thing. You should only live and let live. You should do your designing and you should let everyone else do his job. That's not sensible?"

"Morris, you're a good production man." Phil undid Morris's squeezing hand from his arm. "But you're a lousy philosopher, sweetheart. What's to worry about? Things can't get worse around here, can they?"

"Nu! I suppose not." Morris followed Phil down the narrow corridor that led from the design room past the duplicate makers' room on one side and Lincoln's shipping desk on the other. Now it was Link's turn to stop Phil. He set a pile of corrugated boxes down, smiling deferentially as he did so, his ginger skin creased along old familiar lines.

"What are you doing, Link? First it's Morris, and now you're setting up roadblocks. What the hell's going on here?"

"He's waiting for you in the showroom and you know he's waitin' on something important. I been with him long enough to know that expression on his face."

"So? What's your advice?" Phil sighed. "I might as well hear everyone's philosophy."

"I ain't got no philosophy. I ain't paid enough for philosophy. Just don't want you to go messing with A.F. He's in a bad way already." Link raised his head toward the ceiling, embarrassed by the tears that had sprung into his eyes.

"You're too big to cry, Link, and I'm too short to mess with anyone, including A.F. I'm only the designer around here, that's all. I don't own a thing. Not even myself." He pushed his shirt sleeves higher into a crush of Oxford blue that held above the elbows. "It'd be a good idea if I did own something, though. None of this would be happening. I can assure you of that."

Lincoln sat down at his desk, let his hand rest in the wicker reorder tray. There were no requests in it.

Again Phil shrugged Morris's hand from his arm. "Don't you have anything better to do, Mr. T?"

"Sure I got. Morris Trebnitz always got what to do. But the question I'm asking is whether it's smart to do it. I got garments, plenty garments your room finished, to make duplicates for the road salesmen. Only the question I'm asking is if those salesmen will ever go on the road." Once more Morris reached out to stop Phil. They had moved from the corridor into the square of desk space outside the two offices: Alex Fleiss's large one; Robert Fleiss's cubicle. Marsha Katz, the once respected bookkeeper-goddess and now the entire office staff of Mr. Jack, pointed a finger of warning at the door to the showroom. "In there," she whispered. "Both of them. Be kind, Philly."

"You too?" Phil touched the brass knob of the showroom door, frowned at Morris. "Do me a big favor, please. Just let me talk to them and then I'll tell you all you need to know. Go to the men's room. Take a crap. Relax. Read the paper. Do anything. Only don't follow me around. Don't you think I know what I'm doing? You think I want the business to fold? You think I want to be out of a job? At this time of year? In April?" Phil pinched Morris's sweat-shiny jowl. "Don't worry, Morris, because when I see you're not smiling my ulcer starts ulcering. So smile, Morris, smile."

"You know, Philly"—his face did break into a strained smile—"I love you like you was my own son."

"Yes, Papa darling. That I know." Phil scratched his jutting chin to show Morris he wasn't going to leap into battle. Much more than Morris and Lincoln, infinitely more than Marsha Katz, he dreaded what might happen when he stepped into the showroom to speak with Alex Fleiss.

12

For four years he had been dreading this moment. From the very first week he had started working at Mr. Jack the signs of downhill, baby, were obvious in every corner of the place, especially in the clothes the former designer was doing: price clothes; copies; meaningless for a prestige label. So he had been hired to design Fleiss-Jack, Inc., out of the red, which he thought he could do. But, if he had followed his friends' advice, if he had paid attention to the Dun & Bradstreet report that his own father had gotten on the company in 1961, he wouldn't be locked into this predicament right now. Even so, he was glad that he had done what he did. *He* wasn't in trouble; Mr. Jack was. And no one on the Avenue could really blame *him* for that.

"At sixty-four I couldn't retire already? Of course I could." Bubbles of saliva were collecting at the corners of Morris's rapidly moving mouth. "But who wants to! Not me, sonny boy. I'm what you call a *shtarker*. Hard work agrees with me. All my life I worked hard. I got a good reputation as a worker. I'm proud that wherever I worked I gave each boss my best. All my bosses liked me. Here too. I did *my* job. A.F. says that. You did yours. So who's to blame? Not me!" He thumped his chest. "Not you!" He poked at Phil's disheveled shirt. "So tell me then. What happened to Mr. Jack?"

"I don't know, Morris. Lots of things. It's too complicated for now."

Morris raised his arm, let it slap heavily against his leg. "*Nu!* All right. Go. What'll be will be. Dot, mine fine sir, is life. If we close, I'll sit home in Brooklyn and watch my wife play canasta with her lady friends and I'll play pinochle with mine." He turned away, his straining smile fading fast. "Or I'll get another job." He leaned against Marsha Katz's desk. She raised her head, nodded consolingly. She understood Morris better. Of course she did. On Seventh Avenue a worthwhile bookkeeper is supposed to understand everything and everyone better. That was one of the commandments of the garment center: Honor thy bookkeeper. Phil had learned that lesson a long time ago. And, apart from that, how could he, at thirty-five, really know how a man of sixty-four feels about something, an era, a job, coming to an end? Unless the man was your own father. And even that was hard. Everywhere he went since becoming a full-fledged designer, there were always older people crowding around him ready to be his father. A crazy thing what these Jewish men will do to find a son everywhere. Phil didn't have it, that thing, that drive to be a father to someone. Unless, of course, owning your own business on Seventh Avenue, becoming a manufacturer, automatically cast you in the role. That's the only kind of father he'd ever be. The father of a business. That *thing*, that *shtik*, that bag he did have. It was the next logical step: the Father Superior of Phil Hanssler, Inc.

The showroom was a morgue when he stepped inside, but anyway he corrected the droop of his shoulders, flexed his muscles, readied a seductive smile that, until now, had never failed to win support for any cause he wanted to advance. Even if you haven't got confidence, make it seem like you do. Phil had been told often enough that the one thing he wasn't was a loser. As far as he knew, he didn't have an enemy in the world. Not yet. The closest to that category was his designer friend—a real pal—Monsieur Aram LeGeis, né Aaron Siegel. The thought of Aaron brought on a real winner's-circle smile.

Which he needed! To face the dirty beige carpeting. To stop and straighten the tangled summer samples hanging on a rack in the aisle between the rows of empty buyers' booths. To move around the boomerang curve of the room to where A. F. and Robert were waiting. To where the staff of Mr. Jack—the three road salesmen, the two showroom girls, the two head showroom salesmen, Michael Morgan and Andrew Berns—were busy doing nothing but smoking nervously—plenty of unnecessary overhead right there—the smoke spiraling above their tense bodies.

When he saw Phil, A. F. nodded at the group. They stood up, filed past him, silently moving to the other side of the showroom and into Andrew's small office. Phil's laughter was cautious, was meant to buoy their sinking spirits. He did feel sorry for them all. What special talent did any one of them have to fall back on if things went from bad to worse? Nothing. Anybody could be a salesman on Seventh Avenue if he dressed sharp enough, if he had good white teeth. But to be an Alexander Fleiss, that took something extra. Close to near disaster as he was, A. F. nevertheless had a smile ready for Phil, who sat down then, received the inevitable arm behind his neck, let himself be rocked back and forth as if A. F. were urging him to pray along with Mitch at the Wailing Wall. Another one of his fathers! Phil tried to disengage himself gently. It was embarrassing, this affection, especially in front of Robert, blond, pudding-face Robert, gray-mohair-suited Robert. A.F. should treat his real son half as good as he treated Phil. But his own son was twice Phil's size and blubbery, going to fat too soon. Too big to cuddle or chuck under the chin. Anyway, those demonstrations were reserved for designers. After all, designers were queer, weren't they? They understood men touching men, men kissing men, men sleeping together. "Mr. Fleiss." Phil leaned back, folded his arms across his chest. "I'm glad you called this meeting. We needed to sit down . . ."

"It's not a meeting, Phil. It's a talk. That's all it is. Talking." With elaborate, determined effort he lit a fresh cigarette from the one that had burned down in his water-filter holder, ejected the stub of the Salem into a Mr. Jack ashtray, inserted the new one. But the trembling fingers, the tremor of his tanned, well-oiled head told the truer story, not the words he spoke. "From now on you'll buy fewer sample cuts. You've got enough sample fabric already to open a new company. You'll use some of it up. You'll economize a little. You'll tell your girls to stop telephoning so much. We're running up telephone bills as big as the Pentagon. You'll have to stop using a fitting model. She charges too much, that Cindy. And she's getting too fat anyway. Also, you'll have to forget about the raise I promised you. For a while only. Until we get back on our feet. You'll have to . . ."

"Mr. Fleiss!" Phil had to stop that flow of panic. Robert winced, the pale face forced into a brief moment of animation. No one ever interrupted A. F., except Phil. Phil always did these days. It was the only way to point out to his boss what needed to be pointed out. A.F. wasn't talking to some shipping clerk or salesman. Phil had a contract, a contract that promised certain things. Every worthwhile designer had a contract that promised certain things. Mr. Fleiss understood.

"All right, Phil. So I'll admit it. Only to you I'll admit it. We're in trouble. Serious trouble."

"That I know. I've known it for a long time. Everyone's known it but you. The question is finally whether the trouble can be solved or not." Phil slumped forward onto the beige formica table, looked up consolingly at Robert. Poor Robert who always meant well. That was the source of the trouble: Robert. Not all of it, but a big chunk of it. "Look, A. F. I'm well into work on the fall line. Morris needs to know about making duplicates for the road salesmen. As far as they're concerned, they don't give a shit. They'll drop us and get other accounts. Sure you'll tell me they're loyal. But you know what loyalty's worth on the open market? Not a thing!"

"Loyalty's worth everything. I've always tried to build up loyalty. Right from the beginning. Mr. Jack isn't one of those Broadway *shlock* outfits. It's a class business. With personality. When we started out we had class first of all. That counts, Phil, just as much today as it always did. I can remember . . ."

Alex Fleiss was off and running at Hialeah. Phil sat up, sighed his loudest sigh of the day, but the words kept coming anyway. Every important discussion at Mr. Jack ended with an A. F. monologue, a remembrance of things past, a lament over the dead body of his young, carefree, golden-egg days when everyone in 498 Seventh Avenue knew who Alexander Fleiss was. He wasn't just a manufacturer—Phil nodded, grinned; A. F.'s words had just coincided with his own thought—". . . because I was trying to do more than just make money. Making money was the easiest part if you had brains. In those days . . ."

"In those days"! Shit! Piss! That phrase was the one they should string across Seventh Avenue instead of the United Jewish Appeal banner that was always there, in rain, in sleet, in snow, during Market Week, during slump seasons. It should even be on the masthead of *Women's Wear Daily*. The "In Those Days" A. F. was talking about for the umpteenth time were the same as those Phil's first boss-father, Carl Kalb, always talked about, the same every other boss meant, the same his own father meant when he launched a sad *boruch ataw Adonai* for the way the piece-goods business used to be. And it was all so fucking simple! A two-year-old baby could understand it: those lousy days were gone forever, replaced by other lousy days; those days were the ones before, during, and after the Second World War, when a manufacturer didn't even have to hire a designer to design a dress. All he needed was to get his hands on a piece of fabric, any *shmatte*, have a seamstress sew up two side seams, and toss the garment into the stores. Women bought anything then. They had money. Everyone did. And men like Alexander Fleiss, Carl Kalb, all of them, thought they were brilliant businessmen, the chosen ones. All geniuses. They ran their opportunity into ten-million-dollar operations and they called that brains, know-how, class, style, any word that came into their semi-educated, money-blurred minds. And now, today, April, 1966, Vietnam notwithstanding, there they sat, dreaming, while the walls of the past were crumbling around them. For Christ's sake!

"You see this suit, Phil? This suit that I'm wearing today?" Robert reached across the table to touch the material, but his father flicked him away, waited for Phil to feel it. Okay! So I felt it! "This is the same-style suit with the same-quality fabric I wore in those days. Exactly the same. Two-button roll. I've had hundreds of them. A plain glen plaid. With blue in it. Modest. In good taste. The same blue silk tie to go with it. Every day. Hundreds of the same tie. And why? Why did I do that? I'll tell you why. I did it because I was building an image. An image I was going to live up to. Dependable. Honest. Steady. An image to maintain for a long time. For a lifetime. And I did. When I go into the elevator today everyone knows me. I'm proud of that. I'm proud of what I accomplished. The only thing I'm not proud of," he jabbed his cigarette holder at Robert's averted face, "is what my son here did to it all. How my stupid son ruined a ten-million-dollar business, how he pissed it away, how he . . ."

"Come on, Dad. Please."

Even that had been said too often for anyone to hear it any more, except Robert. "Look, Mr. Fleiss, what Robert did or did not do isn't the issue right now."

"Sure it's the issue, Philly. It's exactly the issue. Would we be sitting here right now if it weren't for his mistakes?"

"Yes." Phil spoke so quietly that A. F. paid no attention. Nor would he, ever. He couldn't. If he did agree, who could he blame for his troubles? Phil? Never happen!

"If I had a son like you, then it would all be different."

A. F. draped his arm behind Phil's neck, rocked him, kissed his cheek wetly. Everyone kissed Phil's cheek. Of course. Because Phil Hanssler still looked like a beautiful little baby, cute and cuddly. Who could believe he was thirty-five? Not even himself. Once more he removed the arm from his back. Damn it! He didn't want to hurt A. F., but neither did he want to hurt Robert. Robert meant well. A little thick in the head. But well-intentioned. Robert looked the other way, toward his father's office, turning the other cheek, enduring what he had to endure.

"For a change, Mr. Fleiss, we're not getting anywhere. And we don't need any more nostalgia. Let's try and be practical for a minute. We're living in 1966, remember. But I *do* understand how it used to be. It *used to be* in every walk of life, but used to be is not now. In my sample room I've got four sample hands left out of the eight I used to have. Good ladies. Every one of them. Great workers. I've got a finisher who's more like a mother to me than my own. I've got an assistant—the best in the business. I've got a girl Friday that works like a horse. Every Wednesday all those people have to be paid. I've got to put dresses into work for them to work on so you'll have a fall line to sell. I've got to buy fabric for them to make the dresses from. I've got to get fabric for Morris to make duplicate dresses from. I've got to do all that . . . or not! One or the other. Either I keep on working or I don't. Either you have the money to stay open or you don't. And is it worthwhile for you to try to stay open and get deeper in debt? It's a decision only you can make!"

Alex Fleiss was crying quietly. So was Robert. Only Phil wasn't. He wasn't about to cry either. Sympathy? Yes! Understanding? Yes! But tears? Absolutely not! Never! Not for this! There were too many other more important things in his life to worry about, too many more important years ahead of him to fill up with some kind of success. He hadn't come as far as he had so he could sit in the showroom of Mr. Jack and cry about the way it was, about how sad it was that it wasn't that way any more. Damn it! Sure he pitied A.F. Sure he realized that in the four years he'd been at Mr. Jack the man had gone to pieces. But it wasn't Phil's fault. When he signed his first contract, the one thing that made him willing to forget everyone's pessimistic advice *was* Alex Fleiss. A. F. *was* a class manufacturer compared to some of the others. He wasn't a big shot. He wasn't greedy. He gave extra to everyone when he had it to give. More than the union said he had to. A bonus here, a bonus there. And if Mr. Jack made the slightest bit of profit during a season, he gave it away, without a thought. Even Marsha, the guardian bookkeeper, had to remind him of the facts. Phil himself had heard her say to him hundreds of times, "You keep this up, A. F., and the books'll always be in red Technicolor." And, when he gave to others, he treated himself right too. Only now it was different. Now when he gave it was his wife's he gave, his wife's he was losing. She had plenty, A. F. told everyone. Don't worry, he said. Her family owns Christmas-tree-ornament companies. There'll always be Christmas.

So Phil waited now for an answer, knowing what, logically, the answer should be.

And, as if to help his father avoid making a decision, as if in that way he could atone for his mistakes, get his father to love him a little bit, Robert began to speak. A.F. blew his nose loudly into one of his imported silk handkerchiefs. "It's not as simple as you make it out to be, Phil. It's very complex. You can't make that kind of decision so easily. First of all . . ."

"What do you know about decisions?" Mr. Fleiss waved his handkerchief at his son's face.

Out of habit, Robert flinched and, just as much out of habit, went on talking in circles. "First of all, there are the factors to consider. Those men have to be paid back first in order to borrow more. So far they have no complaints. My father's hocking my mother's jewelry to pay them, and to pay us as well."

"That's not Phil's concern, so shut up!" Mr. Fleiss stood suddenly, buttoned his two-button roll glen plaid. He always kept it buttoned when he stood up. Robert and Phil followed him around the curve of the showroom to the rack containing the summer line, waited behind him while he lovingly touched each garment, nodding yes, it seemed, to each printed cotton, each linen, each voile. "I don't understand it, Phil. These are good clothes. At the showing the buyers loved them. They told me so." He touched his jacket buttons, patted his hidden paunch, surprised to find it still there now that he was standing. His head moved slowly from side to side. The mysteries of Seventh Avenue, the vagaries of fortune and misfortune were beyond his, beyond anyone's reason. And yet he continued the debate; a silent speaker spoke to him. "They applauded. Remember, Phil? Remember you did a funny commentary? Remember you told your mother to stand up to show the buyers who shouldn't wear Mr. Jack clothes. You remember, don't you?"

"I remember, A. F."

"So what happened?"

"It's slow all over right now, Dad."

"You shut up!" Mr. Fleiss regained his anger instantly. "What do you know about this business? What did you ever know? You should have been an accountant. Why didn't you become an accountant? That's a simple question. Answer it!"

Wearily, Robert moved off to one of the booths.

"Mr. Fleiss, the buyers don't buy our clothes for a number of good reasons. And, let's face it, the styling's not to blame. They see the sample dress in the showing. It looks like a million dollars—my girls make a fabulous garment. But when the stock gets into the stores it looks like shit. And why? Because to save money you substitute lousy fabric. You take the guts out of the dress. The fit gets ruined. Customers won't touch them. Since you hired Morris, the product *has* gotten better. I admit it. But the buyers can't take chances. They have to meet *their* figures too. They have to sell clothes." Phil touched A. F.'s sleeve to steady him, to comfort him. "There was a time when they *had* to buy Mr. Jack. When the company was the leading junior dress resource. When the customers went into the stores and asked for Mr. Jack clothes. But not any more. Not at the price you ask. Not the garments you're giving them."

"Morris is going to change all that. He promised me."

"Sure he's trying. But how can he change it? Be realistic, A. F. Our union setup is against us. The buyers are against us. Not us personally, but against the product. The markup you need to keep us floating is against us. I can't turn out a price garment—"

"The markup! That's his fault." Mr. Fleiss pointed a trembling finger at his son. "He's the one made me go into a knit division. And what happened? It failed. Everyone else makes millions in knits. But not us. Thousands of dollars spent on the wrong colors. Then it's missy clothes he wants. Higher-price clothes. To get us out of the red. And that fails. He hires a rotten designer. The only thing that succeeds at all is what you do, Phil. And now even that's failing." He buried his head in a crush of print voile dresses—one group that was selling—sobbing now. "If only you had come here sooner, Phil, we could have grossed even more than we used to after the war." He looked down at Phil, tears glistening on his oily cheeks, and then, suddenly excited by a fugitive illusion, the kind that raced through his and every manufacturer's heart, he rallied. "What we need to do . . . what you need to design is a quick transition line. Early fall clothes. Get the clothes made and into the stores early. Get reorders on five, maybe ten dresses."

"That's exactly what I'm trying to do. A back-to-school group. Only you'll have to get your salesmen off their asses. If they don't go out and get the buyers up here, nothing's going to work."

"They will. That I'll see to personally."

So, once more the final solution, the big decision, was postponed. "You really are something, A. F."

"All I know how to do is keep trying. And this time I'm going to plan right. You'll see. I'll talk to the factors. I'll get an extension on the loans. I'll talk to my *other* son. My *smart* son. *Joe*." He yelled the name. Robert studied the crease of his gray mohair trousers. "On Sunday I'll see Joe. He's having a party at his house in Westchester. Maybe even . . . Listen, Phil, maybe you'll come up there. Maybe you can talk to Joe. You can convince him to help. Come, Phil. Sunday. Bring that girl friend of yours. Bring all your friends. I'll call Joe. He won't mind. You'll have drinks and dinner. You'll talk to Joe. All right? You'll come, Philly?" Mr. Fleiss kissed Phil's cheek, hugged him tightly. A father's kiss. A father's hug. A father's pleading, and Phil gave in.

"All right. I'll come. But this time we really will talk seriously. No reminiscing, remember."

"No. Absolutely not. A promise." Smiling, A. F. went off toward his office. Robert stood up, shrugged his shoulders, sat down again. Slowly the salesmen filed back out of Andrew Berns's office, smiling tentatively, inquiringly. Once more they had gotten past a crisis, but it had to be a temporary calm. Stopgap. Phil knew it. Why the hell did he let himself get trapped into Sunday? Damn it! It's impossible to go on designing good dresses that won't sell. It's impossible for A. F. to go on hocking his wife's jewels. "Okay, kids," Phil shouted to the reassembled staff at the other end of the showroom, "we're still in business. For today, that is." Defiantly, his stubby fingers rested along his wide hip-hugger belt. "And you people are going to have to help a little. To do more than smoke cigarettes." No answer, only the scratching pop of matches being struck.

Phil's fingers dropped from the belt. He stared over at the rapidly sinking shape of Robert, glum, beaten Robert, and then up to the plaque on the far wall, the plaque that held the symbol of Mr. Jack, the symbol that appeared on every label, on every advertisement the company ever placed during those years when there was lots of money available to place them. Those hot years before Phil appeared on this scene. *Harper's Bazaar,* *Vogue, Mademoiselle, Glamour,* the *New York Times,* even *Life* and *Look.* The ads were always in. Everyone in America knew Mr. Jack. And that was it! Phil admitted it, mostly to himself, sometimes to a friend, never to his family, that that was his reason for working here; he thought that image on the plaque, that symbol, that damn logo could never fail: a faceless silhouette of a woman's curving figure, and in her outstretched slender fingers the label, with Mr. Jack, in elegant script, superimposed across a faceless silhouette of a woman's curving figure and in her outstretched slender fingers the label. A label within a label within a label— how could it ever fail! A good, old idea, one that worked for so long. Jack Farbstein's idea. Jack Farbstein, once A. F.'s partner, long since departed to Broadway, bought out, but waiting for the chance to get his name back —Mr. Jack—along with his ashtrays, pencils, gold logo pins, balloons, stationery, matchbook covers, all of it marked with his blood. Mr. Jack: a faceless silhouette of a woman's curving figure and in her outstretched slender fingers a label. . . ."Shit!"

Robert jumped. Phil made his way out of the showroom, passed Marsha, her plump fortyish face exploding with puffs of pleasure, passed Link, who patted him on the back. Phil's design room was the only sane, safe spot in the entire organization. That's where he wanted to be. Up front is where they institutionalize you. He was a long, long way from being ready for that.

Cindy Rubin always arrived late for fittings, but once she got there, she worked her ass off. If you are thirty-three and a model, you have to have special qualities to stay with it. By that age the waist has begun to spread, the breasts to sag. But Cindy had extras, and so, as long as she kept her size 7, Phil would put up with her being late. For one thing, she could undress—didn't matter how many people were in the room—change her brassière faster than the fastest gun in the West. And she was clean. Never smelled, even when she was having a period. She always wiped her armpits with Kleenex, sprayed herself with perfume before she would step into a garment. Those were plusses, plusses to cherish, those and the fact that she spoke up about the clothes she put on. If she didn't like the idea of a dress, she told you why. Most models never said a word one way or another. Some of them couldn't talk. They weren't paid $20 an hour for fittings, $40 and $50 an hour for showings to have lifelike opinions about anything. Cindy did. And not just opinions, but convictions. When she worked, she was a star, a pro, and temperamental. She would claw any assistant designer, any seamstress, who stuck her with a pin. But her most important extra was that she had no distinctive look. She tried to have one. She redid her exotic Jewish nose, cut her hair Sassoon short, darkened it, whitened her makeup, but no matter what she did she ended up becoming whatever dress she put on. Phil valued that—he could really *see* the dress he had designed—more than he hated her chronic lateness or the fact that during a fitting she was umbilically connected to her answering service. A telephone cradled between bent head and soft shoulder kept her plugged in to the real world beyond Seventh Avenue, at the expense of Mr. Jack. But, like any with-it girl, Cindy just had to provide for her own perhaps husbandless future—she had been through number one early on; now she slept around for fun—by conducting a small-scale, but growing interior-decorating business. A thirty-three-year-old divorced Jewish model with convictions about what *good* taste is and with contacts in the trade succeeds. She doesn't sit around waiting for telephones to ring. She calls out.

"Cindy, you really are a ball buster! Didn't I scream at you yesterday to be on time? I've got a lunch date at one. It's now twelve-thirty. Ginny's gone out—I can't fit the clothes without her. The girls are into their yogurt. You were supposed to be here at eleven. Do you remember that?"

"I just couldn't get here a minute earlier, Phil. Honestly. I had a meeting with a client. . . . I did get that account, Pat."

Patricia Pearson, Phil's new design starlet, clapped her hands. "You didn't! That's fabulous city!" Finished clapping, she rushed her fingers through the tumble of long chestnut hair. Pat Pearson looked like a beautiful lioness. Phil's first impression when he hired her fresh from Parsons School of Design was that she was all hair; her face was barely visible. She stalked people tenaciously, but she wasn't built like a killer. She just enjoyed looking the part. "How will you do it, Cin? Lots of color? Imagine! A museum entrance in Deal, New Jersey. That's absolutely gloriola."

"Knock it off. Both of you." Phil sat down at his desk, brushed pins, sketch paper, fashion magazines, *Women's Wear Daily* onto the floor. "It wouldn't hurt if you cleaned this desk off once in a while, Miss Neat One."

"I did clean it. This very morning." Pat bent to retrieve what interested her.

"Never mind that now. How the hell did she get that telephone. I thought I hid it. Damn it, Cindy! I'd appreciate it if you would leave your decorating crap for *your* free time."

"Scowl. Harrumph. Grrr." Pat moved behind Phil, massaged his neck. "Boss man angry today, Cindy. So watch out. He beautiful when angry, but dangerous."

Phil lowered his head to the desk. His anger was a joke for the people he liked and they knew it. How could a man who looked like a little boy be angry? That's what they said to him. That's the way they treated him. He *was* still a boy at heart and until now that's the way he played it. So far it had worked. If you're born with certain equipment, you might as well use it. If you're fortunate enough to have a body that's wide at the shoulders, that tapers to a narrow waist, use it—he leaned up into Pat's strong fingers; Cindy was still on the telephone anyway—and wear suppressed jackets and hip-huggers and bell-bottom trousers to hide your thin ankles. Thin ankles. Short legs. His two bad features, but both of them coverable, except during the summer tanning months.

"I think I can be there at four. Hold on. . . . You want me back later, Phil?" Gracefully, like a fall of chiffon, Cindy's dark hair spilled over the telephone. Phil nodded, held up three fingers. "Make it four-thirty. And please have the lamps ready for me to look at. I've got a wallpaper appointment at five."

"Phil, love," Pat rested her head on his, "I must tell you once again that if you were just a head taller I'd be your slave for life. Absolutely would. No questions asked. No holds barred. A total slavey." She straightened, still massaging. "Your shoulder muscles just turn me on. And that face! It's the very same Greek face that launched a thousand ships. I just know it is. I've seen all those statues. I've read all the books. There's absolutely no gainsaying it."

"I'm going to lunch." Phil stood abruptly, his energy restored, finger-combed his silky thin hair at the models' full-length mirror, stuffed his shirt back into his short-crotch pants, smiled at his reflection. "Yes, I suppose I could have been a movie star. In the old days. I should have been. Only I'm nine feet too small." He tap-danced away from the mirror. "Fill Cinderella in on the A. F. meeting if she ever gets off the telephone. Go to lunch. Come back and sketch. Do something to earn your money, Patricia. I'll be back at two-thirty. . . . This jacket's too tight!" A black-and-white houndstooth, at least five years old. "I must get some new clothes. I'm such a *schlump*."

This time Phil avoided Morris's grabbing hand at the door. "Talk to Pat. She loves you." He raced down the corridor, thinking of fresh air.

The entrance of 498 Seventh Avenue during lunch hour, if the day is sunny—Phil had forgotten it was—is like what a mosque is to a Moslem when the muezzin calls him to prayer. Not that there was ever going to be a Moslem on Seventh Avenue. Who would allow it? The tribes, the lost tribes, were gathered on either side of the revolving doors. The tailors, old Italian and Jewish men, shortened, even shorter than Phil, by a mysterious process of natural selection dating back to an antique time when tailors sat cross-legged on Persian pillows, needled the air with thin fingers and whined as if the air were a boss and they were getting revenge by sticking him. The production men, artists of a second order, circled near the curb, leaned against the illegally parked trucks, smoking cigars. Pattern makers, precision men, nervously peered down at their shoes, whispered while they pushed bits of debris away. Feh! Dirt! Waste! Cutters waved their arms in wide arcs, lifted them toward the sky, yelling, always ready to fling out a bolt of good crepe or silk or velvet, God—and a healthy cutting ticket—willing.

The April breeze was strong enough to flap the U.J.A. banner strung out across the avenue. The bright sun held warmth and Phil had time to linger at the entranceway, to melt his depression a little before the next onslaught. More than anything else that happened on Seventh Avenue, the people happening made him savor his career. They burst out of buildings, congregated, whispering shreds of gossip, moved haphazardly across the street to Dubrow's cafeteria, zigzagging in and out of the unpredictable paths of tarpaulin-covered rolling racks—"Keep them covered, the racks; you want someone should copy and knock off a style before it's in a store already?"—Those rolling racks! Pushed by thick-muscled Negroes or lean, tight-dungareed Puerto Ricans. For vengeance! The occupational hazard of life on this street. A rolling rack was a weapon. The pushers wanted the enemy's blood. Mr. Goldstein was their enemy. Yid-talking Mr. Goldstein better be on his toes, better be careful every second he shows his face, especially at corners where the curb sends the racks out of control, where trucks and cars, turned impatiently into double-parked side streets, fart posion gas, accelerate pointlessly, screech to a sudden stop, stopped by a solid ribbon of stalled crosstown traffic. Go. Stop. Go.

You had to learn agility on Seventh Avenue if you wanted to survive upstairs in the showrooms, downstairs on the sidewalk. You had to learn how to drink an egg cream at the corner candy counter at Thirty-sixth Street—window open to the weather in winter, spring, summer, fall—to wolf down a chocolate-sprinkled marshmallow cookie, three cents each, to swallow a frank with kraut in two bites while the racks rolled, grazing your legs, while the trucks turned corners as if they planned to go right through the store. And all the time you had to worry with a smile, to down your egg cream before the foam settled flatly, to belch loudly, to cradle, if you were a salesman, your sample case, your treasure chest of buttons, belts, buckles, embroidery, zippers, fabrics, before racing on to your next appointment. How long can a simple man stay in the race? How long before the first heart attack?

Only the designers and the silver-suited salesmen and manufacturers had time to loll in the sun. The silver-suiters! Indomitable in their armor: glistening $250 mohair suits from Mannie Walker, clothier to Seventh Avenue's finest. The racks kept their distance from the silver-suiters. The cutters, pattern makers, tailors, sample hands kept their distance from the racks and the silver-suiters. The models didn't. They sidled past, brushed the armor indifferently, vinyl raincoats—they're in this season—flashing in the sun, silk babushkas tied tightly beneath their pale, mask faces like tourniquets cutting the blood supply to their heads. No wonder some of them are so dumb. You have to have blood to think with.

Phil plunged his hands deep inside his jacket pockets. This whole thing's some kind of circus, a fairyland, a nutcracker world complete with phantoms dreaming *Women's Wear Daily* dreams. *Women's Wear!* The trade paper! The Bible! The Who's Who of what's ready-to-wear! The record of the fashion industry stars for the receptionists and bookkeepers, the stylists, the salesmen and the silver-suiters, the designers and their assistants. "Who was quoted today? . . . When's Norell showing? . . . You think we could maybe copy the Galanos sketch that's in today's paper? For 19.75? . . . Never! . . . Sure we could. He's using eight-ply crepe. So we'll use rayon acetate. They'll never know, the buyers. What do they know? It's an easy knock-off garment I tell you. . . . Forget it. Let's go to Lou G. Siegel's for a corned beef. . . ."

And more. The young salesmen starting out, aspiring, neatly nose-bobbed, man-tanned, but with cheaper suits and smaller paunches. Elbow pushers, model escorts, disturbing the order on the sidewalk, breaking into and through the circling tailors, the ancients, the product of a mysterious process, the chorus on Seventh Avenue. "What are they? They! Punks! *Gornisht!* Not so much as a fly! All they know is to be fancy-schmancy. Like the designers. Let me tell you, if my designer knew how many dresses I saved for him, how much I cut the cost of the garment by doing it *my* way instead of *his* sketch—well, what's the use of talking! They all think they know better." "Shah! Not so loud. That's one there," needle finger pointing at Phil. "So who's he with?" "Mr. Jack." "Mr. Jack's? They're finished anyway. It's a rumor in *Women's Wear* yesterday. I seen it with my own two eyes."

Phil shoved off, broke right through the mumbling group, headed north past Mannie Walker's at Thirty-seventh Street, past 512, 530, 550. Not too much loitering in front of the better buildings. It wasn't chic to stand around where Norell and Donald Brooks and Tiffeau lived. With a frozen smile Phil quickened his pace, greeted a clump of fabric salesmen he knew. He always walked faster past those buildings. He was in transit upward, sure, but it looked like it was going to be a longer while than he had ever planned before he got to where he was going.

At any rate, at least, he had arrived at the door to Ted's, a restaurant across from the hole in the ground that once was the Metropolitan Opera House.

Ted's was the current spot for young designers with pizzazz to be for lunch. Their pictures were hung on the walls: a certain inducement for them to eat there for a few months, at least. Before the pictures went up on the walls—there was one of Phil on the back wall—designers of forty-five and beyond, those who made lots of money working for old established companies but who never expected, didn't care any more for name credit on a label or a percentage of the profits, were the steady patrons. Now both groups coexisted, drank, usually at separate tables, through their long lunch hours. By definition and not by temperament, Sanford

26

White, Sandy, belonged to the latter group. But Phil and he had bridged the generation gap years before. Sandy knew Phil's real age. "I got here early because I like to drink my first few alone. But of course you know that. I've had just two Beefeaters and my vitamin pill so I'm set up fine, baby. Even got this perfect table. Sweeping view of the panorama." As if he were pointing out the pleasures of the Grand Canyon, Sandy's conscientiously chewed fingernails—the accompanying fingers, the whole hand served only to remind him of just how far down he could bite—indicated the bar opposite their banquette table. The serious eaters made for the intimate back booths hidden from the outside sunlight by a row of louvered partitions. "Don't you look beuatifully glum today. Is it over yet?"

Phil shook his head no to Sandy, nodded yes to the waiter. "A Scotch sour on the rocks. On the sour side . . . He's still hanging on. By his toenails, but he's hanging. When he slips you'll hear it loud and clear all over the Avenue. They had a rumor in the Eye yesterday."

"Saw it, but then I never believe what I read in the newspapers. Especially *Women's Wear*. According to them we've gone out of business fifteen times in the last year. And you know that's just not going to happen to Ann Topper, Incorporated." Between sips of his gin, Sandy nibbled his nails. "Of course in your case I hope the rumor's true. The longer you stay there, the harder it's going to be for you to come out smelling like roses. . . . Ah! Here's your drink, Phil. Sip it now. Don't gulp. That's a good boy. Smile. Yes. Like that. The orange is good for you. Beautiful. That's my good little boy. Now Mama's happy." Sandy ordered another gin.

The bar filled up rapidly after one o'clock. The stools, the bodies on them, most of them trim, suits and accessories color coordinated, the faces tanned by sun lamp or St. Thomas, were twisted around to check the crowd. Everyone knew, or knew of, everyone else. The clientele was inbred like the Yale Club, but with unwritten rules and regulations. Sleeping partners were left alone to sigh behind the partitions; those who were obviously on the make were accorded squatters' rights at the bar; those like Sandy and Phil who wanted to eat, drink, and be miserable in full view were left alone. "All's right in heaven and hell. The congregation's arrived. Drink, Phil."

"I can't drink at your pace."

"I don't want you to. You're a fine Jewish lad. You're used to sweet red wine. By the by, how are the stepmother and father? The brothers?

27

The assorted wives? In good health, I trust?"

"Fine."

"Snap out of it, Philip. I need gaiety. News of the Rialto."

"You've come to the wrong man then. You should know *that* by now."

"The story of my life. I always go to the wrong man for the right reason."

"Let's not start that business, please. I'm not in the mood for it today." Sitting alongside Sandy this way, looking out on the passing scene, Phil always felt himself to be at a disadvantage. Sandy was totally tactile; touching was the way he demonstrated his friendship and touching, in this kind of place, meant too much. Sandy knew that, knew that Phil didn't like being arm-held or chin-chucked in here and so, of course, did it as carelessly as he drank his Beefeaters on the rocks. That was their way together. After all, Sandy *was* a friend. *Just* a friend. An old friend, the one who had given Phil his first break on the Avenue. Having done that, Sandy had the right to tease and taunt, and Phil had the right to grow annoyed, then angry, then finally turn away guiltily. Sandy enjoyed that treatment, that reward for a game well played. A sex game. A kick. Open and aboveboard. Sandy never hid his preferences. Phil did, most of the time. Sandy performed best under bright lights. No dark-street cruising for him. His current kick was cultivating the acquaintance of black subway-change-booth cashiers. Tricky, he called it, but original. He was always poor in math. And in New York City there were enough subway stations to last a lifetime. At forty-three, a shock of camel's hair still spilled rakishly onto Sandy's forehead. His wax-works face wore a perpetual smile, but the skin, the often swollen features looked as though they had been carved out by the sharp knife of each new novel kick. He maintained that he liked his life just the way it was, and only his nails said he wasn't totally resigned. But his way was *his* way—no one else had to like it—and for most of the nine years Phil had known Sandy he had danced down his solitary path denying, with every step, the need for permanent or even semi-permanent partnerships. There had been moments of panic though, like at the beginning when he had tried to get Phil to bed. Not that that was ever a serious attempt. Sandy did it for fun. Teasing. Testing. Another kind of kick. Now all he wanted from Phil was his presence at a party or two, to show Phil off to his acquaintances. That was all. And Phil usually went. Why not? It was just another part of their game, another role for Phil to play for Sandy's benefit: the designer, a museum exhibit, who wasn't, or wasn't yet, gay. Some kind of freak. Watch him closely. Watch him move. Look for a sign. A giveaway. He's got to be lying. But Sandy, knowing all he knew about himself, knew better than to think that, to sum someone up too quickly. After all, Sandy knew Wilma, and knowing her, he also knew the hardest X sign to solve in Phil's algebra.

"I hear that your friend Aram's having another one of his gala showings in June."

"Let's order, Sandy, and skip Aram."

"Are you in a hurry? I wanted to linger a while."

"I've got fittings and a fabric appointment."

"Be late for once. Hold *them* up. Be temperamental. Learn how to be a star. I thought I was a better teacher than that."

"You're a great teacher. I'll have just one more drink. If I have too many I can't concentrate for the rest of the afternoon. How the hell can you go back to work after four gins?"

"Sometimes I don't. I have *other* diversions. I do my hard work in the mornings."

"That's why you are where you are. Talented and nowhere."

"Don't be cruel, Philip." Sandy lifted his drink, saluted Phil first and then the faces at the bar that had turned to stare. "Those sidelong glances are for you, of course. Such longing looks. They're certainly not for me. But since you steadfastly refuse to honor them, since you're so rude—only the beautiful can afford to be that rude—I must take up the slack. Noblesse oblige. Compromise with any principle you have, Philip, but don't compromise with admiration. Use it. Admirers count for more on the open market than any amount of talent. You, luckily, have both. Your friend Aram only has one: talent. When forced to I'll admit that much. But he doesn't have an admirer, not one."

"He does have a lover."

"Yes. That he does. Rich and old. But there isn't a buyer who'll support him when the chips are down. You, on the other hand . . ."

"I don't have a lover."

"What do you have, Philip?" Sandy was slipping into his Bette Davis sound: staccato, curt, world weary. Sometimes Phil thought Sandy maintained their friendship just so he could say the name when he got drunk enough.

"Talent. I have that. And ambition."

"But sexually, Philip? What do you really have sexually?"

"Fun. Don't you?"

"No. But I don't value fun. Excitement, yes, but not fun."

"Let's change the subject." Phil turned away, dared to scan the bar, recognized the eyes scanning him, gazed sharply toward the daylit street, letting the eating, talking, silverware sounds of the restaurant slide past hearing. Somehow, drinking at lunch, when you could see the sun, felt like a monstrous sin, almost as sinful as going to a movie on a Saturday afternoon when he was a kid. In Teaneck, New Jersey, every kid went to the movies on Saturday afternoons, except Phil. He went in the evenings, with or without permission. His stepmother screamed about it, about why he couldn't behave like the others, about why he couldn't do what he was supposed to do. And, when she had finished screaming at Phil, getting no other response but a smile, she would turn on Phil's father. "Your son! Your rotten son! See how he treats me! And the other one's the same. They're both rotten. Only mine behaves." Phil's father, always slow to anger, seemed to listen, to accept the verdict, to nod, and only when, finally, she lowered herself over his chair, blocking the light from his *Bergen Record*, was he forced to react, his scream matching hers, moving her back, surprising her as much as himself. And, once they were at each other, Phil left the house quietly, unnoticed. Week after week of the same screams, and the picture, the sound of those repeated scenes of what he thought then were his victories, lingered in his memory as dim funny-bone sensations of loss, sensations that rose and receded at surprising moments like when he thought he was drinking too much at lunch.

"Philip, you're not paying attention. I had to send the waiter away. What's wrong with you today?"

"Nothing new. Just impatience." The Scotch of his two sours, the events of the morning were eating away at the knot of control that Phil imagined had to be there inside himself; otherwise, long before now, he would have, he should have, leapt up and away from a situation which he —there was no one else to blame—had let himself live with for too long. "If Fleiss would only give up and let me go . . . the timing is right for me. Every magazine editor I work with keeps telling me that. Now. The propitious moment."

"And I agree."

"But I've got a contract. I can't just leave in the middle of the season. Fleiss would sue me, no matter what he says."

"Phil, honey, you know designer contracts are worthless. They'd never stand up in a court of law. You just use that bit because you're afraid to move."

"Afraid?" Phil stared Sandy down and into a fury of nail biting.

"What have I got to be afraid about? I've got solid contacts. The buyers like me. And that's without paying them off, without wining and dining them. I design good clothes and the buyers know it."

"But what if you don't for a season or two? What then? It happens, love. It happened to me, God knows. The older you get the harder it is to have new ideas."

"New ideas? You've got to be kidding. There are no new ideas, only old ones made up to look new. With new fabrics. A future full of synthetics. And if you can stay one step ahead of which old idea the magazine girls and buyers are going to want redone, you're a success. That's all it takes. And enough money behind you. Some stock-market money. Some of that war money. The old-guard bosses like Fleiss are for the birds. The whole industry's changing but some of them are still trudging off to Paris twice a year to buy new styles when all the time right here in New York City they've got twenty better designers for every one of those French beauties. It's a joke, this business. A fantastic put-on. Not that any other business is any different. It's all a bunch of crap. You know it is."

"Yes, I do know it is. That's why I think I'll have another gin."

"Can't you talk seriously for a minute without a goddamn drink?" Phil forced Sandy's signaling hand back down to the table. Sandy stared back attentively. "I'm only trying to make sense out of something I already said was a joke. But the saddest joke of all is being played on us and the women we're supposedly designing clothes for. We all think we're tastemakers. Leaders of trends. Bullshit! The buyers lead us around. We lead the women around, by their hems. Raise them! Drop them! Get a whole new wardrobe! We're all crazy!"

"You're shouting, Philip."

"So what. A little honest noise in here wouldn't hurt. This restaurant's for the birds too, sweetheart." Phil stood up, placed a five-dollar bill on top of Sandy's glass. "I'm going back to the office."

Saluting Phil with his glass, Sandy stuffed the five dollars into the breast pocket of his blue jersey suit, waved languidly, happy that, if nothing else, he had brought on a state of siege. Battles were so much more interesting than rumors of peace.

At times like these a hot dog with sauerkraut, a root beer at the corner of Thirty-sixth and Seventh in the sunlight was the best medicine. No doctor would have said so, but Phil understood his sleeping ulcer better than his doctor. Anyway, every ulcer is different. Milk always made him sicker; tea soothed him. It wasn't supposed to, but it did. Raw carrots, tomatoes, green pepper, cabbage were on the poison list, but they did the trick for him faster than those baby foods one doctor told him to eat. And the ulcer was cured. For now, at least. Probably, it was giving up cigarettes that helped most of all. Three years now without a smoke. Just like that. No sweat. But what if he had to give up hot dogs and mustard and sauerkraut and pickles? Impossible. Not even if his life depended on it. Or if someone told him to give up designing and you'll never be sick another day in your life. He'd have to choose sickness. After all, you don't tell a singer to stop singing or a painter to stop painting. It's all the same.

"Phil? You're dreaming about a print, maybe?" A thin, short man with a gently fraying old-world look stepped out from the flow of walkers, settled his sample case between Phil and himself. "I'll knock it off for you. Cheap. Cheaper than anyone else."

"I don't do many prints, Koenig, but if I did I'd call you first." Phil gulped his root beer.

"I've got a beautiful line in this case. Can I come up this afternoon to show you?" Mr. Koenig removed his homburg, wiped his forehead with the palm of his hand. "Hot for April, no?"

"Hot for April, yes. So I'll need some fall woolens." Phil laughed. The salesman replaced his hat. "And you've got the best woolens in the market. I know that already so don't say it and waste your breath. I won't buy them. I'll buy anything from you that's not German."

"All right, Phil." Mr. Koenig raised his hand deferentially. "I'll never push. I respect your opinion. You told me how you feel. I understand. But if I, a Jew from Europe, am willing to sell the goods . . ."

"That's your problem, sweetheart, not mine. I've got my own." Phil spoke gently, as gently as that pale, thin face deserved. They had been through this exchange too many times for it to cause anger. Koenig was one of the few gentlemen in a trade that was noted for cut-throat competition. "But if you want to come up later to talk opera, come. That I'll be very happy to do."

"If I have time, I will. But for now," he lifted his case, "I've got a living to make. Goodbye, Phil." Quietly unnoticed, Mr. Koenig rejoined the walkers crisscrossing Thirty-sixth Street.

Phil moved off to the 498 entrance, sat on the gold sprinkler pump. A few more minutes of sun. A week of sun. In St. Thomas. El Perfecto. Just go upstairs and tell A. F., I'm off. Carry on without me. Like Sandy said.

And when he brought his beautiful tanned face back, he'd make his move, right out of the junior dress market into the higher-priced missy market where he belonged, where all his training had been. Why the hell had he let himself get stuck in the medium-price range anyway? Confess, Philip. Confess. Five hundred a week is why you got stuck. Mr. Jack was why you got stuck. A sucker for big things. Because you're short, as Wilma always said. And she was a sucker for small things. Because she was bigger. The great leveling-off process, love. Or its facsimile. And Howie? His bosom buddy Howie? His intellectual advisor. What did Howie always say? He said too much. About everything. And especially to Wilma. Because, for Howie, the process, the leveling-off process wouldn't work properly.

Phil rubbed his eyes, stood up, leaned against the dirty gray concrete façade, folded his arms high up across his chest, straining the seams of his houndstooth jacket, dizzied himself with the sight of the revolving door that never seemed to stop turning. . . . Maybe I should go back into Broadway. Do summer stock. Be a gypsy . . . One of his showing models, Nancy Harris of the alabaster skin, waved her wicker tote bag at him, slowing the doors purposely, glided up to the pump. After years on a runway she never walked like a human being.

"Philip. You trouble me." She kissed his forehead. "You look sad. Take me to Arthur tonight. I'll make you forget everything."

"Can't."

"You take Cindy places. You never take me anywhere. That hurts me, darling."

"Take two Anacin."

"Phil!" She stomped her Capezio sandals, laughing so that the alabaster skin creased at the corners of her pale-painted full lips. "You don't love me."

"No. I don't love anybody."

"What'll I do? And I've wasted all these years for nothing." Nancy pulled at a loose fringe of her jet-black Persian-lamb hair.

Phil shrugged.

"I'll die. But you'll call me to do the next showing, won't you?"

"If there is a next one."

"Somewhere there will be." One more kiss and she was gliding back into the crowd, but not lost in it, with that skin, that hair, a head taller than every tailor, duplicate maker, cutter, taller than every rolling rack.

. . . Or maybe I'll launch an opera career. A few more years and I'll be ready. Go to Europe. Audition in every German opera house. Be discovered. Return triumphantly to the new Metropolitan. Become the first singing designer in Seventh Avenue history. Open my own business on the strength of that. Sell out to one of the giants like Jonathan Logan. Make a mint. Retire at the age of forty-five, at the peak of my form. Like Garbo . . .

It's sunstroke is what's happening.

Phil lifted his arms toward the U.J.A. banner, let them fall heavily against his hip-huggers, his palms slapping. For a still moment every milling member of every tribe that belonged to 498 turned to look. Every glamorous—hoo ha—model *en passant* posed in tableau. Every bored out-of-town buyer raised clip boards for protection from a New York sniper. And during that same still moment Phil, satisfied, raced for the revolving doors.

The afternoon was no better than the morning had been. But Phil was. A little dreaming never hurt. Morris was in and out of the design room, flashing his smile of resigned gloom. No matter what Phil said about prospects, Morris knew the real truth. "Listen, my darling boy, I have lived through it before. Whether it's here or somewheres else, I know what I'm talking. But if you'll tell me, if A. F. will tell me, to do duplicates, I'll do. So is so."

"So do, Morris, do."

Pat Pearson, following orders, had sketched her way through an entire pad. Her small desk was littered with crumpled balls of tracing paper. "You've had calls of every description, Phil. Your *mère*. Followed by your *père*. You apparently must be home for Friday dinner. It sounded like a direct order from heaven. *Women's Wear* wants a quote about paper dresses and our rumored demise. I said never to that one. *Glamour* called and *Mademoiselle*. Monsieur LeGeis. Et cetera. Et cetera." Pat never looked up. She was deep inside her hair, still sketching.

In the sample workroom next door to his office, Phil's ladies were bent over their machines, sewing as if their lives, their futures at Mr. Jack depended on the speed used to finish a garment. Ginny Jackson was cutting her patterns, the shears sliding lovingly through precious sample cuts of fabric, stopping only to help her ladies with a new neckline shape or the kind of stitch to use for a tucked bodice or the correct fall from a shirred seam, ready, whenever Phil called, to drop everything, and able to return to her own work as if she had never been interrupted.

If Phil had to lose everything he owned in the design world, the one thing he would fight to salvage would be Ginny. A sample-room assistant, once the designing is done, is the one person who can make or break a collection. And no one knew better than Ginny how to transform a sketch into a dress, no one knew better how to trace a pattern, how to cut fabric to match the pattern perfectly and then give it over to a sample hand to baste up the pieces, how to guide it through a first fitting—with Ginny a first fitting was always enough—how to finish it up, finally, resetting a detail, a bow, a zipper, a pocket, so that the finished product, the sample, looked as if it had never been worked on, as if it had just happened. But that moment when the assistant's eye scans a sketch, seizes the idea, knows how to translate the idea into a pattern without distortion or fussiness, that's when, for Phil, working on Seventh Avenue offered up its greatest prize: a combination of creative effort whose yield was a private, quiet joy, like giving birth.

Ginny had been Phil's prize ever since his beginning at Carl Kalb's. By now he could sketch on a circle of paper no bigger than a half dollar and she understood what he wanted. Their eyes saw the same things. No husband and wife were in deeper daily communion. They didn't even have to pick their way through words; pictures told the entire story.

Whenever Phil walked into the sample room his gloom lifted for a while. Carmen Ruiz had her transistor tuned low to the Spanish station. Somehow she managed to sew in time to a cha-cha-cha, and when she rose from her machine to change a bobbin, she danced a few steps without ever losing a thread. Anita Mangiapane, big-bosomed Neeta, pulled the patterns under the clicking needle as if she was yelling at her son, the one that was forever in trouble with the sisters at the parochial school, but the garments she worked on never showed the strain. They ended up full of love, just as her son, hopefully, would. Evelyn Washington used an earplug for her transistor. She sat opposite Dorothy Krakauer and Dorothy couldn't stand gospel blues so Evelyn, from Mobile, Alabama, with a lifetime of experience in the art of compromising with whitey, accepted the earplug solution. She still had the music, which is all she wanted anyway. "Besides," Evelyn had told Phil, "Dottie's the nervous type. Been through those concentration camps and all. You just got to humor her." Phil doted on Evelyn. She smiled without having any reason in the world to smile. Why would anyone give her a hard time? Only Mildred Berkowitz did. Not intentionally, Mildred swore. "Black is as good with me as anything." She insisted that she did the same to everyone. If your job is to be the finisher, to clip threads from dresses, sew on special buttons, neaten a buttonhole, check on hem lengths, a person tends to get picky, and imperious Jewish blonde-mama Mildred, naturally blonde, was blondely imperious, always immaculately coiffed, her corner of the room near the steam pressing iron a triumph of will over limited space. She kept order over her pins, her buttons, thread, needles, zippers as if she had a whole ballroom to herself.

It had taken Phil and Ginny months when they moved over to Mr. Jack to organize their special kind of sample room, hiring and firing until the union got angry. Carmen Ruiz was the last one in, but she had worked out beautifully. And with Ginny there to direct traffic, to kiss and persuade Anita to go easy with the chiffon or to calm Dottie whenever she began to tremble over a hard garment, the room had functioned for almost four years without a major incident. As long as the work kept coming, they did it.

So naturally, watching them made Phil feel better. "Cindy will be here at three, lovely ladies." He hoisted himself onto Ginny's work table, sat down on a pattern. Instinctively her eyes widened with horror, as if someone had suddenly squashed a rose. But in the next instant she grinned, understanding Phil's way of stopping her work.

"Lovely ladies!" Phil had to yell to be heard. The machines stopped in unison. Evelyn removed her ear plug. Carmen palmed her transistor. Only Mildred continued to sew, but her piled blonde hair jiggled a nod so that Phil would know she was listening. "You've probably been hearing rumors on the Avenue—I heard them myself during lunch—about what's going on at Mr. Jack. And you're probably worrying about it. Well, honestly, so am I. But I'm still designing. You've still got garments to work on. So we're still in business. As of this morning Mr. Fleiss says we're okay." Phil slid from the work bench, grabbed Ginny, danced her toward Mildred's corner.

"Mr. Philip, I'm busy and you're dancing."

"So stop being busy and watch me dance."

"I got no time to stop being busy. Cindy'll come and you'll yell for the clothes and they won't be ready and then you won't dance so much."

"I'll always dance for you, Millie. All you have to do is ask me."

Mildred blushed, smiled, waved him away. "Oy, Mr. Phil."

The machines started up again, all except Dottie's. She motioned Phil over. "Is it really true what you said? At the union when I go to a meeting they're constantly asking me what's what." Dottie's lined face, made even handsomer by concern, twitched its distrust. If a person has lived through a concentration camp, words are no relief for fear.

"Don't worry, Dottie," he whispered, "even if we do close here, you'll work for me no matter where I go. I promise you that."

She readied herself for sewing. The lines around her mouth eased. They would always be there, but Phil had learned to read the difference in the way they were set. She had been with him since Carl Kalb's. She was the best worker in the room, the most intelligent, and the most neurotic. He tried to honor all three qualities, but it was never easy.

Back in his office, Phil sifted slowly through Pat's sketches. "Not bad. At least you're on the right track." He sat down opposite her at the desk, picked up the sketches once more, began to squint at them, focusing, trying to block out the sight of everything else, to measure the worth of what he saw against some numberless internal yardstick of rightness.

"They stink." Pat slammed her pencil down on the pad. "I know what you're after but I can't seem to make it work out. I just don't feel tents any more. I want some shape around the body."

"Not yet, sweetheart. Another season or two, but not at this juncture. Tents are in. Tents are what the buyers want, and the way this firm is right now tents are what we're going to have to do."

"But that's not right, Phil. You've got to design what you feel, don't you? I mean, if you have to do just what *they* want, what's the point?"

"My dear, you've got a lot to learn yet."

"I hate when you say that."

"I did too when a boss told me that. But he was right. I did have a lot to learn about this business. So do you. And I learned it even if I didn't like it." Phil picked up the sketch pad, turned it to a fresh page, smoothed down its silky translucence, back and forth, squinting at the emptiness. He reached for a Pentel, a red one that he enjoyed using these days—last month it had been green—poised it over the page while he nibbled his lower lip, waiting for some mysterious switch to go off inside, some hidden circuitry to mesh and light up an idea. He began to draw, starting, as he always did, with the head, the hair, an outline of a long face, while the idea grew inside his eye, his stubby hand tracing bold red lines, never stopping, moving down to form a neck, swanlike, curving the way a real neck never did, and then, suddenly, there was the silhouette of a dress, tucked seams over the bodice, the lines of the tucking moving in toward the waist, letting out there to form the shirred top of a free-swinging skirt. A tent and yet not a tent. The suggestion of a waist. Quickly, decisively he sketched in the sleeves, full length, two buttons on each French cuff. His wrist slid down the page to draw the legs: two wide swathes of red reaching to the bottom. "In gray flannel. Buff-colored satin for the cuffs. Great silver buttons. Over-stitching on the tucks with the thread showing. No darts." He ripped the page from the sketch pad, held it up, still squinting, waiting for the switch to go off. When it did, he leaned back in his chair. "You like?"

"Like is not the word. I'm absolutely devoted to it. Won't rest until it's on my back." Jumping up, Pat paced the small space between the desk and the full-length mirror, between the shelves of fabric. "If that dress doesn't go on the line, I quit. I absolutely quit." All the petulance had left her face, replaced by enthusiasm. And all because of one sketch.

"Not too chic?" Phil let the page float to his desk.

"How can anything be *too* chic? It's a Mr. Jack dress if ever I saw one."

"Wrong again, Patricia. It used to be, but Mr. Jack can't afford it any more. It's not safe enough. It won't have more than a limited sale. If we manufactured that style it would end up retailing for over seventy dollars. Mark my words well, sweet girl." His Pentel glided back over the sketch lines, retracing, emphasizing what he said. "See these seams, the tucks, the letouts, the shirring? Each one of them," he motioned her closer to the page, "each one is labor and labor costs. A.F. will tell me to make it simpler. Take out the tucks. Morris will grab for his heart. The salesmen will say *feh* and belch at it. And it will end up that the two of us and Ginny will cry our hearts out over it because it'll become a discard from the line. I'm right. I know I'm right. That's what's happened to Mr. Jack. A discard Cindy will want to own, so she'll seriously tell me to put it in work. Therefore," he dropped the Pentel, "don't ask her this afternoon if she likes the sketch. Sure she'll like it."

As if he had just finished lecturing a class of would-be designers at Pratt or Parsons or New York's own invention, The Fashion Institute of Technology, Phil sighed, bored by a truth he knew so well, not depressed by it, only resigned. "Those, Miss Sketchbook Queen of 1966, are the facts of this business today. If I try to fight it—which I do every day of my life—I get kicked in the ass. So will you, eventually. The moderate-priced junior dress market has had it. Every personality junior house is on its last leg. We can't use great fabric. Costs too much. We can't design a dress that has real fashion news because that's too risky. All we're supposed to do is the impossible: make cheap dresses *look* expensive and new. And, while you're doing that, while I go around this country screaming to ladies that a junior dress isn't how old you are but the size you are, what's happening to us personally, I mean as designers, as—and you should excuse the expression—creative people? I'll tell you what! Nothing. Not a goddamn thing. Maybe you should design sportswear. Slacks. So the ladies can show off their big asses."

"Stop it, Phil. I can't stand it. I'll commit suicide. Why sketch at all? Why not just let everyone up front rehash any old model that sold well?"

"Because they don't want that either. They didn't hire a high-priced designer to do rehashes. On Broadway they do that. The giants get stylists instead of designers, who shop the stores and watch what the ladies buy. Then they go back to their offices and do the same thing. They copy. That's all. And they get paid so much money for it that it would make your hair frizz up permanently."

"Why go to school at all then? Why train for anything?"

"Who knows! Except what you get then is a title. You're a professional. It's prestige. A stylist is always a hack. A designer can get star billing, which every designer starts out wanting more than he wants money. Everybody wants star billing. That's the American way. A famous designer can make a boss feel he's different, cultured, an appreciator of the arts. The Louis B. Mayer of ready-to-wear."

"Phil. Please."

"Don't Phil me. Just sketch. The one thing we do know from all this is that a group of dresses is going to be done in gray flannel. Maybe, just maybe, it's not a promise, we'll do this dress anyway. But only if we can get two others that have at least a chance of selling. This one," he waved the sketch through the air between them, "we'll try to get featured in *Vogue*, for status, for us. . . . How come the telephone didn't ring once during all this? You think Bell shut it off for not paying the bills?"

Morris, like the ghost of sadness yet to come, appeared in the doorway. "I want you should come check the duplicates, Phil."

"Don't fret, Pat." Phil smoothed back her hair on the way out. "After all, there's always a brighter tomorrow."

Holding on to Phil's arm, Morris led him into a long narrow room off the main corridor. Running the length of the room was the cutting table and on it, spread out, stacked in fluffy layers, was a green-blue printed voile. One of the better-booking numbers on the summer line. The cutters, two of them, were ready to start cutting into it, to trace the outline of the oak-tag pattern pieces laid out carefully on top of the stacked fabric. "You sure you got maximum out of it, Morris?"

"Maximum? You're asking me maximum? Personally I myself put the pattern so one inch wastage there wouldn't be. But a print, Philly darling, a print you got to have a little wastage. You got to match and match. Where the seam shall be . . ."

"It's a tent, Morris. A bias tent. What are you worried about the seam?"

"You don't understand what I mean. There's all kinds considerations. Listen to me. Do I know what I'm doing?" Morris waved to the two men. "Cut already." The hand machines buzzed into life, sliced forward irrevocably. Phil moaned.

At the end of the room was the duplicate space. When Phil started at Mr. Jack there were three duplicate makers; now there was one, and she, Maria, was overworked, but stoical. She put up with it because she was a Mr. Fleiss loyalist and because she liked Morris. They worked late together many nights. Maria's husband had died in a Mafia fight during the twenties in Hoboken. She still wore black.

The headless, armless bust and waist padded forms that represented the *special* Morris Trebnitz-Phil Hanssler-Mr. Jack *fit* were dressed for summer. The production man before Morris could never get the form padded the way Phil wanted; that was when things started sliding. There were so many store returns A. F. opened an outlet to sell off the garments at a terrible loss. When Morris took over, Phil made a vow that he would personally check every duplicate before it went into production. The fit improved, but it was too late. The buyers had been burned.

One form wore lilac linen. A-line skirt. High seaming, under the bust. No bust dart. *Empire.* Halter-type neck. Sleeveless. Phil couldn't feel very proud of it. Every designer in the market was doing the same kind of basic linen, but the color choice had news in it.

The other form was done up in birdseye piqué, black, a summer coat dress without sleeves, rhinestone buttons, no lapels but a great V plunge neck. A sharp dress that any healthy company could run like a Ford, get fat cutting tickets on, even re-orders. Not Mr. Jack. The labor setup and A. F.'s markup made the dress too expensive. But some of the buyers were willing to try. *Glamour* had it full page for June. The *New York Times* had picked it for *Fashions of the Times.* Phil was proud of that dress.

While he studied each form silently, squinting, Morris pulled at the linen, trying to settle it without any buckling. "You know it's Moygashel linen you got here. It's not soft goods. You can't get it to stay flat."

"Stop squeezing it so much." Phil pushed Morris's nervous hand away, smoothed the fabric. "You followed the sample pattern exactly, Maria?"

"Of course she followed. What else!" Morris always defended his charges, but usually because he was guilty of having ordered some kind of change from the original. "It's beautiful, this garment."

"Beautiful? What happened here? Under the bust? We had the fullness coming from nowhere. Higher up." The construction of the sample dress that Ginny had labored over, getting just the right smooth fullness where the waist would have been, was missing from the duplicate.

"You wasted fabric, Philly." Now it was Morris's turn to push hands away. "You didn't see how the sample wasted fabric?"

"The sample was perfect. You screwed up the whole thing. You took out so much you made a different dress out of it." Phil slapped his forehead, whined. "What's the use of telling you anything. I design and you destroy."

"So now you don't like my work? So go complain. Get me fired. I should worry."

"Can't I criticize without you telling me to get you fired?" Phil turned Morris toward the other form. "Don't be so touchy. Live and let live you told me this morning. Temperament's supposed to be my department. I'm the artist around here, don't forget. . . . But *this* dress! This dress you did beautifully, Maria."

She nodded gratefully.

"Sure it's good," Morris moved his hand so-so back and forth, "but rest assured on one thing, sell it won't. How could it sell? Too much labor. Too many buttons."

"You depress me, Morris. I can't talk to you any more. If I do, I'll scream and I've screamed enough today for a whole week. So we'll just try them on Cindy when she comes and forget about them." He walked away from the dresses. And why scream at Morris anyway? Those duplicates would never have a chance to be anything more than relics, mementoes of the death throes of Mr. Jack. What he might be able to do when the place finally did close was to take all the patterns for the fall line, sell them free lance to some manufacturer, and start on his own that way. No overhead. Nothing but the patterns. Maybe A.F. could be persuaded . . .

"Your mother's calling again." Pat was lowered over her sketch pad, trying once more, extending the telephone with her free hand.

"Where the hell is Cindy? . . . Yes, Mother . . . I'm fine. . . . Everything's fine. I don't have a worry in the world. How's Dad? . . . Good. How's Glenn and Betty? . . . Good. And your mother? . . . Excellent . . . Yes, I'll be home Friday night. I promise. . . . I don't know about Wilma. I'll let you know. . . . Pot roast is fine. . . . Yes . . . I've got to go, Mother. I'm very busy. . . . Friday. Positively . . . Yes . . . Goodbye."

"I must say those conversations with your mother are models of excitement. Every time you talk to her I want to howl."

"Can you blame me for being the way I am?" Phil slumped behind his desk. "She's like Cinderella's stepmother. I can't take her. I can't take anyone any more. I've got to change my life. I've got to get some kind of reason for taking all this shit here."

"Why don't you marry me, Phil?"

"Why would I want to do anything like that?"

"It'll give you a reason. A *raison d'être*, love, as they say." Pat thrust her arms toward him, wiggling her fingers. "You need to be turned on. You need to swing."

"And you need to sketch."

The telephone ringing, not Phil's command, settled Pat down. ". . . Lovey? Yes, he's here. Hold . . . Lovey Gray."

"Hello, Lovey . . . Yes, she told me you called. Sorry I didn't get back to you. . . . Paper dresses? What *I* think of them? . . . Well, let's see what might be printable in *Women's Wear*. . . . Paper dresses . . . Lovey, why don't you come up here later. By then maybe I'll have an inspiration. . . . Good. And you can get a sketch on a new dress we're doing. A divine dress. Lots of news in it. You haven't used a sketch from me in a long time and right now, honey, we can use some space. The market thinks we're shut down already. . . . I'd appreciate it, Love. . . . Five's fine . . . Thanks . . ."

Two more calls came in. One from Wilma about dinner plans. "The steak place is great. Seven-thirty. And Wilma, call Howie for me. Tell him where. I'm just so busy . . . Good. Until later . . ."

The other call was from Alice Cristabel, junior dress editor at *Glamour*, telling Phil that they were going to fly his knit dress, the one with the jeweled seams, to Zagreb to be photographed, and to swear to Phil that the sample would be back, within a week, a solemn promise.

"Zagreb? You people are nuts. Why Zagreb?"

"Because I want to go there with my husband. He's got a week off and

I've always wanted to go to Yugoslavia. Zagreb's supposed to be divine. . . ."

Stealthily, Cindy entered the room during this call, stripped to her bra and half-slip in seconds, brushed her hair until Phil was ready.

Pat put her pad away. Ginny entered with the garments to be fitted, helped Cindy into an orange knit. Silently, each of them paced behind Cindy's posed figure, occasionally scanning her reflection in the full-length mirror, Ginny with her tray of pins and yardstick ready to take the final hem length. Phil stopped pacing. Pat stopped. Ginny stepped back, all of them, Cindy too, trying to gauge the dress's possibility now, each in her official capacity and each ready to collaborate as soon as Phil spoke, as soon as Phil broke the locked stance that matched Cindy's: one leg thrust forward, the body leaning backward, defying gravity, like the tower at Pisa, stomach jutting out, chin lifted rakishly, nostrils flaring, eyes squinting, studying this orange knit with its inverted front kick pleat as if it were a piece of sculpture being considered for museum purchase, no longer just a dress to set before the world, which the world's women would, if they ever got the chance, yank from a department store's rack, measuring its worth against the illusion of their own worth, sometimes trying it on, even buying it sometimes, taking it home to try on again for their husbands' and/or boy friends' approval or disapproval, sometimes keeping it to wear for this fall and maybe the next, finally forgetting it because it was out of style, because the designers were up to something new, something much more exciting in fabric and silhouette; but often—almost as often as buying it, if the department stores' 30 percent return statistic was correct—bringing it back to Lord & Taylor or Bergdorf or Bendel or Saks Fifth Avenue or Bloomingdale's, where it would end up its life on a markdown rack.

Phil tried, always, when he leaned back to look, to maintain that balanced image of the world, that honest picture of what this fashion industry was really like: big business, one in which, as in any other big business, your product either sold or it didn't. But, no matter how hard he might try to bury it, another image, one that showed him as an artist, as college-trained, as a craftsman applying abstract absolute standards of taste, color and construction, harmony, wholeness, beauty, that image fought for projection too, behind his squinting eyes. Mostly, it lost the battle. It had to lose. He wasn't involved in a fine art. The world didn't see designers as artists. They were queers, sissies, making Brenda Starr cutouts for the *Daily News* comic strip. And both images of himself, both judgments, like every judgment in his life or anyone else's, were beside the point anyway. Art and business were only small clumps of people in big cities with the power to make judgments for the rest of the world about what was right for this moment in time and space. That's all. Well, for right now, at this moment, in this space, he had some power, and he and Pat, Ginny, and Cindy were going to make a judgment, an estimation of whether one lousy dress had the potential of making thousands of dollars for Mr. Fleiss, whether it should become part of the fall collection of Mr. Jack, whether it was good or bad.

"Cindy? What do you think?"

She maintained her pose, scanned her reflection. "I like it. Very much. Love the color. Very flattering shape. It has action, spirit, a point of view."

"Pat?"

"It's too tenty. I don't feel tents. I told you before . . ."

"How would you like a strait-jacket? Just knock it off about what you feel. Tents are in. I told *you* that before. Listen once in a while."

"Why bother to ask me then? You know what's righter better than I do."

"Because I want your approval. Is that what you want me to say?"

"Oh, Phil! It's not that at all. I'm not paid to . . ."

"You're not paid to look at clothes the way I do. That I know. And I also know that you better start learning how, and fast. You can't be fresh out of school for more than five minutes in this industry and become a designer—which you'll be. And a good one. And when you are you'll want everyone's opinion, believe me. . . . Who made this dress, Ginny?"

"Dorothy." Ginny knelt at the dress's hem, waiting, taciturn, but having knelt to measure, she was indicating her approval.

Phil leaned over, kissed Ginny's topknot of hair. "It's beautiful. Thank God for you and the girls."

"What length, Phil?" Ginny's yardstick, her weapon, was poised.

"Short for the sample. Two inches above the knee. By next year they'll be wearing them just below their business." Phil toured the dress, satisfied. "But that's next year in America. In England they're so far ahead of us it hurts. Our stock dresses—if we ever have any stock!—Morris will cut below the knee anyway. Come to think of it a middle length might be fun. Call it demi or midi."

Ginny measured and pinned. Cindy stood straight. A.F. appeared in the door, watched, nodded.

"You like it, Mr. Fleiss?"

"What's it, knit, Phil?"

"You wanted knit for an early group."

"It's a good dress. But what color is that? Orange? I've got all that yardage in storage. It's in brown. Beautiful shade. Why don't you cut it in brown instead of orange? Women love brown. Years ago the hottest dress I had was a brown."

"I don't feel brown for fall, A. F. The magazine girls want brights."

"Magazines!" Mr. Fleiss waved his empty water filter dangerously close to Cindy's new nose job. She flinched, respectfully moved his hand away. "Sorry . . . Magazines don't buy dresses, Phil. I keep telling you that. Women do. Women buy. And women love brown. . . . Can I see you out here a minute."

They moved back from the door. A.F. pulled Phil close to him, whispering, "Couldn't you stop using Cindy for a while? She's too damn expensive. You could just as well fit on a form. Think of how much money I'd save. Do it for me. Just until we catch up. After that you can use all the models you want. That's a promise, Phil."

"I can't. A form is a dummy. It's not human. I'll never make clothes on a form."

Tears welled up in A. F.'s sunken eyes. He turned away. "All right. But think about it, Phil. You might have to do it. Give it some thought. Also, think about brown knit. Women love brown. At least cut one. A simple dress. No pleats. No buttons. No labor. Just two side seams." He walked slowly down the corridor, mumbling something that sounded to Phil like "Think about it. For my sake, think about it, Phil."

Phil did think about it, even past the time it took him to lock into his model's stance before the next dress that Cindy quickly slipped on. A pink wrap knit. "How do you think this would look in brown?"

Pat laughed, but when she realized that Phil was not joining in, she shook her head vigorously. "You can't mean it. You can't!"

"I could mean it, but I don't. Not this dress anyway. However, my dear, if your boss asks you to do a dress in fabric he stupidly overbought years ago, you should at least entertain the idea. Ginny? What else have you got done in this group?"

"One more. And one more in muslin. You weren't sure about going ahead with it." Ginny adjusted the side hook of the pink wrap, paying no attention to Cindy's shiftings inside the dress.

"Well, loves, the fourth dress is going to have brown on it somehow." Phil reached for a sketch pad, began to draw an idea that had burst out of his annoyance with A. F. "This is right for the group. Ties it together. Pink and brown. We'll call it the . . . the arrow dress. Brown, with a pink arrow going down each side seam. You like it?"

Pat studied the sketch. "Won't be cheap. It'll be hard to make."

"Will it be hard, Ginny?"

"Not for us, but for stock it might. How's this one? Okay?"

He nodded. "Same hem as the other. I'm sold on this arrow knit. It's got a sense of humor." He squinted, studied the sketch some more. "We'll do it. What the hell." He placed the sketch in Ginny's open palm. "Next. The white one."

Cindy stepped out of the wrap, brushed her hair some more, dabbed under her armpits with Kleenex, squirted a vial of cologne under her chin, was ready when Ginny held out the white knit for her to step into.

Then there were the duplicates to fit. Morris hovered over them protectively, and Phil put a check mark next to the dress number in the production book. Might as well. No point in fighting about the linen. It was cheap enough to sell no matter how much the original idea had been distorted. Pat moaned. Ginny sighed. And Cindy? She had to rush; she was overdue at her next appointment. A.F. reappeared in the doorway, frowning openly now at Cindy. Every extra second she was there cost him.

"I really must fly." Cindy gathered up her work tools: extra bras, hairbrush, comb, paisley-print appointment book, make-up, stuffing all of it neatly inside her straw tote bag, bending so that the black shiny hair spilled into disarray, a disarray which she worked very hard to accomplish. "Need me tomorrow, Ginny?"

"No. Come on Friday."

The telephone rang. "Phil Hanssler's room." Pat became formal for A. F.'s sake. "Yes. Hold on . . . It's *Vogue*."

Phil covered the mouthpiece. "Four sharp on Friday, Cindy," he glanced at A. F., "unless you hear otherwise." Cindy retrieved her appointment book, scribbled, blew a kiss to all, and was gone, with A. F. following, the distant squeak of her black vinyl boots assuring Phil that she did make a getaway, that A. F. had not caught up to her. "Ginny, you'll cut the pattern of the sketch." She nodded, grabbed up the fitted dresses carefully, making sure none of them dragged on the floor. "Sorry to keep you waiting, Sally . . . You're dropping it? But why? . . . You changed the story? . . . Okay. Yes. Well, please send the dress back no later than tomorrow morning. We need it for the road salesman. . . . No sorrier than I am . . . Sure. I understand. . . ." The receiver crashed into its cradle. "Damn idiot girls. They keep a dress for a whole lousy week. Photograph it in West Berlin. Send it back. Call for it again. Rephotograph it in Helsinki. And after all that expense they drop the dress from the issue. They changed their story again. This time it's Africa. Marrakech! And you want to be a designer, Pat? Don't bother! Go get married. Live a normal life like any other twenty-one-year-old girl." Phil lowered his head to the magazine-fabric-card-littered desk top. "It's no use. I've got to take a rest."

"Poor Phil." Pat took up her hairbrush. "It's just the end of another glorious day here at Mr. Jack. Look at my hair. It's all frizzed up, damn it. And I'm going out tonight. To Arthur." She lowered her brush. "Come with us, Phil. Do you good. You can sweat it out on the dance floor."

Phil lifted a copy of *Elle* and threw it at Pat.

"That's gratitude!" She stroked through snags. "I'm only trying to help you out of your *brown* study."

Morris appeared in the doorway. Phil sat up. "The return of Morris Trebnitz, angel of mercy. What now, Morris? Now you really look worried."

"Worried? Sick is better." He cupped his heavy chin, moved his head in a wide arc, an arc describing indescribable pain. "The voile is damaged goods. They cut already and it's damaged." The head stopped moving. Pat stopped brushing. They waited for Phil's total collapse. Instead, he was laughing, quietly at first, then louder and louder until he reared out of his chair, moved toward a stunned Morris, clutched him.

"You're *mishuga*, Phil."

"*Mishuga?* Sure, I'm crazy. I've flipped."

And at that moment Lovelady Gray arrived. Phil rested his head against her rust tweed suit jacket. "Flipped, Lovey. Gone. Mad."

"Not yet. Don't. I need a quote first." She led him back to the desk, supporting his chin between her strong thumb and index finger.

"So, *nu*, Phil? What should I tell A. F.?" Morris spoke quietly, his voice drowned by agony and fear.

"Don't tell him anything. Salvage what you can. It doesn't matter. It's no greater tragedy than anything else that's happened here today."

Wearily, Morris shrugged his hunched shoulders, trudged off, mumbling, "I'll retire. Who needs to work."

"Phil? What about paper dresses?" Lovey Gray removed a huge gold spear from her neat bun, shook her head. The black hair fell grudgingly into freedom. "Just look at these gorgeous colors the manufacturer sent me." She spilled pieces of saw-edged paper swatches onto his desk. "Aren't they marvelous? I think they're so exciting. Don't you, Phil?" He remained transfixed, thinking of damaged voile. "Aren't they sensational colors, Pat?"

"Just absolutely devoted to them." Pat, pug nose scrunched in an ecstasy of disgust, lifted them as if they were cancer cells, shuddered, let them float downward beneath Phil's following stare.

"They'd make great toilet-paper tints." He fingered a brown one. "My mother would love that. She's got this rhinestone-studded toilet-paper cover in her downstairs bathroom."

"Be serious, Phil. Say something I can print." Lovey opened her writing tablet to a fresh page, smoothed it. "Shoot."

"I'll trade you for them, Love." Slowly, he picked up each piece, shook them together inside his palms, transferred them from hand to hand, mesmerized. "They are pretty. Imagine them in crepe and chiffon. Be great colors for the holiday and resort line. Can I keep them?"

"Yes, you can keep them, only give me some kind of quote for the column. As you said, you can use the publicity, sweetheart. The word about Mr. Jack is all over the market. Everywhere I went, I heard rumors."

"We'll be okay. Never fear. Philip's here." He splayed the swatches across his desk, studied the red, the moss green, the lemon, smiled up at Pat, who had by now applied her white lipstick. The girls from the sample room were leaving, stopping to lean respectfully into the room, to wave their goodnights to Phil. Distracted, he failed to wave back. "Okay, Miss Lovelady Gray. Here's the bargain. A sketch in the paper in exchange for a quote and these pieces of paper? That fair? Pat, do a sketch of that flannel dress for Lovey before you go." Pat nodded happily. "How about it, Love? Is it a deal?"

"It's a deal. I can't promise—I don't *own* *Women's* *Wear*—but I'll try, if I like the dress. So start talking already. I'm due at Tiffeau fifteen minutes ago."

"Shouldn't keep him waiting. He's a star. I'm not."

"You will be." Lovey smiled consolingly. "I wouldn't be here if I didn't think that."

"That's the nicest thing anyone has said to me for months. Thank you, Lovey."

"And I mean it, Phil. I go from place to place. I see what everyone is doing, and I know that you really are a designer. The others . . . well, they just want to make dresses that sell. They want to make lots of money. Couldn't care less about good taste."

"I want to make lots of money too."

"You will. Just be patient."

"I've been patient. I'm thirty . . . well, never mind. Let's just say that I'm of a certain age where the possibilities begin to narrow down to a precious few . . . ." He sang the next few words, "For it's a long, long time from May to December . . ."

"Don't get sticky, boss man." Pat handed the sketch to Lovey. "Sure you won't come swinging with me tonight?"

"Sorry, but I'm otherwise engaged."

"Ta, ta, all." She kissed Phil.

"Make sure you're on time tomorrow. And no hangover. We've got plenty of work to do."

"Oui, oui, sahib." She shook her hair free of her ears and watusi-ed out of the room.

"Paper dresses, like hula hoops and yo-yos"—Phil approached the full-length mirror, still holding the colored papers in his palm. He placed them in his wallet carefully, placed the wallet in his back pocket, where it always bulged temptingly—"are doomed to walk the earth for a certain time—that's Hamlet, I think—then die quietly, having made someone a vulgar new millionaire. Frankly, the thought of paper rubbing against the skin puts me in mind of something unpleasant. And what happens if it rains?"

"Excellent." Lovey scanned Pat's sketch quickly, her reporter's eyes accustomed to rapid-fire judgments. "Great dress. I'll try getting it in the Best of New York forecast." She joined Phil at the mirror, rising a full head taller than he. "What I'll do is cut all my hair off. It's a drag this way and it's a drag done up. I look like a horse's ass."

"There's nothing wrong with your hair. Just teach it how to hang loose, like Pat's."

"I'm too old for that. Not to mention the fact that I don't have her kind of natural beauty." She kissed him with warmth. "Must run or I'll begin to slobber."

Ginny entered. She had changed from her smock into a gray sweater dress, and with that change the look of a handsome forty-year-old woman had returned: the tight topknot, the smooth wide forehead, the high cheekbones seeming to rise higher, unsquaring the hard set of her chin, allowing room for a smile, for the softening of her no-nonsense control.

Phil motioned her onto the arm of his chair. "Can you join me for a drink?"

Alone with Phil, Ginny indulged a fugitive illusion of adolescence. "Sorry, but I've got a dinner and theatre date with my beau." Nevertheless she blushed.

"You go ahead then. I wanted to talk to you but it can wait until tomorrow."

"I can stay a while longer. Talk. You look too sad to leave."

"I am sad, but I've been sadder. You go ahead."

"You sure?"

"Positive. I've got a date later. And send my regards to your beau. Why the hell doesn't he marry you already?"

"And spoil it all? We've only been engaged for three years."

Another kiss and Phil was left alone in his own room. He stepped to the door, watched Ginny stride down the corridor, heard her say goodnight to Link and Marsha, listened for the whine of the showroom door opening and closing. One more day almost done.

Instead of returning to his desk, he walked into the sample room, lazily examined the basted dresses hanging on the forms near each girl's machine, studied the half-done muslin for the arrow dress on Ginny's workbench. That girl never stops. But in here was where work *would* stop last. In here everything went on undisturbed, like a fairyland. For how much longer was the question? And if it did stop altogether what would happen to the girls and to Ginny? Another job. Another company. Another day, another dollar. The closeness of four years would dissolve in a second. Out the window. And himself? What about himself? Another what? His next step was the crucial one and so far all he knew was that it had to be a change, had to be a few steps up, maybe all the way to 550. A new firm. A new price range. Better dresses. Sharper buyers. More money. A better life. It had to be. But it didn't necessarily follow that it would be. It didn't necessarily follow that he would be able to make it happen.

He reached for his wallet, removed the colored papers, let them float freely down to the workbench, studying their fall, squinting their colors into a blur of brightness that blocked the view of anything real in the room, that blurring together of color and energy, the habit of his life. The falling papers became his own descending possibilities that might settle finally to a dead stillness. If he wasn't careful that's exactly what would happen. If he didn't break certain habits, he'd sink beneath the daylight instead of moving up toward its source. . . . But habits are so hard to break. Like Wilma and Howie. Sandy. Aaron. All his friends.

Habits. His family and the way of thinking about them, a habit, full of weight, hanging on to him every step of the way through college, the army, his career, right now. Making him stationary, the fixed center of a blur, with everyone and everything spinning around, pushing in on him. Traps, he felt, and all ready to spring shut . . . if he didn't begin to sort it out, didn't begin to act. He poked at the squares of paper, shuffled them around, finally gathered them up, squeezed them into a ball and threw the ball, like a fancy lay-up shot, behind his back into the wastebasket next to Dorothy's sewing machine.

When Link entered broom in hand, he was still standing above the wastebasket, staring down at the ball of color. "Got to sweep up in here, Phil."

"Sure, Link. I was just going. It's been a long day. Is A. F. gone?"

"They all gone." Link swept the pins, the bits of fabric, the threads into a pile in the center of the room.

"Morris too?" Phil finger-combed his hair forward. Link nodded. "Good." Now he could leave without having to face anyone. "Night, Link."

Link mumbled, bent to scoop up the pile of dirt.

At five o'clock the elevators are crowded with sample hands, but at six the pattern markers and the cutters, some worried bosses and their salesmen, a few designers, pass through the marble lobby of 498.

Outside the rolling racks are gone. The fabric men, the button men, the belt men are gone, home to an early dinner. The corner candy stores are pulling in their chocolate-sprinkled marshmallow cookies for the night. The egg cream hours have passed into cocktail time. The silver-suiters and the young salesmen mill in backslapping clusters, discussing what the day has done to them, before crossing the Avenue on their way to the darkly lit bars and restaurants along Thirty-sixth, Thirty-seventh, Thirty-eighth streets between Seventh and Broadway. It's make-out time in the Garment Center, the commingling of new tribes, the new breed: the Broadway sharpies, the ones who are really into the big-volume money there, sleek and young, like Thunderbirds, nails polished, Man-tanned; the beehived, bleached-blonde showroom girls; the swinging young bookkeepers and receptionists. And the class salesmen from the Avenue, quieter now, suave for nightfall. After all, they're the ones with the reputations, and now they're mixing with the Broadway pushers. They have to set the style. Style counts; style will out; style gives the best lay.

The Avenue quiets down. Traffic has thinned. Taxicabs become available. Copies of *Women's Wear Daily* are gone from the newsstands.

And in the bars it's an April evening, it's the time between collections, between seasons, when the salesmen talk over Pernod martinis and Chivas Regal Rob Roys about how they'll make a killing with the next line on the Coast, or in Dallas, or Chicago, if the faggola designers will only stick with the work. The early fall line's going great. Salable merchandise, none of that fashion crap . . .

Phil knew those bar monologues and their sidewalk equivalents. He had nightmares about them and tried to walk by the groups tuned out, his volume dial turned down to six. For a while he had been a part of this evening scene, back in the good old idiot days of his beginning when he was fresh out of the army, fresh from the separation of himself from his father and stepmother in Teaneck, New Jersey, and his father's begging him not to move, please not to move. "Dad, you're going to have to face it once and for all. I'm not your little baby any more. I wasn't in the army so I could come home and live in New Jersey. I'm only going across the Hudson River, you know. And there's a tunnel and a bridge . . ." And it was Aaron Siegel, Monsieur LeGeis to the trade, who saved Phil from the ravages of the barroom soliloquy, that fate worse than death on the Avenue for anyone with real ambition, that suction cup of seven o'clock drunken sex. Phil had met Aaron by accident, at the Plaza bar, where Phil had gone, all innocence, one night, as a novelty, a change of pace. Like Jesus saved, Aaron saved, demanding, however, displays of faith and adoration, dumb shows of subservience. So Phil displayed his faith and his smile, without forcing. Then, at that beginning, he had faith in everything, especially himself. Anything was possible. And, sure, he could design or sell, go into advertising or show business, act or sing or both, even dance, anything that would get his ass moving forward. Aaron steered Phil away from the Broadway sharpies, the Seventh Avenue pretenders he was working with in those days, led him instead in the direction of the Park Avenue smoothies, the sophisticates, the name designers, the sex sharpies. "After all, Phil," slim but pear-shaped even then, his words sounding in memory still juicy, pregnant with expendable promise, Aaron pontificated then, "you do have a degree in the arts—more than I had. And you can go to one of those specialty schools if need be. I'll call my friends. They'll take *you* in hand. You can sketch, can't you? because it'll be a while before you do more than that. But you're beautiful so it shouldn't take *too* long. I'll introduce you to everyone."

Phil stepped from the curb. A taxi tonight. No subway as long as there was some sun still left over. And just to think about Aaron made the subway gauche. "Subways get you to places on time. Never get to places on time, Philip. It's rude." When Aaron and he had their first in a series of fallings-out, it was about being late. Aaron was an hour late for the theater. Phil waited outside, angry, but determined to be cool. And then the inevitable cab had arrived. Dressed in one of his little Lord Fauntleroy collars, a waist-suppressed suit—the suppression close to suffocation like Scarlett O'Hara's corselette—Aaron's incredulous annoyance had turned Phil's ice into fire. "You silly little fool! Why didn't you go in and leave my ticket at the box office? That's what you're supposed to do if you can't learn to be late for anything." They didn't speak to each other for a year that time. Currently, they were talking—occasionally. Because Aaron, now Aram, was on a down swing. Aaron had gone up too fast not to slide down. Progress was much slower for Phil, but when *he* finally got there, he'd stay, no matter what.

The cab bumped in and out of potholes, sped past the steam-cleaned Statler-Hilton, past the gutted Pennsylvania Station, with its sign announcing the NEW MADISON SQUARE GARDEN, the sun's rays touching where they hadn't for so long and wouldn't again soon, probably forever, pointing to doom in the dusty air above the construction site, their message lost, suddenly, behind the modest old buildings of the fur market that came next—pelts on a string to be pulled down like Penn Station. And Twenty-third Street. A quick, leaning-forward view of the Chelsea Hotel, where the old writers and the new artists lived in peace and harmony, for the moment. And Barney's! Seventh Avenue and Seventeenth Street! The only store of its kind where you don't just settle for . . . Fourteenth Street, crossroads into the outer edges of Greenwich Village. West on Thirteenth. The Van Gogh Apartments. The artist comes home for a while to the fifteenth floor and his Hudson River view, to the westering sun. Four years of the same horizon. Four years at Mr. Jack and in an L-shaped 3½ rooms with a real tree, a real piano . . .

All right, Philip! Enough. Say hello to the doorman. "Evening, Mike." Get the mail. More bills. Another elevator. Nod at the passengers. Don't stare. The dog's barking. My only pal. Walk her. Then a Scotch and a shower and to dinner before Wilma calls to find out why you're not fifteen minutes early. "Yes, you're a good dog. Sure you are. Good girl, Liffey. Yes. Left all alone. All day. Without a friend. Just like your father. Yes . . . And tonight too. Don't bark. We're going out. Sure. Good girl . . . Sit for the leash!"

Chapter Two

Wilma Pasternack and Howie Goldstein were the south and north poles of Phil's slowly revolving planet, the light and dark sides of its moon. For years, and in a way much different from Aaron and Sandy and Carl Kalb, they had kept him in continuous orbit. For years he had quietly kept them in check, in apparent separate-but-equal balance. They were for him the friends that really mattered. And he was for them a center of gravity, their middleman, their big dipper in the business world, their wheeler-dealer, their "hoo-ha," as Howie put it.

A private secretary for a political fund-raiser, Wilma, at thirty-two, had weathered a few thousand minor crises, emerging from all of them remarkably unscathed. She always snapped back. Fortunately, her skin was resilient. It resisted anxiety lines. Its texture was as smooth, its color as rosy as a baby's behind. Her teeth had been capped in youth by her brother, the dentist, and their whiteness remained, more than the blemish-free skin, the breathtaking challenge of her face. "Impossible for anyone to find whiter teeth anywhere in the continental United States. I defy anyone to try." Actually, the whole face was pretty. Not gorgeous, but glowing, the parts at peace with each other so that passersby did stare and think they had seen a great beauty. Her body had the same kind of *almost* about it. But with the help of the Kounovsky gym—once, sometimes twice a week—and a psychology-major, N.Y.U.-trained mind, she had learned to create an illusion of lightness, as a five-to-ten-pound-overweight ballet dancer might. Not as limber as in the good old days, but still able to maintain the same position on her toes for long periods of time. The position she maintained, would go on maintaining forever, if necessary, was that she loved Philip Hanssler, "and someday, God willing"—she said it every time she was hostess at one of Phil's parties—"he'll break down and marry me."

Howard Goldstein, on the other hand, had been through, in rapid succession, during his twenties, the two major crises that occur, ultimately, in everyone's life: the death of a mother and father. And, unfortunately, everything about his face showed the strain of those events. At rage or at rest it was like a gray day, permanently overcast. Even his smile, the lips too heavy, the nose too long, too humped—he refused to allow aquiline—the nostrils too wide, the cheeks too sunken, that smile was almost always splashed with rue. Only his high-blood-pressure ruddiness, the honesty of his efforts, the length of his hair saved him from obscurity. He taught high-school English in Westchester County, which was fine— for someone else. "What's the point of a B.A. from Brooklyn College, an M.A. from N.Y.U. if you're not prepared to teach in a ghetto school! I'm a coward. I know I'm a coward. But if I majored in English literature, I want to teach English literature. Can you blame me? I don't want to be a policeman. I hate policemen." Howie maintained himself, alone, in an apartment not far from Phil's on Bank Street. Early every school-day morning when Westchesterites were coming into New York City for Madison Avenue or the stock market, he was driving out of it. And every school-day afternoon when they were going back home he returned to Bank Street. All his life had been spent driving against the flow of traffic. He was proud of that and not much else. Except for one fugitive fantasy, his aspirations were modest and realistic: he too loved Philip Hanssler, had loved him ever since the day they met at Fort Dix. Howie, however, was never co-host at one of Phil's parties.

For that night, as on many other nights, Wilma had chosen her favorite weight-watching restaurant, a steak place. Every time they met there she felt obliged to sell its virtues all over again, trying to make each meal seem like a new discovery, another first time. "And it is centrally located, you realize. A block from me. Just a few more for you and Howie. And I can wear slacks there too." Not that anyone really fought her choice. Howie didn't care. As long as he was included, they could eat at a Chock Full o' Nuts, and Phil's only objection was that it had the look of one of those hooker joints near the Avenue: sunburst clocks; wrought-iron booth dividers; elaborate fake flower arrangements. On a few occasions he even had to greet some silver-suiters and their models who had somehow drifted off the official circuit while drunk and had ended up in the Village.

". . . even how dark it is is a pleasure. It shows my teeth up to great advantage." Wilma's bracelets jangled to rest near her elbow-propped arm, her cigarette spearing the air as punctuation for her monologue. ". . . and it's been such a hard day I can use the advantage. Cloak me, darkness." She lifted her arms to Allah, shook her bracelets some more. "Cloak me."

"Cloak me too." Howie, facing Wilma and Phil, kept his cigarette low and away out of consideration for Phil, who had given up smoking when his ulcer struck. "Another department meeting this morning. Another fight with the arch-fiend herself. If I have to sit through many more of her we-must-keep-*Silas Marner*-safe-for-the-tenth-grade, I'm going to take up weaving myself. To be a department head and to be so dumb is appalling. All I have to do is mention *Catcher in the Rye* and she acts like I said 'fuck' or something. Just two more years—I should live so long—and she's retiring. That will be the happiest day of my life."

"Me too." Phil sipped from his third Dewar's and soda.

"You too what?" Bending closer, Howie palmed his cigarette, urged his hair forward onto his forehead.

"Me too I had a hard day."

"I'll bet you did, love." Buoyantly affectionate, Wilma leaned against Phil. He supported her claim by patting her arm. "Anything new happen? Will I be getting summer dresses or not?"

"As they say, only God knows the answer to that one. Shouldn't we order dinner?"

"Yes. Let's. I'm starved." Wilma allowed herself only one drink before dinner—"thousands of calories in a Scotch"—and with that one she had long since reached the ice-sucking stage. She grabbed the last green olive in the relish tray. "Had to skip lunch today."

"One more drink, Phil?"

"I've had enough, Howie. You have if you want."

Howie shook his head no. Phil motioned for the waiter. Wilma, as a mother might for her children, ordered all the dinners. White teeth flashing, tight curls springing as her head moved back and forth above the huge menu, she obviously enjoyed this part of their ritual meetings much more than the drinking stage. A single drink is no help. "I'll have sliced steak. Very well done. No potato. Hearts of lettuce. Vinegar. No oil. Not one drop. And he'll have"—Phil, content to be relieved of this traditionally masculine responsibility, closed his eyes—"sliced steak. Medium, but on the well side. Baked potato. Sour cream and chives. Hearts of, with Roquefort. And he," she twisted toward Howie, but didn't bother to look at him, "sliced steak too. Blood rare. The rest is the same." She thrust the menu at the waiter.

"Just for that, I'll have another Scotch and soda." Holding up his glass, Howie darkened his rue, but Wilma refused to look. She busied herself by smoothing Phil's hair for a moment, by examining his fingernails.

"My mother and father want us for dinner next week, love. We haven't been for over a month and . . ."

"No!" Phil's eyes opened. Wilma's hand hovered, surprised, retreated. "I'm not going to Brooklyn. It's bad enough I've got my own Friday night to do. No more. Forget it. Uh-uh." He swirled the ice in his drink. "I've got too much on my mind to have to smile at your mother for a whole evening. They'll both start in with the getting-married routine and when they're finished you'll start. So let's leave well enough alone for right now. Okay?"

"In the final analysis, I suppose I'm the fortunate one. No family." As if toasting himself, Howie lifted his new drink to his lips. "On the other hand, for a young Jewish homosexual to be without an old-fashioned Jewish mother poses problems. No father . . . well, that's a different story. *That* I can manage to find when I feel the need."

"Howie, sweetheart, make the most of your situation." Phil clanged Howie's glass. "You're free to do whatever you want."

"I hate when you talk that way, Phil." Wilma's words were couched in menthol-filtered mildness. She smiled, asking for amnesty. "Howie can't be content to live the way he does. Everyone needs some kind of combination. Everyone wants to procreate. I mean, that's just nature's way, after all." She turned to Howie, waiting.

"After all what? After all, the world only screwed itself to death with that nature crap, with that procreation bit. And so what if I'm not particularly content to live the way I do. Are you content living the way you do, Wilma?" Anxiously, Howie glanced across the table, but Phil seemed calm, attentive. "Sure, you *get* it regularly. But you don't *own* the giver. And in our great civilized world you're supposed to *own* what you love. That's where the power is. *And* control. In ownership. That's what combination means. Is that what you think is so healthy?"

Wilma's big bright eyes narrowed menacingly. "Look, Howie, your insights are part of an essential sickness which I've confronted many times during my short and—"

"Well, if you've confronted it many times, then the sickness must have reached epidemic proportions. I'm not the only carrier, remember. I'm only another victim and I . . . I don't want to fight with you, Wilma but—"

"No fights, please." Phil leaned back against the banquette, closed his eyes again. "My ulcer's beginning to hurt."

"No. I promise. I won't even raise my voice." Even though Phil wasn't watching, Howie brushed the hair back from his forehead, deferentially. "You're a victim too, Wilma. Just because you get *it* and get enough of *it* doesn't mean—"

"Why you so afraid to say 'sex,' Howie?" Phil's voice was the raised one. "Don't be afraid. Say it. Sex. S-E-X." He spelled loudly enough for nearby steak eaters to turn and frown, to turn and smile. It depended on what kind of steak they were eating: rare, medium, or well done.

"All right. Sex. But getting enough of it—sex—doesn't mean all you think it means. You're not thinking of a baby everytime, are you? You're thinking of yourself. You're thinking of your partner, maybe. You're thinking about how you look. How pretty you are. That's the real point. How you look. Everything's geared to that idea. How to look better. Because if you look better you'll get all the sex you need. If you're a stunner, you can get plenty. And you need it the least. You always have yourself. If you're so-so, you get so-so, but always enough. If you're unfortunate looking, like me, you have to struggle. Combination's best for the last group, whether they're homosexual or heterosexual. Any group of people that have to struggle to get what they need usually ends up thinking that if only their lives had some kind of center to it, some kind of order, then their worries would be over. They're trapped, those people. The rest don't have to be. Phil doesn't have to be, for example." Triumphantly, Howie drank a series of quick sips, expecting Wilma to lash out, but before she could respond the salads, the breadsticks, butter, a replenished relish tray arrived. For the time being, Wilma wanted to eat more than she wanted to talk. Some more celery and carrot sticks, another scallion kept Phil silently content. Only Howie went on talking.

Whatever Wilma was not doing, Howie did. That was part of the process, letting Phil have the opportunity to make his free choice of activity according to his mood. That, more than anything, was their path to a peace that passeth understanding. Gladly, Phil traveled it. He listened to Howie. He watched Wilma. He munched a breadstick. Whether or not he could get through life that way was questionable, and at times, when he was home alone with his dog, he questioned it. And the answer so far, the only answer that satisfied what he understood to be the present condition of his life, was that all Howie said and all Wilma did mattered less to him than getting something more, much more than they wanted. Sex mattered. Of course it mattered and had its own special problems—regardless of what Howie thought; he should know better—but those problems mattered less than all the other things. That, at thirty-five—count 'em, kid—was what every bit of schooling, in Teaneck or the University of Syracuse or the American School of Design, every bit of his *thing* with people made him feel. And now, living in the age of *Who's Afraid of Virginia Woolf*, he assumed that was the only sensible way to feel. Marriage, honestly, as an institution, was a drag. Dragola! So, carry on. Have a ball. Show it hard! What he did privately was his own business. As long as it didn't hurt anybody else. Not Wilma. Not Howie . . .

". . . and I'm not trying to sound intentionally flip, Wilma. Your labels are obsolete. They're only fit for politicians, priests, and moral entrepreneurs. I predict that by the time we reach that mythic 1984 the family unit as you know it, sex as you know it, will become an unsung part of the historical record. Just remember that I told you so. One way or another the hippies, the flower people, the New Left are going to get the power in this country. And I, for one, am glad. Maybe they won't last, but at least they're attacking the crap around you. That's what counts. That's what real love is about. The establishment will dissolve. Giant industries will crumble. The military complex will be defeated. Real, uncategorized love will emerge and be more powerful than all the H-bombs put together. I believe—"

"Why don't you eat, Howie!" Wilma tried to shove a carrot stick in his mouth. "Eat anything. Only shut up already." He pushed her hand down roughly, spilled part of his drink, but remained semi-silent during the main part of the meal. They all did.

And after the third cup of coffee, Wilma's fourth cigarette, Howie's first Benedictine, when the chance the evening had held for fun had long since been frittered away; actually long before Phil's three and Howie's four Dewar's, Wilma's one, back before their separate afternoons and mornings, back even to the moment when Phil met Howie or the moment when at the acting class he used to go to he had met Wilma, the failure of this evening had begun. It grew out of exactly what Phil thought he wanted from it most of all: simple affection. But they, each of them in their separate ways, wanted love—whatever that was—from him. Love! Like a bill forever being presented, month after month, year after year, because he wouldn't, couldn't pay it. A nightmare debt, recurring. So, for the second time that day, he wanted to get away. First from Sandy. Now from Wilma and Howie. From everything. "I've got to leave." He stood before either of them had a chance to object, waited only long enough for the waiter to return with his American Express card, but too long to escape Wilma's question, "I thought you'd stay with me tonight?" or Howie's pathetically persevering, tacit pleading. Nevertheless, and no matter how they tried, he was leaving. As long as he paid *this* bill, he had some rights. "I'll call you tomorrow, Wilma." He squeezed Howie's thin shoulder on the way from the booth.

They watched him twist through the maze of tables, stop to tip the maître d', and then disappear.

Five minutes later Wilma left. Her goodnight was a nod. Howie drained what was left of his Benedictine and ordered another. It was still early. Maybe he'd go out hunting . . . for a father.

Phil tried not to answer the telephone. It would only be Wilma and he didn't want to talk to her. Or it might be Howie calling to apologize for whatever imagined mistake he'd made that night to spoil the fun. But when the phone rang for the tenth time—he was counting them in the dark—and his dog started growling in her sleep next to him on his pillow, he had to answer.

It was Aaron. "You're not sleeping yet, are you?"

"As a matter of fact I was trying to."

"Well, don't try any longer. Come up to this marvelous party I'm at. There's someone here I'd like you to meet."

"I told you I was in bed already. I'm too tired, Aaron. Another night."

"Stop acting like an old man. That's the trouble with you. Just get dressed and come up here. It'll be helpful. I promise, And you can use some help."

As he always did, Aaron won. Phil did get out of bed, went up to Seventy-eighth Street and Park Avenue. It was just before midnight when he arrived. The guests were all male and they were all either approaching or deep into constricted drunkenness. Becomingly, Phil frowned—lingering handshakes seemed to say they liked the frown—through the introductions being made by Aaron, in lieu of the host, an old-time continental designer who had long since—Aaron smiled, lusciously lascivious, when he explained the absence—"gone to bed . . . with someone."

For Phil, a queer party at the end of the kind of day this had been was not exactly exciting news. But here he was—it was his own fault—and here he would have to stay, at least for a reasonable period of time, to smile and chat, always alert, ready to draw back from anyone who tried to make a claim. Those were the rules, as Aaron would be sure to inform him if he so much as looked as if he were ready to break them. The mentor always knows the rules; the pupil always acts *as if* he enjoys obeying them, the *as if* becoming finally the only gratifying element of the game.

"Why'd you get me up here, Aaron?" They stood at the side of a large-mouthed, white-painted brick fireplace, between the end of its photograph-laden mantel and a tall potted palm. "I told you I was tired. This kind of thing takes energy for me. It's easy for you. You forget that all the time." Phil drank too rapidly and Aaron had fixed the drink with too much Scotch and a splash of soda, just the reverse of Phil's request.

Aaron drank sherry, never anything stronger. "I don't forget a thing. I just insist that your life needs this," his sherry hand indicated the softly murmuring men. "Look at all these gorgeous people. How can you resist them?"

"It's simple. They don't interest me."

"But that Wilma does? Howard Goldstein does? Is that what you want for the rest of your life? To be observed by them instead of participating with something better?" Aaron held his glass close to Phil's nose as if to let the fragrant scent of sherry speak for that something better. "I told you a long time ago you won't amount to anything until you begin to distinguish the winners from the losers. You have a talent, darling, but your taste—in everything—needs improving."

"Thank you, monsieur. I'm happy for that lesson. But your trouble is you keep giving me the same homework."

"That's because you simply won't learn. You must be retarded."

"That's it. I'm retarded. And you've taken on my case. I'm grateful. Medical science is grateful." Phil moved from the potted palm to stand behind the nearest of the two extra-length, identical, beige antique-velvet sofas that stood at right angles to the fireplace. Everything in the enormous, high-ceilinged room was beige or white or cobalt blue or magenta. Everything was exquisitely ordered, manicured, including the plants, the vases of flowers: peonies, lilacs, roses, beach reeds, dried and brittle brown. All very . . . something. Chinoise? Neo-chinoise? Or early Flatbush Avenue. A mixture of modes. Very modern. Very daring. Very beautiful. There was no denying it. Color was beautiful. Ordered or disordered. And the apartment was beautiful. He wouldn't mind, someday, living in a place like this. Voluptuous luxury. A maid, a butler, a cook. And people of all sorts, sizes, shapes, professions. A salon. An at-home. With women, however. With old Wilma officiating, pouring from the brass coffee table in front of the fireplace, twenty years from now, when I'm wealthy, a famous designer of *better* clothes, not a cloak-and-suiter but a member of the new American haute couture, a new-breed designer, married, with a few kids, instead of one of these types hanging on. He stared at them, at the stylish way they crossed and uncrossed their slim legs, displaying their soberly dark Italian and French suits, suits that were impeccably tailored, the best-dressed people in New York City, beautiful, as Aaron would have it, gorgeous. And they were. Well coiffed. Well oiled, not slick. Properly noisy. Murmurous. Suspiring, *ensemble*, at the end of a long hard day.

So live and let live! As Morris would have it. But *they* wouldn't just let live. They stared back at him. That was the point of it all. And, in spite of everything he ever said to Aaron or Sandy or Howie—Howie, who was supposed to be one of them, would rush howling out of a room like this —he was pleased that they looked at him, admired him, pleased that in a short time after his arrival some of them had gotten up from the sofas, had started circling him, smiling at him, coyly. Not the young ones. Almost always the older ones, the fifty-year-olds, sixty-year-olds. If only they would look, without touching, without talking, he could perhaps enjoy being at this kind of party. But they did touch and they did talk and, almost always, apart from the habitual inanity of opening gambits their mouths were trained to recite, it turned out that the ones who spoke were the nicest. They were no hungrier for sex than anyone else you passed on the street. Probably less. Probably had more sex in a week than other people had in a month. More than he had. Although, he liked to think, at least he had what he wanted when he wanted it. For them, sex was like a horse race without an end. They selected the healthiest, prettiest horse, part of the sport to do it that way, then bet on it, followed its progress twenty-four hours a day, for a few days, maybe a week, only to look up one evening somewhere, like here, in this apartment, and spy a prettier horse. That was what he hated most of all, that, and their urgency about doing it, about grabbing for a chance of victory over something unnamable, someone unknown that they just had to have, even for ten minutes, or die.

Finally, no matter what they talked about, the theatre, the opera, the galleries, the stars, horoscopes, the restaurants, the bars they liked, their summer homes in the Hamptons or on Fire Island, what they were really saying was "Go to bed with me. I command you to want to go to bed with me." Why else take the time and trouble to anoint a body with unguents, creams, cologne, to dress it to perfection, if they didn't want that commandment to be the coda of their conversation? The only topic— even with politics, how attractive a candidate was became the issue—that didn't end up meaning bed was designing. That was work. So Phil tried, whenever he was getting in too deep, to steer for the shore before the wave struck, to talk about fashion, about the Avenue. Sometimes it worked. With this kind of hot house assortment it almost always worked. With someone like Howie who wanted, needed to talk, nothing, no ploy, could ever work for long.

"You're being admired." Aaron stood behind him, whispering, pushing against his ass. "And by just the one I thought would admire you. He's a manufacturer. Better market. Smile back. Don't be afraid."

Phil did more than smile. He walked directly up to the man. "I'm Phil Hanssler." He extended his hand.

The man took hold of it, held it while he spoke. "I know your name. Aaron has talked about you. You're with Mr. Jack. I know Alex Fleiss quite well. Known him a good many years, long before he made his money. Sad that he's losing it so quickly."

Phil tugged his hand free. The man's palm was repulsively smooth, like melted butter. "And your name?" Phil didn't want to be polite. Not to this sixty-year-old fool. This Adler-elevated fool with wispy bleached-blond hair that was brushed forward like a monk's across his high forehead.

"My name is unimportant for the time being." He touched Phil's arm, frowned at the black-and-white houndstooth, rubbed his fingertips together as if they had just come in contact with poison sumac.

"Not appropriate attire, Mr. . . . ?"

"Charles Dietrich. Whatever you choose to wear is appropriate, Philip. I'm sure you couldn't care less. You don't have to. You'd be handsome in a sack." Charles brushed the front of his Cardin blazer.

"You shouldn't wear Cardin clothes. You're too short for them. Like me." Phil stepped back, readying himself to return to the field of action, to the sofas. But Charles grabbed the back vent of his jacket, pulled him to a stop.

"In addition to being quite handsome, you're also quite rude."

"I make a point of that with people who start out ruder than me."

"It's not to your advantage to be rude with me. Aaron has told me you could use some help. I happen to have some influence on the Avenue."

"Not with me you don't." This time Phil pushed Charles's hand from his sleeve. It was kneading flesh too vigorously, with too much pressure. "Didn't Aaron also tell you that I wasn't a paid-up member of your . . . club?"

"He did, but I don't believe it. And I don't care."

"You should because I do. You should also feel flattered. Aaron isn't usually so honest. . . . Look, Mr. Dietrich, I'm sure you're a well-intentioned gentleman. So am I. I'm also a candid guy. Sex is out. If you want to talk about business, I'm at your service. I do need help."

Mr. Dietrich stepped around Phil and away. Phil followed, moved close to Aaron. "Thank you for nothing." He handed Aaron his drink. "My respects to the host, but I've got to get the hell out of here. Why don't you call Howie Goldstein next time, or is he too queer for your crowd?" Phil didn't wait for, nor did he want an answer. Smiling, he bowed low before each of the stuffed sofas, before Mr. Dietrich, and even lower before the white brick fireplace. The moment of leaving was his only triumph of the day: Aaron was red with rage.

But the moment was, after all, just a moment, and in the taxi taking him back downtown, the cool April breeze blowing against his sweaty face, the pleasure of that kind of oneupsmanship felt as tacky and empty as Park Avenue looked at 1 A.M. Winning at that kind of game was the same as losing. It took precious adrenalin and hot blood just to contend. It took the same length of time to calm down no matter what the outcome.

And, by the time the cab hurtled across Fifty-seventh Street, before it reached the Lever House and the brown-stained Seagram's Building, Phil was just as angry with himself, felt as guilty as he would have felt if he had stayed, if he had let that letch feel his muscle all night.

"I don't believe it," Dietrich had said about him. The *schmuck* was probably right. Why should he believe it? If Phil let himself be conned into going to the party in the first place, why should anyone think he couldn't be conned into more? The con game was the oldest one going. Everyone, everywhere, knew how to play it. You traded. You swapped. You give me what I want and I'll give you what I've got to give. Money. A body. A favor. Happened every minute of every day. Fuck your way to stardom. The American Way. Free enterprise. Make me President and I'll make you Secretary of State. Raise the price of steel and I'll build you a recreation center, for nothing. Give me off-shore oil rights, airplane contracts, napalm orders and I'll do you a Head Start, a Peace Corps, a Vista.

64

Even Doris Day was in it, right up to her touched-up freckles. So why couldn't a good Jewish boy like Philip Bernard Hanssler relax and play the game the way it was supposed to be played? Because even if he wasn't exactly like Aaron or Sandy or Dietrich or poor Howie, a part of him was, a part of him did belong to them, maybe as much as another part belonged to Wilma and her kind of con game. Both parts were inside him all right, but neither one, so far, had really claimed him. They were only different stripes of color—one dark, one light—on the bouncing ball of his confusion, that blur of instincts leading him down or up, no matter what he thought he wanted. Wanting was just not enough to change the way things happened to him. Everyone moved around him. He kept on bouncing, admitting very little, looking for a place, a way, to stay *in between*, to go in and out, from sun to shade to sun again. One thing he did know—the years with Carl Kalb had taught him that much; Wilma had taught him more—was that he wasn't a queer-queer. He wasn't a homosexual like Howie. He was a . . . what? What label fit him? It was about time *he* tried to know.

The cab slowed, curved beneath Grand Central, the new Pan Am building, headed down Park Avenue South. "Driver. Instead of Thirteenth and Eighth take me to University and Eleventh." The driver shrugged without turning, without saying a word.

That's how he gets by, Phil thought. That's his *shtik*: indifference. Who really cares what anyone else does or doesn't do? What possible difference does it make to anyone what Phil Hanssler does in bed, what friends he has, what people he's seen with? None. Not now. Not yet. Except perhaps in Teaneck, New Jersey. It makes a difference to his father, his stepmother, his brothers, their wives. And what mattered to them was if he got a picture of a dress in a magazine, with name credit, if he was quoted in *Women's Wear* or had a sketch in it, if and when he was going to marry Wilma. That being the case—Phil leaned back, rolled up the window—the only thing that really counts is how much pleasure you get from doing whatever it is you do. Not sick pleasure, but pleasure-pleasure that lasts for a while longer than stepping into a taxi. And, also, how much abuse you have to take. That's more important. How far you get before you die. How many people you have to hurt. How many people you can help in a system that honors and pays only the makers, that honors and pays for the way things and people look, that doesn't really give a shit for the way people feel or are beneath the way they look. There isn't a system anywhere that cares too much about that. Power doesn't breed too much compassion. So, all things considered, I'm glad I'm a designer. What else I am is secondary. A statistic in a new Kinsey report. Before I know it I'll be another kind of statistic, a member of a higher tax bracket. Then, being married or not will mean something. So live and let live!

Instead of ringing the bell, Phil walked the one flight of steps to Wilma's apartment, used the key she had given him for just this kind of change of heart.

The light was on in the living room, out in the bedroom. The door to it was ajar. He removed his jacket, loosened his tie, sat down on the foam-rubber Danish-modern sofa, listened for, heard no sound that indicated Wilma knew he was there. A few more minutes before the encounter. A few more minutes of dumb stares at the bookshelves, the hi-fi speakers, the fake, dusty leaves on the corner plant, the coffee stains on the travertine table, the filled ashtrays, the spare ugliness of this room that always seemed to him furnished, except for the books, so that at any moment Wilma could be ready to stuff everything into a pocketbook and leave, move in with him, where there was the permanence of a piano and a real tree, of real window shades and not Venetian blinds. "Be ready to move in a sec, Phil. Just let me get my shower cap."

He left his jacket on the sofa, twisted in a heap that would surely crease it permanently before morning, slid his tie through the bottoned-down tunnel, removed his shirt, got up, still weary, but determined.

Wilma heard him as he entered the bedroom. The door squeaked. The light was behind him; she knew the silhouette. She didn't jump up or scream. She sat up slowly, yawning, lifting her arms toward him, and he moved to sit at the edge of the bed, kicked his shoes away, tugged off his trousers, left them where they fell. Wilma's hand rubbed his back in circles, gently, with just the right amount of pressure, not demanding anything yet, just assured because, after all, there he was. His free choice to be there. Without her nagging or making a scene in the restaurant. So the socks came off, then his wristwatch, his undershorts.

He fell back heavily against the pillow. Wilma propped herself over him, her nylon nightgown brushing across his skin, her other hand moving lightly, brushing back and forth across his chest, patting the hair there with hurt, touching tenderness. "I called you . . ."

"I went to a movie."

"Why did you get so annoyed at the restaurant?" She cradled his head.

"Don't ask me now. I'm too tired to talk about it." He felt her breath on his cheek, in his ear, a satisfied, sleep-warmed breathing.

66

" 'Kay," she whispered. "But I want to know. I deserve to know."

"Did Howie leave with you?"

"No. He had another drink."

"Poor Howie."

"He's not so poor." Her voice moved higher than a whisper. "He's lucky. You're his friend."

He nodded, would have nodded then at anything she said. He rolled on his side to face her, saw, in the semi-darkness that his eyes had adjusted to, that she was smiling. Once more she sat up, pulled her night-gown over her head, threw it from the bed, pushed back the cotton quilt. "I'm always thankful I bought a double bed. My one luxury." Quickly, she moved from the bed to the bathroom, skipping, her *almost* body a blur to Phil's squinting eyes. And almost as quickly she was back, snuggling alongside him, whispering, "Had to you know what." She kissed each of his eyes, his nose, his mouth, his chin. And, without having to force, he did begin to feel her nakedness against his, to feel her under-nourished breasts pressing hard onto his chest. She pulled him closer, not awkwardly, accustomed to the need to do that, the need to lead him to her, to wait, just as he had to wait, for the immeasurable fragment of a moment when the mind, if it is going to at all, shuts down, when the skin leads, pulls, takes over, as if millions of tiny threads were winding around his, hers, everyone's, separateness, binding bodies together, so that the bodies will do what the skin wants them to do, what they exist to do: to lock together, to move beyond that fragment of time, beyond the will-you, won't-you, can-you, can't-you, when the skin does freely what the mind only thinks about doing or thinks it can't do. And if that switch doesn't trip off, as sometimes it didn't for Phil when Wilma led him that way, the mind, its will-you, won't-you remains stronger than the skin, and what you do then is ordered, cold, habit, necessity, solitary, no more pleasurable than urinating when you feel the urge to.

This day's people, pressures, flights receded smoothly now. Wilma's touching led him closer to leading her, and, without thought of what she was or what she hoped for from him each day, he moved over her, stretched the length of her, his body taut, his toes reaching downward, his head upturned toward hers to kiss, scrambled within the fury, the passion, of his shortness that never reached each end of her, lifted then, straight-armed, over her to find her face smiling with love for his effort, encouraging him further, rising to meet him, winding her legs around him so that she was smaller too, mindless too, her hands pulling at his shoulders, straining, forcing, pulling him down against her, into her. Shuddering, squirming with a graceless, dumb strength higher, as he reared, she attached to him and his strength and his weakness, his pushing, pulling, straining to hold back, his delaying the moment for each of them when the skin had to give up once more, yield to the mind, to the tripping switch, to the images of the day flowing back, focusing, becoming, once more, this bed, this room, this semidarkness, these separate bodies panting side by side, settling down against the pillows, the twisted sheets, each listening, waiting for the sounds, the murmurs of satisfaction, hands touching with leftover force, fingers clutching the quieting, slowly cooling, finally silent skin.

Wilma rolled closer to him, kissed his cheek. "That was good. And you were so tired. Sleep. Stay tonight."

"I can't."

"Why not?"

"I can't."

"Please. Stay. We'll have breakfast together."

"I've got to be at work too early for that. Next time I'll stay. Over the weekend." He removed her hand from his. They remained silent, breathing deeply, and then he sat up at the edge of the bed, began the search for his shorts, his socks, his shoes, turned back to kiss her before, carrying his things in a heap, he left the room, finished dressing in the living room, called out, "Good night. Go back to sleep," and left the apartment, locked the door, tried it, hesitated in the corridor before descending the stairs.

Only when she heard his steps sounding in the courtyard beneath the bedroom window did she believe he had actually gone, that he would not change his mind once more and come back.

She got out of bed, resigned to his going, familiar with the fatigue of that resignation, but angry, nevertheless, as she entered the bathroom, ready to cry there, but not in bed. Never in bed. "I'll never win. Never." She opened the medicine chest so she wouldn't have to see her tangled hair, her sweat-glistening skin, her trembling lips locked over those white teeth. "Damn him anyway!"

Chapter Three

One of the promises Phil made to himself when he finally moved from Teaneck into Manhattan was that he would never again travel back there on one of those choking, fume-filled buses that groaned their way across the George Washington Bridge. When he was younger, in his teens, and a bus was the only way he could get into Manhattan with his friends, more often than not he stayed home. Loss of their company was a small price to pay for his comfort. He had kept that promise, even though it meant buying a car which he seldom used, paying for the garage in his apartment building, as well as waiting for the rush-hour traffic to thin out on those Fridays he felt trapped into going home. Waiting meant staying later at work, sketching dresses he would never put into work, but saving the sketches anyway, just in case, stuffing them into a drawer of his desk marked, when Pat discovered the pile of them, THE PERSONAL FILE OF PHILIP HANSSLER, DESIGNER.

This Friday night staying late gave him a chance to talk to Ginny. A. F. found them together when he came into Phil's room to remind him about Sunday afternoon, at his son Joe's house, ". . . and you come too, Ginny. My son has a beautiful house. Beautiful. You'll enjoy it."

"Thank you, Mr. Fleiss, but I've got another engagement."

"I should have asked you before but I've got so much on my mind I can't remember. . . ." His voice trailed off, his gaze shifted from Ginny to the fan of sketches under Phil's hand. "What are these sketches?"

"They're sketches. Just sketches."

"For the line?"

"No. Not for the line. They might have been, but they won't be." Phil closed the fan, carefully straightened the pile.

Relieved, A. F. grinned. "Thank God." He flicked ashes from his blue tie. "So I'll see you Sunday, Philly?"

"Yes. You'll see me Sunday. With a few friends."

"Good. Bring all you want. The more the merrier. Joe's a good enter-tainer."

"I figured we'd need more to be merrier." Phil stuffed the sketches into the special drawer.

"So I guess I'll say goodnight." He moved toward Phil to kiss him. Phil extended his hand. "Goodnight, Ginny. You have a good weekend. Rest up. Plenty of hard work ahead of all of us for the next few weeks." But he was looking down at Phil, was squeezing Phil's shoulder, mumbling: ". . . all of us . . . with hard work . . . we can save it still." He moved as if to leave the room, stopped to touch, to lift, to inspect a mound of tangled fabric in the bin near the doorway. "Too much, Phil. Too many sample cuts here. You'll never use these, but you still buy. Thousands of dollars wasted on sample cuts." He slapped a trembling hand against his cheek, shook his head, discouraged suddenly by the thought of loss, as if these five-yard cuts of fabric were the only reasons for that loss. "Too much. It's too much." He didn't look back as he stepped into the corridor.

"I can tell you, sweetheart, I'm not looking forward to Sunday. He thinks his son Joe, the smart one, is going to solve everything for him. It's pathetic, really pathetic, because from what I hear Joe's a bastard. He won't give a damn about any of it."

"At least you'll be in the country."

"Some country. Scarsdale ain't country, honey. It's just where Jews go when they make it and turn Republican. Either there or Fair Lawn, New Jersey. Where *you* go is really country."

"No place around this city is like country anymore. Not even Goshen, New York. When my man Jim bought that house they practically gave it to him. Now he could sell it for five times the original price. In the Cat-skill Mountains yet. The Gentile part. He probably will sell and then we'll never move up there and get married."

"That's an artist type for you. Do it all the time, Virginia. Just rather go on living in sin."

"Sin-schmin. Who cares. No matter what it's called, I love it." But Ginny blushed because at forty a miracle had happened and she had stumbled on the affection, the excitement that most people hope to find at twenty. And, having found her Jim, her artist, at a time when she least expected it, nothing else came close to mattering, especially work. "My

Catholic mother should hear me say that. *Oy vay!* She'd have a conniption fit. I don't care about getting married really. As long as I didn't have to die a virgin, I'm happy." She burst into nervous laughter, but then, realizing that Phil did nothing more than smile, she stopped abruptly. "As you were saying before A. F. interrupted . . ."

"It can wait until Monday."

"No. Now. I've got time. I'll just take a later bus."

"Well, all I wanted to say, Gin, was that if we close down, I don't want to lose you."

"You think it's certain we'll close?"

"He can't keep it going. His son's not going to help and A. F.'s used up all his money already. Now he's started on his wife's. Which she's sure to put a stop to. She's had it too long to let him piss it away. So what I'm trying to say is that you should be prepared, only don't say anything to the girls yet. No matter what happens, at least they'll get unemployment money. It's you that could have a rough time of it. You're the one I'm worried about."

"And what I'm worried about," the remnant of Ginny's smile dissolved, "is what you're going to do."

Phil leaned down toward his desk, rested his chin on top of clenched fists. "I don't really know. The last few months I feel as if everything has turned to shit. I know what I'd like, but whether I can get it or not is another question. . . . What if it took me three or four months to get someone to back me in a business? Could you wait that long?"

"I'd try to, but I can't promise." There was no hesitation in her response. "As long as I'm a working lady, I want to work for you. You're the one who gave me a break at Kalb's. You made me an assistant. I'd still be a sample hand otherwise. I owe you something."

"You don't owe me a thing."

"But I do as far as I'm concerned. I owe you a lot. But I also have to be realistic. Jim's no earner. He might never be. I am. All my life I've been. I had to be."

"But you'd try to hold out? Right?"

"Right. I'd try."

"That's fair enough."

"No, it's not, Phil. I'm old enough to know that. Nothing's fair. Nothing's fair about life. When you get over your disease—"

"What disease?"

"Being in your thirties. That's why they say life begins at forty. It

71

really does. It's a shorter one, but it begins. Everything gets so clear. That much I can promise you." She stood up, her movement as precise as her words or her work. "It's way after six and if you're going to get home for dinner . . . I'm glad you spoke to me, Phil. I wouldn't have said a word, no matter what I was thinking."

"That's one way we're very much alike."

"Not really. We're that way for different reasons. You have to be, but I'm not ambitious. I don't care about anything any more except Jim. It's the honest-to-God truth. And I don't even feel guilty about it."

"I don't care about anything but myself and I feel guilty about that all the time."

"That's not true, Phil. Everyone loves you. You're good to everyone. Your friends . . ."

"My friends? Some of them love *me*, I suppose." He stood in front of the mirror, flattened his hair into place. "But who do I love? Do I love anything or anyone? That is the question. That's my whole thing."

Characteristically, Ginny didn't try to answer the question. Instead, she held his jacket, smoothed it into place across his shoulders. "Don't worry. If and when Mr. Jack closes, you'll find out in a hurry."

"I hope you're right, sweetheart."

Only Link was left as they walked down the corridor.

Phil noticed a crumpled ball of colored paper on the corner of his packing table. "Where'd you get that, Link?"

"I found it sweeping the other night."

"Why you keeping it?"

"Don't know. Just like the way it looks."

Phil held it in his hand, studied it, tossed it into the air. "Someone's going to make paper dresses out of that stuff."

"Who is?" Link settled the ball back on his table.

"Some smart manufacturer who wants to make a quick killing."

"Will, too." Link held Phil's arm. "Whyn't you do it? Solve all A. F.'s problems."

"No thanks. That's too easy. I never do anything that easy." He moved Ginny forward. "Night, Link. See you Monday."

First there was the dog to walk and then a quick change of clothes, a sport shirt. Wilma managed to squeeze in a call from Brooklyn. "Mama sends her love. And me too." Then there was the Corvair to maneuver out of the crowded garage. It was after seven as he started up the curving, cobbled lane of the West Side Drive. Here caution, only caution, saved. There were still knots of traffic. On Friday evenings there was always traffic, no matter what time. But it kept moving. Very slowly, but moving.

Liffey had her head out the half-opened window alongside the other bucket seat. Occasionally she turned toward him, asking for more speed, more wind. "Sorry, kiddo. Can't go any faster. Good girl. Yes. Look at the scenery." The luxury liners docked. The sky-darkened inky river. The polluted smell of it. The just-greening trees and grass in Riverside Drive Park. The old grime-ruined rococo façades of the apartment houses, once the most stylish dwelling places in Manhattan. High ceilings. Big rooms. Lots of them. Spectacular river views. But the section became unfashionable and the natives' migration across town to the barren East Side began. "See it, Liffey? See?" Her head darted in and out, frantic, looking. Then came *West Side Story*. And Lincoln Center. And another migration back west, but across the river, to the Palisades this time. To Fort Lee, where the living was easy and the taxes were lower. A smart operator could lead a whole city from place to place like a Pied Piper.

Great care on the maze of twisting lanes that led to the bridge. And on it, finally, squeezed between trucks and buses, their exhausts farting down on his compact Corvair, Phil felt his stomach tighten. The span of the George Washington, the cables, the arch, the busses towering above, pressed down. The traffic picked up, slowed down. Car-framed patches of river showed free, briefly. Northward, red lights on the Tappan Zee Bridge winked. And then the automatic tollbooth. Fifty cents in the wire basket. A new game. Perfect shot, a star. "Thank you" flashed in green. Go. Weaving into position, cautiously, for the right lane to Teaneck. The acceleration. A forced speed now that he was on it. Why hurry to get home? But if he slowed, the danger from other cars increased. Trapped into going faster. No pleasure driving on Friday nights in New Jersey. Nothing to see anyway. Neon. The biggest speed-limit signs—50 MILES AN HOUR. THE TOWER OF PIZZA. 50 mph. Everyone was going 60. Which made the short trip to Teaneck even shorter, much too short for the transformation from worried designer to smiling sonny boy to take place.

And after the usual fuss was made over Liffey and she was led to her water bowl and another bowl of shredded chicken in the kitchen—"Off the furniture, Liff. Off!"—and Phil was kissed by his father, stepmother, his half-brother Glenn, Glenn's wife, Betty, after he had shaken hands with his brother Paul and Paul's wife, Andrea, his father urged him into the dining room, whispering so no one else should hear, "You don't look so ay-ay-ay, my sonny. It's bad there?"

"It ain't good." If he didn't turn into a grinning idiot his father would be noodging him all evening. Phil kept on walking, out of the dining room, to the bathroom, where the first item that helped bring on the life-saving grin—a first-aid Scotch he wasn't going to get—was the rhinestone-studded pink and blue toilet-paper cover that matched the pink and blue tiles, the pink and blue towels, the pink and blue magazine rack, the pink and blue ruffled chintz tie-back curtain on the small window, and, of course—Phil stood before it, sighing—the rhinestone frame of the medicine chest. Gorgeous. Every bit of it. Just like the rest of the house. Color coordinated. From top to bottom. He frowned at his reflection—cool it, calm it—forced a smile. Better. Fingers through the hair. "Fuck it!"

They were all seated and silent, impatient—Phil's always being late delayed every meal—except his stepmother, who usually spent most of a meal on her feet, serving a course, then trying to catch up before she had to shuffle back out to the kitchen in her flannel Indian-work slippers to get the next course. "Gefüllte fish. Your father made it especially." As quickly as a big-bosomed, stoopingly tall woman could, she made her proud way around the table. "Be careful of the horseradish. Go ahead. Start. Don't wait for me."

"We can't start before everyone has some, Ethel. When they have, we'll start."

"They'll all have in a minute, Herman. Don't rush me. You're in such a hurry to go somewhere maybe? Relax a little." She shuffled off.

Mr. Hanssler at the head of the table, his hands gripping the armrests —his chair was the only one in the dining-room set that had arm rests— was satisfied. He nodded his satisfaction to the left, where, next to him, Phil, then Betty and Glenn were seated, and to the right, where Paul and Andrea were. They were eating. "It's very good fish this time. At least I *think* it's good. Start, Phil. Don't have to wait for Mother. Just be careful of the horseradish everyone."

But Phil waited anyway, wanting a drink badly but unwilling to stop the action to get one, to slow things down so that it would take even five minutes more to finish dinner and get back to Manhattan. He leaned over to scratch Liffey's pompadour, got her settled at his feet. Waiting. Not for everyone to be served—there had never been such a rule in their fam-

74

ily; his father only acted as if there were—but for his stomach to loosen. Each time he came home, it took longer for him to become a sonny boy. A time might come, maybe when he was fifty, when his father would be willing to admit, "Okay, so you're a grown man and I'm old enough to retire. I won't work. I'll stop riding my horses. I'll sit home with my wife in this house and I'll . . . I'll . . . do what?" Phil wondered what. Look at the gold damask wallpaper? The crystal chandelier? Fall asleep in front of television?

"Eat, Phil." His stepmother, seated for the moment, called out, staring at him anxiously from the other end of the table, but never anxious about anything more than that he eat, that he rave about what he was eating, that he like whatever new *chotchke*, new decoration, she had added to an already over-*chotchkeed* house.

This time he did start eating. Everyone else was eating, everyone but Betty, who poked at the cooked carrot resting on the untouched oval of fish. The fish was good. So tell him so, sonny boy. "Excellent, Dad. Better than the last batch."

"I don't like fish." Betty stopped poking, moved the small plate from her server. "It smells. And I don't like those little yellow beads. They're so ugly."

"How can you not like fish?" Stupefied, as if she were hearing this incredible news for the first time, Mrs. Hanssler frowned at her daughter-in-law.

Betty folded her arms defiantly across her flat breasts. "It's very easy. I just don't."

"Try it at least." Mr. Hanssler spoke up, obliged to speak rather than concerned that she didn't like his fish. As long as his sons ate. That's all that mattered.

"Never. I'd rather die first."

"Leave her alone, Dad." Glenn's fork stopped in mid-air. "You know it is just possible that someone really doesn't like gefüllte fish. She's not used to it. Her mother never made it."

"Her mother's a very good cook." Mrs. Hanssler spoke to the entire group. Since she had wanted the marriage between her son and Betty, it was her duty to assure everyone else that Betty and her mother were worthwhile additions to the Hanssler family.

Paul laughed first. "I'm sure she is, Mother." His wife, Andrea, tried to stuff back her smile with the napkin.

Glenn's fair skin—he had his mother's coloring, her auburn hair, not the Hanssler swarthiness, nor the dark brown hair—paled. He glowered, thin-lipped, across at Paul and Andrea, turned to make sure that Betty did nothing more than pout.

Now, at last, Phil felt he was at home. The brilliant conversation would sparkle with new luster. Paul would start baiting Glenn and Betty; Andrea, lovely, red-headed, Jewish-model chic, quiet bitchy Andrea, would look on amused. His stepmother would settle into her role of public defender and kitchen slavey. His father would stretch his arms out in supplication. "Please, children. No fights. Sssh. Quiet. It's Friday night." And he? Eldest son Philip? What was his role? "Dear Rose Franzblau and Dear Abby and Joyce Brothers, I need help from all of you. I am the product of a fairly well-to-do Jewish family. An average ship of fools. And that's my problem. They own this here beautiful split-level in Teaneck, New Jersey, not far from the George Washington Bridge, in the shadow of Manhattan, you might say. Anyway, my stepmother keeps the house spotlessly clean. Never allows clutter in it like books and records. Only *Look, Life,* and *Cosmopolitan. House Beautiful,* of course. *Photoplay. Screen World.* She loves Cary Grant like a god and, no matter what I tell her, she thinks he's really married to Doris Day. She spends one whole day each week taking apart her crystal chandelier, washing each piece in ammonia, drying them, studying the rainbow in each before she puts it back together again. Other days she dusts, vacuums, scrubs her pink-flecked kitchen Congoleum. My father is a good man who lost his first wife when his two sons were twelve and nine respectively, so he got married again—what else could he do? His second wife is a good housekeeper, but a lousy cook—he does most of that. She's also a lousy decorator, but all she asks for is enough money to go on decorating her house until the day she dies. My real brother is jealous of me. He has reason to be. I left him alone in the lion's den. I did other things too, but I won't go into that now. My half-brother is jealous of me. He has no reason to be. At twenty-three he earns $350 in my father's business, never went to college, really wants to be a car salesman, and owns his own home outright. Although he kisses me affectionately each time he sees me, no matter where it is, I think he really hates me. He knows, because I said it often enough before he got married, that I believe his wife is subhuman. For example, she won't eat tomatoes because they have seeds in them. Therefore, my question to each of you ladies is whether you think third-generation Jews are going to have to fight harder to make it into the mainstream of American life or if they're going to wake up in time to stay out of it, by choice. Which will it be? And, also, what's going to happen to gefüllte fish if they do? Let's hear from you kids soon."

"Phil, your chicken soup's getting cold already." Mr. Hanssler touched Phil's arm. "What are you dreaming about, boychik?"

"Nothing." That was his role: to say nothing; to exercise the power of silence but to lead them all to vicarious fame and wealth, while he went on living in self-imposed exile. Paul and Andrea lived in Manhattan exile too, but Paul wasn't the eldest and therefore was not automatically the just and wise son. Paul was in advertising. No matter how many analysts Paul went to, no matter how many art classes he took at the New School, he would still, and forever, be the middle son, the poor doomed son. Phil slurped his soup. Mrs. Ethel Hanssler was making her accustomed rounds.

"What do you think of my new hairpiece, Phil? It's a good match, isn't it?" Betty poked his arm to make sure he did look. And that was his other role: tastemaker, by royal decree, to the Hansslers. But that, that was a tricky function because if he really told the truth, as he saw it, then he jeopardized his silent power, he became engaged, committed, as the existentialists say. Then they would all be one step away from open warfare and annihilation. Tonight, Phil was relieved of the responsibility of decision. Paul led the attack.

"Tell me, Betty. Is a new hairpiece all you've got on your mind?"

"No, smart aleck! I've got other things, if you'd really care to know."

"Like what?"

"Pot roast!" Mrs. Hanssler shouted on her way in from the kitchen, bent beneath the weight of a platter so filled with thick slabs of meat and potatoes that a battalion of soldiers would have been hard-pressed to finish them. She had missed the news of the hairpiece. "And I've got a beautiful Jello mold. Everybody take. There's plenty. Don't wait for me."

"We're not waiting for you, Mother." Once more Glenn's face whitened with anger, once more his fork was poised, pointing across the table, the food-barricaded buffer zone between natural enemies. "We're waiting for an apology."

"Which you won't get." Perhaps, more than what he said, it was Paul's self-confident smirk, the cool, cruel, perfect oval of his darkly handsome face that set Glenn off. It did that to Phil. Paul was too gleeful, too intent, in a boy-prankster's way, on chipping away—for the sport of it—at the status quo of a family that would never—certainly not at this stage of the game; they were into the late innings—be able to use the honesty of breakthrough, of confrontation. Just because Paul's analyst was leading him to liberating insights didn't mean that everyone could or had to be led to the same place. Live and let live.

"It's a very good match, Betty. You can't even tell it's fake. And I'm also glad to see you're wearing a Mr. Jack. Looks great." Phil watched her puff victoriously, saw, out of the corner of his eye, Paul's lightning flash of hatred, Andrea's cat-eyed contempt, their combined look saying silently, "You lie, Phil Hanssler. Why do you lie? Why?" And his wordless reply: "Because my father is relieved, because he deserves some relief, some rest." Phil directed Andrea's attention to that fact by jerking his head around toward the head of the table. But she wasn't buying any of that crap. Defense of her husband came first. A good quality. Her husband needed help. Admirable. Wilma would probably do the same thing. And once having thought of Wilma, as if it were an ESP implant, the next question out of his father's chewing mouth was, "How's Wilma? Why didn't you bring her tonight?"

Adhering closely to the agenda, that would, of course, be their next item for consideration. Phil readied himself, speared a square of over-cooked pot roast, commended his stepmother, "Excellent. Just right, Mother." Might as well go all the way now. The deeper in you get the easier it is to lie. And, besides, she wouldn't start eating unless he said something.

"Yes. How *is* Wilma?" And it must follow as the night the day that Paul was representing the prosecution, now that he had been betrayed once again. Over and over again. The smirk, the sneer were there. Andrea was beaming the smoldering pleasure of her complicity.

Okay, brother mine, let's wing it. "She's having a period."

Betty slapped her legs, Glenn's, Phil's food-filled fork hand, upsetting it, laughing so that Phil thought he might have to, at any moment, apply mouth-to-mouth resuscitation—a repulsive thought. Fortunately, she remembered that talk of periods should embarrass her. She stuffed her fingers against her mouth, bit them.

"That's not exactly what Paul meant, Philly." But, nevertheless, Mr. Hanssler was grinning too, his cherubic cheeks puffed into brilliant red circles. "Seriously, I'm asking to inquire how she is."

"How come no one's touched a pickle? Usually you eat all of them. And I cut up so many. Aren't they good?"

"Will you keep quiet, Ethel!" Mr. Hanssler slammed the armrests of his chair as if they were a prayer desk at the synagogue. "I'm trying to talk to Phil."

"Pardon me, your highness. I didn't hear you open your mouth."

"You never hear when I'm talking."

"She never hears when anyone's talking." Paul was letting the choke out all the way. "It's impossible to communicate with her."

Mrs. Hanssler's lips quivered. She poked distractedly at her blond-streaked auburn hair, hair that was just too much for the big shell combs she used to hold it in place. Poor thing, Phil thought. She just had too much of everything: too much breast; too much height; too much nose; too much hair; but not enough brain to know how to strike back. In addition to which, she dressed like a *schlump*—the final indignity for her stepson the designer. She bought her clothes in every tacky Tall Shop in Northern New Jersey instead of going to the places he wanted to send her to. She had the money, but she lacked the nerve. It was pathetic. Sad. So Phil felt compelled to exercise the power of his divine right, to try to maintain the precarious peace for another night. But he had the feeling, judging from Paul's mood, that nothing was going to help; kindness would not prevail. Immediate escape was the only answer. Which was impossible. Escape, yes, finally. Immediate, never. When the pot roast and potatoes were removed, when the Jello mold stopped quivering, there would be tea and cake, nuts and raisins, fruit in season, formal debate, playing with Liffey and then, only then, and only if the stars were on his side, Manhattan. "I'll take Manhattan, the Bronx and Staten Island too/ It's lovely going through the zoo. . . ." "Mother," her lips stopped gnawing plaintively, she exhaled, certain that he would help her, "perhaps you should listen a little bit more to what's being said."

"I hear everything perfectly. I was only asking about the pickles and . . ."

"Ethel!"

"Don't Ethel me, Herman. Just let me finish what I started to say! Usually, you all eat up every pickle I cut up. I always have to cut more. So I only wanted to inquire if these were maybe not good. That's absolutely the only thing I wanted to know. Is that so terrible a thing to ask?" She forced her shoulders up and back, but the strain of having said what she wanted to say, the weight of her breasts, dragged her down, returned her thought to what hurt her most of all. "I have a right to speak too, you know, once in a while."

Paul's charitable smile flashed on; his arm stretched toward her along the littered tablecloth: gestures of a recently discovered awareness, a concern for *some* of those less fortunate than himself. Phil watched, absorbed by the breathtaking display of sudden affection. Next would come a com-passion-filled explanation and then—"You have a perfect right to ask about the pickles, Mother. No one denies you that right. It just happened that as you were asking that question, Dad was also asking Phil some-thing. About Wilma." The smile dissolved; the arm was withdrawn, and with it went charity. "Now, perhaps, we *can* hear about Wilma."

Phil shoved his plate away. The slabs of meat, all of the undercooked, tasteless potatoes were still on it. "What's all this sudden interest in Wilma? Why doesn't anyone ask me what's happening at work or what I think about Vietnam or black power? What's all this concern for Wil-ma's condition? Because if you really care that much, Paul, I'll give you her mother's telephone number in Brooklyn. That's where Wilma is to-night. You can call her yourself and find out how she feels."

"Boys." Mr. Hanssler raised his arms, extended them toward either side of the table protectively. "Please. Not now."

"Can't I ask Phil a question, Dad?"

"Of course you can ask. But a real question. About something else. Phil, you didn't finish. Don't you like it? It's not good meat?"

"It's too dry."

Betty stage-whispered to Glenn, "See! I told you. Your brother *Phil* al-ways tells the truth. Just like *I* want to do."

"Don't copy me, Betty. You'll get into a lot of trouble that way."

"Telling the truth?"

"Yes. You're supposed to lie and like it."

"Well, I won't."

"It's not necessary for anyone in this house to lie." Mr. Hanssler slammed the armrests. "It's possible the meat is a little dry. It happens . . ."

"I thought you said it was excellent, Herman?"

"I did. *I* think it is. Phil thinks it's dry. So is that anything to make such a fuss, such a *tsimmis* over? More important is whether you're boil-ing water for tea."

"Just hold your horses!" Nevertheless, she stood up, began collecting the plates.

"Andrea? Betty?" Phil lifted Liffey to his lap to guard her against fall-ing missiles. "How about both of you getting up off your asses to help your mother-in-law with the dishes?"

That remark Mrs. Hanssler heard. She stopped shuffling, trapped and sputtering. "It's . . . it's not necessary for anyone to help me."

"I don't help in someone else's house." Betty glared across the table at her sister-in-law, not at Phil. "And they don't have to help in mine."

"I work all day. I'm tired." Satisfied, Andrea smoothed the long red bang back from her eyes.

Mrs. Hanssler set herself in motion once again, turned a deaf ear on the proceedings, carried her load out to the kitchen.

A temporary truce followed, a silence punctuated by belches, teeth sucking, chair twistings. Hands brushed crumbs over the table. Mr. Hanssler, in exaggerated circles of satisfaction, rubbed his stomach, gazed out at each of his sons the wan, lost smile of a sixty-four-year-old man whose life had been derailed suddenly years ago, too many years ago to remember exactly, and whose every effort now was aimed at making appearances appear as if he had worked since then uninterruptedly, unselfishly to achieve the family harmony that existed in this dining room tonight. And maybe, just maybe, Phil thought, he believes that everything *is* harmonious. After all, he goes to synagogue every high holy day, he makes gefüllte fish and pickled herring, he's generous to his youngest son, who will someday inherit a small, but solid business. So how could anyone dare to say, dare to think, that God isn't good to those who sacrifice for others? Of course God is good. Just look at all the happy faces in this room. Just look at all the looks of love and human kindness being exchanged beneath the sparklingly clean crystal chandelier, ricocheting off the gold damask wallpaper. It's a pleasure to relax in such an atmosphere.

And, as he always did on these glorious occasions, and always without wanting to do it—what's done cannot be undone—Phil imagined what his life, his father's, Paul's, might have been like if his mother had lived. Thinking that thought was like dreaming a recurring nightmare with your eyes wide open, and so never being able to shake free of it by opening your eyes on a new slant of sunlight, by leaping out of bed. What if. What if. Over and over again without wanting it. A thought suspended, stretched across all the time of his life between then, when it happened, and now. What if? One thing, he wouldn't have ended up as a designer. That was certain. Designing was no profession for a Jewish boy. Jews were manufacturers. The money men, the power behind the throne. They made stars out of Gentiles, made them world-famous designers. They didn't promote their own. It wasn't kosher to play favorites. Such scrupulous people. Snobs of self-righteousness who always got the shitty end of the stick.

And Paul? An advertising exec if she had lived? Never. That beautiful child using his beauty to sell ads? Of course not. A dentist, maybe. A movie star.

And his father? His father woudn't have that sad, self-sacrificing smile on his face. He'd be angry; he'd be yelling the way he did years ago. They fought a lot. Phil could remember that. Good fights. Not about pickles. The kind that ended up somewhere else different from where they started, that changed things, that moved them all closer together inside a house that had books in it and music—his mother played their piano every day—and comfortable furniture to jump on instead of the phony museum pieces his stepmother collected which no one was supposed to use, only admire. And when he and Paul were growing up they could have masturbated properly behind closed doors instead of having to hold one hand against a door without a lock. His stepmother had removed the locks from every door in the house except the outside one. For what reason she never said. For just that one thing Phil, even now, could never forgive her. The older he got the more he resented it, remembered it. Her screaming, her slaps, her pinching, her lousy cooking, her making him into a mother's helper when Glenn was born, all that he could forget, but not those doors. And neither, he guessed, could Paul.

When they were on friendlier, more brotherly terms, Paul often recalled that lovely period in their lives. It was when Phil fought his way out of the house and went off to Syracuse that Paul turned on him, as if he felt that his older brother, his ally, his only link with a buried world of feeling, was deserting him, leaving him stranded all alone on a crowded, emotionally barren suburban island. Well—Phil shifted Liffey to another uncomfortable position on his lap, watched his stepmother sorting teacups, looked across at Paul chewing hard on a nut cake—wondering *what if* isn't going to change a thing. At least Paul is married. He isn't alone. He's got another ally and a much better one than his older brother had ever been. So, Mother mine, rest in peace. You're just a what-if, a waste of time now, with a dim face, a short, slim, beautiful darkness that's all so hard to recall. The only clear memory is of being twelve, and of the death, and her few angry words at the end: "Not now. Not now. . . ."

"So Philly, what are you dreaming about again?"

"Nothing Dad. Nothing at all."

"Phil. Take some raisins. You like raisins."

"I don't want any, Mother. I'm getting too fat."

"You? Fat?" Glenn leaned in front of his wife, smiling in disbelief. "Never. Paul's the one who has to watch his weight."

Paul dropped a piece of apple cake onto his plate. "That's my own private business."

"Sure it is, but I only think a friendly reminder once in a while . . ."

"My wife is here to remind me. As long as she doesn't object, that's all that matters."

"Well, I *am* your brother, after all. I'm allowed to comment—"

"My brother? What's that got to do with it? I don't sleep with you."

"Paul!"

"Oh, come on, Dad. Don't be so afraid to let people talk. It's healthy once in a while to talk about serious things instead of . . . of . . ."

Mr. Hanssler nodded benignly, waiting to hear what serious topic Paul would propose. It was discussion time.

". . . of cars and hairpieces."

"I didn't bring up cars once tonight." Since he wasn't holding a fork, Glenn pointed his finger, but not directly at Paul, at something on the wall to the side of Paul's head.

"No. That's true. But your wife did ask about her hairpiece."

"She asked Phil. It's natural that she would ask Phil, isn't it?"

"Yes. I suppose so, if that's all she could think of. If she couldn't ask him about a book she's read or a play she's seen or a museum she went to then a hairpiece will have to do. But it's a pretty sad substitute."

"We can't all be as cul-tur-al as you are. Not *all* people have to like the same things you do."

"That's true, but if they knock something, they should at least know about what they're knocking. Betty, when was the last time you and Glenn went into New York to see a play?"

"I don't like to go into Manhattan. It's too crowded."

Paul slammed the table. "You're kidding me. You have to be joking."

"I am not joking." She folded her arms across her breasts. "I just don't like to be pushed around by strangers and I don't like driving on bridges. Can I help that, big shot?"

"Don't call me a big shot. I won't take that kind of talk from you."

"Whoa! Slow down." Mr. Hanssler grinned conciliatorily, lifted his arms.

Phil forced them down. "This is the most fun we've had all night."

"If you want to call anyone a big shot, just speak to the man at your right, Betty. *He's* the big shot."

"I figured you'd get back to me somehow, Paul, old kid. So go ahead. Tell me about big shots. I'm enjoying myself."

"Herman! I don't like this kind of talk. Eat your cake, Paul. You're not getting fat."

Paul's look was anything but charitable now. "Will you just please stay out of this! I'm talking to Phil. And he *is* a big shot. Thinks he's superior to everyone else. So *above* the rest of us . . ."

"You're describing yourself, not Phil." But Glenn's hiss of hatred went unnoticed. Paul had no time to waste now on minor irritants.

". . . and where does that so-called superiority come from, I ask you? From making more money than anyone else? And how? Doing what? Designing dresses! While the rest of the world goes to pieces. Some profession!"

"Paul, now even I don't like this kind of talk. It's not nice." Mr. Hanssler covered Phil's hand as if it were a pair of eyes that he wanted to shield from an ugly sight meant only for grownups, never for his sonny boy. "As long as women are wearing dresses, someone has to design them."

"A woman should. They know how clothes feel. A man who thinks he does can't be very much of a man."

During the expectant silence that followed, Phil, weary but calm—this was not the first time Paul had launched such an attack in full view of the family—removed his father's hand, put Liffey back at his feet, straightened, still smiling. That was essential: to smile confidently, even while his ears clogged with anger—it only hurts when I laugh. The topic *was* tricky. It *did* reach down to a chamber in the heart of the matter. And if Paul would just raise it once and for all somewhere privately for any other reason than vindictiveness, Phil would be glad to talk about it openly, understanding brother to understanding brother. They had shared enough lousy meals together in the past, in this same damn house, for each of them to try to salvage some affection now. But no. It was always raised in front of his father and stepmother, in front of Glenn and Betty. And what point was there in that? What could they know about the real situation? For them "not much of a man" meant a sissy, someone who rolled his eyes and his hips. A hairdresser. A female impersonator. A ballet dancer. A designer. But not their son and brother. Never that. Anyone else, but not Philly. He didn't look like one, not like the kind they saw on television or in antique shops or their friends told them about seeing in a nightclub in Miami. Of course not. "All right, Paul. Now it's my turn." But he paused, wanting a little longer to sort through his thoughts with care, to balance, beforehand, their silent weight against their spoken impact on his stepmother's dumb, determined grin, his father's downcast, balding head, Andrea's knowing, spoon-turning embarrassment, Betty and Glenn's immovable ignorance. No way to calculate anything for sure. People felt words only to the degree that they were equipped to feel them. Here the risk was hurt, not comprehension. So shoot. "If you're trying to force me into some kind of confession, I'm sorry to disappoint you. There's nothing much to confess. But what if there was? What pleasure would it give you to have me say it right here? Would that help anything? Would it make *you* feel superior to me? Is that what you want? Because if that's the case then I really feel sorry for you. You're a lot less intelligent than I thought you were."

The silence filled with nervous squirmings, creaks of discomfort. They were listening. So far, so good. "Without sounding malicious—I don't mean to sound that way—I can tell you that I know a number of queers who have it all over you in brains and ability—maybe not in looks—who don't go around the way you do, forcing their point of view on everyone else, insisting that what they think about the way to live is the only thing to think. They've got better things to do with their time." Phil saw the sad smile return to his father's face. The threat of being told something he didn't want to hear was passing. Now it was Paul's turn to be downcast. "And as far as Wilma is concerned—I bring her up because when you asked about her earlier you were really asking the same question you're asking now—if I get married at all, which I'm not sure I want to do, it'll be Wilma I marry. But—and I might as well say this as long as I'm saying—if I do get married it's not going to be so you can have a grandchild, Dad, or for Mother to buy presents. Paul and Glenn can give you all those prizes. That kind of crap doesn't interest me. And I'm sure it's no special news to anyone that some people, including me, feel this isn't such a hot world to be born into."

"What the world's like doesn't matter, Philly." Mr. Hanssler's hand returned to cover Phil's, pleaded by its gentle patting to be allowed to stay there. "A boy, a Jewish boy, grows up, gets bar-mitzvahed and married, earns a living, buys a house, has children—"

"In Teaneck, Dad. In your world. It may come as a great shock to you and Glenn, not to Paul, I hope, that for a lot of people, Jews and non-Jews, white *and* black, life's bigger than that, a lot more complicated. Which is why I know that the future's going to be different, whether you or anyone else likes it or not. It'll take a while. A long while. But it's going to change and I'm glad it is. It should change. The only thing I'm not glad about is that I'm too old . . ."

"You're young. What are you talking old for?" A father's hand patted.

". . . I'm too old to change the way things influenced me inside. I keep trying, though. And as for my being a big shot, Paul, and a designer, all I can say is that if you think I'm such a big shot, if you think my profession is so worthless and making money and success are worthless, why are you jealous of me?"

"I'm not jealous." Paul did not look up.

"You are, sweetheart, whether you admit it or not. I think that's a good topic to talk to your analyst about. You might have a major breakthrough." Phil stood up. "The most amazing thing about this entire evening is that not once did any member of my loving family bother to ask me seriously about Mr. Jack, about what I'm going to do if it closes."

"I did, Philly. Right when you came. But I didn't want to bother you with questions."

"Bother me? Come on, Dad. Tell the truth. You're afraid to ask me. You're afraid you'll hear something bad. It's better not to know. That's the story of your life." Phil moved away from the table, Liffey following obediently at his heels.

Mrs. Hanssler sprang up. "You can't go yet. I'm going to make coffee. You didn't eat any fruit."

"I'm going, Mother. I'm tired and I'm disgusted and I'm not in the mood for coffee."

Glenn and Mr. Hanssler hurried to their feet, both of them trying to hold Phil back. Liffey growled, confused by the hugs, the kisses. "I didn't say anything to offend you, did I, Phil? Betty didn't?"

"Of course not. You never do. Which is *your* problem. Neither one of you ever says anything that matters. That's one thing I'm in agreement with Paul about." Glenn shrugged his shoulders, moved off. "But don't worry, Dad. Everything's going to be perfect for all of us. You raised healthy children. You've got a fine wife and a beautiful home. Only don't expect me here next week or the week after that or for a long time. If you want to come into New York, fine." He turned back toward the fruit-and-nut-filled table. "Good night, Andrea, Paul." They remained motionless. "I'm sure nothing's changed between us."

And as if, in fact, nothing unusual had occurred for her, as if she had refused to hear Phil's promise, Mrs. Hanssler accompanied him to the front door, kissed him, thanked him for coming home, apologized for the meat, "it'll be better next week," stood outside on the red brick porch, waving and grinning as Phil and Liffey raced down the neat, shrub-lined walk to the car. As a parting gesture, Liffey stopped long enough to squat and squirt out a half dollar's worth of water on the lawn.

"Good girl." The car door slammed. Mrs. Hanssler waved her arm in wider arcs. Phil pressed down on the accelerator. Up, up, and away.

Chapter Four

Probably it was a mistake to ask Cindy Rubin up to Joe Fleiss's house. Pat would have been a better choice. Natural instant-swingers always help crucial situations. One of the magazine gals would have been more politic. But Pat was unavailable and it was too short notice for anybody else, so Phil had to settle for Cindy, and Cindy made four, a good number, two couples: Cindy and Howie; Wilma and himself. *Oy vay* Psychopathics anonymous. A taut string quartet. Cindy, seated in the back with Howie, spent most of the trip applying make-up and complaining monotonously about how narrow the seat was. "Really, I can't imagine what those designers in Detroit know about human proportions. I've never thought of my derrière as being oversized. Nobody's ever told me it was. Do you think it is, Phil?"

"You've got a great ass, Cindy. Best in the business. It's the car that's to blame."

"Why don't you get a new one?" Cindy's hairbrush sliced through her Sassoon spillway with professional abandon. "A Mercedes. They are darling cars, don't you think?"

"Not exactly darling. Good-looking, handsome. Not darling. But no matter what you call it I wouldn't buy one."

"Why not? They're so chic."

"Well, I'm not chic. I don't buy German products." Phil sighed. Wilma leaned across him for the cigarette lighter, smoothed his beige hip-hugger leg. They smiled. Wilma was happy today. Last night Phil had stayed with her, all night, had had breakfast with her. Next to that, she loved a car ride in the country more than anything he could ever give her. Especially when the day was as sunny, as cloudless as this one. April, the way it is never reported to be, but almost always is. May is when it rains.

"You know, Phil," Cindy's brush stopped brushing, a sure sign that she was momentarily puzzled by something, then resumed its sliding path, "I really don't understand your attitude. I mean, being Jewish doesn't seem very important to you and Germany is, after all, a friendly nation now."

"Cindy," Howie, his friend the teacher, took over for Phil. A person couldn't talk and drive at the same time. Not seriously, anyway. Not on a Sunday, and Howie enjoyed trying to reconcile a paradox. The greater the paradox, the better the explanation. If Howie became talkative, then maybe the afternoon would succeed instead of making them feel like they were all on their way to a wake or a sympathy call. ". . . and what I'm getting at, Cindy, honey"—Howie cleared his throat, hoping to lure her attention from her mirror and her jiggling lipstick brush—"not every friend of your friend is a friend of yours, is he?"

"No, but I really don't see what that has got to do with it. Really I don't."

"You really don't?" Howie uncrossed his legs, a preliminary to further explanation. In his classroom he would have been pacing back and forth, energetically pursuing an idea. Here energy made no sense. There was no room for it. His long legs made contact with Cindy's beauty equipment. Reflexively, he squeezed back into the corner. "Let me put it another way, if I may . . ."

"You certainly may." Cindy continued to struggle with her lipstick brush.

"Thank you." He fought the desire to yield to the peace of watching her single-minded pursuit of glamour. But no. Having spoken up, he was honor bound to continue. "Germany *is* a friendly nation. So was Russia during the Second World War. America decided to make her enemy an ally, and her ally her enemy. Given Germany's history I would call that a dangerous choice and one I don't happen to accept. And, yes, my Jewish background is relevant. Why shouldn't it be? Germany is *my* enemy. Always will be. Phil and I were stationed there in the army. We both have some personal experience with the German mentality, some very strong reasons for not buying their products."

"You too? You don't buy?"

"No. And there are a lot more of us than you might think."

"Well, I think it's ridiculous."

"So do I." Howie turned quiet, finally hypnotized by Cindy's attempt to get her false eyelashes on in a moving vehicle. A valuable skill, more valuable than thinking in a moving vehicle.

"Look at all those yellow . . . what-do-you-call-'ems?" Wilma's white teeth flashed for Phil inside her expanding smile.

"Forsythia."

"Well, whatever they are—forsythia? lovely name—they're just grand. Absolutely grand. Why don't we stop and pick some?"

"We're on the Hutchinson River Parkway, Wilma. You can't just stop and pick. There's a fine for that. The Westchester County expert, Howie Goldstein, told me so."

"A fine? How horrible. Anybody that would arrest anyone for picking flowers has got to be corrupt. This whole world is corrupt. Completely corrupt. From my boss right down to the police. Why, just the other day I tried to make a citizen arrest on University Place, near N.Y.U. Someone was exposing himself and the policeman I called over said I shouldn't be looking. Said it's none of your business, lady. Well, if that isn't, what is?"

"What is?" Howie leaned forward, his chin coming to rest on the back of Phil's bucket seat.

"What is what?" Wilma twisted around, ebullient, sun-inspired, ready to talk, even to Howie.

"What is your business?"

"Justice is my business. Justice, baby. Liberty and justice for all."

"Well, that's a conversation stopper all right. No arguing that endeavor." Howie slid backward, scrunching up, avoiding Cindy.

"Do you think this culotte outfit is right, Phil?"

Wilma answered for Phil. "You look divine, Cindy. If I had one I would have worn it instead of these stretch pants."

"They're charming, Wilma. Just charming. I love stretch pants—for when I go to a ski lodge."

"Not to ski in?"

"I don't ski. I just go skiing. I love to look at snow. It's so . . . so pure." Cindy began a fastidious repacking of her gear, dismissing Wilma.

"Remember, honey, justice for all," Phil whispered, the sound concealed beneath the chug of the Corvair's back-pushing engine. "Just stare out at nature. You love nature. Count the forsythia. We'll be there before you know it." She nodded obediently.

"I'm so glad you asked me to come, Phil." For some mysterious reason Cindy had resumed brushing her hair. "I've been dying to see Joe Fleiss's house. Robert tells me it's magnificently decorated. Very sumptuous. Westchester people let their decorators go wild, I hear. I'd love to get a few commissions. . . ."

"Didn't you brush your hair already?" Howie tried to sound ingenuous.

"I did, but hair is a model's chief asset. It can never have enough care. Without it you're nothing."

"Without it you're bald." Howie leaned forward once more. Wilma suppressed her sense of justice behind a handkerchief. Phil sighed, but Cindy went on brushing and talking single-mindedly.

"Not really. Nowadays there are marvelous wigs and falls. Perfectly matched pieces . . ."

So, from Friday night to Sunday afternoon, I've gone full circle, Phil thought. Nowhere. He accelerated, then had to brake sharply.

"What are those gorgeous trees, Phil?"

"Those ain't no trees, Wilma baby, those are hairpieces." He gripped the steering wheel tightly, knuckles whitening, but, in spite of everything, kept on smiling.

And he kept right on smiling through the introductions, through the Cindy-inspired tour of the three-story nineteenth-century house, and through the first drink. Standing at the back of the back lawn—"It's like July weather," Rosalind, Joe's wife, repeated to each new cluster of guests, of which there were millions, many more than a small gathering, "exactly like July, so I thought we'd drink outside. Like a lawn party, you know"—Phil spied A. F. and his wife moving toward his hiding place behind a willow tree, and at that point his smile unfroze. It never returned, except for a moment of hysterical laughter, until he got back to his apartment very drunk and very much later that night. Howie had to drive home, help him upstairs, walk Liffey.

Actually, the crowd wasn't a bad one. It was intelligent, chic, integrated, Jews, Gentiles, a dash of Blacks, escapees from Angola, heteros, homos, independent Republicans, a stimulating mixture—of wealth, of everyone vomiting money at you, not in a vulgar, obvious manner, but managing to slip that fact about themselves in sideways, like a quick lateral pass in a football game. "On our trip through Mexico to Acapulco this winter—we own property there—the one thing that appalled us so was the condition of the poor Mexicans. Unimaginable squalor. I said to Peter, my husband, I said I didn't think I could stand very much more of it. So we canceled the touring and went right on to Acapulco. That shoreline is breathtaking. . . ." Wilma got stuck with that one on the house tour. For openers, and, as it turned out, for closers, Cindy attached herself to Joe Fleiss. Cindy forced the group to linger in the second-floor sitting room while she oohed and ahed over the colored cushions. "They're just the perfect accents for the wood paneling, Joe. Your wife must be so clever." "My wife didn't do a thing. Some pansy decorator did. Charged plenty." "From the look of it, I'm sure he must have."

Phil dragged Howie from the room, led him through the maze of corridors and out to the portable bar set up on the back lawn where, to Howie's obvious chagrin—his mouth opened in a silent, howling O of anguish —Joe Fleiss's effeminate high-school-senior son—there was another son and a daughter darting nearby—cornered him. "You teach in Mamaroneck, don't you, Mr. Goldstein. English, my mother said."

So that left Phil alone with his first drink. Not alone in fact—fifty milling guests nearby isn't really alone—but alone in feeling, the way it was when he walked through a crowded bar. At least this bar was al fresco, sunlit, life-giving. He made it to a willow tree unattached, with the chance for a few moments to size up the situation, to plan his next move. One thing was quite clear: Joe Fleiss was a big-timer, a smart operator, just as A. F. said, the opposite of Robert. From this temporarily safe distance, Phil saw Robert and his chopped-liver-luscious Israeli wife being turned in circles of introduction by Rosalind. Like blind man's buff. And it's true that no matter where Robert went he was always being turned in circles, either by his wife or his father or his sister-in-law or by anyone else who wanted to act as official circle-turner. It was Joe—Robert would go on gyrating for the rest of his life—who could, probably, with one of his smallest bank accounts, save Mr. Jack. Plan One now in operation, sir. Well, A. F. old boy, you better leap off that mountain of dreams you're standing on. Your sonny boy won't dig it. This kind of layout—a Tudor mansion, three cars, three dogs, servants, a tennis court, a swimming pool, a spur-of-the-moment decision to move a buffet dinner for fifty-odd from the inside to the garden—all that didn't happen because Joe could feel sentimental about a father's dying business.

Even A. F. sensed that whenever he repeated the Joe Fleiss Saga. There were always tears in his eyes, but the tears were for what he had failed to hold on to, not for the affecting, bigger-than-life details of his son's rise to affluence. That old American Dream come true ain't no romance, Papa. No sirree. It's all about this here power. Heartless, defeating-other-people power that gets you to the right place at the right time, that makes you look like some kind of marvelous, blue-eyed god when you get there. Joe Fleiss got there just before the building boom began in New York City. What was he before? A small-time contractor who gambled, who bought up all the heavy equipment he could find and then rented it out. "Smart, my Joe. Very smart." Next came real-estate speculation and after that the stock market and while that was going on there were the moves: from Central Park West to the East Side, a Gracie Mansion–area cooperative, and, finally, on to Scarsdale, to a green shade beneath a big green tree, and a big house, an art collection, Rosalind's pride and joy. Phil knew it by heart. When he arrived at Mr. Jack, it was a lunchtime story and an over-drinks-at-the-club story. A proud father crying: "And the schools in Scarsdale! The best schools in the country, you know. Better than California."

Phil gulped his drink. A.F. had appeared near an iris patch. A person could spot him on any crowded back lawn in America: the glen plaid; the blue tie; the sun-lamp glow of health; the image sustaining, but wearing thin. And he was looking for his Philly. That was clear. He stopped to ask Wilma, herself alone—no, she was being circled by what had to be a loose husband. Wilma smiled no, shrugged, peered, pointed to the house. No. You're cold, A.F. He stalked Cindy, laughing Cindy, Joe-touching Cindy, who was being introduced to potential customers. She pointed to the bar. But A. F. had toured that area by now. No, Philly wasn't there. Still cold. And another no from Rosalind, who pouted when her father-in-law pulled at her Pucci print from behind. That's the way to see it all, Phil baby, from an unengaged distance. Through a glass lightly, so it all looks like a mirage, a pantomime, with the volume turned down low, so low you don't have to pay no nevermind to any of it, while the spring sun explodes overhead, promising a westering, a setting later, much later, and the trees budding, forsythia yellowing peacefully like dabs of melting butter, clarifying, for Julia Child, a jug of wine, a loaf of bread, a wire whisk —but no, *sonnele*, there is no safe distance. He *was* engaged, had to be, wanted to be. His future depended on the right move from behind this tree. So stop hiding. Stop running from everyone, the way you've been doing all week—sure you have—with the exception of last night when you stayed warm with Wilma. Move to meet A. F. and his wife, Clara, halfway. If you're seen—which he was; "So there you are!" they called— so be seen already. Cut velvet! Jump!

Clara offered her round, blond cheek to be kissed. "Phil, let me look at you," at arm's length so that her Chanel suit could be surveyed and appreciated along with the color of her beige and blue hair. "Why, you look marvelous. Alex told me you didn't. He told me he was worried about you. Alex, look at him. He looks beautiful. Such a smart sports coat. It's

English," rubbing the sleeve of his itchy Harris tweed, a jacket even older than the houndstooth. "I know English styling when I see it. Why are you hiding down here?" She took his arm. A. F. took hold of the other. Together they led him up to the crowd, toward the bar. The volume came up, blastingly loud, like going from a quiet bedroom in an old Hollywood movie to the outside where drilling was going on. Everything suddenly amplified: the laughter, the shouts, the women's bracelets banging.

"Another, Philly?" A. F. took his glass, but didn't let go of his arm. "Scotch here, bartender. A little soda. Lemon peel, Phil? You want some lemon peel?" A. F. yelled, "For my designer, a toast!" Alex and Clara turned Phil to face the nearby faces, whose mouths froze mid-word. Glasses were raised, including Wilma's and Howie's. Phil sought their eyes for help, but they wanted help too, they wanted to be sprung from their traps. Irritated, polite sipping ensued, and then a general lowering of glasses. Faces turned away; suspended syllables dropped; mouths resumed chewing their cud of party conversation. A. F., Clara, Phil were forgotten. The three musketeers moved into the eye of the sound. "Well, certainly Scarsdale's changed. All of Westchester's changed alarmingly. . . ." "The Turner exhibit at the Modern Art is breathtaking. You must see it immediately. Never mind how crowded it is. Go . . ." "I only buy Jerry Silverman's. I can count on his dresses being sane! No need for my clothes to be avant-garde, really. Comfort and chic. That's the way I dress. That's always in style."

They were advancing toward Joe and Cindy, a stationary pair on the fringe now, moving through loops of people, cutting through the rain forest, inching forward. ". . . But I do appreciate the great poetry, Mr. Goldstein. I only question Shakespeare's relevance for now. I really prefer Brecht. Didn't you love *Threepenny Opera?*" "No. As a matter of fact, I didn't." Poor Howie. "You live . . . alone . . . in Manhattan, Miss Pasternack?" "No. As a matter of fact, I don't." Keep lying, Wilma honey. That's the way to win. They arrived behind Joe, undetected. "What you need is someone to set you up, Cindy. A shop. A classy East Side shop. And work out of there." Cindy, facing them, smoothed back her spilling hair, lifted her grass-stained culotte bottoms, leaned away from Joe in warning, but he misunderstood the signals, took them as gestures of desire, stepped closer. A. F. tapped his back respectfully, frowned at Cindy. Clara hopped into action, outmaneuvered Cindy, cut between Joe and—her face showed it to her son clearly—this cheap, overdressed model. "Joe darling, did you meet Phil yet. I'll bet you didn't with all these people here. A gorgeous party. Absolutely—"

"We met before, Mother." He tried to move around her, but Clara Fleiss was no pushover. No son in the world could neglect her wishes, not even Big Joe, handsome, oiled, manicured, perfumed Big Joe, ascoted, Italian double-knitted, baby-blue-sweatered, gray-flanneled Joe. He was just another million-dollar son to Clara. But, at least, while the jockeying for position went on, Phil was unhanded, freed to gulp his Scotch, which he did then with alarming speed, while, grudgingly, Joe yielded temporarily to his mother and father. Cindy, demurely decorous, stepped aside. Joe wouldn't forget her. That much even Cindy could decipher from Joe's raised eyebrow. Phil watched her departure, a slow sidle, a stumble—the grass was a little tricky for gracious exits—a hair-controlling hand shooting up through the rosy light. You're doing it all wrong, A. F., baby. You should know better than to interrupt a pointer pointing. What's he going to care about your troubles if you break his point? A sputtering father? A mother's sacrifice? Never. Come on, A. F. Act your age. . . . Phil strolled onto the stage. He had to, to speak up for the cause of decency, the ten commandments: Honor thy father and thy mother! "You've really done a job here, Joe. A great house. Can't get over it. And you too. How the hell do you stay in such great shape through the winter?"

Joe, deflected, twisted his ascot beneath his heavy earlobe so that the flow of its loose knot pointed out over his sweater, down toward his flat stomach. "Thanks for the compliments. I've been working out daily. Joined the New York Athletic Club. Jews are in there now, you know. I led them in, and out of Egypt." He laughed, choked briefly on some loose phlegm. Clara and A. F. took their stand now on either side of their big boy. Another grouping. A classic grouping. A Henry Moore made flesh. Phil gulped. He was striking ice. Steady, boy. Joe counts.

"Is today's party for a special occasion, Joe?"

"Didn't Dad tell you? It's my twentieth anniversary."

"You're kidding? You're too young looking for twenty years in bondage." Phil, playing an embarrassment lesson from his acting-school days, extended his hand. "Why didn't you let me know, A. F.?" A. F. kicked the ground, anxious to get to the point. "Congratulations, Joe."

Joe's hand grabbed, toppled Phil against him, Indian-wrestle style, straight-armed him upward. "What you need is another drink, Phil. . . . Where the hell is Rosalind?" His head held high, higher than most—tall is tall, Philip; there's no gainsaying that, and Joe is tall, a giant among men—Joe scanned the proceedings. "Let's get over to the bar before these booze hounds drink it all."

"Joe. One second." A. F. held him back. Clara followed suit. "I'd like us to have a talk—later—with Phil."

"Sure, Dad." He tried to break away. Clara squeezed, held on, shot him a womb-suffering glance. A beautiful look: pain amid plenty. What a lady. Joe rested between tugs. "Not now, Mother. I've got guests."

"You promise you won't forget?" Clara breathed heavily, stretched her swan neck, bringing her fair face closer to his tan one.

"What is this? Some kind of a vaudeville act? Don't gang up on me." He tugged free, started moving. "I don't like the approach. I'll talk—but later."

He knew what was afoot. Phil knew he knew. A.F. knew that Phil knew that Joe knew. Clara knew that A.F. knew that Phil knew. . . . "I need another drink, A.F. I should also pay a little attention to my friends." And Phil was free, back-stepping, bowing to Clara, as if in homage to deposed, but still revered royalty. The Tsar is dead! Long live the Tsar! "Don't worry, A.F. We'll talk. I promise. I won't leave these grounds before we speak to Joe."

Clara glowed gratefully. A.F. looked crushed, brought low. A Job about to be lowered into still another whirlwind.

Phil dribbled slowly downcourt, backward, ass-bumped a few big-assed ladies, golfer types, turned to apologize, and lost control of the ball, but started after it again, bravely, his throat desert-parched, his straining eyes searching for the distant bar. Was it a mirage? The bar? The conversation? The jumping-jack people? Hallucination? Yes. It must be.

". . . but marijuana, Mr. Goldstein, liberates. It's not, ultimately, a depressant like alcohol is." "Yes, I know that." "But you don't, Mr. Goldstein. You don't know what I mean because you're drunk right now. You wanted to get drunk. Why don't you let me help you inside? You could rest up in my room, if you'd like." "No thank you. I'm not drunk. I'm always this depressed. . . . Phil! Can I see you a minute?" Howie hung on to Phil's jacket. "See you later, young man. It's been very interesting. Very interesting . . . Phil, what did you get me into here? I'm in a jungle I tell you. I am actually being seduced, and by a minor yet!"

"Just shut up and follow me."

". . . Listen to me, Wilma. Married or not, I dig you. D-i-g! You're a free spirit aren't you? My wife does have *her* lover so I should have mine. So who cares?" "So no one cares, Barney, only, as I previously stated, I'm not at liberty . . . Oh, Phil love, can I see you a minute." Wilma grabbed the seat of Howie's baggy corduroy pants and hung on. The train began to pull off. "It's been swell, Barney. Really swell. See you anon. . . . Why have you forsaken me, Phil? Why?"

"Just shut up and follow me."

Cindy beat them to the bar. "It's a lovely party. But my culottes are absolutely ruined, Phil. Look at those stains! Ruined!"

"They'll all come out in the wash."

Before they had a chance to redefine the strategy of the upcoming moments, but after each of them had received a new drink, Rosalind approached with a carefully selected escort: an oldish, red-eyed designer for Phil; a young, eye-glass-slipping Wall Street type for Wilma; a middle-aged and tweedy lady geometry teacher for Howie; no one for Cindy, an intentional omission which ardent Cindy accepted with graceful, ladylike shiftings of her weight from one pose to another. After all, Rosalind, rose-red and forty, was the hostess, a meticulous, unharried hostess until this moment, and Cindy was nothing if not polite. Rosalind moved from the bar. Obediently, the semicircle moved with her to the center of the lawn, at which point, having passed an imaginary Go, they were set free to play the rest of the game according to Rosalind's house rules.

Just before dusk a cooling wind started up from the northwest, blew away the thick haze of cigarette smog, brushed loudly through the budding trees. Conversation faltered. Mouths moved. Their sounds were silent in the wind. Expertly the tables which had held the shrimp, the cheeses, the olives, the hot hors d'oeuvres, the dips, the herring squares, the caviar, the crackers were reset by a staff of six. A stroganoff, a chow mein, a ham, a turkey, a roast beef, long French breads, salad, mounds of steaming vegetables were wheeled out. Hushed by the sight of so much food, the crowd remassed quickly, formed a snaking line before the tables. Rosalind and Joe acted as flankers, kept it moving smoothly. "Eat it all," Joe yelled. "This kind of day comes once in a lifetime. Enjoy yourselves, friends. Our pleasure. Happy to have you on the team . . ."

Phil was back near his willow tree, semidruink, breathing deep drafts of darkening air, trying to sober up so he could deal with what was coming next. And once more A.F. found him. Clara had attached herself to Wilma on the chow line, so A. F. had a clear field now.

"You should eat, Philly. You feel sick?"

"Never. I never get sick from drinking."

"But you look pale. Come eat a little."

"In a while, A.F. Can't stand lines. Never wait on lines for food or the movies. Never."

"Your girl friend's there. See. Talking to Clara. And that . . . that boy. What's his name? And Cindy. Why did you bring Cindy? Rosalind doesn't like that type of girl. She already complained . . ."

"You said I could bring friends so I brought. You didn't specify what types Rosalind likes."

"All I want is for you to stop with Cindy. I asked you just the other day, remember I said—"

"And I said just the other day that I wouldn't stop fitting on her. Remember?"

"All right. Have it your way. I give in. Only don't get yourself in an excited state. Come eat something, Phil. I want you to be sober when you talk to Joe. It's very important you should be sober. I can't talk to him unless you help me. He's such a hard person to talk to."

"He's your son."

"Sure he's my son, but he didn't used to be so hard. Years ago he never raised his voice to me. Never. In all the years he was growing up. Not once. Robert did. All the time. But him I slapped down. That worthless good-for-nothing. He ruined me, that Robert."

"No *one* person ruined you, A. F. You're old enough to know that."

"Old enough? Sure I'm old enough. That's how I know what I know."

"What do you know? Why don't you let me in on your secret?"

"Because it's a secret. Secrets a person has to learn for himself."

Phil, trapped once more inside A.F.'s arm, sighed, let himself be moved forward toward the food. If nothing else, the draped arm straining behind his neck offered support, for a while longer. They walked slowly, Phil stumbling occasionally, turning out a thin ankle, cursing, straightening, sensing the cooling grass.

"When you talk to Joe, you'll tell him for me, Phil, how we could fix everything with one good season. You'll tell him how good the new clothes are. Which they are. So it's no lie. The best clothes you ever did for us. When you started at Mr. Jack you had what to learn. And you learned it. You know how. You'll tell Joe. And if he'll help us get back on our feet, I'm going to change everything. Morris'll do his production perfect. It's lucky we got him right now. I'll lower the markup a little like you always told me to do. We'll sell more. Some volume sales. And in a few months we'll show a profit. And the first thing I'll do then—a solemn promise, Philly, and for me that's binding—is I'll draw up papers to make you a partner. You always wanted that, right. So you'd be working for a reason? So you'd be part of Mr. Jack? Right? You still want that, don't you?" A. F. stopped, grabbed Phil by the shoulders, squeezing them as if to force out the answer he wanted. They were close to the food line, within the murmuring presence of real people being as real as they knew how to be. And Phil looked up at this aging man's handsome, sweating face, saw in the tear-filled eyes the only reason to read his lines the way they were written, the only reason that made saying yes worthwhile and harmless: A. F. might fall in a useless heap before him if he didn't. And A. F. didn't deserve a no at that moment. In a while, when they finally spoke to Joe, he would get enough noes to last for the rest of his life, enough to cancel out all the years of yesses. Phil, wearily on his way to being drunk, could still figure out that much. "Yes, I'd like that, A. F. I'm grateful for that offer. Even if it doesn't happen exactly like you think, I'm grateful you made it."

A. F. kissed him loudly on the cheek, hugged him tightly, released him only when Clara approached with filled plates for both of them.

The meeting took place while the guests had dessert and coffee. Joe led his father, his brother, and Phil to the second-floor den, a room fitted out with hi-fi equipment, ebony paneling, leather-bound books, and hard chairs of aluminum tubing and foam rubber. Clara had wanted to be part of the sitting, but Joe said his first no, made it an absolute condition of his having the meeting at all, so she had to give in. Perhaps that—Phil held on to that wandering strand of thought for support as they marched upstairs—was another first for the family.

Joe sat behind his semicircular ebony desk, lit a cigar, puffed it vigorously, adjusted his ascot, while the rest of them dragged chairs closer, forming an arc of dispensable human satellites around the rim of drifting smoke. A. F. leaned an elbow on the desk, cupped his chin, hid his eyes behind spread fingers. Robert, in the middle turned half away from his brother, fixed his gaze on Phil, who, feigning good spirits, sprawled in his chair at the other end. Big Joe wasn't going to get the best of him, although no amount of drink or food would make being in this room bearable for long. Whatever else Phil knew himself to be, one thing he wasn't was the kind of guy who could watch someone about to be beaten up and stand around smiling, as if to say, well, hell, it's all right, let it happen, doesn't matter. Goes on every day to someone. That's life, baby. Because if that's life as we've come to know it and expect it to be, then let's forget the whole thing. The human experiment's finished. It's kill or be killed. Every man for himself. So come out fighting. All right. But not yet, not here. Nothing was going to make him close his eyes to what was about to happen. Even if he was offered *all* of Mr. Jack in the next instant, no strings attached, a bloody A. F., a crumpled old man, was not something he could step over lightly. And there's a tidbit of truth for you, Philly-willy. A simple truth to remember about yourself, drunk or sober.

Joe's cigar glowed red. "Just so we don't have to waste too much time up here, I'll tell you how I size up the situation. If you can convince me I'm wrong, I'll do my best to try to change my mind, but I promise nothing." He lowered the cigar, settled it in the free-form ceramic ashtray beneath his father's face. "And we're not going to take all night. I've got guests. As it is, Rosalind's fuming about this thing. For once she's right. Anyway, from what information I've got, from what Robert's told me—"

"Never mind what Robert's told you because—"

"And don't interrupt me for once, Dad! I don't like that. You interrupt me again and I'm walking the hell out of here." Joe half rose threateningly. A. F. nodded inside a rush of flailing arms. Joe sat back down. "From what Robert told me—it happens he knows what's going on, Father dear. He's an interested party. A very interested party." Robert turned then to face his older brother, grateful for the recognition. "Also, from the account books I saw last time I stopped up there, your days as an owner of a business are numbered. You owe out much more than you can possibly make back in profit this year. Every stop-gap measure you've taken so far like opening the knit line and the other thing—what do you call it?"

"Missy," A. F. whispered.

"Missy line. Anyway, both of them were so mismanaged that in the end they only got you further behind. My advice is that you declare bankruptcy and get the hell out from under. You're old enough to retire, Dad. I'll send you and Mother to Florida. I'll pay for anything you need for the rest of your lives. I'll buy you a house even." Calmly, Joe rounded the gray ash of his cigar along the edge of the ashtray, leaned across the desk closer to his father. "But I will not, I repeat, *will not,* give you a cent more to invest in that business. Most of the factors you have now are my friends. I told them, every single one of them, that you were good for the money. So they loaned you. They got a right to expect it back—without having Mother hock her jewels to do it. You're running a business, not a pawnshop. And whatever money you make from whatever bookings you get on any new line that Phil is designing has to go to pay off the factors first. If you paid them off, if there was anything left, you'd still have all the other debts. It's absolutely no go." He sat up, pointed his cigar at himself. "But that's just the way *I* see it. There's a lot more I see, but the other things belong to the past. Ancient history. Whatever you did, you did. It's too late to change how you did them. So am I right or wrong? You tell me now."

"I can't, but Phil'll tell you. Phil tell him!"

But Phil remained motionless, weary, depressed. He sighed. "What can I say, A. F.? He told it the way it is. He's right."

"Tell him about the new line! Tell him! It'll book millions. If I learned anything from my years on Seventh Avenue, I learned what will sell and what won't sell. I know—"

"With all due respect to your years, you know nothing!" Joe waved him back against the hard chair. "And that, I'm afraid, is the truth. You *knew*, maybe, but you don't know now. The way it is now, I mean. The concept of Mr. Jack is a dead issue and it's going to get deader. It's a fairy-tale left over from a different era. Any independent business based on private capital is going to be choked out. It's gotta be. Labor demands alone will make it happen. So if you don't have corporation money behind you, forget it. Which leads us to the next point. In order to get that kind of money you have to have something to sell to one of the giants. And what company on the board is going to buy a sick business even with a name like yours? They'd have to be nuts to do it when every day in the week they can get a healthy one. Which leads me back to my original point. End it, Dad. Give in already. Go enjoy the rest of your life. Retire to Florida."

"I don't want to retire to Florida." A. F. sagged against the curving desk, his hidden paunch straining the buttons of his glen-plaid jacket. He tried to light a cigarette, but the water-filter holder with its long cigarette trembled out of reach of the match. Joe didn't offer his lighter. Robert folded his arms obstinately as if by that unfamiliar defiant action he was saying to Joe, okay, so now I'm on your side, fine, and all I'll need is a job, something to tide me over. . . . But then Phil, suddenly recovering some of his drink-buried instinct, jumped up, grabbed the lighter from the desk, lit A. F.'s cigarette. He remained standing, leaning at his end of the desk so that he faced the three of them. "What the hell are you doing here, Joe? Even if what you say is true, which I agree with you that it is, why do you have to treat him that way? Send him to Florida! That's your answer? Florida?"

"That's none of *your* business!" The cigar waved dangerously close to Phil's face, but he didn't flinch.

"Excuse me, buster, but it *is* my business." Phil folded his arms defiantly. "I've got a contract with your father. I've got some life ahead of me. I've got a career to think about. Your father's been good to me. What happens to *him* is the most important business I've got."

Joe rose slowly, moved around the desk, stood next to Phil, looked down from his height at him. "First of all, little boy, no one calls me buster. I don't like it." His hands came to rest on his hips, elbows leaning in at Phil. "Secondly, no fairy designer's going to tell *me* how to treat *my* father! Understand?"

As if by reflex, A. F. stood, but he did not move from his chair. Robert unfolded his arms, turned away once again.

In that instant of silence before Joe, having paused as any sport would, went on talking, Phil shaped responses in his mouth, responses that he had to reject, none of them being sensible or practical, what with Joe towering above him. That was a situation which Phil had faced too often in his life—the long and the short of it—not to have learned the safety of retreat. You don't fight when you know you have to lose everything you have. And to deny Joe's accusation would just be child's play, irrelevant. The moment itself, the dare, the silence, was some kind of joke anyway. So, although not at all expecting to, he began to laugh. Maybe sober he wouldn't have. Maybe tomorrow or the day after that he would regret not having kicked Joe in the balls. Lots of times he'd regretted not having kicked someone in the balls. His laughter gained momentum and volume. Lots of volume. So much so that it had an unpredictable effect: it surprised Joe. Even as Joe began speaking again, surprise diluted the force of his words.

". . . and thirdly, I don't give a shit . . . about *your* career. . . . Your kind . . . of career . . . is peanuts . . . to me. . . . Oh, the hell!" He shouted, moving back to his chair. "I'm not getting sidetracked with that crap."

Phil started toward the door. "Neither am I." A touch of swagger. Unconcern. More laughter. A. F. called out to him, pleading for him to stay, that Joe didn't mean what he said—yelling louder than his father, Joe said he did—that they had to talk more, that Phil had to help him, that, remember, they had a bargain, about the partnership. Remember his promise . . .

"Forget it, A. F. And whatever your son has to say doesn't interest me. He's your son. You listen to him. Get Robert to talk for you. I'm going back to the party. And if I don't see you later, I'll see you at work tomorrow." As he closed the door behind him there was silence, and then, immediately, A. F.'s voice screaming, "Listen to me, Joe. Listen . . ."

It took Phil a long while to round up Wilma and Howie, to fight off Clara's requests for information about what had happened—"You'll see your husband soon enough. I guarantee it"—to locate some more to drink. By now most of the guests were lolling in sitting rooms sipping more coffee, more brandy, hoping the piped-in music—Greek, *Zorba*— would rouse them, help them put off the need to call it another Sunday night, just another Sunday night before another Monday morning. And when he did find Wilma and Howie, he couldn't find Cindy. At least, by then he had had two more drinks and was working on a third. The three of them began a new search. Rosalind joined them, tireless Rosalind, looking as fresh as she had at the beginning, but anxious to get them, especially Cindy, on their way back to the big city. It was no way to end a twentieth-anniversary celebration—poking through a littered mansion for an aging model. "A garden party. A garden party!" Howie's words and laughter were hysteria. "A surprise garden party in Westchester County. In April. It's the end of another era, Miss Mansfield, April in Scarsdale. . . ."

"You're drunk too, Howie." Wilma led Phil, who led Howie, all of them trying to keep up with Rosalind.

"No I'm not. Not the least bit drunk. Just nostalgic."

"For what?"

"For man's hope. And sad. Sad about his fate. About the boring way he celebrates himself. Getting drunk. Fun, he calls it. Getting laid, he calls it."

"Mr. Goldstein! If you don't mind! You're supposed to be a teacher, I thought." Rosalind halted in the painting-lined corridor, detoured them through the dining room, out the French doors and onto the back lawn, where it had all started, where now only glowing bits of white refuse remained in the darkness, an unfamiliar darkness for Wilma's faulty vision. But not for Rosalind. She knew exactly where she was headed. Steadily walking and steadily talking, "Watch out for the hole there; be careful of the begonias," her voice growing louder and louder as they approached a modest thatch-roofed summer house. Cindy was there. So was Joe. The only unsurprised person was Rosalind. "Your friends have been looking for you, Miss Rubin. *They* want to leave. I suggest you should too! And, Joe! Your mother is looking for *you*. Your father is not too well. He's got gas. Goodnight, all. It's been a pleasure having you." She held Joe's arm firmly, steered him clear of the group and back up the lawn to the French doors and inside to the light.

"They're absolutely ruined!" Cindy bent lower to inspect her culottes. "Ruined, Phil!" But Phil was being led out of earshot. Cindy had to run to catch up.

Howie drove back to the city. In the rear of the car Wilma cradled Phil's head beneath her neck, smiling, glad to guard his worried sleep. In front Cindy twisted the edges of her hair, stared straight ahead at the spotlighted darkness of the road. There was little traffic and the trip was mercifully fast, a fact that saved Howie from the responsibility of further conversation. Not that Cindy seemed inclined to talk. She dreamed instead, sighing right up until the moment they arrived at her doorway. "Just a heavenly afternoon, except for the damage to my culottes. Thank you all."

Wilma tried to insist that she should see to Phil's getting upstairs safely. Howie thought that, under the circumstances, parking the car, walking the dog, he had better do it. "It's so much closer to home for me afterward, Wilma." She acquiesced. "All right. But you're to call me when he's settled, Howie. Remember!" She kissed Phil's closed eyes. Howie waited until she was safely inside her building.

Phil was in some control by the time Howie led him onto the elevator, and almost sober by the time Liffey had been walked and given her bedtime biscuits. Howie, having dog-sat whenever Phil went on vacation or on the road with the clothes, knew the precise routine. Liffey raced into the bedroom, nuzzled her nose and biscuit next to Phil's pillow. He was awake then, totally awake, breathing rapidly, turning his head to watch every movement of Liffey's munching mouth, of Howie's collapse into the swivel wing chair near the casement windows, intent, it seemed, on cataloguing details for posterity, but, in fact, concentrating on nothing but the flow of his own thoughts. Howie knew those private signals of his friend's distress, had deciphered them long ago and many times since, was not deceived by them now: the deep breaths; the glazed, piercing, unblinking stare; the sad, self-accusing smile. Howie couldn't leave him alone when he looked that way. Never. That's when a friend was necessary. That was the whole point of affection: to intrude, to speak, to break in on quiet desperation, expose it to the light, loosen its hold, even just a little bit. Doing that had always helped him. Whether it really helped Phil was hard to know. Phil said it did, but saying was so different from feeling. Anyhow . . . "Quite an afternoon and evening, eh what?" Irony was usually good for openers. "Full of frivolity."

No response. The gaze followed the crossing of Howie's legs. "You okay, Phil?" At the name, Liffey lifted her head alertly, waited for action, let it fall back against the pillow when none seemed imminent. "You want me to go?"

"In a while. I'm not sleepy yet."

Howie lit a cigarette, swiveled so that he could view the few river lights, the glowing boat docked on the Jersey side, the tall building far off, deeper into the Jersey marshland, with the red neon cross of JESUS SAVES on top blinking off and on. "Do you want to talk, Phil?"

"What time is it?"

"Close to twelve."

"You better go then. You'll have to get up in a few hours."

"When I finish the cigarette." He swiveled back, smiled. "Their son's queer."

"I figured that out."

"He did everything but proposition me."

"You should have done it. He sounded semi-intelligent."

"Never, Philip. I have a strong sense of propriety. Besides, I don't dig young boys. That's how come I can teach high school and observe the laws."

"Whose laws? Joe Fleiss's?"

"He really is the shits, isn't he? No gainsaying that. And his taste! *Feh!*" Howie slapped his knee for emphasis. "How did that secret meeting turn out? What do you plan to do about Mr. Fleiss?"

"Do? What *can* I do? I'm trapped for right now. I'm always trapped. By A. F., by my father, my stepmother. By Wilma. Everyone traps me. That's the kind of *schmuck* I am. Always trappable."

"Do I trap you?"

"You try not to. You're about the only one."

"That's because I really love you."

"Don't start that business tonight, please. I'm too tired for that."

"I won't start. I promise. I was only thinking out loud."

Phil raised himself higher, sank back against the headboard of his double bed. "You see," he pointed to the other pillow, "if you weren't so outspoken you could sleep here tonight."

"I'm not outspoken. I'm just honest. I have no reason to lie about anything."

"Even at school? Do you go around telling everyone at school about yourself?"

"That's different, Phil. Be fair now. That's another kind of world. Joe Fleiss's world, where you deal with the American Dream. Not with the American truth. No one could teach otherwise."

"You didn't use to talk that way. When we were in the army you didn't make compromises so easily."

"True enough. But that was because no one was really interested in what I had to say, except you. If it wasn't for you, I would have gone crazy. Stark raving mad. You saved me. But, obviously, I didn't do such a good job of saving you. I made everything worse for you, didn't I?"

"Who the hell knows what you did to me. Whatever happened to me would have happened no matter what. I'm convinced of that. In the army you woke me up. That's all. While you sank into a protective sleep."

"Star-crossed lovers."

Phil shifted Liffey onto his bare chest. "Do you always feel miserable, Howie?"

"Most of the time. But I'm not unhappy. One thing, at least, I know and admit something important about myself. That helps. And knowing it doesn't hurt. Being alone does. That hurts. But there's school. I'm never alone there. I've got a hundred kids each year. Different kids. So my ego stays in one piece. You're actually more alone than I am. Which bothers you, doesn't it?"

"No more than it bothers you. I enjoy being alone, frankly. I'm surrounded at work too, every day. And I love my work as much as you do. I complain of course. But so what. Everyone complains. Even if I were to get married—which is what you're really questioning—my wife is going to be secondary. That's what Wilma can't stand about me. She says differently, but she cares all right. She wants to be first."

"I can understand that. If I put myself in her place—"

"Don't put yourself in her place."

"I only meant it as an analogy, Philip."

"Even as an analogy don't. You're always putting yourself in someone else's place. Even in Liffey's place. All through the army you did that. When I worked for Carl Kalb, you did it, the worst of all. Not that you

106

were wrong about that particular episode so don't get pouty. It's just a fact. And Aaron you hate. Which is another fact. And Sandy. And Wilma too, I suppose, just to keep the record straight. What you do is put yourself in someone else's place with me and then you try to get rid of them for me. Or be like them, if I happen to care for them. You have to stop doing that, Howie." Phil sat up for emphasis. "I'm saying that for your own good."

"I'm trying to. You have to admit that at least I'm trying. I've never once interfered with you since you've been at Mr. Jack." Howie leaned toward the bed. "But you! You're actually the one who sets me up for those things. You're always inviting me to those Christmas parties at work, to other places with your friends, to things like today. You can't expect me to just sit around and smile. That's not why you invite me, is it? . . . Or is it? Is that the reason? Why do you invite me? Tell me that at least?"

"Because it's my habit."

"Well, there's your answer for the way I behave. Behaving a certain way is instinct for me too. I have as many habits as the next guy. I don't lie about that. I keep telling you how I feel. You keep telling me not to start that business and then you force me into situations, no matter how hard I try to avoid them." Howie was alert now, as if the day were starting, not ending. "Why do you want me for a friend, Phil? Answer that honestly. It's my most important question."

"And my most important answer. Because I care about you and what happens to you. Because I think you're the only honest person I know. Because since those times in the army you've never tried to get me to have sex with you. Those are pretty good reasons for wanting you as a friend, aren't they?"

"Yes. They are. But they're selfish ones. Just like mine, I admit. The difference is that you take advantage of my being honest. I always hoped that you'd be just as honest. Like right now. But you won't. You won't give in to something that might end up being the best thing for you." Howie stood up suddenly, moved to the edge of the bed, but sat down tentatively, losing his courage just as suddenly as he had gained it.

"Go home, Howie. Call Wilma like she asked you to do. Tell her I'm sleeping already. I've got some things I need to think about. Other things."

Howie propped his elbows on his knees, cupped his chin, urged his hair forward across his eyes.

"And don't start crying, Howie. Just go home."

"I'm not going to cry. I don't cry about things like this. I told you before I wasn't unhappy about you. Just frustrated. Being frustrated isn't the worst thing in the world. A person can live with that. For how long I don't know. But what happens in the future is the last thing I care about. For you it's the first." He stood up once more and then, before Phil knew what was happening, leaned down to kiss him. "That didn't hurt, did it?"

"That? That never hurts. Men kiss me all the time. A. F. kisses me every chance he gets."

"Only when I do it, it matters?"

"That's right. It matters, Howie."

"So life isn't a game?"

"It's a game. Whatever you say it is, it is. A game. A bridge. Anything."

"I'll call you tomorrow."

"Go, Howie. Goodnight. Thank you for helping me. And don't worry about a thing. Not a thing. If you ever need a friend . . . if you ever need help, as they say in songs, I'll be here. Don't worry about that." Phil turned away.

Howie nodded at Phil's back, walked slowly out of the bedroom, turned off the lights in the living room, and left the apartment.

Chapter Five

Right up until the first Friday in May, Alex Fleiss kept trying to persuade the factors to extend a little more credit, a little more time, to invest a little more money. That's all the company needed because the new line was fabulous. A real winner. If he only could have a little more time to show it to the buyers, it would sell. No question about that. He invited the factors to have a look for themselves. Triumphantly he would unlock his office door, march the uninterested men out into the showroom, send Link to go get Phil to bring the clothes out, with basting stitches still showing and sleeves pinned on. Andrew Berns and Michael Morgan were instructed to talk it up, pour it on as if they were selling to customers. The showroom girls were also forced into the act by A. F. Sizes 12 and 14 respectively, they had to model the dresses, sucking themselves into size 7 samples, for the factors, for any would-be investors. But the factors didn't want a fashion show; they wanted their money.

Then A.F. decided that maybe if he offered a percentage of the business, a small percentage, to some money man, he could save the day. Suddenly there was more traffic through the showroom than there had been for half a year. A.F. had lots of friends whose friendship he was counting on. Each evening, after a day of disappointment, he would guarantee Phil that tomorrow, one more day, and everything would be fine. Just wait. "You keep on doing your work, Phil. Even if we won't be able to afford a formal June showing, we'll get the buyers up here anyway. Andy knows how. Mike I don't know. What does he care? He's too young. He's a Benedict Arnold like all the young ones. But if all of us work together—if you, Robert, would do something else for once instead of following me around all day lighting my cigarettes—we could get somewhere. And tomorrow I've got my dearest friend coming up. He's got plenty of idle money and he already told me he's interested, so we'll see."

And then it was tomorrow evening, a Thursday, and A. F. and Robert were back in Phil's room, A. F. talking about another dearest friend and his same worthless son and how tomorrow was certainly going to be the day they reached a turn for the better and asking Phil if he had told his girls about using the telephone too much and if he had stopped using Cindy temporarily, "just temporarily. Until it's all straightened out."

All week, every evening, Phil had nodded, no matter what A. F. said. Nothing good was going to happen. Everyone left at Mr. Jack knew that, everyone but A.F. Like a man who finds out that a loved one is dying of cancer, A. F., right up to the ugly, screaming end, would go on not believing the truth. To anyone else it could happen. Not to him. Impossible. Who cares what the doctors say? What do they know? There's plenty they don't know. Every day you hear about new cures. Those fools don't even want to try anything new.

That Thursday evening when A. F., obsessed, had once more counted the pieces of sample fabric on Phil's shelves and walked off down the corridor, mumbling, Phil, still nodding, as if an engineer had forgotten to push his STOP button, began laughing, quietly at first, but riding quickly up the madness scale. He laughed a lot these days, ever since that night at Joe's Fleiss's, hysterical laughter which a slap would not have stilled.

The sample hands had left; Pat and Ginny remained, more for moral support than because they had work. Phil had stopped putting new sketches into work on Tuesday of that week. No point in wasting ideas. They were good ideas too. Excellent, in fact. How strange that just because he knew the company was finished every sketch he did was great, dresses that, if they were manufactured, would sell thousands. Obsessed himself, he kept sketching all week, and not just fifty-cent piece circles but ones with details and color and fabric swatches attached. Each one a winner. "It's a tragic sight." Phil, having watched A. F.'s stumbling departure, turned from the doorway.

"Tragic, no. Pathetic, yes." Pat, wreathed in smoke, slumped forward, searching for fresh air. "He doesn't even chase me around his desk any more when I go to his office."

Ginny leaned against Pat's desk, still in her work smock, waiting for instructions. Phil's laughter didn't upset her. Anything he did that week would have seemed normal.

He returned to his desk, rubbing his hands together, shouting, "Okay, kids. Let's consolidate our defenses. I predict that by tomorrow evening we'll be unemployed. Friday night. The traditional firing time. We have to work out some kind of strategy." He rubbed his hair as if to get the blood circulating to his brain. "The first thing to do, Pat, is collect all our sketches. Especially the ones in the bottom drawer of my desk. Next. Ginny, do you have all the muslins for the samples?" She nodded energetically. "Good. Because what we could do is alter them slightly and offer them free lance. Do you think you could reconstruct them?"

"I could, but who's going to sew them up? Who's going to pay for the fabric?"

"I will. And you can make them up—not all of them, just a few groups —and Pat can help. She learned how to sew in Parsons, I hope. And meanwhile I can be out looking for a manufacturer."

"Where will you make them?" Ginny led Phil to a chair, forced him down into it. "Calm down, love. It won't work."

Like a sinking plumb line, his head fell forward. The laughter creases disappeared from around his narrowed eyes, replaced by tiny wrinkles of an old, familiar despair. "Well, then that's that. It was great fun, but it was just one of those things." His head bobbed up. "Okay! Only prepare yourselves, because tomorrow will be the day."

And tomorrow it was. The last, dearest friend had come, listened, looked, and left. A.F. called a meeting in the showroom for four-thirty. The famous Friday-afternoon routine: the death hour on Seventh Avenue for a faltering business that was struggling to stay afloat between seasons, that two-way stretch between the summer line that didn't sell and the fall collection that might.

Silently, not even mumbling, out of respect for a death that was close at hand, those that were left, those happy, loyal few, entered the showroom, took seats at the buyers' tables as if they were entering pews at a funeral parlor. Phil's sample hands had changed from smocks into street clothes for the occasion. Morris Trebnitz, Anna, the duplicate maker, the two cutters tiptoed in. The glum showroom staff, Andrew, Michael, the two girls surrounded a separate table. Link sat alone until Phil insisted he join Pat, Ginny, and himself. Marsha Katz, pencil stuck through her beehive, sat with pale Robert and A. F. across from the nervous mourners. No one looked at anyone else. The staff was a dwindled shadow of its former strength. No shipping clerk. No packers. No tailors, graders, cutters, receptionist, house models, secretaries. No strength in numbers. Phil steadied his gaze on the plaque, on the unfailable logo that was about to fail, the faceless silhouette of a woman's curving figure, arm outstretched,

imagined he saw the ghost of Jack Farbstein, the original Mr. Jack, pluck-
ing the label from the outstretched arm, forcing its arm to bend at the
elbow, its featureless face to accept its shroud, while Jack howled glee-
fully.

A. F. got to his feet somehow, tottering, but pacing the dirty beige rug,
smoothing his jacket, stopping to pop a dead cigarette from his filter, adding another one, lighting it, pacing once more. There were no racks to
block his path. Where were the clothes, just as a matter of fact? Phil stood
to peer around the boomerang curve. Nothing. Gone. Probably locked up
in his office. A.F. was planning something. The old thief. When he
asked for the new clothes that morning to show to his last dearest friend,
they had never been returned to the sample room. Locked up, out of
reach. So, he's still got a few tricks left to pull. The bastard, and here I
am spending my every waking minute worrying about him.

A.F. cleared his throat. His voice, at first, was a whisper that everyone had to strain to hear. He tried clearing his throat once more,
stopped pacing entirely, stood, stooping, with his back to Robert, blocking him from everyone's view.

The listeners remained motionless, waiting for simple words to be spoken quickly, words that, after all these anxious months, would finally free
them from limbo. But A. F. didn't know how to be quick, didn't understand mercy. If it was going to be his final speech, he had the right to deliver it in his own, inimitable style. He might never have such a chance
again. ". . . yes, it is close to fifty years I've been on Seventh Avenue, in
one capacity or another," the group sighed in chorus, sank back against
their chairs for support; so it was going to be that way: through history,
"from the lowest shipping clerk right to the top. . . ." He paused, lowered his gaze, not for effect, but because there were real tears in his eyes
which he had to wipe away.

Phil forced himself to watch now. No matter how long it took A. F. to
tell the story—obviously, he was going to tell it all—Phil would listen,
force himself to listen and to watch . . . and to learn, learn exactly what
it was he would never let himself become: a tired, deluded, indomitable
stick-figure ego with arms and legs flailing, with a mouth panting for air,
surrounded by people hired to keep that ego from falling apart.

". . . For close to fifty years, mind you, and everything I've done in
this industry I was proud of doing. I never cheated the public. I never
paid under the table to get buyers to buy. Never. I never underpaid my
workers." The cigarette holder punctuated each item of his virtue. He

had rallied strongly, the pre-death delusion of recovery suddenly brightening his smile. "Any garment produced by any company I owned was really *made*; it wasn't just slapped together for a profit. Even when there was no Seventh Avenue, when whatever industry there was, was still downtown, right during those years after the Triangle Fire and the unions were just beginning to get stronger so they could take over and drain a manufacturer dry. Because if you want to know the real truth they're the ones who are ruining our businesses. They cut off the nose to spite the face. And what'll they be left with? What?"

The sample hands, Dorothy Krakauer especially, the cutters, looked up then, ready, at once, to fight for their unions.

But A. F. only lit another cigarette. No disagreement was possible. "Facts are facts! I saw all of it happening, years ago." He paused, looked toward the ceiling as if he were studying the display of stars at the Hayden Planetarium, but instead of stars, he saw the details of those days. "In those days . . ." Phil froze. Pat moaned, a respectfully quiet moan, rolled her eyes at Phil. Ginny tapped the formica table top patiently. "In those days there wasn't such a thing as a labor setup. Who needed it? Who needed the union to tell you how much to pay for a buttonhole, a seam, a top stitch, a pocket? No one needed it. A girl got paid by how many garments she made. The more she made, the more she got paid. And I'll tell you one thing, I always paid the highest. All my friends did. We didn't have to be told what to do. We all paid for quality. That was the whole thing. Quality! Quality made Seventh Avenue what it is, not the shyster businesses that make a million and disappear overnight. . . . But that's another story. That's not why I called you all together this afternoon."

The fidgeting stopped. And what was surprising to Phil at that moment was that A. F. suddenly seemed relaxed, almost serene. The tears were still there—his handkerchief kept wiping them away—but his smile grew wider, more wistful, as if he were shuttling back and forth through time so fast that the memory of "those days," those good, successful days, was overwhelming his sense of what was happening now, today. "I called you all together this afternoon to tell you exactly what's what with us. I know, I know very well, you're hearing plenty of rumors on the Avenue. I hear them myself. All the time I hear them. For every day and week and month in my life I went up and down the elevator in this building I heard rumors. If it wasn't about Mr. Jack then it was about another company, companies that were the healthiest in our business. Rumors. Just rumors. Let me tell you, I can remember"—the quiet dissolved like a jet breaking through the sound barrier—"when the one-piece dresses began, back to the First World War—that's long before your times—how there were rumors that such a garment would never sell. And in the twenties? The flappers? Crazy clothes, everyone said. Never catch on. Never. Well, let me tell you, my friends, I've lived long enough to see the flapper clothes sell, disappear, and make a comeback. Just like the Carole Lombard clothes from the thirties and the Joan Crawford clothes and the long hems from Dior after the war. All of it comes and goes. And each time are the rumors. Rumors and more rumors. Remember during the Second World War how they had the posters LOOSE LIPS SINK SHIPS? Well, that's a slogan just as true for today. Rumors kill businesses. Which is what happened here!" A. F. slammed the table behind him.

Phil, startled as they all were by the sudden force—unless he was talking to Robert, A. F. never spoke much above a confidential whisper—jumped, suddenly released from the stupor, the lullaby of A. F.'s mishmash of nonsense words. Anything might happen next, anything but a clear-cut announcement of the facts.

"So rumors you can disregard. All week I've been having my friends up here to check over the situation. My truest, dearest friends from way back, men who made successes of themselves just the way I did, by hard work. We didn't have time to go to school." He twisted half around to leer at Robert, the arch-enemy, and that helped him locate new stores of energy. "We didn't need to. We learned our trade by working in it. Each one of them and myself got where we are today by doing. Each one of them I'm proud to call a friend. They looked over the books for Mr. Jack. They saw that right now things aren't so good. But not one of them said, 'Alex, give up.' Not one. They looked at Phil's clothes. They were impressed. Just like I'm impressed. Because Phil has turned into one of the best designers on the Avenue. I'm proud to have him work for me. In all my years I never hired a designer I wasn't proud to have working for me. In all these years I never had to fire one. Until a few months ago I never fired anyone who worked for me. And I'm proud of that record too. All my friends know that about me. All of them know how bad times only make me feel stronger. During the Depression I held on to a business that another man would have given up. I don't believe in quitting something I start, especially a company with the reputation that Mr. Jack still enjoys. Women all over the country know our label. Every day I get letters from customers wanting to know what's happening to our dresses?

Why aren't they in the stores, they want to know? And you know what I answer them? Marsha can tell you. I answer them that they should go to the department-store buyers. *Ask them* why the Mr. Jack clothes aren't on the racks. Ask those bitches!"

"Dad! Take it easy." Robert rose from his seat. A.F. shrugged the offered hand away.

"But that's another story too." Another cigarette. Phil watched the trembling hand light it, saw the wistful smile wane, the wiping handkerchief hand cut through the new ring of smoke. Everyone in the showroom was attentive now, but no longer trying to attend to the words, only studying the man who stood before them performing these last rites as if he were an absent-minded priest unwilling or unable to offer final absolution. Phil stood up.

"What, Phil?" A.F.'s fading smile flickered brighter. Phil moved to meet him, to steer him back to his table. "A.F.," he whispered, "do yourself a favor and get it over with. It's five o'clock. Tell them already. Should they come to work on Monday or not? Just answer that. Please." Phil looked past A.F. to Robert, requesting help, but Robert and then Marsha shrugged. Not even they knew what A.F. might do next. He hadn't even told them for sure.

But what A. F. was finally doing next was suddenly crying, beyond control. He dropped his arm from Phil's shoulder, turned back to the averted, embarrassed faces, and managed, through the sobs, the gulps, the coughing, to say what nothing in his entire life had ever prepared him to say, to admit that, for once, he had failed—he said it just that way, leaning against Phil—and that the company would declare bankruptcy, that on Monday the doors would be closed for the first time in fifteen years, ". . . and whatever money is coming to any of you, you'll get, no matter what—a promise," that there was no other way out, but, "this I promise too—that before you know it," he straightened himself, pointed his cigarette holder at them, "I'm going back into business. . . . A new Mr. Jack, better than it ever was. Jack Farbstein will never get control again of that label. Each one of you here today should remember I said that. . . . Each one of you here today will work for me again. . . ." Phil tried moving him out of the showroom, but his body had gone limp, a dead weight of despair. The others were crowding around Robert and Marsha, trying to get the facts. Ginny tried to help Phil, but it was Link, crying himself, who led A. F. out of the room.

As he watched them stumble away, Phil's thoughts leaped to the poor dresses. Where were they? Locked up in A. F.'s office? Why should they be? They belonged to him as much as they did to A. F. What would he do without them? He had to have something, something tangible, to show for his years here too. He had to own something, to have some rights too. And out of the confusion behind him grew a panic of sudden certainty, a clear, dark imprint of the truth. He had nothing to save that mattered. Not even himself. Nothing that he might do next mattered. The tears that sprang up then, that rolled down his cheeks to his mouth, that entered it as a hot, bitter taste, were for the sudden knowledge of that personal nothing, not for the death of Mr. Jack.

And if you're hit by a taxicab or a car, if you're in an airplane crash, that's one kind of event, the kind for which, afterward, no one could accuse you of being unprepared. Those are accidents. They happen to the best of people, like heart attacks. Go know! But the closing of a business? That's a different event entirely. Anyone could, everyone should, accuse him of having failed to act before it was too late. For too long a time all he had done was wait. Not as A. F. had waited—Phil had never expected a miracle. His waiting was more like a general paralysis, a blockage in the blood supply to the brain. And, of course, he did have a contract. Some contract! Now that Mr. Jack was finished, it offered about as much protection as a nail clipper would in a Harlem riot. The contract routine that he had used, especially for his father's benefit, was nothing more than a baby's pacifier, a toy that calmed the face of things. And, child that he was, he was the one who ended up believing in the myth of the calm surface more than anyone else. Idiot. Fool. *Schmuck*, who, for believing, was, as of 6 P.M. Eastern Daylight Saving Time, on the first Friday in May, unemployed—and unemployed during the worst possible month on Seventh Avenue.

Well, so why had he waited for it to happen? That was the important question. Why? That was always the question to ask and never answer. Why did he wait for everything in his life to happen *to* him? Why did he have to? Didn't everyone always tell him how much they loved him? How talented he was? How handsome? How generous? How good? Yes! They all *told* him, but listening to that was like listening to nothing. He didn't believe it. All that was, was crap. Flattery. Somebody wanting something from him that he didn't want to give. Any smart ass could work it so that he looked like he had those qualities. The point was, and always would be in this fucking world, to have *something more* than all that, to know what that something more was, to know how to get it and keep it without losing the other things. Which was why he had waited: to find out what that *more* was. Which was why he always waited. If he could figure that out, then everything else in his life would finally fit into place. Only now, while he was waiting, there wouldn't be any money coming in. And there was the apartment to keep up, there was food to buy, a maid to pay, people, especially now, who would have to be entertained, and clothes to buy. Clothes? An unimportant item. Ironical for a designer to be that way. But he was a *schlump*, and, like every one of his debits, the schlumpy look had worked, until now. It was the people item that would be the trickiest to manipulate. Manipulating anyone was not one of his best things.

Earlier Pat and Ginny had wanted to take him to dinner for once. For morale. For laughs. No, he had said, but gratefully, and insisted they go on home, not worry about him. He'd be fine. See them on Monday morning. That's when they'd really have to get down to the nitty-gritty. Pat and Ginny, the sample girls, they were a special category of servicing, people he needed and had to hold on to through loyalty, the decent, good way. The others, the magazine gals, the fabric *yentas* who went from design room to design room showing their wares like Fuller Brush men, trading bits of gossip for an order, the teams of buyers and their powerful offices that could control who was *in* that season and who was going to be *out*, they would need shrewd handling. They were some of the contact people who would—or wouldn't; don't forget that possibility—help him get placed fast because by placing him they helped themselves. They obligated him; he obligated them. They gave him a break; he gave them a break by making up some, as few as possible, of the ideas, the fabrics, the clothes they wanted. That was the simple arithmetic of big business, any kind of big business. So, just to take on another job, if he was lucky enough to get one, had very little to do with the something more he was after. Doing it that way was only maintaining the balance of a tired equation. That led to a life like Sandy's. There were other ways, ways that people like Aaron knew about. Aaron hadn't called since the night of that faggot party. A bad time to get him pissed off.

Phil swiveled away from the bedroom window, moved slowly to the bar in the living room. The sun had just about had it anyway. The smog took over about seven-thirty, like chiffon covering a spotlight. Another Scotch and his brain would be smogged in, but he wanted it anyway, for courage, for apologizing to Aaron. Aaron's answering service informed him that Mr. LeGeis was out for the rest of the evening. Great. A reprieve. Eventually he'd have to contact Aaron, but not tonight. Tomorrow. Wilma and Howie tomorrow too. Being alone was necessary. Drinking alone felt even more necessary. The rest of the night had to be his to use in whatever way he wanted to use it. He deserved that much. If the telephone rang, he wouldn't answer it.

Liffey followed at his heels lovingly, love without complications, from the kitchen phone to the corduroy club chair in front of the living-room windows. She insisted on being picked up as soon as he sat down. Poodles have that sixth sense, like cats. They know all about anxiety. Must be some kind of smell the body gives off. "Good girl. My best girl." She licked his fingers, settled to rest on his lap. How easy. He sipped his drink, swished the coldness through his teeth, bathing his gums. Wallowing. Which is what he wanted tonight: to be indulged or to indulge himself and not with anyone or anything he knew. To get drunk anonymously. That's what he'd do. Just go out, treat himself to a great dinner, like before going to the electric chair, and see what came along. No reason why he couldn't do exactly that. The only thing he ought to do was call his father first, before he got too drunk. In a while . . .

He left the lights off in the apartment. All the better to study the sky with, the flow of river with, the river dimming rapidly to ink, the marshmallow twists of moving cloud in the west darkening, a soundless jet vapor trail stream cutting through them, disappearing with them, where the sun was still shining. The windows needed cleaning. The windows always needed cleaning. Dust city when you lived high up. But if you lived low down, you lost the view, the perspective, the essential place of yourself in all of it. So don't complain. Get the windows cleaned. Enjoy the view of the view you have. Enjoy one thing at a time, one minute at a time. Now. Stretch it out. Linger. Wallow. Alone. Expectant. And afterward, tomorrow, Monday morning, there'll be time enough to start all over again. . . . Maybe even a new profession. Show biz. A star. That's a *more*. But probably less. Risky. Very risky. And if he had really wanted that, he would have stuck with those acting classes he took after college, and the singing lessons, hundreds of them, would have yielded more than just a good voice. So designing was it. Owning his own business was it. Being a Joe Fleiss, whether he liked it or not, was it. It *is* too late to be anything else. At thirty-five it is too late to re-do the inside of the package, to rearrange the furniture stuffed inside your brain.

But if you had to pick the worst possible moment in history to be stuck with being over thirty, 1966 had to be it. All the old labels were lies. Justice for all. Liberty. Equality. God. Crap! The American Dream was a nightmare that only the young and the black had the guts to laugh at. Because if you were over thirty and not Paul Goodman or Norman Mailer where were you? What were you going to get in place of what was? Another suffocating system? New labels for old things that hadn't ever worked before? The New Left? Students for a Democratic Society? Black Power. Italian Power. Jewish Power. Tyrone Power. Okay. All of it. Fine. And peace in our time. Hallelujah, baby. And violent nonviolence. Go get it, kids. Only don't kill me first just because I don't have the courage to fight right now in the streets. It's not my fault it worked out this way. I just want to live my life. My time is limited, the same as yours. Three score and ten. I mean well. I'm on your side. I'm drunk.

Outside the windows now was the luminous darkness of a Manhattan night, the dark aura that blotted out any sense of sky. Street lights. Neon. Apartment lights. JESUS SAVES.

He put his tie back on, splashed cold water on his face, rubbed some life back into it with the nubby towel. Maybe a little vacation was in order before he started searching for the big break. Some tan. A glow. Right now the only glow his face had was the yellow reflection from the shower curtain. Made his bloodshot brown eyes look like he had jaundice. Got to get rid of that curtain. And the eyes. Get new eyes, a new brain. That's the only change the face needs. And a haircut. Napoleon's fringe is getting out of hand. Or maybe let it grow long, very long and silky. Become a Rolling Stone. With that nose how could anything go wrong? How fortunate to be blessed with a straight, classic nose—and be a Jew at the same time. Even a WASP couldn't match it. "You never had it so good, Phil-up!"

With her master about to leave, Liffey retired to the bedroom and the pillow. For her a fact was a fact. "Take care of everything," he called from the door. "Watch television. Answer the phone. Tell old Dad I'll call him later."

He walked into the Village, down Greenwich Avenue, weaving in and out among lounging young queens, prissy and sibilant, preening, stalking him as he crossed to the corner of Eighth Street and Sixth Avenue—Avenue of the Americas to out-of-towners, never to a citizen. The Village show had started early tonight, what with the good weather holding; Friday night was dressy: make-up, teased hair for the boys; leather and stretch pants for the tough little girls; some chains, some brassy buckles on wide belts; some love beads, beards, and bare feet. The Al Fresco Follies, more spectacular than any uptown Easter Parade, had begun. And the tourists from New York City's own provinces, the junior hoods from the Bronx and Brooklyn, the young-marrieds from Queens, high-school boys and girls from everywhere outlying, on foot or in flashy, souped-up, roaring cars were there to hoot and holler, to observe the *paso doble* up and down the sidewalks, in and out of handicraft shops, sandalmakers, costume-jewelry fronts, bookstores, delicatessens, the Village Barn.

Phil turned right at MacDougal Street, out of the mainstream, breathed easier at Washington Square Park, glanced up at the spotlighted Arc de Triomphe and then down the park paths patrolled these days by policemen on scooters. Make the parks safe for democracy. Make them safe for the residents of the high-rise luxury apartments of Lower Fifth Avenue, who came to take the spring air along with the junkies, the hustlers, the drifting Bowery bums, dispossessed ever since there was no Third Avenue El to hide under, along with the folksingers around the circle fountain in the Square, with the beautiful mix-matched strolling couples of silky-long-haired white girls and frizzy-natural-haired black boys who collected at the fountain to sing if they felt like it, to protest if they felt like that, freed for the weekend from a worried mother, a tired father, from the hard weekday thoughts of how they would make it into the future and make that future different, better, more responsive to what *they* wanted. As if they knew. As if anyone really knew anything more than what they didn't want. It was enough to know that much. It was even enough to be able to pick a place to eat in. Like now, which was what he had better do in a hurry. He decided on Granados at Third Street and MacDougal.

Another Scotch, first, then paella and a whole bottle of the easy-to-like Spanish white wine. He was quiet, not stoned. He felt drunk and sober simultaneously, the canceled-out feeling of zero. He was there inside the noisy ring of the restaurant, sitting still and alone, lifting a hand to eat or drink, aware of the waiters rushing by him, the diners laughing, whispering, kissing. He was being squeezed between the dropouts outside and the holders-on in here, between one job finished and another one to be found, between being young and being middle-aged, between Wilma and Howie, between Teaneck and the Village, between knowing and not knowing, between trying not to care about what he wanted, and caring more than anything else in the world. Well, then, it's all very simple. If you're in between everything, the thing to do is move away from the center, in one direction or another or in both—some people can manage that. Only move. Don't stop! Don't stop moving until you've arrived somewhere that feels comfortable. To hell with any other thought. Go. Get.

And, suddenly feeling elated, not a zero, but drunk, loose, Phil believed that the going and the getting would be simple. Just the steps might be hard. But this time he would take them. One at a time. He really did like to walk, to run into opposition. Most of the time no one offered enough of it.

He got himself out of the restaurant, retraced his path out of the Village to the quiet zone of St. Vincent's Hospital. Then he hailed a cab for uptown, for the East Side, for the other world, the world the "theys" said was saner and cleaner. The theys! All the theys that made this great grand city, this great grand nation the way they were: the smiling white liars and leaders, the money men who kept everything as close to their idea of heaven as possible, who drank well, remembered the old Guy Lombardo favorites, saluted the flag, hid their sex from sight. And that, Philly boy, is how they hold on to what they've grabbed. So say *they!* Say uncle. Shout hallelujah. Fall on your knees.

He went to Sandy White's apartment first. A party was in progress, the beginning of an orgy for eight or nine. Stupidly Phil wanted to talk about his day, but Sandy was preoccupied with a black subway cashier who, when he was introduced to Phil, wanted Phil instead of Sandy, or wanted both of them together. Phil left. That would be too much movement too fast for one night.

Aaron was still not at home, nor was he at the Plaza bar. But Mr. Dietrich was and very happy to see Phil. A few more drinks and Mr. Dietrich led Phil out of the bar and home to his apartment on Park Avenue. Of the events that followed all Phil could somehow manage to remember when he awoke in his own bed in his own apartment with his own telephone ringing the next day was that when Mr. Dietrich had begun to undress him he offered some resistance and then, totally drunk, gave up.

It was Liffey barking, more than the telephone ringing, that roused him. Of course it was Wilma. "Call me back. Later. I'm still sleeping."

"Sleeping? It's two o'clock in the afternoon, Phil. Get up."

"Call back later." He banged the receiver into its cradle and fell instantly to sleep again.

But Liffey's barking and the ringing telephone returned. Pat called. ". . . Yes, I did get drunk . . . sleeping it off . . . thanks for calling. See you Monday." And Ginny, content that she had found him still alive, just told him to go back to sleep. And Howie. "Later. Please." At four Wilma broke through again: ". . . But you just can't sleep all day, Phil. The sun's out."

"I can see that even from bed."

"Well, don't you want to get up and be out in it? Maybe go for a walk in the park?"

"No. Not particularly."

"What is it, Phil? What happened?"

"They closed Mr. Jack. Bankruptcy."

"Finally." A sigh. "Thank God that's over with. Now, perhaps you can begin—"

"Is that all you can say? Thank God?"

"What do you want me to say? I'm glad it happened. Now you'll be forced to decide a few things."

"Yes. Now I'll be forced. Thanks a lot." He disconnected even while her protest started up. He would have to call her back later and apologize. Not now. Now he had to try getting out of bed. No headache. Stomach rumbles? Yes. Dizziness? Yes. But fortunately no headache. Never did get a headache. He even felt a kind of exhilaration, a lightness like being in an airplane that would never arrive. Well, at least he was still alive. "Never again, Liffey. No more drinking like that. It's a promise." Liffey whined consolingly. "You have to go outside, don't you? Okay."

Down—heaviness, guilt began to throb in his head—and up again. A shower. A cautious, trembling shave. It always shows in your fingers. Tomato juice. Hot coffee. Slowly. A can of dog food. The smell caused him minor retching. As long as Liffey liked it.

The telephone again. His father. Well, here goes. ". . . Yes, it finally happened, Dad. Friday at five. The usual way."

"What will you do now? Do you have enough money in the bank?"

"I have enough money."

"How much is your idea of enough?"

"Enough, Dad. It's my business how much."

"Why don't you just get in your car and drive out here tonight? Mother'll make you a good dinner. We'll be able to talk things over and decide what—"

"I can't." Why not say, "I won't. I don't want to." Remind him I'm thirty-five, not thirteen?

"Why can't you?"

"I've got a date."

"With who?"

"Don't do that, Dad. I hate when you do that. Just leave me alone."

"Leave you alone? That's what you are is alone. That's why I'm worried. You don't know anything about money. I'll bet you haven't saved a penny since you've been working for those bastards."

"Why are they bastards all of a sudden? The other day on the telephone you were telling me what a nice man Mr. Fleiss was, how good he's been to me, how I should stick with him, not be ungrateful. And now he's a bastard. Why?"

"Because he didn't give you notice. You probably didn't even get paid for the last week."

"I got paid."

"Do me one little favor, sonny boy. Drive home. We'll sit down. We'll talk. We'll—"

"I already told you no. I can't."

"All right. I heard you. Don't have to yell. Only promise me that you'll come home next week then. Monday. Tuesday. Name the day. Whatever's best for you. Whatever you like. Just say what."

"I'll call you on Monday, Dad. Take care." A pause. Silence. "I'm going to hang up, Dad." Silence. "You know by now I'll never do what you want if you treat me this way."

A sigh. "Okay. Just take care of yourself. Make sure you eat. And, Phil, do me one other favor. Don't drink too much."

"I won't, Dad. So long." The heaviness, the throbbing *had* turned into a major headache and the telephone was ringing again. Aaron.

"So you were out last night, Phil darling."

"Yes."

"And you were a naughty boy, too."

"Knock it off, Aaron. I'm not feeling well enough for those games."

"It's no game. When you do something you say you'll never do again it's much more than a game."

"Look, Aaron. Mr. Jack folded yesterday. I've got a lot on my mind so don't start with that naughty-boy crap. I'll bet he called you first thing this morning. Told you a story about all the things I did in bed. As far as I'm concerned I didn't do a thing. He did it all."

"But you must have let him. Or are you going to claim that you were too drunk to stop him?"

"So I let him! Whatever he says. What does *let* mean on the open market? Nothing!"

"It means a lot. But calm down for now. Call me when you're in better control of yourself, if that's possible. We'll talk about your future then."

Revenge, they call it. A kick in the balls after you're shot, they call it. But at that moment Phil was too sick to worry about anything else but throwing up, which he did in the bathroom with unusual care, his head bent over the cool rim of the commode, on his knees. He settled against the soothing tiles, heard the telephone ring and stop, ring and stop. He slept and woke, threw up some more, slept again. The telephone kept ringing. By the time he crept out of the bathroom and managed to stand up in the living room, it was turning dark outside. And he did feel better, convinced himself that he was better. He even called Wilma. It was she for sure who kept telephoning. Howie would have given up. "I'm just not feeling well, that's all. It's my stomach. My ulcer's acting up. . . . I really don't feel up to going out, Wilma honey. Just let me recover in my own way. . . . I'm sorry I yelled at you before. . . . No. It wasn't your fault. It's mine. All mine. I'm not a hundred percent. But by Monday I will be. So promise that you won't call me until Monday. That way we won't fight. Promise?" She promised. She also insisted that she loved him, that she didn't mean to hurt him, that she felt guilty. Why should she feel guilty? Because she loved him enough to blame herself for anything that went wrong for him. She didn't say that, but that was what she meant.

Two more calls before he was able to get back to bed. One was from Sandy, who was apologetic, who did remember what Phil had said about Mr. Jack and who assured Phil that it was for the best. "We'll have lunch next week. I'll help you any way I can, Phil. I promise that. Everyone will help you. Don't worry."

And, finally, Howie. He had spoken to Wilma. He knew. He understood how Phil felt. "But if you need anything, if you want to talk, Phil, call, please. I won't be a drag. I promise."

"Thanks, Howie. I appreciate it. But I'm okay for now. Speak to you soon."

On Sunday it rained. He spent the day back in bed with the *Times* and Liffey, ate lots of spaghetti covered with butter and ketchup, the way he liked it best of all, watched television, and by the time a rainy Monday morning dawned he was completely recovered, full of plans, remembering the only part of Friday night that mattered, the part when he understood how he had to move out from in between everything to an open place. Only now he realized, sober, that the going and the getting would be hard, hand over hand, slow and tiring, but it had to be and it had to be up, past everything he used to be, past Joe Fleiss and all the others like him, onto some kind of high plateau where, sure, there would be obstacles, but at least they would be new obstacles, not the same old sand traps. He couldn't be Norell—if that was to be a goal—in a day, but he certainly could be an Aram LeGeis, né Siegel. He could be much more than that. He could be a Phil Hanssler—whatever that was.

When he got off the elevator at the Mr. Jack floor all the others, the loyalists, were waiting glumly. A. F. was missing, but Robert, circling among them, was there. The doors were locked. The representative of the factors was the only one who could unlock them and he was the last one to arrive. "Remember. You can only take out personal items. I'll have to check everyone before they go to make sure. Those are my instructions so let's not have any arguments."

Phil led Pat, Ginny, and his ladies through the dark showroom, down the corridor to their rooms.

"Wouldn't you know it would be raining? It's uncanny." Pat wondered about turning on the lights. "I mean we're not exactly criminals. We could be treated with a little more *esprit de corps* or something. Even a cup of coffee would help." The others, including Phil, were bunched up at the doorways, reluctant to move forward for the mopping-up action. "This place is a shambles." Pat poked forward with her umbrella. "They must have been here on Saturday looking for diamonds. Ladies! To your posts. Take only what's yours." The groups separated, brave smiles lightened the atmosphere. Ginny led the ladies into the next room.

Phil, energetic now, pulled off his raincoat. "First thing, Pat, highest priority, is to find out what's happened to the samples. Track down Robert. See what he's up to. Reconnoiter. We need to use strategy. And tie back your hair. It gets in my way."

"*Oui, mon capitaine.*"

Alone, Phil dug deeply into the drawers of his desk, piled everything in separate mounds: old buttons and belts—the tent had made them obsolete; beading he had liked once but never used on the line; newspaper clippings, pictures of himself, sketches announcing fashion shows he had done in Pittsburgh, Cleveland, Atlanta, Kansas City, Richmond, Denver, St. Louis, San Francisco—at least he had seen America; personal telephone books, engagement books, a trade book listing addresses of Who's Who in the industry; and sketches, hundreds of old sketches, rejects, all of them useless, out-of-date, but good, full of ideas. Determinedly, he dumped them all into a wastebasket, but then, compelled, leaned down to leaf through them, wanting to pick just a few to save.

And Pat, returning, joined him over the basket, silently, as if they were poking over the pieces of their bombed-out home. She stopped first. "No use thinking yourself into the glooms, love."

"You can say that because you're young. You don't have things to save yet."

"Yes sir, *mon vieux*. Obviously you're gnarled before your time. Bent over your basket. Slipping into senility. Age. Age. Age." Phil pushed the basket away. "Anyway, A. F.'s office is locked tighter than a vestal virgin. Robert claims that officially the samples are lost to us *and* to his father. Whoever gets them, if they have a smidge of brain, gets a business is the way I see it. But *we* most assuredly do not. We may have the patterns, but they, whoever *they* are, have the real goods. Which leaves us with a binful of sample fabric. What are we going to do with it, Phil?"

"Nothing. We can't touch it. It's part of the inventory by now. And that man out there's going to check everything we take out."

"All these gorgeous woolens! Lost! No fall! Summer goes on forever." The glooms suddenly breaking through her joking self-possession, Pat moaned: "What am I going to do, Phil? I mean, what about the future? How long will it be before you're ready for me again?" But Phil had no chance to respond. Her self-possession surged back. "Never mind. Disregard what I just said. I'll wait. I absolutely will not take another job. Starvation first. And there's an end to it. No rebuttal possible. So don't even try."

"Catch your breath, sweetheart. It's too early to be turned off and on so fast."

"It's all that watusi I'm doing. Shakes all my marbles loose." She rocked her head violently, hair falling freely, then stopped abruptly. "I'm crushed, Phil. Absolutely crushed. I mean, what is the point of this effort to get ahead? I should just get married and go live somewhere with cows. Because this whole thing has got to be ridiculous. It's beyond sanity. And, believe me, we are not alone. No sir. I don't see how anyone can deny the whole world's in trouble. I don't see how mankind stands it. How can *you* be so calm? Just answer that one question! Just that!"

"If you'll zip up for a minute I'll be happy to try."

Why, Daddy? How, Daddy? Her wide eyes questioned, daring him to summon up some reason for this event. That's life, baby, made no sense at all. He should have something more to say than *because, that's why.* But what? "Look, Pat, this isn't the first time I've been dumped. It's just the first time I let things slide so long. It's my fault, so how can I be anything but calm? Angry, sure. But calm angry. And if I learned anything from Friday, I learned that I'm never going to let that kind of thing happen to me again. Never! I swear it. I'm not working for another boss. I don't have a single clue about how long it's going to take me to get what I want, but I'm going to hold out until I do. And, as far as you're concerned, whatever I do I would like you to be with me. I want everyone left here. . . . Let's go in to the girls. Might as well say what I have to say to all of you."

He led; she followed. The girls had packed their old wedgies, their smocks, transistor radios, plastic spoons and forks, their personal coffee cups into Bloomingdale shopping bags. The coffeepot had been dismantled. Since Phil had bought it for them, it would be his to take home, Millie Berkowitz whispered, sitting in her corner, crying. One hand held her hair in place, the other circled Ginny's waist. Dottie's head nodded down at her possessions, at the number tattooed on her arm: of course, of course, what can you expect from a world that makes concentration camps. Anita sighed, then smiled, and sighed again. Evelyn hummed her hymns. Carmen looked out at the rain. I like to be in America. Everything's free in America.

"Now hear this, ladies! It's not the end of the world." He hoisted himself onto Ginny's work table, swung his legs energetically. Pat faced him, smiling bravely. Everyone seemed determined to smile, even Dottie. "Ginny will pull the plug on the steam iron here and before you know it she'll push it back into another socket somewhere else. I can't promise you exactly how long it'll be, but whenever and wherever it is it's going to be mine. I'm going to be your boss. Nobody else. And I want every single one of you to be with me."

Millie sobbed, surprised by the noise she made. "Excuse me, Mr. Phil."

He jumped down, hugged her. "Don't worry about a thing, Millie. You'll be on unemployment. You've got a union, and a husband who still pinches your behind. You'll be fine. And me, I've got . . . I've got your telephone number. As soon as I'm ready you'll hear from me. All of you'll be hearing from me. Even if you're working somewhere else, I'll haunt you until you come back to work for me."

Before another hour was up, each of the ladies had come to Phil in his room, had kissed him, and left silently. Nothing more had to be said, not even by Ginny when she was ready to leave. Phil had told her earlier that he was giving up the idea of keeping the patterns. That was that, except for a final hug.

Then it was Pat's turn. She didn't want to go, but what else was there to do? Whatever they had decided to save was stuffed into Mr. Jack shipping boxes. ". . . and if I stay any longer I'm only going to cry. I refuse to cry. It's not part of my code. Hard rock is my style. Why don't you come down with me, Phil? We'll go get smashed."

"I can't. I've got to see Morris and the others. You just go mosey along. I'm fine. Really. Don't worry. You'll hear from me every day. You'll know exactly what's going on. Just keep on sketching. And if you take another job I'll kill you. You hear?"

"I hear, love of my life. I hear every syllable your sweet lips utter. Kiss me quick." Her hair enveloped his shoulders. She was crying, mumbling, "Leave soon, Phil," and then ran out of the room.

He took her advice. The silence that filled his room then had nothing to do with the energy he felt inside. He wasn't depressed and didn't want to be. A little sentimental, maybe. But why not? He was entitled. He was also ready for action. The weekend had done that. Letting loose for a few days always did that. So go home, start the telephone calls, make the contacts. That'll be the first step and, hopefully, the first of many.

Moving up the corridor, lugging his boxes of junk, Phil stopped to watch Link shovel piles of Mr. Jack pencils into Mr. Jack envelopes, stack the Mr. Jack ashtrays into neat piles, sort the Mr. Jack order pads, the Mr. Jack matchbooks, the Mr. Jack pins fashioned out of the unbeatable logo. He studied the crumpled ball of colored paper that Link had saved —paper dresses, paper dresses—to use at the end of the pull string for the overhead flourescent light. Those damn cheap colors. Instead of fading they seemed only more brilliant, more beguiling. He flicked the ball with his finger. Link turned in time to have it graze his face. "You really are a saver, aren't you, Link?"

"Things like that I save. That don't cost. Money I can't save worth a damn. Never got enough to save."

Phil undid the string from around the crumpled paper ball. "Can I have this?"

"Don't know why not unless that there man up front's liable to take it from you."

Phil stuffed it into his raincoat pocket, put his hand on Link's shoulder. "Don't you worry about a thing. Before you know it . . ."

"Before you know it, Phil, I'll be dead. That's all I ever worry about. Never had a chance to worry on anything else. I'll get me another job the same as this here. A. F. says he'll get me one right away. But, if he don't, I will."

"Better not count on A. F."

"I got to. He's about the best I ever had outa my fifty years." Link raised his head, stared into the flourescent brightness as if he were searching for a new sun, a new chance there.

"A. F.'s gonna watch out for me."

"I'm sure he will. You just take care, Link."

"You too, Phil."

In the empty showroom Phil settled his boxes on the dirty beige carpet, and saluted the logo that would never bear his name now. A. F. would never have done it anyway. It would have been like getting the Pope to remove INRI from the crucifix.

Morris and Michael Morgan surprised him from behind, each grabbing an arm, steering him to a corner table.

"Philly, my boy, you shouldn't look on this that you did wrong. You didn't."

"I don't, Morris."

"Good then. Because what I got in mind for you, you'll be happy to hear from me. I got a proposition already."

"Keep it down." Michael Morgan whispered, annoyed; twenty-seven-year-old Michael was ordering Morris Trebnitz, the ancient, the venerable cut-velvet production man, to keep quiet as if he had, over that past weekend, been transformed from fledgling salesman into the impresario for a conspiracy; the same Michael Morgan who had been with Mr. Jack for less than a year, who had acted during that time as if he were a humble apprentice cobbler and who was now stretching his legs, lighting a cigar like an instant *macher*. "Let *me* tell it to Phil. You don't understand the entire plan."

"*I* don't understand? Me?"

Phil laughed. He was witnessing the return of Abbott and Costello.

Who's on first . . . ?

"That's enough, Morris!"

Surprisingly, Morris did sit back, quiet and contrite.

"Phil, I've been watching you since I've been here and—"

"You have? I didn't realize that. And what did you see while you watched?"

"I saw that you've got plenty of ambition. Which is why I want to talk to you about this proposition my friends and I have got hatching. It's a big one. Very big. A. F. has got wind of it. I suppose he told you—"

"All he told me was that he didn't trust you. You're a Benedict Arnold, he said. Was he right not to trust you?"

"Perhaps." Michael paused to let the implication take root. His boyish square face, a face which, like his name, seemed to have been tailored to meet Gentile business-world specifications, nevertheless contained a certain style, a confusion of candor and calculation.

Phil saw that Michael Matthew Morgan had no intention of turning into a dime-a-dozen silver-suiter. Gold maybe, but never silver. So Phil decided to sit still and listen for a while even though there was a liberal sprinkling of dandruff on Michael's blue serge shoulders. A loser's flaw?

"What my group is planning to do is buy the name Mr. Jack."

"They're what?"

"I thought that might get you."

"It gets me all right. In the gut." Phil punched at his tightly belted Aquascutum.

"Anyone could have seen this bankruptcy approaching." The cigar glowed brilliantly, was moved carefully back and forth with a style that a Joe Fleiss would never have. It included; it had nothing to do with keep-your-distance. "I just put my friends onto the idea of stepping in at the precise moment to snap up the name. Mr. Jack is still a powerful drawing card, you know. It draws all over the country."

"I know, but it might not be able to draw shit a month from now. Big names come and go. As soon as the ladies find out the label's gone, they'll latch onto another one."

"That, of course, is the great risk. We—my friends and I—realize that, so we want to get back into the stores before the customers know what's happening. And we want you to go on designing for us."

"For you? For your friends? I don't even know you, Michael. I don't know those friends you keep mentioning like they were some new breed of Mafia."

"They're all wealthy boys. Fine backgrounds. My age. In real estate mostly. Or the market. Banking. Big money all around. I guarantee that. I'm the only one who's poor." Michael lowered his cigar, leaned forward as if he were suddenly drawing the curtain of conspiracy more tightly around them.

"Philly, darling boy," Morris could contain himself no longer, "it could be a *mitzvah* to everyone. Even to me it could be. At my age to start again with a new company that has money—well, what should I tell you? It would be . . . it would take twenty years from my life. If you want I should give you my advice, my advice is you should say yes before you leave here now."

"Morris, sweetheart, don't tell me what I should or should not do. That's out! No more of that crap." Phil stood up, eluding Morris's grabbing hand. "When you can offer me something more than talk, Michael, call me. But you might as well get one thing straight right now. I'm not working *for* anyone. Tell that to your wealthy friends. I don't care how much money they've got. I'm the one that has all the contacts. I'm the one who's got the talent. And, if they want it, they'll have to give plenty. I'm the one who's known on the Avenue. Not you and not them. They better recognize they won't get anywhere with an unknown if they buy the label. So keep in touch, Michael. And be careful. Jack Farbstein probably has his own plan to get *his* name back, and A. F.'s got *your* number. It's getting to be a familiar one these days. They used to call it *chutzpah*. Now everyone's so elegant they call it better business bureau."

"Philly, listen to me." But Morris's plea went unattended. Michael, on the other hand, didn't seem at all disturbed. Smiling coyly now, he looked for a moment like a winner.

Dragging his boxes, Phil made his way over to Robert and Marsha, seated at the remotest corner of the showroom. He didn't look back at Michael. Always leave 'em wondering.

"I see you were in conference with the opposition." Robert was glum. "Those bastards don't even have the decency to wait until after the funeral. The body's still warm and they're planning."

"That's the time to plan."

"You too, Phil? I didn't think you'd align yourself with them."

"I'm not aligning myself with anyone. Morris is no bastard. He's a frightened old man. But you, Robert, you're a *schmuck*. If no one ever told you that before, let me be the first. Why don't you just cut out this sentimental crap? People have to live. They have to earn money to live."

Phil leaned down, kissed Marsha dutifully on the forehead. She was on Robert's side. "Please tell your father I'll be in contact with him. Not that he'll get anywhere with any ideas he has. What he should do is retire and live on your brother Joe's money. The new Seventh Avenue is something he doesn't know anything about. And neither do you." Phil touched Robert's shoulder, walked off, imagining Robert turning in a series of circles, too dizzy even to respond to insult, propelled only by the motion of someone else's movement. A hopeless case. Hopeless.

In the hallway in front of the elevators the representative of the factors had set up an inspection table. Phil refused to step up to it. "They're sketches and I'm not about to open these knots for you or anyone else."

"I'm supposed to check everything that goes out of the place."

"Well, buster, you'll have to fight me to get to see what's inside these boxes." Phil rang for the elevator. It was only fitting that this should happen. No leftover sentiment at the end to weaken anyone's will. A clean, deep incision. Just business as usual.

The bald, thin man raised his thick eyeglasses onto his forehead. "No fights, mister. I don't fight. You don't want to show me, so don't. To me it's nothing. As long as you're not taking out a machine."

The elevator arrived. Phil got on. The doors closed. No regrets. No sighs. Just relief that felt like freedom. The express elevator rushed him downward, away from Mr. Jack and the months of living with mismanaged loyalties. The days of A. F. were over. And if Philip Hanssler had let himself go down this far with A. F. it was only so that he could make sure there was another, better way to climb up again. Just as long as he climbed up, as they say in the army, smartly. That's what counted.

The lobby was crowded with obstacles: flapping umbrellas blindly stabbed across his path; rain-soaked salesmen who knew him smiled sadly; buyers, trying to push their rain-ruined hairdos into some semblance of order, offered their sympathy; and, damn it to hell, Jack Farbstein— wouldn't you know he'd be there?—was pacing the space in front of the revolving doors. There was no escape for Phil from that stalking, gleeful advance.

"So! It finally happened. Now it's my turn again. I'll get back what belongs to me. I'll get even. I guarantee you I'll get even with that thieving old bastard."

"I'm not interested, Jack. That's your problem." Phil tried to step around him, but Jack Farbstein had waited too long for this moment to lose it in a revolving door. Jack Farbstein was lean and strong, possessed by a vision of revenge. Like a swooping hawk, he plummetted and held on to his prey.

"He outsmarted me once, but never again. He bought *me* out, *my* ideas, *my* business when I had no money to stop him, when I had so many debts what else could I do. And who would believe that that man, that gentleman he calls himself, could do such a thing, could force me out of what was mine? Well, you can tell him for me that now it's my turn to kick. I'll get my name back even if I have to send him to his grave to do it. Tell him for me. Tell him." His long fingers squeezed through Phil's raincoat to the bone.

"Get your goddamn hand off my shoulder, Jack, and then go fuck yourself. I'm not your messenger boy." Violently, Phil jerked himself free. "If you want to tell A. F. something, do it yourself. I'm out of it. In the clear, baby." This time Jack made no attempt to stop him.

Outside, he stopped because now he had to, because Jack Farbstein's eyes had burned holes in his elation, had reached to where his fear was kept buried. Suddenly he felt panicky, paralyzed by the rain, by the massive slate-gray buildings, by the gray sky, by the weight of his boxes of old sketches, by the tarpaulin-covered rolling racks. Almost noon on a splashing, traffic-jammed Seventh Avenue, where nothing, not even himself, was allowed to stop. The world was waiting for the garments. So move, Philip, move. Get in there and step your way up to where you're going.

He walked to the corner of Thirty-sixth and Seventh, wolfed a hot dog and egg cream for good luck, continued on to the subway at Thirty-fourth. First thing when he got home would be the start of the telephone campaign. The quicker he was launched, the better. And once he was launched there'd be no stopping him. No sirree. Because that's the way you get the prize, baby. *You* go after it; it doesn't come to you. That's life. That's what you're supposed to do with your time: use it up.

Chapter Six

Each morning of each day of that first week without a job he prepared a list of important telephone numbers. He went through his personal business book checking off those he thought might be the most helpful names: the fashion-magazine editors, the ones who had always told him how simply marvelous he was; the buyers who had had success with his clothes; the fabric salesmen he trusted to understand what he was after: ". . . And not just another job. Something special. I want backing for my own business. . . . What am I offering? I'm offering talent *plus* business knowhow. That's what I'm offering. And let me tell you it's a rare combination. Easily worth a million dollars in sales potential." He called some of the manufacturers he had met who impressed him as possessing more than the routine amount of adventure and imagination. They set up appointments. They talked. To a man they said they liked him, liked his ideas about medium-priced fashion, but it took time, you couldn't just leap into a new business without a solid production package, a top-notch sales force, not with the way the market was at that moment, not with the goddamn Vietnam war getting bigger every goddamn day; they'd let him know; he'd hear from them, when the time was right, in a month or so. Lovey Gray at *Women's Wear* he called every afternoon, just to check in, to find out who was leaving where and why.

By the second week he was onto acquaintances, people who called him when they needed a favor. He was merely reciprocating. That was part of the system too. And then he decided to stop calling out, to sit down and wait for a few responses, to reap the benefits of old praise and old affection.

An old habit, the oldest one of many that had served him for so long, got him up early each morning. As far as his nervous system was concerned he was still expected and needed at the office just as years before he had been expected at school or at an eight-o'clock class in college or at five-thirty reveille. He couldn't remember ever relying on his mother or stepmother or an alarm clock or a barracks shout of "Up and at 'em." Never, with the possible exception of those mornings after drunken nights. Those didn't count against his record. So there he was these days out walking Liffey to the newsstand even before the doorman had finished his container of coffee and the *Daily News*, and then back upstairs to make a sensible breakfast of eggs and toast, after which there was still a long enough stretch of time left over to sit in the swivel chair in front of the bedroom window, to read the *Times* at his leisure, to sip a second cup of tea while he waited for . . . waited for what? For the telephone to ring. That was all, really, to do. And it did ring, but those were the daily calls from Wilma, happy to know that she would find him home, from an anxious, solicitous Howie, from Sandy who was trying to help, from Pat, from Ginny, from Teaneck, his father, worried, urging him to take a job, any job, just for the time being, just so there's money coming in. The more Phil tried to reason with and convince his father that money coming in was not the point, the more Mr. Hanssler said it was, the more he insisted that he knew his sonny boy all right. Sure he knew how his son spent money left and right, how he never saved a penny. Even when he was a child he spent. Not that he ever asked for more than his allowance. That he was willing to admit.

At first Phil's optimism hardened into something like a protected, fixed point in space around which his drifting mind could anchor, but by the last week in May the hardness, the fixed point, the anchor were weights more than they were supports, were the products of swollen obstinacy rather than conviction. His will, as it always did, wavered, damn it, and worry worse than his father's set in. Worry was even more contagious, more resistant to treatment than all the assorted communicable diseases assaulting man, spreading as it almost always did—not just in himself, either, but in everyone—to the deepest, most inaccessible areas of a mind, burrowing even deeper into the oldest, least-explored black landscapes there, acting like the fuse for a chain reaction of remembrances, of sudden glimpses of other worried times, forming a color-coded symbiosis between the surface he could see and the subconscious he could only guess at. The more acquaintances and friends offered consolation, the more rampant and raging the disease became, the more futile became the attempt to contain the contagion. The low-grade fever mounted. The sickness spread faster than any galloping cancer, slowed him, stopped him, until, finally, he felt that nothing but a miracle would help. And he didn't believe in miracles. To get out from under, to get up there where it was all supposed to be happening and where he wanted to be, would take hard work, not miracles. Horatio Algers died from heart attacks today, were buried along with Edgar A. Guest and Whistler's Mother and Herbert Hoover. Fairytales, all of them, useless metaphors, mixed into manure at Auschwitz, into a pile of bones at Hiroshima, gunned down in Mississippi. From rags to riches had happened in the rag business, had happened to men like A. F. and Carl Kalb, in the good old days, before the truth set in for everyone else but them and people like them to see.

Not that everybody looked. Most people didn't, or wouldn't. They turned their backs on it all and forgot. They went on watching Johnny Carson for comfort, reading themselves down into the *Valley of the Dolls*, crying for Marilyn Monroe, calling those the great American success stories while the really big success stories, the really spectacular killings on the market, went on behind closed doors, got reported quietly in the silky pages of *Fortune* or in the second section of the daily *New York Times*, where a small picture of a frightened, surprised face hailed another executive made, packaged, shipped skyward by American Express. So who's selling miracles! Apparently no one Phil knew, except maybe Michael Matthew Morgan. "I tell you my group is going to buy that name, Phil. Why fight it so hard? Think about our offer. Join us. In a few weeks everything at the Mr. Jack office, including the name, is up for auction. We've got lawyers working on it day and night. A. F. can't possibly get it back. He's trying, but I can personally guarantee that my friends are going to win out. So be prepared to start rolling again. You'll work for our combine. . . ."

When A. F. called to report on what's what, he used "Jewish Mafia," not "combine." "That little punk and his Jewish Mafia are trying to ruin me, Philly. Stay away from them. Listen to my advice. They're none of them any good, especially that shitheel Morgan. What does he know about Seventh Avenue? When I was working on my first million he wasn't even born yet. . . . One more week and I'll be refinanced. You'll be working with me all over again. That Benedict Arnold! There he was working for me, taking my money every week, and all the time he was stabbing me in the back. He's a Pearl Harbor. In all my years of being in business I never met anyone like him, that I can assure you. So come have lunch with me, Philly. Forget them. We'll talk. I'll explain what the new business'll be. Separates, Phil. Sportswear. That's where the next big money will be made. I know those things. Maybe instead of opening on Seventh Avenue we'll go to Florida. How does that sound? The sun you'll get. The beaches."

Phil didn't meet A. F. for lunch. He didn't meet anyone for lunch. He waited at home or he took Liffey out for long walks to Washington Square Park, where he sat on a bench and worried. And in the late afternoon he was back on his swivel chair peering into the sun setting behind the Palisades.

Sure he received some calls from the trade, but they were condolence calls, the kind you make when someone dies. "I'm trying, Phil, but the Avenue's in very bad shape. Everyone's tightening up. As soon as I have a lead that's right for you rest assured I'll call." Or, "If only it was another time of the year, Phil. It's impossible right now. Nobody's buying clothes. My sales figures are way off last year's. If it continues this way, I'll be out of a job too." Or from Lovey: "Why don't you put some kind of dramatic ad in *Women's Wear*? Something like, 'Talented designer seeks talented new breed manufacturer.' You've simply got to approach this thing in some truly creative way. Why not get yourself some free-lance work until you really connect?"

Once June began and the weather held warm, warm enough for him to recall, without wanting to, other years when Carl Kalb and he would have been spending long weekends in the Hamptons, or Wilma, Howie, and he would have started their summer treks out to Fire Island, he was frantically looking for free-lance work. Nothing materialized. The people who interviewed him wanted cheap gowns, cheap suits, cheap dresses, and wanted his services just as cheaply. Yes, they liked his concept of medium-priced fashion, but they wanted their clothes to sell for twenty, twenty-five retail, not sixty or seventy. They wanted volume. So what if the dresses were made out of cheesecloth? As long as they sold!

The disease spread into his arms and legs; he felt a semiparalysis take hold, began to imagine himself a person with a legitimate, officially undiagnosable illness who *could* move if forced to, but only with great effort. He refused to drive out to Teaneck in that condition. He refused to meet Wilma more than twice a week, and when he did she talked, tried to help, but he didn't respond. They went to bed. Sex was bad. Lust was out of the question. Only habit and biology helped him perform. He turned away to sleep; she cried. He heard her crying, but what could he do? He was the one in trouble. It was harder to shut out Howie and not just because Howie had a key to the apartment, but because Howie had been there when Phil was being led into experiences which, years later now, seemed to be forcing his life out of shape, to be dragging him along a faint, but emerging, dotted line, a tracing of the past that had been, until then, feeble enough to fight, that Phil said he wanted to fight but somehow didn't or couldn't completely. No one else knew about those things, not even Wilma. So only Howie understood, in that woebegone, born-to-suffer way of his, that what was wrong with Phil was so much more than being out of a job; it was everything; the works. The dots were darker. The pencil picture was almost in place. The connection of then to now was surfacing. Howie said it that way, asked if he was right. Phil admitted, yes, it was everything, so would Howie please just leave him alone for a while, let him think it all out, keep tabs on him, sure, but not interfere? And, of course, Howie would, would do whatever Phil wanted him to do, would do anything except stand around to witness Phil's complete breakdown. *That* he wouldn't do. But that, Phil said, wasn't about to happen. Don't worry about that.

The fuse was still hissing, burning, yes, but it was a long fuse, the steady sound of it in his ear an accompaniment as he stepped through the apartment or when he listened to Pat say that she didn't know how much longer she could be without work but that she promised to hold out somehow because she wouldn't work for anyone else, she just couldn't think of it; or when Ginny called to say that she had taken a job because Jim insisted. He was planning a one-man show for the fall and one of them had to be working steadily. Phil understood. Yes, certainly he did. But he didn't understand why Aaron would choose this time to be his bitchiest, why he would call and tease, tell him to come out and join "the club." That's how he'd get what he wanted. And Aaron, the person Phil cared least about, did the trick. The fuse burned out. The hissing stopped. A thudless explosion took place in his head. He didn't break down, but he was forced to sit down, to sit still, to listen to the reels of words, to watch the pictures spinning through his mind, grainy pictures, sepia-tinted, distant and lost, he thought, of forms and faces, voices, thrust suddenly nearer, distinct, alive again the way they once had been. He couldn't stop the spinning reels of his life. There was nothing to press. And, perhaps, if he sat perfectly still, unresisting, all that he saw now as a jumble would, finally, fall into a new pattern, a new design.

It was bound to happen sooner or later, this looking inside yourself, this taking stock, as Howie liked to call it, this sudden sensation of seeing all at once, and then separately, all the selves he'd ever been, like studying a color wheel at school, squinting his eyes—it was mauve-red, a deep pink, a deep blue sunset outside his bedroom window—scanning the endless flow of intensity and combination back and forth, from pale to dark to pale again, those triangular wedges of the wheel that could be slipped out of order, examined, turned over, dropped back in their proper places. So each part of himself, now, felt that it was being picked up by a robot's fingers inside his mind, examined, turned over, dropped back into its proper place.

The yellow-white-green-blue of those summers along the Jersey shore. Belmar. Bradley. Asbury Park. Tan sand. Towering waves. Crests curling downward. Spray. Foam bubbling out of the rocks. A beach ball bouncing. A chipped red shovel scooping the wet sand, the sand spilling onto his brother's blond curls. Paul smiling, happy, flinging sand back.

"What are you doing, Phil? You mustn't do that to him!" His mother calling from the circle of shade beneath the beach umbrella, the umbrella a wheel of colored strips that seemed to spin in the hot sun as she dropped her magazine and walked slowly to them, removing the shovel from his hand. "Please don't do that, Phil. That isn't playing nicely. And you stop throwing sand, Paul." But she wasn't angry, really. She was smiling. She sat down between them, pulled them against her body, her head bent between theirs, her cheeks tan and warm, her arms firm but short, barely able to go around both of them.

"Ma, look. I can get my hand around your wrist almost."

"Almost is right. And I can get my hand around your ankle. See?"

"But you're old, Ma. You've got bigger hands. That's not fair. How old are you, Ma? Tell me. I want to know. Are you older than Daddy?"

"No. Of course not. Your father's thirty. I'm only just twenty-seven."

"And I'm seven. And Paul's just four. When I'm thirty, Ma, will I be what Daddy is? Will I be married? Will I own a store like Daddy does? Will I sell material to people?"

"I hope not." She let go of them. "You'll do more than Daddy. So will Paul. I'll see to that. That much I can safely promise. . . . Come. I'll take you into the water."

"I want to go far out. To where the waves start."

"I can't take you that far, Phil."

"Neither can Daddy and I want to go. Uncle George is the only one who takes me." The chipped red shovel was raised.

"Then you'll have to wait for Uncle George to take you."

"No! Now!"

"I can't, Phil."

"But I want to."

"I'm afraid you'll just have to learn to wait. I'm sorry. Come, Paul. Come with Mother."

The shovel struck Paul's cheek, the flat part of it, so his mother wasn't even angry then. She laughed and shook her head so that the beautiful tight curls bobbed like springs. But Paul cried. Not hard though. And he cried, off and on, until the next day when Uncle George came to visit. Uncle George was the best one in his mother's whole family and the only one who could really swim. Phil loved to be close to him, to sit on his shoulders in the water, to hang on to his neck when he swam far out to where the waves rolled like the rollercoaster at Coney Island, so far that it was even before the white started in them. His uncle floated. Phil hung on, pressed against the black hair on his chest when a wave lifted them high, lowered them as it rushed past them toward the shore, hiding in its height his father's arms motioning from the beach for them to come in, come in. And then the wave broke and there was his father again. But his Uncle George paid no attention to anything else but the water and the new wave that was coming and Phil, who felt safe and warm, warmer than the cold of the water. Carefully he stretched out on top of his uncle, let go of his neck, turned over and stared up at the sky. His uncle never stopped him. His uncle never sank. He couldn't sink. And the waves kept rising and falling beneath them. Up and down. Back and forth. His uncle moved him lower down, over his belly. They floated that way until, when the next wave was just beneath them, his uncle turned suddenly, grabbed Phil around the waist, started swimming with one arm toward the shore.

"No, Uncle George. More. More."

But he wouldn't stop swimming. "Your father wants us."

"No."

"Yes. Be ready, Phil. I'll be holding you. Here we go." They went down, beneath the water. Phil closed his eyes. His uncle's arm tightened around his waist. The explosion, the weight of water pulling them back. And when he opened his eyes again they were standing at the edge, on the rocks, in the boiling cold foam.

Uncle George never took him out again, except once, a long time after that day. Phil's father wouldn't let him, but George never tried to make him change his mind, or joke about how nervous Herman was being, the way he always had before. Phil didn't understand why his uncle didn't try any more, but somehow he knew enough not to mention his disappointment to his uncle and certainly not to complain to his mother or father.

The next time, the last time, they went in the ocean together was just after his mother died. Uncle George drove Phil and Paul down to Belmar and took each of them swimming far out. Phil was twelve then and George was married, out of the army, finished with the war. They swam out side by side, but when they got out there and George floated and Phil tried to hold on to his neck, to press against the black hair on his uncle's chest, George stopped him. "No sir, Phil. You're too old for that. Swim on your own."

Phil took the next wave back to shore, ashamed of whatever it was that had made him want to hold on to his uncle's neck, to sit on his belly. His father wasn't on the beach then, motioning, but Paul was. Phil took his brother's hand, walked with him back to their blanket where there was no beach umbrella, no mother waiting.

He never went back to Belmar. His new mother didn't like the ocean. She liked hotels in the Catskill Mountains. The green was shady there, mossy. And the white was plastered buildings. The sky was a blue that never seemed to change the way it did over an ocean, always too deep to be real. Even the gray, when it rained, was dead gray. And the pool was chlorined and it was crowded, any time of the day. He wouldn't go swimming. Paul went at first, but then he stopped going too. Whatever Phil decided to do, Paul did. If Phil sat on the lawn away from everyone and read comic books, Paul followed. If Phil played baseball and handball and ping-pong with the other kids, Paul tagged after him. If Phil went to the casino at night to dance with the girls, Paul went too and watched, never interfering, just watching. Wherever their stepmother was, neither of them wanted to be. They didn't say that to each other. They didn't have to. It was just a thing that happened, that had to happen because she wasn't any of the things their mother had been. She wasn't tan and warm and small and pretty. She didn't talk softly. Especially at night, when she rounded them up for bed, when they had to be where she was, she didn't talk softly. She yelled everything she ever said. "Your father's going to hear about the way the two of you behave. Don't worry! When he gets here Friday night he'll hear plenty. You can rest assured on that. I'm surprised how you won't listen to me. Both of you. And you're the ringleader, Phil. The troublemaker. Instead of setting a good example for Paul, you make trouble. A bar-mitzvah boy already and you still act like a two-year-old. I never heard of such a thing. Swimming is swimming. You don't need an ocean—"

"I do."

"So do I."

"I want both of you to stop that immediately. Do you hear me? Immediately!"

She had red hair and it was very long. She kept it coiled on top of her head, but when she hit them, it shook loose and fell around her face. Neither one of them would cry when she hit them and that made her scream louder and hit harder. "Your father's going to know all about this. Believe me. Just you wait. You're both terrible to me." She was the one who ended up crying.

"And you're terrible to us." Phil pulled Paul against his side, covered him so that when her hands landed the long nails couldn't get at him. Until then Phil didn't know how much he loved his brother. He hadn't ever really thought about it. But now he did. Paul looked so much like their mother. Phil had to take care of Paul; otherwise, no one would. Paul couldn't die too. That first summer they went to the Hotel London in the Catskill Mountains and the summers after that the two of them slept in the same bed. And if Phil got a hard-on, they laughed about it. But Mrs. Hanssler knew why they were laughing. "Your father's going to hear about this too. I guarantee it. That's absolutely disgusting!"

The third summer Paul was sent to camp. Phil wanted to go too. He fought with his father about going. But she said that Phil was too old to go, and, besides, he had a new brother, Glenn, to take Paul's place. His father tried to get him to see it that way, but Phil saw it the real way: she needed someone to help her take care of the baby, someone reliable who would wheel the carriage when she was busy with her friends playing mah-jongg on the lawn, or when she went in to eat her meals in the adult dining room. So Phil was picked. Phil would go on eating his meals earlier, in the children's dining room.

Glenn was actually an easy baby. Phil didn't dislike him. But he hated how much Glenn looked like her: the same red hair, the same freckles; and he hated the stinking lousy way she had of guarding him from people and bugs and the weather as if he were a crown prince or something. It was embarrassing to have to wheel that carriage with the mosquito netting all over the front of it and not let people come too near. But nothing was as embarrassing as the way she screamed, in front of anyone, whenever Phil had to pick Glenn up, "Don't touch his soft spot. Hold his neck, not his head. Be careful of the soft spot. You'll kill him that way."

And the other lousy thing was the nighttime. She didn't want Glenn to be left alone before he was asleep, so Phil had to stay in the room every night.

If he was too old for camp, then he was too old for that kind of crap, he complained to his father. He was supposed to be in the casino at night. His friends were there waiting for him. He wanted to dance. Betty Steinberg was waiting for him, and she was the best dancer of all the girls that fooled around with him. A lot of them fooled around with him. He was very good-looking, they said, and not stuck up. He also did the best Lindy Hop. No one had to tell him that. So, during the week, when old Ethel came in to see how Glenn was doing, Phil, fully dressed and waiting, would rush past her, out of the room. She could scream as loud as she wanted to and wake Glenn up. That was just tough. Glenn was hers. She could take care of him. Let her tell his father. Phil didn't give a damn. What would his father do, except yell louder than she did? His father certainly had learned *that* from her since they were married. How to yell loud! First he would yell at Phil—he wouldn't dare hit him—and then he would yell at her and they would end up fighting, ignoring Phil, which was just what he wanted anyway. Most nights he got past her without a battle, but sometimes she caught him. She pinched; she scratched; she twisted his skin until it was black and blue. He would scream back, try to push her away, but when she held on, she held on with everything she had, and what she had were the longest arms and fingers in the world. He was too small for an equal battle so, finally, he had to slap her in order to get free. That, of course, his father couldn't let him get away with. Phil would get no allowance for a week, but, anyway, at least he got to dance with Betty Steinberg and, afterward, go off to behind the hand-ball court and feel Betty up. He wasn't going to be a kid any more even if that bitch screamed her head off. Who the hell did she think she was, anyway?

She had him trapped all winter in Teaneck. But Paul was there then too. And his best friends. Which he needed because Teaneck was gold damask and ugly pink and blue tiles in the bathroom. Teaneck was a house filled with *chotchkes*, hundreds of little odds and ends that served no purpose except to collect dust. She collected them because she liked them. That was her reason, and for the same reason, only in reverse, there were no books in the house, just schoolbooks and movie magazines: she didn't like to read and, anyway, books collected too much dust. Also, no one was allowed into the living room. Everything was covered in plastic, including the lamps there, expensive lamps—she only bought expensive things—that were turned on and off every night but whose light was never used for anything more than show. Just like the sofa pillows which she set on end, fluffed into enormous piles so no one would dare sit on them. Everything that was supposed to be home was in the finished basement, except there was no rug to stretch out on, only cold, speckled chartreuse linoleum. At least, though, there was a real bathroom down there, with a door on it that could be locked. So he had to jerk off down there. He had to leave Paul and Glenn—Paul listening to the Benny Goodman and Harry James records, Glenn trying to break them—and go into the bathroom when he got the urge.

"What are you doing in there, Phil?" Now how the hell did she know where he was? He never slammed the door. Why couldn't she just concentrate on doing the dishes upstairs? She had eyes in her feet. "I want you out of there this instant!" By then she was on her way down.

"Drop dead!"

"Herman!" She shouted back upstairs to the kitchen. "Herman! Come down here immediately."

"I'm listening to the radio."

"I don't care. Come down here this instant. I want you to hear the way your son talks to me."

But by this time Phil had finished and come out, and then the pinching, shoving, slapping started. She never knew what else to do. It wasn't only her fault. The poor thing. Instead of just getting married, like other women did, she had inherited two sons as a prize. Well, that's what happens when you don't have the equipment to know better, when you have to accept what you can get, not get what you want.

One thing he was going to do, come hell or high water: he was going to get away to college even if he had to rob a bank to do it. Not that money was a problem. His father had enough. It was just that she tried to prevent it.

"Why must he go to college, Herman? Just answer that one question. Why can't he work in the store and learn your business? Is that such a terrible thing to do?"

"For me, no. But for him, yes. He's going to go to college if that's what he wants. Nothing—I'm warning you, Ethel—nothing's going to stop that."

"And so who's going to take over the store from you? Who's going to learn the business? All those *schnorrers*—don't yell because that's what they are, those leeches—in your family. Your oldest son should be the one."

"He doesn't want to do that, Ethel. Can't you understand that? It's very simple. ABC."

"It's not up to him to decide. He's too young to know what's best. He shouldn't go away to school. I forbid him to go away."

"You can forbid all you want to, but he's going away to school. That much he absolutely will do. He's too smart to do what I do and I don't want to hear any more about it. Also, we can do without those remarks about *my* family." She made her biggest mistake when she talked that way about his family, but it was the only thing Phil ever heard her say that was right. Herman did all the work, the hardest work, and his three brothers lived off the earnings.

"And I suppose when your other son is old enough he'll go away to college too?"

"If he wants to, he will."

"I want to." Paul had learned well enough from Phil.

"Then he'll go."

"And what about Glenn?"

"He too."

"You'll see when the time comes that of all your children Glenn will be the only one to stay with you. *That* I'll make sure of."

"It's a better idea, Ethel, if you wait for him to decide that question."

"Don't *you* tell *me* what's a better idea. What do you know about except fabrics and piece goods? What kind of businessman are you? When we got married you told me that in a few years you'd own the whole business. Sure! But I don't see it happening. No sir. Your brothers own it. Not you. So how can you afford all this college sending when you don't even give me enough to redecorate this house? Answer *that* question."

"If you want to redecorate, if that's what's going to make you happy, I'll get the money. I've got enough. Only stop yelling? I'm tired of this yelling every day." And down he went to the finished basement to his Relaxolator chair, his radio, his Bergen *Record*, pale, with a quiet anger, beaten, even in victory.

Phil went to Syracuse University because two of his best friends were going there, and at Syracuse the colors of his life changed again, merged with new hopeful hues, vivid ones, intense living colors of autumn in up-state New York and the huge heights of elm trees, the burning maples edging the squares, the rectangles of brown farm land, all of it looking like the Mondrian painting in his art history textbook; pure moments, when he was alone, of seeing things he had never seen before, balancing what he saw on a scale of ocean and not-ocean; new sensations and new people to meet and like, to make like him. The green-yellow-white-blue of Belmar were gone, and, finally, that was all right. He couldn't help that. He couldn't, even when he consciously made the effort, re-form the image of his small tan mother. She was sand, waves, sun-warmth, not a face, not a body any more. Only when he looked at the sepia-tinted wedding picture, his father standing rigidly, his slick hair parted in the middle, smiling proudly—he never smiled proudly now—his hand resting lightly on the lacy shoulder of his seated bride, could Phil know his mother as a fact. She had been there, once upon a time. And beautiful, fragile, smiling gently, looking then like a child, a child who, it seemed so true whenever he looked at it, couldn't live much beyond the taking of that picture. He imagined dying already there in her half-closed eyes, or turned into the folds of the tulle train that seemed to be pulling her small body forward while she tried to resist, tried to prevent the incipient fall from the ornate throne to the dark carpet. A freakish death George called it. People didn't die of pneumonia any more, not unless there were complications. It was crazy. But it was just as crazy that anyone who looked like that had ever lived at all. Those first months at Syracuse Phil kept the picture on the bureau in his room at the fraternity house, and when he stared at himself in the mirror above it, he studied those other two faces at the same time, saw how he resembled both of them, a combination of possibilities: he had his father's smile; his mother's oval face, her narrow, straight nose; his father's lips, full, but not too full, good healthy teeth; his mother's slightly jutting chin, just right in profile. The only fear in his face was in those half-closed eyes, her eyes. And it came from the same fear of dying that she must have had; it came with the sensation of his short body, a body like hers, which no amount of stretching and exercise and hard muscle would ever make taller. And his mother was in a grave which his father made Paul and Phil visit every Mother's Day, never telling his new wife that he did.

So Phil put the picture away, inside the bureau, underneath his socks and underwear. He wouldn't think about her dying or his own. He wouldn't think about missing anything or anyone. There was no one to miss at home, or anywhere. He was free, and he would never be unfree again. He had sprung himself from the Teaneck trap by persisting, and if he continued to persist he could become and do anything he wanted.

His school was Liberal Arts. Fine Arts became his major. He wasn't a great student. He had the brains, but he didn't have the time to use them properly. He enjoyed college first and passed his courses second. He joined every group on campus that mattered. No one could ever really call him *big* man on campus, though, without laughing. But he did become the biggest little man on campus: the best character actor in the drama group—leading roles were for the tall guys no matter how hard he tried; the spark plug of the Sigma Alpha Mu, the Sammies, a Jewish fraternity; the leader of all the football pep rallies; the best tenor in the all-male glee club. A Mickey Rooney type, right out of *Girl Crazy*, and the girls were crazy about him. Some mothered him; some loved him; some slept with him. All of them wanted to be around him. So did the fellows. Some of them from the glee club and Art League wanted it *too* much. That kind Phil made fun of, mimicked for his frat house, included the routine in a skit for the Drama Club Revue.

When semester breaks arrived, he and his Teaneck friends went touring instead of going home. Up to Rochester and Buffalo. Chicago. Detroit. Anywhere they felt like going. They saw the sights; they tried to make out. The Korean War was on, but who cared about that? Eisenhower guaranteed he would end it when he became President. If it was that simple to end, why should anyone worry about it. Eisenhower was a general, wasn't he. He knew war, and Stevenson knew . . . what? Peace? War and Peace. Attaboy, Tolstoy. Hold that line.

Summers were the only hard times for Phil. He had to go home then, but he refused to work for his father or to go up to the Catskills where his stepmother and Glenn were, where Paul was being forced to go. Some weekends he did drive there, weekends when his friends were busy or his father pleaded, "Do it as a favor for me, Philly. I don't make you do anything else, do I? So do this one thing for me. She keeps asking and I keep lying. Please, Philly. You can do the driving."

The swimming pool had been enlarged. Now there were an air-conditioned dining room, a bar in the new, potted-palm casino, tennis courts, a golf course, a roller-skating rink. There were things for him to do. He had even developed a way of listening to Ethel without hearing a word she said. She didn't yell at him any more. She had Paul. And Paul had Glenn. They hated each other. They both loved Phil. They *both* wanted to be with Phil, which made Paul hate Glenn even more, but Phil wouldn't take sides. Glenn was just a child. Glenn's mother wasn't his fault and they all had the same father. Paul remained obstinate; Phil did too. He always ended up taking both of them for rides in the car, into Monticello, past all the name hotels. He had become, finally, a big brother, along with all the other roles he was learning how to play, and that role pleased his father, unintentionally made his stepmother happy at the same time. She was free in the afternoons to sit on the lawn and *yenta*. What else did she need out of life but the chance to gossip, to show off her children —"college has really made a man out of my Philly"—the money to refurnish her house? Which, of course, she kept spotlessly clean. Never trusted a maid, she told the ladies. They won't do what you'll get down on your hands and knees to do. She never stayed around for the cooking talk. That she would never master. But cleaning? There she was a star.

During his junior year at Syracuse Phil shifted from Fine Arts to Applied. It turned out he was a great designer of things. Maybe he'd become an architect. Everything was still a maybe, not a yes. The colors and shapes of buildings, of things, of nature interested him. People, how they looked, how what they wore brought out so many different things in their personalities, interested him. Maybe he could design clothes, create a new way of dressing that let people live freer lives. Appealing, very appealing, that idea, except for one thing: too many of the guys he met in those design courses were fairies. They latched onto him. They even showed up at the frat house. His brother Sammies ribbed him, but only up to a point. Phil was going to be president of the fraternity. That was his protection. "Why do you guys carry on so much about them? Who they hurting? You? You afraid of them?" And during that last year at Syracuse Phil realized that what those guys in his design courses thought about, what they knew about—music, serious music, art, the theatre—was far more interesting than all the talk about new cars, football, baseball, movies, getting laid. They dressed well. They looked handsomer, cleaner than any of the slobs who lived at the house. As long as they didn't try to touch him everything was kosher. Some of them tried, but he developed a very graceful, harmless way of saying no: he made them feel that he was the one to blame, that he wasn't up to their standards, that they were actually freer than he was, that that kind of sex, however exciting it might be—he could see where it might be—was just not what he had in mind. They ended up wanting him more, but got even less.

Not until he was in the army, not until after he met Howie Goldstein, was Phil willing to pick up that dark-colored wedge of his own possible sex problem and examine it. The things he had done with the guys in Teaneck like jerking off together, the times he had gotten an erection when he slept with Paul, those were the kinds of things that happened to every normal guy. Or something like them. No one called that being queer because jerking-off-together days had no connection to the real world of what you were going to be in life, how much money you wanted, when you were going to get married and have children. Those were the big questions, Phil had thought before he met Howie, not sex questions. One thing had nothing to do with the other.

Those two years in the army after graduation were, as he remembered them now, two that changed him. Their color was a pearl-gray and brown and a lot of snow for beauty and a gold too for beauty, a gold which was his friend Howie. They met during basic training at Fort Dix by accident at the Service Club. They were shipped out together, ended up, again by accident, being stationed in Germany, in the mountains of Bavaria at a place that had been a Hitler youth camp. There was so much time, all the time they needed during those startlingly quiet, clear mountain nights, to talk and think and compare who each of them was and how they had gotten to be that way and what they would be when they went back to New York. Just what he was doing now, in front of this dark bedroom window with Liffey curled on his lap, Phil had done with Howie back in the middle fifties in Germany. Only then he hadn't been forced to. Then he had wanted to because it was the most exciting thing he had ever done, to stop, to have the time to stop, to take stock of yourself, Howie called it, to move out of the flow of time, to sit still without turning away from anything Howie said, to see yourself like the trunk of a tree that's been sawed across, revealing circles around circles around circles that spread out from the center, that ended, finally, at the bark, the bark covering all the circles, as skin covers the many selves Phil learned he was, each self a different color, a different sound, a different mood, each self contained, hidden from view, but continuing to live on undisturbed, hibernating, even the child part, waiting for the proper moment to show itself, whether you liked it or not. ". . . And it's all there inside you," Howie would say as they sat out on the balcony that fringed each floor of their Kaserne high up in the dark and white mountains, "all the pieces you've told me about yourself, and all the things I've told you about myself are inside me. Sometimes certain facts erupt, force themselves to the surface, like an island shoots out of the ocean. You can't push them back inside again. Do you know what I mean, Phil? Does it make any sense?" Phil would nod and then, as if he were unsure of why what he thought would matter to anyone else, Howie would always add, "at least that's the way it seems to me. That's what happened to me."

Howie had that habit, the habit of people who speak only to those they care about and even then with considerable effort, of asking if he was being understood. He needed to make sure. He wanted to clarify, to chip away at stony thoughts, to reveal what he found it essential to believe, that the only real joy, excitement, beauty in life grew out of the attempt to trace to the source the form, the pattern of what you thought, to find there—who knew if it was even possible—some truth larger than yourself, that made sense, at least, for two people. That was enough for him: two people trying. It was Howie's official disease: talking. And Phil listened, believing that while he listened he also learned, believing that there *were* things to learn for no other reason than that, suddenly, a word, a phrase could settle comfortably inside yourself, explaining a part of yourself that insisted on being explained, like that memory of his uncle and the ocean. "George knew what he was doing. He knew it *then*. I didn't. But the important thing is why a person can't forget it. What in hell good does it do me to think about it now, Howie?"

"It might do a lot of good if you were willing to admit what it really means. Then it would stop bothering you so much. At least I think it would. Your uncle wasn't doing something horrible and wrong. He felt something so he acted spontaneously for a minute. And in the next minute he must have said, 'Christ, what am I doing, it's my nephew,' so he had to stop and take you back to shore. The point is that it didn't make any difference whether he stopped or not. It had its effect on you anyway."

Phil nodded, started at Howie's intense, wide-open eyes staring back at him, at his thin body huddled, hunched protectively against the chill night air. No matter how cold it got, Howie would sit there as long as Phil wanted him to. "But my brother, Paul. That worries me. I didn't *stop* with him. What's going to happen to him?"

"Who knows? You'll have to wait and see. Not everyone gets . . . damaged—psychologists love to use that word as if a person turns into a reject—by things like that. You don't think that all the friends you jerked off with are going to be queer, do you?"

"Since I'm not, I suppose they won't be either. But you never know. That's what you keep saying all the time. A person never knows for sure. With Paul it's something else again. I'd *like* to know . . ."

"But you can't. Again, that's the point. You'll have to wait and see. I'm no authority, you understand, but I think or I believe—if I believe in anything at all—that very little of it matters in the grand, chaotic scheme of things, and at the same time the slightest little thoughtless gesture matters more than anything else—to yourself. Does that make any sense?"

Phil squinted, turned to look out at the snowy mountains, up at the frost-silver moon. It was too cold out there. Their breaths were smoky. The fur-lined fatigue jackets crackled when they moved. They could have been two tubercular men taking the cure high in the German mountains, as in that Thomas Mann book Howie talked about so often. "Immensity and smallness, Phil. Those are the elements of everyone's life, and everyone has to struggle to keep them in some kind of balance every day. So my father tried to have sex with me when I was a kid. That means something to me. It would mean something to my mother if she ever knew about it. Which she won't. It's an immense thing to me, but it's a small thing, almost nothing, to anyone it hasn't happened to. Why should it be more? Or the man who tried to feel me up in the movies when I was eleven. I wasn't looking for anything. It just happened. Or the older kid who tried to make me blow him when I went to the boys' room in the first grade. They're all pieces of *my* experience. Important pieces. Immense to me. Bigger than a god or a government, but at the same time so small I can't imagine they're inside my head at all. But they happened *to* me and they stay with me. I can't really wish them away. A lot of people go through their lives acting as if things like I've told you never happened at all. That, I think, is the great danger. And I'm talking now only about you and me. On the open market nobody else cares. If you were to have sex with me, for example, what difference would it make to anyone else? It certainly wouldn't change the world and it might even be right for you."

"It might be. But I'm not going to do it, Howie. And don't start making me analyze why I won't. If I did this kind of thing at all, you can be sure I'd do it with you."

Howie laughed quietly, a derisive sound, directed more at himself, at his own self-doubt, than at Phil's statement.

"It's true so don't laugh. I'm being perfectly honest."

"No you're not. But you're not lying either. There's an in-between. If you felt it, if the feeling was strong enough, you wouldn't be able to talk about not doing it. You'd have to do it. So the fault, dear Brutus, is in me. I think that's the real truth, the objective truth. I'm not exactly a romantic-hero type."

"Look, Howie, if that's the way you want to see it, okay, but I think you're being a *schmuck*. I don't feel anything about anyone. And that *is* the truth. If I *feel* like having sex, the easiest thing is to have it with a woman. I want it to be easy. That's what my Fräulein's for. I do it and it's over with. Sex is just not one of my big things. It's in about third place."

"What's before it?"

"Being rich. Being famous."

"If that's the case, what difference does it make who you have sex with?"

"Logically it shouldn't, but it does. I don't know why," Phil turned away from Howie's scrutiny, "but it makes a lot of difference. If you could solve that puzzle you'd really be helping me. I'd like to end up someday feeling for people as much as the next guy does."

Howie sank back in his chair, shivered and sighed. "No. I think you'd rather end up feeling *more* than the next guy. That's the price you'll have to pay for *your* past."

They became silent then and stared out at the mountains, the snow, the sky, the stars, overwhelmed—Howie thought that; Phil was determined not to be—by the immensity.

At first, whatever passes or furloughs they had, they took together. They went to Paris, then later to Venice and Rome. Wherever they went, eventually people introduced themselves to Phil, certain kinds of people, ones that Howie understood. He warned Phil, warned him again when an invitation came to go to Capri, but Phil went anyway. Howie chose not to go. It seemed pointless. He'd only get drunk and stay drunk. He always did that when there were other people around who admired Phil too much.

And when Phil returned from Capri he swore that nothing had happened. Those guys just liked him. That was all. It was fun. If Howie wasn't jealous of Phil's Fräulein, how could he be jealous of something that didn't even happen? It wasn't being consistent, Phil pointed out. And Howie, in order to be consistent and honest, admitted that he was jealous of both, of what did happen and what might happen. The admission changed nothing; it only made their friendship stronger. Frustration was, after all, the heart of their affection. By then they could even joke about it. For Howie, frustration was the way he had of showing Phil how much he loved him. It was no different from the long, empty plain of his life up until then. He had always been frustrated by the things he cared for most: books, music, art. None of that helped really, that culture business. It didn't change how hard it was to live for most people. It only made despair calmer, bearable. So if Phil's image had entered the plain of his life, if only as frustration, it still had to lend a brightness to the darkness there, a brightness that was something like hope or the knowledge that, in any case, he could and would go on waiting, even though he doubted that the waiting would lead to any place better than where he had always been. At least now, he told Phil, I can make believe I have something to look forward to.

Which he didn't. Phil admitted one night out on the balcony that something had almost happened at Capri. One of the guys was nice and he was insistent and "I was drunk enough. But it just didn't work. I couldn't."

"Not now, maybe."

"Never, Howie. Never."

"We'll see. We'll wait and see."

Howie was still waiting, and *never* for Phil had come and gone. Howie knew it. Howie knew everything. It had made him bitter and bitchy, but it never made him stop caring. That kind of feeling, that kind of loyalty Phil doubted he would ever experience. And so what, really? What did it accomplish? A waste of time. Howie was still waiting and so was Wilma. Wasting their time. His whole small world was waiting for Philip Hanssler to emerge, to walk away from his window. Of course it was.

"Right, Liffey?" She looked up from his lap, her eyes glowing amber in the reflected light of outside, yawned, sniffed the knee of his dungarees, and went back to sleep, content. He swiveled gently as if rocking her, enjoying the darkness of his room. Darkness was appropriate—all the better to see with, my dear, to see the dark end of his memory's color wheel, the triangular wedge of black time right after the army when, still uncertain, he waited some more for something to happen to him that would make him decide.

Actually, what happened then happened to Howie. First his mother died of cancer, and a few months later his father committed suicide. Howie called it his Greek tragedy and left New York City. He had to get away or he'd just crack up, so he took a teaching job upstate. Phil drove him up there. It was just after Labor Day in 1956.

Two weeks later Phil moved from Teaneck into New York. Mr. Hanssler objected to the move. His stepmother didn't. "Let him go, Herman. He's old enough to provide for himself. We'll see what his college education did. And then Paul'll go and like I always said you'll be left with

Glenn, who won't leave you in the lurch."

Phil lived in a furnished room on the Upper East Side of Manhattan. He had his severance pay. He asked his father for nothing, even though Mr. Hanssler's new piece-goods business was doing very well, well enough so that he could have used Phil's help. He begged his son to at least think about it. He asked it as a favor each time Phil came home on Friday nights. "You don't have anything else to do so why not try it for a while? If you don't like it, you can always stop. You don't have to make it your whole life."

"Never, Dad!" And this time, fortunately, "never" was not a lie. Not that he knew exactly how to proceed. He tried to be organized, to have a plan, but it was just not his style. First he tried Madison Avenue, put together one of those portfolios, using college projects as evidence of his talent. He bought one of those huge, leather carrying cases, but the struggle it was to carry the damn thing made him realize that advertising was absolutely not his field. He began taking acting lessons, made the rounds of casting offices, lying about his experience, got nowhere except for the offers of summer-stock character parts. He was still too short for leading roles.

So okay! He could draw. He could design. He had a college degree. So what next? Designing what? Furniture? Shoes? Fabric? Women's clothes? Where did you go to become a designer of women's clothes? To Seventh Avenue! He put together a batch of sketches. A teacher had once said that if you try for a job on Seventh Avenue you must have sketches. Carrying them in an attaché case was easy enough. He walked up and down the Avenue for a few days, trying to digest the flavor of it. What a way to plan your life! Drinking egg creams and eating frankfurters, getting pushed around by those racks of *shmatas*, eavesdropping on groups of workers during lunch hours. Was there a better way to decide? At least there were plenty of places to eat. There was never a lull. The streets were always crowded. There was action, lights, camera, even glamour. Yes, he liked it. He wanted to join this crowd.

He bought *Women's Wear Daily* every day and every day for a week he debated making a telephone call to a firm, any firm that had a dress featured in the paper, just to see what would happen. Nothing ventured, nothing gained. A stitch in time . . . What happened was that the first call he made was to a company called Janet Dobbs, Inc. Why that one? He didn't know. Chance. Fate. Kismet. The stars. He picked it from the directory of 550 Seventh Avenue. It reminded him of the good day he had driving through Dobbs Ferry in Westchester County with Howie. He asked to speak to the designer. Was he a friend? No. Did he have an appointment with Mr. White? No. He waited. They put him through. What did he want? A job. Who told you to call me? No one. The voice on the telephone was enjoying itself. It said, "Okay, come up. I'll be free in a little while. I love a joke."

Janet Dobbs, Inc., was on the top floor of 550. Even the view from the receptionist's window was exciting. He could see the George Washington Bridge. "I'm here to see Mr. White. He's expecting me."

"Just a minute." She rang him, nodded, pointed, "Okay. Through there."

Through there was through a white door into a white, large, mirrored showroom, beyond that and through another mirrored door—the salesmen motioned him silently when he inquired—down an aisle alongside the longest wooden tables he had ever seen, the tables covered with lengths of piled black crepe, the windows behind the table looking north, up the Hudson River. The view, only the view at that moment, stopped his pace, broke his rhythm, awed him by its immensity, made him consider for the briefest, longest next step what he would say when he went beyond the mirrored door at the end of this aisle. It will be all right. He was equal to it. He was walking forward. The worst thing that can happen is that he tells me to get the hell out.

Sandy White did not tell him to get the hell out. He was friendly, nervous—he bit his nails throughout their exchange of greetings—effeminate in a direct, masculine way. He studied Phil, liked what he saw, nodded as if to say, Okay, I'll take it, and only then asked to see the sketches. He liked them too. "They're college sketches. But they're good. You really do want a job? No one sent you up here as a gag?"

Whatever dumb fate it was that made Janet Dobbs, Inc., his first call and Sandy White the first designer Phil ever met, was pointless, a waste of time, to consider. Accident? Chance? Coincidence? His life had always been that way. It played with him, dealt him good cards sometimes, just to let him feel the thrill of thinking he could win once in a while. He sat on a black leather club chair opposite Sandy, confident that the outcome of this freak meeting would be right.

"Can you do quick sketches? Feel sketches we call them."

"Yes."

"Then here," Sandy extended a pad across the desk, "sketch!"

"Sketch what?"

"Anything. A house. A tree. A man. But preferably a dress. The kind you might see in *Vogue*. That's what we do here." Sandy leaned forward to watch, smoothing the surface of his nails, admiring the assurance—he told Phil later—with which the sketch pad and the thick black pencil were accepted, the way the eyes squinted at the blankness of the paper, the way the stubby hand hovered, fell, drew. Hems were long that year, Dior long, dresses cinched at the waist, but Phil sketched a dress that was short, waistless, glided, slid over the body. It looked new, had a different proportion. Sandy smiled with pleasure. "Where did you come from? Parsons?"

"Parsons?"

"Fashion School."

"I never heard of it."

"You *are* an original." Sandy's smile showed just how much he appreciated originality. He told Phil that *he* didn't have a job for him, but he knew someone who did. "It's a sketching job. That's how you have to start in this business. But are you sure that's what you really want? My guess is that you haven't thought much about it one way or the other."

"I haven't."

"Then why the hell did you call me? Not that I mind."

"I wanted to find out."

"And did you?"

"Maybe."

"That's the way you make a decision? On a whim?"

"Why not? Should I be more calculating? Is that more impressive?"

"Not to me, for Christ's sake! I wish *I* had a job for you. I need someone like you in my life at this moment." Sandy's smile faded, then quickly reappeared. He picked up the telephone, dialed, eventually spoke to a man named Carl Kalb. ". . . Yes, he is, Very talented . . . Experience? Listen, Carl, the way the market is right now wouldn't you like someone without experience? If I see another tight-waisted dress with a long hemline I'll scream. . . . How does he look? It happens that he's beautiful. Absolutely beautiful. Can you see him?"

It was settled. Phil was to go over to 530, twentieth floor, in an hour. Carl Kalb, Inc. Cocktail clothes. "Very missy and expensive . . . but you're also having lunch with me tomorrow. One o'clock. I insist. A place called Ted's on Thirty-ninth between Seventh and Broadway. Be there."

"I will and thank you, thank you very much, Mr. White."

"Sandy is friendlier, Phil."

"All right then, Sandy. Thank you."

"Don't forget your sketches."

And that was the way it all started: a kind of miracle that Phil said he didn't believe in. Sandy, and then Carl Kalb, responded to a part of Phil that he called just being himself. But, apparently, that instinct, that casual boyish, candid manner sold in this market too. What he had always thought of as a coincidence of birth, his good looks, was like a handle that some people would try to grab and hold on to. He had seen some evidence of that in college, and in the army Howie had described it, warned him that a handsome face could be just as destructive as an ugly one if you ended up letting the handle, the label, take the place of what you really were inside.

Mr. Kalb, a romantic like Sandy, but more practical, older, told Phil he couldn't pay much to someone without any experience. "This is all intuition, you know, young man. Mr. White's first, and now mine. I'm willing to test it, however. You'll be working close to me and so you'll have the perfect opportunity to learn every aspect of this business. It's a very complicated business. I've been in it long enough to know just how complicated. Everything about it is demanding. You work under constant pressure and you must be quick. But I can see that you are . . . quick. You learn instantly, don't you?"

Phil didn't move in his antique chair—it had to be antique because it was too old and beautiful not to be—nor did he answer the question immediately. Whether he did or didn't had little to do with the quickness Carl Kalb meant. Just in the way this man's fingers rested securely beneath his square chin, Phil sensed an undercurrent of certainty concerning what he saw and what he knew. They looked across the desk at each other. Phil knew he wanted the job. Carl Kalb wanted him to take it— the unwavering stare seemed to say that. Or, if not that, then it said, job or no job I want something from you. Phil had heard one-half the conversation with Sandy White so he wasn't being crazy to think that was a strong possibility. But Carl Kalb was also a cautious man. The muted, continental cut of his gray suit, the maroon tie, the gray-dappled black hair groomed to a wavy luster; the controlled, gently rocking movement of his swivel chair said that. Nothing was excessive, either about the man or about his surroundings, except perhaps the ego that made it all possible. Carl Kalb, at fifty, fifty-five tops then, was a handsome man. He didn't look as if he lost minor battles like this one, or if he did, he wouldn't be shattered by it for very long. He could easily find someone else to play with. Which was why Phil didn't rush to answer, yes, I want the job. But everything that day had been done for a lark and so he might as well go all the way, risk one thing in order to gain a bigger prize. And if he forced Carl Kalb to play a game with him and he lost, well, Sandy White seemed like the kind of guy who would find him another opponent. "What kind of pressure do you mean, Mr. Kalb?"

"Oh, it's a special kind for me, of course. I'm a designer, but I'm also the boss. We book six million dollars' worth of business a year, which makes us quite big. Therefore, I need help. Good help that understands what I mean when I speak of good taste. That's one thing I won't sacrifice no matter how fierce the competition gets. Never. My customer expects that."

"Well, the pressure doesn't seem to have affected you at all. And the good taste shows everywhere." Phil smiled.

Mr. Kalb smiled back. His fingers moved slowly from beneath his chin, came to rest on his desk. "Thank you, young man. That's the nicest compliment I've received in a long time. I hope that if you work for me— which I would like—you'll continue to feel that way. But I warn you in advance, I do have a dark side."

"I'm sure. That's only natural. We all do, Mr. Kalb, when we're under pressure. But even if you do have a dark side, I'd like very much to work for you. The only trouble is I don't think I could get by on the seventy-five dollars you offered."

"Ninety then?"

"A hundred?"

"It's too much, but I'll risk it." A manicured hand was raised, extended across the desk. They shook hands and Phil felt palpably then what before he had only sensed. The hand held on to his a little too long. But so what? He had a job. The rest of it would take care of itself.

At first he only sketched ideas. Within two months, after Carl had altered details on certain sketches so that he could call the design his own, Phil was allowed to follow and guide one of his ideas from muslin through fittings to finished sample. Carl's assistant in the sample room taught him how to order supplies for her: belts, buckles, buttons, zippers, lining, extra sample fabric. Eventually he stood beside Carl whenever he had appointments with the fabric salesmen; eventually he was forced to decide what goods Carl Kalb, Inc., might consider using, what they would never touch and why they wouldn't, duties which Pat Pearson now performed for him. He learned about the economics of production, how Carl decided on the price of a dress, how the union man fought to raise it by arguing the cost of labor for a buttonhole, a seam, a pocket, a bow, how, after the man left, Carl and the production man found ways of cutting down on fabric for the dress in order to maintain the markup, show a profit.

Phil was taught duplicate making, learned how the sample garment was transformed into the various sizes, how the particular fit of a Carl Kalb, Inc., was designed to satisfy the customer the company wanted. And, as he discovered all the things a good designer with good taste is supposed to know, he also went to a fashion school two nights a week. He got Carl to pay for that, convincing him that it was, really, a sensible kind of investment. After all, the more he learned, the more valuable he was going to be to the company. Carl didn't fight it. He was very satisfied with Phil's work, enjoyed the enthusiasm with which he stayed late to work out a particularly difficult fitting problem, or helped out with billing when the company fell behind on their promised shipping dates. Stores could refuse to accept merchandise if their order arrived late.

Phil tried everything and not because he wanted to please Carl but because every part of the business excited him. What he did never felt like work; it was pleasure. He hated to leave the showroom in the evening, except on those occasions, irregular at first, when Carl suggested they have dinner together. Eventually, coming out of school, Phil would find Carl waiting. Those evenings were like bonuses, extensions of the day's excitement. Carl knew the best restaurants, knew what it was best to order in each one, knew what wines to order, what brandy to sip afterward. And, as they ate, Carl would talk about himself, his career, his success, Seventh Avenue, as if he were a concerned teacher or father rather than a boss. He spoke of the industry, the biggest industry in New York City. But that's what fashion was for Carl, visual history, and serious stuff, the pulse of America and the world, he called it. What a woman puts on her back, what she has always put on, or taken off, is the product of what's happening around her. The Pilgrims, the frontier ladies, the antebellum Scarlett O'Hara clothes, the Victorian influence, World War I, suffrage, flappers, Carole Lombard, Jean Harlow, Joan Crawford, all of it history, showing us the values of people someplace at a particular time. With always the French influence, the style setters, "Because no one can afford to let go of the French couture. The French inspire change, and change is what makes the American ready-to-wear business boom. Without it we would be in trouble. Volkswagens instead of new Chevrolets each year.

159

. . . Your job, Phil, if you want artistic success in this business, is to guess, before it happens, what the French will do next, what the new trend will be. If you can do that, you'll be made."

"I understand, but I don't see where art is really involved. You call yourself an artist. But why?"

"Because I never forget good taste. I never compromise with what I know it is."

"And how do you know what it is, that thing you keep calling good taste?"

"You feel it. You're brought up to feel it. My whole life is based on knowing what it is, sensing it in everything I do. You have it—to a degree."

"Well, if I do, I can't tell you where it comes from. Maybe from my dead mother. She's about the only person I've ever known who might have had it." Phil poured more wine into Carl's glass and then into his own.

"Now that's not good taste, for example. I'm going to tip the maître d' for doing just that." Carl, smiling, wagged his finger at Phil. "Oh, I know this is an unimportant thing, but it's all part of something that *is* important, very important."

On those occasions Phil didn't say what he really felt. He had stopped "just being himself." He liked his job too much to risk disapproval. He liked Carl Kalb and the world that Carl had introduced him to. And maybe Carl was right. He knew he had a lot to learn and not just in terms of business. Socially, too. Aaron Siegel made him aware of that soon after they met at the Plaza bar. Aaron had his own plan for Phil's education, a plan which Phil accepted as readily as he accepted anything which demanded, at first, little more of himself than going where Aaron wanted him to go. Besides, Aaron was very much like Carl. He believed in fashion the way Carl did, became serious when he spoke of it and his career, which he was just about ready to launch, on his own, with the right backers. He even had his new name picked out, "Because Siegel is just not right. It's too Jewish for the couture market. All I had to do was turn it around and it's French. LeGeis. Monsieur LeGeis. Clever, isn't it?" But Aaron's being younger than Carl, much younger, resulted in one difference. Carl was always circumspect about what he wanted from Phil. Aaron didn't have to be. He wanted Phil: "Your body, my dear. Friendship is just too limiting. I know Carl Kalb. He isn't as pure as you think he is. Just because he's married doesn't mean a thing. I could tell you . . ."

"Don't. I didn't think he was, as you call it, pure. I'm not as dumb as that."

"Of course you're not. I didn't mean to imply that you were. But you *are* naïve. You lack the temperament of an artist. I'm sure you'll end up being financially secure in this business, but I really doubt that you'll ever do couture design. You fell into a job, you didn't have to have it as if your life depended upon it the way it does for me. You lack something, Philip. I'm not exactly sure what it is. Chic maybe. Or maybe it's just that you aren't queer, or queer enough. Which is it?"

Why he allowed Aaron, or Aram as he insisted on being called, to lead him around was one of those unknowable facts about himself which Howie, if he had been around, might have forced him to investigate. Since Howie wasn't around and might not be again, Phil let himself be led out of the Village bars where he felt comfortable and into the uptown places where he felt as if he were on display, a showpiece, a curio for the curious who lived their social lives in drunken contentment, in perfectly tailored suits, in carefully lighted apartments, with indirect lighting that protected them the way covered light bulbs protected Blanche DuBois.

Aaron kept trying, and Phil gave in to everything but his seduction. It was easy to resist Aaron in a way that it was never easy with Howie. Aaron's desire had nothing to do with affection. It was simply a matter of acquisition. He wanted to own everything and everyone for a while— or else. He never defined "or else" for Phil then.

Fortunately, there was always Sandy to put everything back into twisted, insane perspective. Sandy plied his trade, received his good salary, demanded nothing more from Phil than lunch once a week, arranged elaborate orgies to which Phil was always ceremoniously invited. If he was drunk enough, he went. Sandy never judged the reasons for his coming, or the way he took part. Phil only let himself be serviced, that's the way he let his mind describe it, a description which lasted until the night Carl Kalb appeared at Sandy's.

Carl had been married for twenty years. The last five of those years he had seen his wife only on weekends. She had moved out to the house they owned in New Jersey, a garden spot very close to Bucks County, with their two high-school-aged daughters. Phil had visited there often and each time he thought he was viewing lives lived in quiet normality. Mrs. Kalb seemed devoted to her husband, made each weekend a pleasant interlude for him away from the strain of city pressure. When Carl left for New York on Sunday evenings, no greater request was made of him than that he call to check on this or that repair to the house, or this or that minor problem of the childrens'. Phil liked the country comfort of the house and loved the aura of serenity which Mrs. Kalb's presence created. She liked Phil, made it clear how happy she was her husband had found someone like him, someone Carl liked and respected. And when she said those things she did it easily, directly. She wore comfort as if it were an old favorite dress. She had always had money enough for anything she ever wanted, but instead of choosing things, she had chosen a life of plain, simple retreat. That was all Phil ever saw. It was all Carl would say of her, except, on occasion, adding how fortunate a man he was to have found so understanding a wife and hoping that Phil would be as fortunate. "Because everyone should get married. Every man should have at least one child."

So, until that night at Sandy's, Phil had almost convinced himself that what he had thought about Carl at their first meeting was an illusion. Aaron's innuendoes he heard as lies. Sandy never said a word. During the year that Phil had worked for Carl nothing the least bit suspicious had taken place between them. Carl was a mentor, wise and fatherly, in control of everything, including his affection, affection which, under the circumstances, seemed perfectly natural. That night Phil learned another lesson, one which had no direct connection to his future on Seventh Avenue: always trust your first impression; it may turn out to be the only one you *can* trust. That night Carl reverted to his position of absolute authority. He was Phil's boss, his supervisor, and his judge. He rushed Phil out of Sandy's apartment and over to his own, angry that Phil had been there at all, that Sandy had invited him. When he was finished being angry, he became solicitous. He didn't want Phil to mess up his life with things like that. If he wanted that kind of activity, if he felt he needed it, then the best way was for Phil to let him, Carl, take care of that too. Phil said nothing, but he didn't object. He thought he was too drunk to object. And there it was, out in the open, between themselves, in the dim light of Carl's living room, on the cream-colored antique-velvet sofa where they sat close together. Carl asked to be trusted, said he would do nothing to hurt Phil, and Phil believed what Carl said, believed he wanted to, needed to have this finally happen as a fact, as a reality to test. He fell asleep dreaming of comfort and softness and pastel colors. He was afraid, but his fear was less than the pleasure of the soothing, fondling, loving hand moving over his body.

Carl Kalb, Inc., opened a new division, a junior dress division, at the beginning of the third year of Phil's association with the firm. Phil was its designer. He hired everyone who worked for him. Carl just looked in once in a while, checked on the clothes that were being made, smiled at the efficiency with which Phil did all the things he had been taught to do. Carl was proud, the way any teacher would be of a good student. Phil had not disappointed him in any way at work, but in their arrangement outside of work—well, that was a different matter. It was an entirely different matter. That did not prosper the way the new business division did. Carl blamed Phil; Phil blamed himself. He hated the new apartment Carl found for him, a furnished one and done like a museum room. It had nothing to do with Teaneck or Belmar or the Catskill Mountains, or the rumpled joy of the college frat house, or the forced neatness of the army. It was posh and he wanted to be a slob, whether or not Aaron or Carl or anyone else liked it or not. So he didn't have their good taste. So what. He didn't want it if it meant giving up every little bit of comfort. Why couldn't the two things go together anyway? And he was growing tired of following Carl—two steps behind like an Indian wife—in and out of good restaurants with rich French food, in and out of the theatre, the opera, art museums, parties for buyers, the house in New Jersey, where they visited too many weekends, while Mrs. Kalb repeated how happy she was Carl had found Phil and the daughters avoided him, back and forth from the summer house on Fire Island that Carl had rented and where Phil when there spent each day getting drunk. He didn't want to be kept —that had to be the word for it—and he didn't want to be queer, not in the way Carl wanted him to be. But the more he complained, the more trapped he realized he was. Carl insisted; Phil had to follow or lose his job, lose all the things he had gained and thought he wanted. There was no one around to help him, no one who began to know what he was like inside.

When he went home to Teaneck every Friday night—Carl insisted on that too; a son and father should never be separated for long—Mr. Hanssler was only proud of how fast his sonny boy had gotten ahead in such a hard field and how kind Mr. Kalb was to help him so. His stepmother stopped yelling at him completely. Now she wanted him to like her, to let her please him. "Just tell me in advance what you want for dinner. Name it and I'll make it. Do you want veal cutlets? The way you like them? With onions?" All week she called him at work, planning for his visit. What else did she have to do? Paul was away at school. Glenn was grown enough to need no particular attention. That left Phil: the star, the success. He made good money. He had good clothes. Before long everyone, except Phil himself, would be proud of what he had accomplished.

Phil dragged his private ache along with him from day to day, each day feeling guiltier about what he didn't do to help himself, thinking that he should quit, go away, hide somewhere. Instead of doing any of that, all drastic measures, he hit upon an old joy, a breather, stop-gap but helpful. He began acting classes again down in the Village, two nights a week, when he wasn't busy at work. Carl objected, said it was a waste of time. Phil was a designer now, and not a child who could play around. Phil won that battle by saying it was only a hobby, exercise, and everybody needed that. It wouldn't interfere with work. He promised that much in return for the chance to do it.

He kept that promise so completely that he never told anybody at the school what he did for a living. When they asked that question, the inevitable ones who were drawn to him, he would only mutter, "What do you mean what do I do, I'm an actor. I don't do anything else. I live off dividends. My father's dividends." And that was that. They stopped asking, liked him even more for that aura of mystery he maintained. Actors and would-be actors respect what they don't know. They wait for directors to tell them about it. Those free nights away from Carl became his college days all over again, the time before the darkness started. When he did scenes, improvisations, he imagined that, yes, there was still time to rearrange events, to shuffle the pieces, to come up with a different picture.

When he met Wilma, a friend of a friend at the acting class, the possibility of rethreading the reel, of running it backward until the frame where it all went wrong was reached, seemed not only desirable, but necessary. And then Howie moved back to New York, got a teaching job in Westchester County, resumed his role as advisor. He heard the Carl Kalb story, met him and Sandy, Aram and Wilma, remained on the outside looking in, suggested that, sure, a Carl Kalb had always been one kind of threat, but if Phil was going to go in that direction finally, why did it have to be with such a hard-on, an American aristocrat yet! Why couldn't it be with himself, for crying out loud? Wasn't he worthier? Wasn't he better equipped to deal with it since he knew *all* the facts? Howie was still pathetic, but he could lead from strength now. He had a profession, a legitimacy. He had enough satisfaction each day to oil his ego. Now he could talk to everyone and couldn't care less if he was misunderstood,

"That's my scale. If they don't understand me, fuck them. I'm decent. What they see when they look at me is exactly what I am. Take it or leave it. Good taste! Christ, that man doesn't even know he's a phony. Which is really sad. And Aram LeGeis? He should be put in a museum or in a time capsule. He's too valuable an example of what this culture can really produce when it sets its mind to it. I mean, what the hell have you been doing with your life while I was away? Donating it to everyone else without letting me know? Your best friend?" Sandy was fine. He was honest. And Wilma? Well, Wilma was a different kind of problem entirely. She was another direction entirely. Howie wouldn't presume to interfere there. That would be dangerous. But with Carl Kalb . . . well, he wouldn't interfere there either. Unless Phil wanted him to.

Wilma entered Phil's life through the principal, customary entrance, knocked the door down, rushed about, once inside, taking charge of emotional property she had no way of knowing belonged to others. There was no sign that said beware of dogs. She assumed that whatever was wrong with Phil came from Teaneck. And why not? Every semi-affluent Jewish boy has a Teaneck in his life. It's a tradition, handed down from generation to generation, like a recipe for gefüllte fish. Later, when she met Carl Kalb, her first thought was he had to be Phil's father. What else would a handsome, going-gray man be but a father? An actor's agent he isn't. That was certain, as certain as the fact that she was a grocer's daughter, a Brooklyn grocer's daughter, which was different from being a Bronx grocer's daughter. Because there was a subtle difference between the two and one that Phil should remember until the day he died. In Brooklyn a grocer uses a fatter pencil when he adds up the numbers on the brown paper bags. Or he used to. Now they have supermarkets and IBM. Only the Chinese are left from the good old days. An abacus is mother's milk to them. She could remember how she'd grab up the profits from the store, Yankee Doodles, bagels, lox, bulk cream cheese, and go to the Chinese laundry and watch them jiggle those beads around. Oh, it was gorgeous, absolute heaven. Until she started getting too fat and put herself on a strict diet. The abacus left her life forever. And what took its place? What? New York University Downtown Center took its place. That's what. And the circle in Washington Square took its place. And journalism and philosophy. Which was ridiculous. Absolutely ridiculous. So she dropped all that to become a private secretary. Not that she could type or take shorthand. Her boss didn't need her for those things. There were plenty of people around who could do that. What he needed was an arranger, an organizer, a telephone personality with a solid education. He was a lawyer. But he was in politics. You know, the kind who raises money for favors. She could get anything, anything Phil needed, for nothing. Flowers for Mother's Day. Theatre tickets for Jewish holidays. All kinds of gadgets that didn't work for long because the companies were only fronts, fronts for other companies that got government contracts. That kind of thing. And if Phil needed money, for any reason whatsoever that his heart desired, she could get that too. All he had to do was ask. Just ask. Just put your lips together and pout.

Wilma went on and on, and she held on to him. Not that she had to; he wanted to stay. He loved her stories. She made him laugh. No one else he knew did that. And she loved him, stated it unequivocally, would swear to it on a stack of Yankee Doodles, a proof of it of which there was none greater. So what if she was a little taller than he was. Who cares. She'd wear flats for the rest of her life. Wilma Pasternack wanted to be his one and only. She had been that for a few others, she admitted. But Phil was finally *it*.

It felt good to be with her. He wanted her. He told it to Howie, over and over again, trying to convince himself that it really was the truth. Howie was forced to agree. Maybe it was. Howie liked Wilma then, and the way he saw it, anyone was better than Carl Kalb. Anyone. Animal, vegetable, or mineral. "Do you enjoy sex with her, honestly enjoy it? Notice I didn't ask you do you *have* sex with her. A good friend knows things when he sees two people together. He doesn't have to be told."

"Yes, doctor. I understand, doctor. And my answer is that I do enjoy it, much more than I enjoy looking on while Carl works me over. Also, my answer to your next question, which I as *your* good friend know you're going to ask, is that she doesn't know anything about that—what should I call it?—back-street part of my life."

"I dig, as they say nowadays. I'm hep. So when are you going to start telling her . . . things? Or aren't you going to?"

"When she asks. She hasn't asked."

"And she doesn't care what you do with your days? She doesn't inquire how you get money to live on?"

"So far, no. She just thinks I'm a struggling young actor."

"She hasn't been to your apartment, I gather."

"No. I go to hers. She thinks I live in Teaneck."

"That's just swell, Philly. Perfect. Only don't forget that underneath that handsome face of hers there's a woman, close to your age I might add, who's going to want to get married. Pretty soon she's going to reach out for something more than your balls. She's going to have a right to do that too."

Agreed. Phil didn't dispute it: Wilma had her rights. And Carl had his too, Howie pointed out, as if Phil needed to be reminded! Of course he knew that. He knew like he always knew—afterward—how when you take the first step, which he managed to do when it counted, and then wait around for what you want to have happen to happen, you end up by letting everyone, except yourself, have rights and claims on your life. That was nothing astounding. Howie was in on that too, damn it. Wasn't he? Yes. Howie admitted it. But he also insisted that he never grabbed, did he? He never forced himself where he was going to create more problems. He only tried to uncomplicate things. Wasn't that true? Phil agreed again. Just as he was going to do now. In some way, Howie swore, he was going to loosen Carl Kalb's hold. If that's what Phil wanted. If that's what he really wanted. Yes. That's what Phil did want. He wanted that most of all. But how to do it. How to win without losing. He was going to have to lose something, for Christ's sake. All right, so he'd lose something, everything. What the hell. He'd lose, and just when Aaron Siegel was winning, was being launched into high-priced couture as he said he would be, getting the backing he wanted: silent partners who knew nothing about fashion and didn't care to know, who just wanted to invest, to gamble and who, if Aaron failed, would have a nice tax-loss situation anyway.

The first thing Aaron did was change his name legally, become Aram LeGeis, designer-owner of Monsieur LeGeis, Limited. He rented three floors of a small building on Fifty-eighth Street, very near Fifth Avenue. He hired a publicist who got his name placed in columns announcing the opening of a fashion house, a French concept, a salon, in America. His first showing, a formal champagne affair, would be held in June, 1960, a fall collection. The better buyers were contacted. Magazine editors were eager for invitations. Society women whose clothes Aaron had been making for five years, custom clothes, one of a kind, would be present. The attack would be massive, organized, certain of success. How could it fail? Or, more precisely, how could an Aaron Siegel fail? He had always had the temperament, the talent, the connections, and now, finally, the connections had produced the money. Who in America doesn't want to see a new star made? "And you'll be at the opening, Philip. . . . Dress suit, remember . . . I want you to see how it's done. And I'll invite Carl, for your sake."

"Can I bring anyone else?" Phil was being taken on a tour of Aaron's apartment above the showroom.

"Who? Because one has to be selective, you know. I keep trying to make you realize that fact but you simply—"

"All right. No lectures. Forget it."

"Don't get pouty, Philip. Just let me know who you want and I'll see if I approve. . . . Isn't this a divine tapestry? A friend sent it from France."

Carl received his invitation and, as he always automatically did, arranged the schedule for the gala evening. "A French dinner. That's appropriate. Of course, I'm shocked Aaron invited me at all."

Phil said nothing about the why of Carl's invitation. He saved everything he felt to tell Howie, about his anger, about his silence, and about his envy, too. "That fucking Aaron's going to make it and all I can do is just sit there and listen to his crap and then I go home and listen to Carl's crap. I know it's crap and still all I ever do is sit there and take it."

Howie moved the Chianti bottle aside, placed a bowl of spaghetti before Phil, handed him the butter and ketchup. They were at Howie's tiny Bank Street apartment for a Jewish spaghetti dinner. "Why did you ask Aaron if you could bring someone else to the showing? Who'd you have in mind?"

"Who the hell knows? I was just dreaming, that's all. I was thinking how I'd rather have Wilma go instead of Carl."

"Why don't you take her then?"

"Don't be a *schmuck*, Howie. Sometimes you come up with the goddamnedest ideas. I can't have both of them there."

"Why not? It's a great idea. Inspired. And I'll go too. The four of us. We'll make a real event out of it. All you have to do is call Aaron and coax him. He'll do it if you get sexy with him. It won't be hard."

"I can't do that to Wilma."

"You won't be doing anything *to* Wilma. You'd be helping her and yourself too. That is if you really want to. All you have to be prepared for is that you could lose a job, an apartment—I've got room for you—a lover that you say you don't want anyway, and maybe, just maybe, a girl friend."

"You're kidding, Howie. You're crazy."

"I'm not crazy. This is a perfect opportunity to face the facts, see what you really want. You can get your whole life straightened out faster than the speed of sound. Do it, Phil. Go call Carl right now. Don't think about it. Tell him there'll be two more for dinner. The rest will happen as it will."

"Sure. And at my expense."

"Who else should have to pay for it? Me?" Howie poured more Chianti, stared above the salad bowl at Phil, silently waiting for a sign.

"Okay! Why not!" Phil went to the telephone, wheedled two more tickets from Aaron, then spoke to Carl, asked him to reserve space at dinner for two more. "Who? Well, my friend Howie Goldstein is one and . . . and another friend."

Fine. Done. But when he left Howie's apartment, started walking down Greenwich Avenue, crossed Sixth Avenue onto Eighth Street, passing the boys in their tight late-spring costumes of leather and nailheads, his resolve flickered, as usual. It was too much to put on the line: his career; his feeling for Wilma, which was real enough but tricky; Carl. Only that was what he was prepared to lose. That part of himself. Maybe he couldn't go through with it. He'd crack up. But he'd crack up anyway if he didn't do something. Even when you tread water you use up time and energy and the water gets colder and colder. So? So sew buttons! That's what. Move. Let it happen. Cross Fifth Avenue now that you've come to it.

Wilma was in one of her Judy Garland outfits when he arrived: a man's button-down shirt, pink, over black tights, her Yoga uniform. Her weather-beaten hair hidden beneath a turban of terry towel, her teeth flashing their white welcome, Wilma yum-yummed her pleasure when he kissed her, sprawled beside her on the sofa. "You smell from sour wine. But never mind that because I've got something so marvelous to tell you. . . . Howie all right? . . . Good . . . Now listen carefully. We're going to be able to have our first vacation together. The boss says I can have his house in East Hampton for a whole week in June. All expenses paid for and even use his food credit cards. Imagine! We can play house and I can teach you how to meditate by the ocean. Meditation is glorious. Better than acting classes. I'll have to give up on that. It's just not me. . . . You aren't listening, are you? You okay?"

"No. I'm not." He twisted, arranged his head on her lap, looked up, smiling, nestling.

"What is it? A mood? I'll stop talking. I talk too much. I know I do." She brushed the hair back from his forehead, left her fingers there to curl it, smooth it. "You have such beautiful hair. I shouldn't tell you this, but

I love you. No question about it. I love to look at you. . . . Don't you like the idea of the house? Is that it? Because if you don't, don't worry. I just thought it might be fun. But we can stay here if you want. Whatever you like. We don't have to go outside, ever. I'm happy this way, Phil. Really . . . Don't you want to talk to me? Because you're making me very nervous."

He roused himself, sat up, told her about this friend he had who was opening a business, a dress business, and that he had been invited to the first showing. Howie was going and would she like to go too? and if she would, well, it was formal so she'd need a gown and another friend would be going, someone she didn't know, someone in the dress business and they'd all go out to dinner beforehand.

"Why should that depress you? I'd love to go. I even have a gown which I bought last year for my cousin's bar-mitzvah and I've never had a chance to wear it since. I didn't know you had friends like that. I mean, I didn't think that was your kind of circle. I'm surprised."

"Don't be. Sure, I have friends. All kinds of friends."

"Well, yes. I assumed that. I just didn't want to ask about them. I was afraid to."

"Why, Wilma? Why should you be afraid?"

"Because you never asked me anything beyond what I told you. I thought you wanted to keep it that way. So I didn't ask. Whatever you wanted to do I wanted to do. If you want to stay locked up in this apartment for the rest of our natural lives I'll do it. Somehow it feels very late in my life these days to take any more chances. I am pushing thirty and I suppose it's ridiculous that I've never felt quite this way about any other man. I didn't think I would any more. So I wanted you to feel—"

"I feel . . . enough. Honestly. Don't be afraid." He undid the turban, kissed her, moved her head onto his shoulder. "Just tell me if you really want to go to this thing. If you do, then we'll go. Sooner or later we'd have to go somewhere. And we'll even go to your boss's house in East Hampton. We'll meditate. We'll smoke marijuana. Anything."

"Can I show you my gown?"

Phil swiveled his chair in wider arcs before his bedroom window, remembering that night with Wilma and how without telling her exactly what to expect he had nevertheless said enough for once to comfort her and himself, how they had laughed over her gown, which had ostrich feathers at the neck, feathers that tickled both of them to passion when she tried it on, a passion that wasn't forced but grew in his skin spontaneously. It included a joy and concern for her which Phil, thinking about it before they slept that night and thinking about it again this night, hoped was the spontaneous instinct of his body, however elusive and hidden and untapped it remained: the sensation that he could feel free to fuck freely, that he had the same equipment to use and feel with that everybody else had but that circumstance, coincidence, only that, had forced him off and kept him off the main line. He still had time to get back on. He could. He would.

But then, on the night of Aaron's showing, another kind of instinct surfaced, the strongest one of all, the one that always seemed to trap him into traveling down side roads and dirt paths, into avoiding obstacles. And it wasn't his fault. It wasn't, wasn't, wasn't. . . .

The night before the showing Phil and Howie went to Wilma's apartment. Howie did most of the talking as usual, and he started talking about New York. He said when most people speak of New York they mean the island of Manhattan, not the four other boroughs, not Long Island or Westchester. Manhattan is solid rock, a fault in the earth that, millions of years ago, split, rolled over onto its side and waited while water rushed around it to give it shape, to protect and isolate it, to form its sea sides, the Hudson and East rivers. When the city began to grow its growth couldn't be lateral like that of Los Angeles or circular like that of London or Paris. It could only grow up. It could only soar to incredible heights, conditioning the people who ended up living there to bend their necks to see the sky instead of shading their eyes to search out horizons. New York was actually the smallest big city in the world, he insisited, a fact, like David and Goliath in the bloodstream, that led to subway fantasies, metaphors of rapid transit, myths about tall buildings and making a name and money in a hurry. The people who come from all over America to live on the island of Manhattan, from as far away as Texas or as close as New Jersey, just across the border, are seduced by the legends. If they remain, the bloodstream takes charge, the dreams sleeping in it wake up. The legends of size become the living truths. The Empire State Building and its TV antennae are there to be conquered after all, like Mt. Everest, otherwise they wouldn't have been built. That being the case, if you live in New York, you have to dream about moving up or moving out. Your mind won't let you live any other way. Reason gets to be beside the point. Anything goes. Everyone's dreaming about getting to the top his way. So shouldn't a person just go into his respective corner, come out fighting, and hope that the best myth wins?

Howie Goldstein felt that way about his life in New York.

Phil felt, yes, he had to live that way too, but *he was* going to win.

Wilma didn't care to listen to what Howie, drunk and slobbery, thought. She was going to go to the bathroom.

Carl Kalb, Howie said when Wilma left, thought he *was* living on top of the mountain as official king. Aram LeGeis, né Siegel, thought he would be living there, and very soon.

When Wilma returned, Phil was saying that he would live there too, damn it. If Aaron could, why shouldn't he? Wilma asked Howie to please go home already. It was late and he was drunk and they were all probably going to get drunk again the following night. Phil agreed. Howie obliged.

The following night they arrived late at the appointed restaurant, and Phil knew this was sure to cause Carl's irritation—Carl believed in promptness as strongly as Aaron didn't. Phil had tried to rush Wilma, but Wilma was not about to be rushed into her gown. A gown was not something she put on every day. So, of course, the gown and Wilma were awarded Carl's second frown. Howie, pulling at the sleeves of his rented tuxedo, received a split-second, disdainful glance. Reserved for Phil alone was the fire in Carl's eyes.

Phil was familiar with the restaurant, austere and French Provincial. He had been there before with Carl. He knew it was elegant—no credit cards accepted, only cash on the line—and he knew it was one of Carl's particular favorites. So what for Carl had begun as irritation, what had developed into anger was now full-fledged fury, necessarily suppressed fury, which made things even worse. When Wilma, seated at Carl's left, reached across him to squeeze Phil's hand, Carl froze, lifted the huge menu in front of his face, his eyes demanding some sort of explanation for all this vulgar activity. Phil got the message but grinned valiantly, hoping he looked as innocent as he was trying to look. Wilma watched the exchange. Her false eyelashes blinked rapidly. Her excited smile seemed more determined. If she had any inkling of what was going on, she wasn't going to admit it. Certainly she was going to talk—her mouth was opening; her white teeth were flashing—but she was definitely not one of the walking wounded yet. "I'm really very happy to meet you, Carl."

"Mr. Kalb! *Miss* Pasternack."

"Oh." Wilma's smile didn't fade. She fluffed the feathers at her neck. "Anyway, it's still a pleasure because I had no idea Phil had friends as distinguished looking as you." But her glance at Howie seemed to say, *Feh*, vile jelly. Howie, equally determined, remained silent, stared bravely back at Carl. "I mean, I always thought of Phil as some kind of waif."

"A waif?" Carl, embarrassed, lifted his handsome head to gauge the effect of this conversation on the quietly murmuring diners nearby. Like any true aristocrat, he accepted the bad manners of others as a cross to bear. He sipped his Scotch. "I'm sure that such a response must be a product of the particular way *you* know him, Miss Pasternack." He refused to look at her. "I have never thought of him as a waif. Do you know him—I'll use an old-fashioned word—intimately?"

Howie laughed. Carl ignored that interruption. Phil shuddered visibly.

Wilma hesitated, but not out of uncertainty. She was no dope. She wanted everyone to know that she realized her answer would, in some crazy way, make a difference. "How lovely it is to hear it put so quaintly. Yes, we do screw, Mr. Kalb. You won't mind my saying that, will you, Phil?" She blew him a kiss, attended to her feathers innocently.

Phil turned finally to face Carl, waiting for what he thought would have to be the death blow.

Carl tightened his grip on the tasseled menu, sipped some more Scotch, motioned for the maître d'. "We'll have to get on with dinner. Service is slow here. Everything is cooked to order."

"I just love this restaurant, Mr. Kalb. It's so . . . so . . . authentic."

"Have you been to France, Miss Pasternack?"

"No. I never have. I've never been out of New York."

"Then how can you know if it's authentic or not?"

"I'm a very big reader, Mr. Kalb."

"How clever . . . I'll order for everyone. Poached fish might be appropriate." There were no objections. "A Pouilly Fuissé. Endive salad . . ."

Throughout the gruelling dinner Phil had the sensation of being rocked back and forth, of being pulled uphill to new possibilities and then downhill to familiar words. Carl said. Wilma said. Howie observed. Time had no forward thrust; he felt as though it never would again, that he was bound inside this still point in space and destined to remain there until friction burned him up. He was embarrassed by all the talk about him. He knew he was getting drunker and therefore more inclined to blurt out all the things *he* wanted to say instead of listening—to Carl's baiting of Wilma and Wilma's counter-attacks—but at the same time, he knew he wouldn't, that the instinct to let others do it for him was stronger, would prevail. If only dinner would be over with. If only someone would help him to his feet, lift him, put him in another place out of reach. Someone would, eventually, but not yet. And Carl went right on showing how much he hated Wilma and Howie, and Wilma and Howie went right on defending themselves, showing Carl how much they didn't care if he did. The bitchier Wilma got, the more attractive she became, the happier Phil was that she claimed him.

Carl fought them off, retreated into indifferent silence. He wasn't going to air his grievances publicly. Later, his angry eyes indicated, later he would have his moment. Phil was going to hear plenty. Carl called for the check. He would see it out. All the way. Even pay for these fools. What manners.

"Superb cuisine, Mr. Kalb." Wilma smiled as if her mouth had been stuffed with alum. "Thank you profoundly for the experience."

Carl grunted, ushered them quickly out of the restaurant. Wilma held Phil's arm, steadied him at the curb, at the door of a waiting cab. "We'll take this one, Mr. Kalb. They don't take four. See you there." She waved. The cab sped off.

Now she could let out some of what she felt: "What a prick that man is. I feel sorry for him. He's your boss? That's all he is? Nothing else?"

"Nothing else."

She reached for his hand, squeezed it. Whatever he said, she would believe, managing to accept the lie as proof that he did care enough and not that he was a liar. Howie would have blurted out the facts, believing that if a person knows then he can make choices. Phil didn't want her to know yet. He didn't want her to choose. He didn't want to choose either. "And you're a designer. That much you could have told me."

"You never asked."

"Do I have to ask everything?"

"Not everything. Only what you really want to know."

"Good. Then I don't need to be told. As long as I know how you feel." She lifted his hand and kissed it. "I'll tell *you* instead. Like I'll tell you that one of my things is endurance so you better be prepared."

"I'm prepared."

"Groovy, because my really best thing is dealing with intrigue. You'll see."

He did, too. At Aram's. Whenever, in the crush of champagne-drinking, expensively gowned women, dinner-jacketed men, Carl tried to isolate Phil, Wilma broke in. Howie helped too. For this evening at least he had become her ally. Instinctively, she understood the rules of the game, knew something big was at stake. When Howie pushed Phil toward her, she pulled. She wouldn't let go of Phil's arm, refused champagne just so she could have two free hands for holding on. Politely, Howie made sure Carl's glass was never empty, that his path toward Phil was blocked by waiters, trays, knots of milling people. Right up until the moment they were all directed upstairs to the showroom, Carl tried. He looked like a person caught in a traffic jam who desperately has to go to the bathroom. He wasn't going to make it there on time either. Phil and Wilma were led to bridge chair seats on one side of the rose-carpeted runway; Carl and Howie were led to the other side. The respectful, expectant hush that descended on the guests prevented Carl from moving away. He would never make a spectacle of himself, not there, certainly, in such an elegant setting, not faced by the endlessly reflecting, mirrored walls, by the restraining power of perfectly placed bronze vases overflowing with white and pink peonies. Never. He accepted his position gracefully.

Phil didn't look across at Carl and Howie. Instead, he surveyed the room, described for Wilma how the models would enter at the top of the carpeted staircase, how they would probably pause before starting down. "One of Aaron's theatrical bits, because he loves effects almost as much as he likes expensive things. The more it costs the better he likes it. The banister, for example, is an antique"—Wilma stood up to check it—"imported from England." Then the models would pass down the runway like show dogs, very fast, return to the staircase, do their thing, depending on what outfit they wore, maybe go down the runway again, slower this time, and then leave by the opposite end.

Wilma confessed it wasn't exactly her scene but she was glad she had come for a visit, only she would hate to have to live in a place like this, and also her bar-mitzvah gown felt very inappropriate compared to the numbers the other ladies were wearing. She wanted to know who those other ladies were. They made her feel like such a slob.

Most of the people, he admitted reluctantly, he didn't really know. He just knew *about* them. They were the big-time buyers, couture buyers from all the best stores in the country, the elite, the legendary ones, superwomen of the trade, who made fashion stars when they felt like it. A lot of the others were the real stars. Actresses from Hollywood and Broadway, ones that Aaron had been dressing for years. "He knows everybody, everybody that counts, and he never introduces *those* people to me." Phil pointed out the editor-in-chief of *Women's Wear Daily* and assorted assistants; and there was Eugenia Sheppard, the baby-faced Hedda Hopper of the *Herald Tribune*, the one who had the most power to elevate or kill if she decided a new designer was gauche, just as long as he didn't have society connections. If he did, he was safe. What she'd do to Aaron Siegel would be interesting. And those bored ones—they were the power ladies from *Vogue* and *Harper's*. Was he jealous of Aaron, Wilma wanted to know. Sure he was. Phil smiled, shrugged, defended himself by telling her that, after all, if a person was going to be a part of all this crap, he had to be jealous, to want the most he could get out of it, otherwise what's the point? Who doesn't want to be a star if they've got all the equipment for it?

Wilma nodded, admitting nothing. Her gaze shifted upward to the top of the staircase. Aram was there. He placed both hands on the banister, smiled down at the crowd, waiting for the murmur to subside. It was time to begin. He was ready and obviously confident. Nothing about his young fair face, his blondined, carefully waved hair, his double-breasted, wide-lapeled tuxedo indicated doubt. Since every detail had been arranged beforehand—publicity, magazine and press coverage, the right people as guests, the clothes themselves—he could afford to wait patiently for a silence that he and his silent partners had paid plenty to make sure they would get when they wanted it. Everyone was expected to be attentive now. Everyone was expected to be conscious of the part he had been asked to play in this fashion event, this reoccurring ritual of self-gratification. If they didn't honor the form of the rite, what right would they have to direct, to select, to name the fashion leaders, the fashion trends for the whole star-struck country? Noblesse oblige, in fashion as it is in heaven, in America as it is in Paris. The people demand an aristocracy, want to give the few the power to choose for them all, and then to adore the chosen as if, in fact, they were responsible for having made the choice. So there was Aaron Siegel, waiting to be chosen, elected, wanting to become a part of the fraternity of the famous more than he wanted anything else, able to measure how successful his life was only by the size of his audience. Phil, hypnotized by the hush in the crowded room, by the sounds of breaths inhaled and held, by the sudden sensation that in one more hour a new *name* might be made, felt more than ever the vicarious body-emptying pleasure that becoming a name must be, would be, for Aaron, would be for himself when it finally happened, an erotic pleasure like no other orgasm he could imagine, one that shot seeds of success skyward. He wanted that, needed that more than he wanted, needed Wilma's, Carl's, Howie's, anybody's love. . . .

Aaron's hand stroked the banister seductively. His gaze scanned, sought contact with, each upturned face. Fingers arched and resting lightly on the polished wood like a pianist's on a keyboard just before he starts to play, Aaron lowered his head, turned, nodded for the first model. As she emerged, he disappeared backstage, where he was to remain, according to the rule book for high-priced showings, until the end. The directress of his showroom, done up in an original LeGeis, replaced him, ready to announce the stock number of each dress.

"Number 100." The model was poised at the head of the staircase, her smile frozen, her amber hair coiled, piled to a pointed peak. "That's Erica," Phil whispered. Erica's legs grew taut against the dress's flare, her stance a challenge, her smile defiant.

The collective gaze shifted upward as Erica stepped quickly down the steps, stopped as she stopped at the bottom, followed as she strode along the runway. She twirled, posed, raced out the door at the far end of the crowded room. Speed counted. Pacing counted. Thoroughbreds were racing. The models knew how long to take on the runway; they needed time to change behind the scenes. When the eighth model, Gia, appeared, the flow had been established. "He fits the entire collection on her." As if Phil's words were the command, Gia began her descent, stepping easily, utterly relaxed, her short-cropped curly blond hair bouncing. Unmistakably, she was much more than just another pretty model plying her trade with practiced skill. She was a young lady proud of and, at the same time, thankful for having been born beautiful. She wore the outfit; it didn't wear her. By the time she reached the bottom of the staircase the evening's first round of applause began. Gia stopped, acknowledging the response as if the audience were only corroborating her expectation: the suit she wore was a winner; it was fashion news. The mauve jacket was held in place by one jeweled shoulder button. It was fitted to fall flat in front and back, with inverted pleats under each arm expanding as the body moved: a new silhouette; the mark of a designer's genius. The *Women's Wear Daily* team greeted it warmly. Gia strode down the runway, returned to the bottom of the staircase, moved briskly back down the runway, disappeared.

From that point on almost every dress was greeted with applause. The showing was a smash. Heads turned admiringly from side to side. Murmurous ahs and ohs grew in volume, became audible comments.

And then came the evening clothes. Number 155 on Gia. Wilma clutched Phil's arm, leaned forward to watch the dramatic moment unfold. Gia stopped in mid-descent, the first time any model had done that.

The floor-length, hooded white silk ottoman coat's folds settled into place. Solemnly, Gia stared out above the heads of the spectators, unmoving, caught in the ecstasy of a private vision which, in an instant, but not yet, not yet, she would be willing to share with the rest of the world. A Brünnhilde waking from a fire-ringed sleep. A Cinderella redeemed through suffering. A Sleeping Beauty kissed into living. Fantasies presented as reality, perfection, life as it should be and not ugly—as it too often seemed to be—was mirrored in her pale face. So swiftly that the eye was unconvinced that it had actually happened, a hand shot up to a single silver button beneath her chin. The hood fell free. The coat moved apart, revealing at first a pastel flowered chiffon gown, and then Gia opened the panels of the coat. The lining was a silk of the same pastel print. The crowd gasped, stunned by the unfolding field of pale flowers. The applause was thunderous. Gia closed the coat as swiftly as she had undone it, moved imperiously down onto the runway, opened it again, removed it, let it drag after her over the carpet as she stepped through the doorway and out of view.

The show consisted of one hundred pieces. The finale was a gown of gold and silver brocade that sparkled sunrise fire as Erica twirled. The audience rose, raised their hands, clapping wildly; some called for Aaron, the call became a chorus. He appeared; the directress stepped back. He bowed low over the banister. The eight models appeared behind him. Gia took his arm, led him to the top of the staircase, where he bowed again. The group started down. Pear-shaped Aram LeGeis, né Aaron Siegel, surrounded by the palpable proof of his achievement, the gowns, the girls, the glamour, had arrived at the first station of his fame. The movie miracle of recognition, the one kind of miracle that everyone there that night believed in as completely as they believed in the incontrovertible fact that all men are created equal, warmed Aram's cheeks, directed his steps downward into the waiting mob. His pink skin glowed. His tears thanked them. He was embraced, kissed, pushed, pulled deeper into the center of their love, their joy, their need. An artist. A creator. A genius. The winner.

Phil moved Wilma toward the surging crowd. Her feathers were being crushed, but she didn't care. Everyone seemed to be carried on the wave of not caring. Spindly bridge chairs were falling all around them. Flowers were pulled from the vases, were flung through the air. It was impossible to get close to Aaron, so Phil rerouted Wilma. Howie gestured from across the room, tried to push through to them, but couldn't. Carl was moving away from the crowd, heading for the other stairway that led down to the entrance foyer. They followed him. Reluctantly they inched their way down the steps and away from the greater noise, the shouts, the massive magic of Aaron's victory toward the drab reality of everyday, of more drinks and more food, of Carl's obvious anger, anger which could only make Phil's distance from what Aaron had won seem, at this moment of following Wilma downward, infinitely remote. He had thrown away, just as if he had thrown away a wad of waste paper, his one chance of reaching the top of his desire. And for what? For honesty? For the honor of honoring what Howie had convinced him was his truer, his nobler instinct? Shit. The true, human, honored instinct, the one that counted on the open market, was what had happened upstairs and not the so-called honesty he was facing now: the four of them forced together in the center of this room by the descending crowd, forced to look at the situation squarely.

"Absolutely breathtaking." Wilma shouted to be heard. "Thrilling. Wasn't it sensational, Mr. Kalb?"

"Yes, Miss Pasternack. Gaudy and vulgar like all sensations."

"Vulgar?"

"Don't *you* know what vulgar means? I'm sure Phil does if you don't." Carl stared at Wilma's flushed, still smiling face, waiting for its expression to dissolve into hurt or anger. But it didn't. It wouldn't.

Wilma was stepping up to the batter's box. "So you really aren't a gentleman. You're the one who's vulgar and insensitive. And here I was thinking that you just doted on good manners."

"I do."

"Then what accounts for the way you're behaving tonight?"

"I've decided my present company wouldn't appreciate good manners, Miss Pasternack."

"And I've decided, sweetie, that your present company doesn't give a shit." Wilma didn't turn away. Carl wanted to, but he couldn't. There was no place to go. They were locked in combat by pushing bodies, by surging tidal waves of laughter and noise. Wilma leaned toward Phil. "Is he always so nasty?"

"Am I, Phil?" Carl's anger grew expansive, generously included all of them now. "Why don't you explain it to her? Go ahead. Tell her exactly why I'm irritated. Or perhaps *you* should, Mr. Goldstein, you pathetic, undernourished . . . teacher."

Aaron's sudden appearance beneath a waiter's raised tray of champagne glasses delayed Howie's attack. Phil, relieved, embraced Aaron, offered congratulations, introduced him to Wilma.

"Aram—I can call *you* Aram, can't I?—I just want to tell you how thrilling this all is. And the clothes! Well, they are absolutely staggering. If I could afford them I'd buy every single one of them."

"Thank you. But just one will do." Aaron removed his arm from Phil's shoulder, and, ignoring Howie, spoke to Carl. "Didn't you like the collection?"

"Yes. Very much. Of course, it's not salable, but you don't care. . . ."

"Seventh Avenue talk is so boring, Carl. But fortunately, as you started to say, I don't have to care about sales."

Outsnobbed, Carl flushed. "Quite true, but perhaps someday you may just have to learn—"

But whatever Carl thought Aaron might have to learn, Aaron did not have to hear. Certainly not that night. He broke away, accepting a glass of champagne from a shrieking well-wisher.

"What a lovely group of people. Wasn't that Sophia Loren with the glass?" Wilma shaded her eyes. "Or maybe it's just her sister. It's so hard to tell off screen. Along with everything else, my eyesight is just not what it should be."

"*You* are not what you should be, Miss Pasternack. The only taste you've shown is in your choice of a lover. I hope you'll both be happy."

"Well, thank you for that, Mr. Kalb. I'm glad to know you appreciate him so much." Wilma kept smiling doggedly.

Carl slammed his empty glass on a passing tray. "I'll leave now. Obviously you won't be coming with me, will you, Philip?"

"No, Carl, but I'll call later and—"

"Don't bother. I'll see you at the office tomorrow." He raised a hand, but it was only to help himself shove off. They watched him push by flailing braceleted arms reaching for new drinks, squeeze by straining bodies reluctantly yielding space to let him pass, move under the cloud cover of cigarette smoke oozing upward toward the high-ceilinged dimness.

Carl's departure closed the curtain on the evening's performance. The meaning of the final speech was clear enough to Phil. What he thought he had been willing to risk had, with almost no effort of his own, happened. The view of the stage from where he stood that night as a spectator to Aaron's success and to his own desire, the view of the stage from where he sat now, not quite six years later, moving back and forth in front of his dark window, still a spectator to the actions of his life, were views of the same moment in time. The grainy pictures of forms, faces, voices from that night shuttled suddenly nearer, retreated just as suddenly, revealing, now as then, the same tragicomedy of his impotence. The wedges on his color wheel of memory went on spinning endlessly, round and round to nowhere.

Then as now Wilma and Howie were nearby ready to love him, ready to help him. Then as now he had lost a job. But then the loss had seemed a profit, a freedom from Carl and sex that had a name he didn't like and didn't want. He was younger then. Freedom at first had felt like power, the power to make all kinds of better, more natural choices. And so he had made the choice of Mr. Jack and had held on to Wilma. He had learned how to sit still. For five years he had sat in one place, designing better clothes, inching his way toward recognition, sleeping with Wilma and—keeping it as much a secret from himself as possible—anonymous Carls, brooding with Howie, fighting with Aaron, lunching with Sandy, letting everyone dangle the diamond of their need for him in front of his glazed eyes, ending up by thinking he enjoyed the sparkle of the diamond.

He was everyone's pretty toy. Everyone had played with him. He let them because he didn't know what else to do while he waited for the time when he would step out on top of the mountain, be king of the mountain, a decent, honest Howie-king and not an Aaron kind, bitchy, cruel, selfish. And now that kind of waiting, that kind of wanting were nose and nose at the wire. Now, and probably for the last time in his life, he had the chance to make a choice. Not what he would do—at thirty-five the *what* was settled—but how he might proceed, how he could use his talent and still be more than Sandy, more than Carl Kalb and Alex Fleiss, more than Aaron, how he could be human and a success at the same time. If that was possible or even worth the effort any more: to force out into the open air the part of himself that, damn it, was decent, that didn't want to contend; to make it operate as a check, a balance against the mindless bloodstream drive of getting, having, owning, needing to be known. This was no spectator sport anymore. It was the rest of his life. It was preparation for the final battle with the giants waiting on top of the mountain: machine-bred monsters, public giants who gnawed on the bones of the past, having fed on the war meat of the forties, the fifties, the sixties; obscene, sexless corporate entities entrusted with the defense of the American Dream turned nighmare. There was no contest, really; but neither was there anything else for him, for others like him, to do but fight. He was one of the other breed, the in-betweeners, the lost spawn of the Snow White, Glenn Miller swing-jazz-love-song era, poisoned by a wing and a prayer and the Truman atrocities and the six million unavailing screams. He was an over-thirty, a generation straddler with aching legs whose memories wouldn't let him be a dropout and who didn't know what else to do but what he was doing, who felt the sand shifting beneath him to form another landscape and who could find nothing else to hold on to but the giant's cold hand. Either that, or go underground, be anonymous, take a job, make a living, protect the old way, make believe none of the new was happening, live happily ever after. . . .

He moved Liffey to the floor, turned the bedroom light on then, and walked through all the rooms, switching on the lamps, the overhead lights. Liffey followed at his heels, whining, watching while he put on his raincoat. "Be a good girl. I'll be back soon."

Waiting for the elevator, his fingers named the junk in his coat pockets: matchbooks, ticket stubs, Diner's Club receipts, a comb, subway tokens, a crumpled ball of paper. He pulled that out, studied it, tossed it into the air. A squashed ball of colored papers. Lovey Gray's last gift to him. Link's souvenir. The end of Mr. Jack. He squeezed it between the palms of his hands, pressing it while the elevator glided down, tossing it, catching it. The doorman didn't nod. Neither did Phil. He was intent on the rising, falling movement of the ball of colored paper. At the corner he tossed it for the last time high into the yellow glow of the street lamp, watched it land—a perfect shot—on bags of garbage in the litter basket. And that's that, Mr. Jack. Paper dresses. Paper moons. Cardboard skies.

So? Now that he was outside, where to? Wilma's? Howie's? Uptown? What'll it be? On just such a decision a future is hung. So go know! He breathed deeply, coughed, his lungs stung by the humid smog of a New York evening with summer just around the bend. But he felt better now. Sure he did. When a person thinks things through, he has to feel better. Just look at all these people on the streets thinking things through and feeling better.

Wilma was at home, her head wrapped in a terry turban, her body smelling of Je Reviens after-bath cologne. She had washed her hair for a change. She was just getting ready to lounge through the night in her frilly pink nighty with *Ramparts* and the *New Republic* and *Vogue* and an extra-strong dose of TV. But if she had known he was going to make one of his infrequent, spectacular guest appearances, well then . . .

"Would you mind lowering the TV?"

"Did you return to the real world of my bedroom to make that request or did you come here for a reason?" Nevertheless, she did lower the volume.

"This time you're really angry, huh?" Phil sprawled face down across her double bed.

"Whatever makes you think that! Of course I'm not angry. I'm absolutely ecstatic you deserted me. My favorite thing is to be abandoned."

"You'd be better off if you were."

"Oh, so my baby isn't feeling well. He's feeling sorry for himself." Wilma leaned over him, rubbed his back. "Is that it? My baby came here to be comforted?"

When Phil rolled over, he was surprised to find tears in her eyes instead of fire. He pulled her down, kissed her eyes. "I'm sorry, Wilma."

"Of course you are. I know that. I always know that. And a lot of good that does me. For weeks I've been languishing here waiting for a sign from God." She tried to sit up, but his arms tightened around her. "So suddenly you appear tonight. Is that a sign? Do you know what you're going to do? With yourself? With me? Are you really going to let me help you or are you just going to go on sleeping with me? Which is it going to be because I feel I've got a right to know. It's about time I—"

He kissed her again, more to stop her words than for any other reason. She sighed, gave in, cried quietly. "No more talking, Wilma. Not now. At least I made it this far. I got out of the apartment. That's a sign. And you're tired and I'm tired. So we'll talk later. Not now. Okay?"

As she nodded against his cheek, her turban came loose. He made a pillow of it for her head to rest on. "Can I turn the set off?"

"Yes," she murmured, "and the light too."

Part Two

Moneybags

Chapter Seven

Popular-price power lives along Broadway between Thirty-fifth and Fortieth streets. Five blocks of tall towers on the Great White Way house the businesses that provide the clothes for no-nonsense millions of budget-basement American housewives and their daughters. Giants of the industry, with a listing on the big board downtown and nourished by volume sales, they watch what the stars wear on television, what the magazines are pushing, what Twiggy wears and Jackie, what Mrs. Paley, Mrs. Guest wear at home according to Eugenia Sheppard, and what designer wins the Coty Award, what collection gets the press in Paris, what fashion trend, after the tent collapses, looks as if it will catch on next. Then they copy, interpret the styles for the real people, for the hard-core consumer, for the underbelly of the nation. Cheaper dresses. Cheaper sportswear. Cheaper skirts and blouses. Cheaper car coats and fake furs. Synthetic fabrics that are better, longer lasting than the originals. Wisely, they watch and they wait for the word from Seventh Avenue, and then they lead the fashion followers of America forward.

On the second floor of one tall building, a building which the business owns, the Greenstalks grow greener: Sam, the father; Gary and Bruce, the sons; Marvin Bernstein, the holy ghost, the behind-the-scenes man who made the Greenstalks giants, got them a seat on the exchange, lifted them into the big money.

Inside a separate entrance to the building is a white-and-black Rorschach marble lobby with a private escalator—mornings Up; evenings Down. At the top of the escalator, above the Thermopane doors that swing open automatically, is the logo, the symbol of their miraculous growth: the leafy green stalk twisting to the top of the neon-lit, pink-edged label, between the G and the R, the huge letters in barnyard red flashing off and on: GREENSTALKS.

The doors swing open on a startling white rotunda with a gently curving white wall, on an oversize white formica reception desk, a white vinyl
tile floor and radiating corridors painted white, all of it awesome, as awesome as total darkness might be, but for an opposite reason. Darkness
hides. Darkness generates fear of what you can't see, what you don't
know. At the Greenstalks there was nothing to hide, nothing to fear, unless the whiteness challenged the visitor's sense of his own virtue, which
it was meant to do. White was for purity. And who was pure? Who
didn't come to the Greenstalks to try to get something for nothing? Who
didn't double-deal? The Greenstalks didn't. That's what the white announced. Sam Greenstalk didn't. He wanted everything snow white so
that whoever came up that escalator would know what was what. The
desk, the walls, the floor, the chairs for waiting, the white carnations on
the receptionist's Nightstalk dress said that this company was on the up
and up. The only colors permitted in the reception rotunda were on the
foam-rubber cushions on the free-form chairs and the leafy green plant
that grew in a straight column to the ceiling.

Nor was there any darkness down any of the five spokelike labyrinthine
corridors, nor in any of the doorless offices that lined those corridors, nor
in the back workrooms and stockroom that began where two spokes of the
fan ended and where in the dead center of that rack-lined space Bruce
Greenstalk's design room and office were located and from which he
could roam at will, bellicose, bullish, in full and instantly threatening
view of all those who were paid damn good money to follow his orders
and who had better be working damn hard whenever he chose to walk
around the place.

Blue-white fluorescent light illuminated every inch of space. The
round, recessed ceiling fixtures glowed inside white Acousticon tiles like
pale moons in a colorless sky.

Not the meeting rooms, not the spartanly furnished showroom, not
even the principals' offices found at the tips of the three other spokes
were allowed to be lit indirectly. One source of brightness for all. Sam
Greenstalk wanted it that way. Every morning at 10 A.M. he arrived at
work to make sure it stayed that way. Not that he had to any more. Gary
and Bruce were there to mind the store. Like father, like sons. If it was
good enough for him, if the path he had traveled for so many years had
brought them all to this happy land of light and wealth why change even
a bulb? Better just to increase the wattage and the output, whenever possible. With Marvin Bernstein acting as official guide of the grounds and

guardian of their present holdings, their books and records, possibilities, growth possibilities, seemed always available for the Greenstalks. Once, already, the company's stock had split. By now, a year and a half later, here in June, 1966, the price per share had moved right back up to where it was before it split. Marvin had all the reports at hand to demonstrate how it had happened and, in addition, he had another report ready—the real reason for this meeting in Sam's office—one that described a gigantic deal, a plan for the future, the kind that everyone on Broadway and Seventh Avenue would be whispering about, that the *New York Times* would do a feature article on. Really big. Gary and Bruce, flanking Marvin, leaned toward their father's desk, watched him leaf hurriedly through the onion-skin pages of Marvin's report. He was frowning.

"Before you say a word, Pa, consider one important point." Gary lifted his manicured index finger toward the ceiling. "If CBS buys the Yankees, if RCA buys publishing companies, then soon, very soon, according to Marvin, companies like that are going to want to buy into the garment industry." Disapprovingly, Sam watched Gary's waving finger. It stopped waving, was lowered, scratched briefly one side of his perfect nose job, came to rest in his lap. "Look, Pa. All I mean to say is that we should be first. We wouldn't be losing a thing. We'd stand to gain. Ask Marvin, Pa. Go ahead. Marvin's been handling the negotiations. Ask him. He'll tell you."

"I don't have to ask, *sonnele*. I know. Don't think I don't know." Sam dropped the report on his desk. "I follow all that's going on. I know trends. I see in the papers everyday. And right now I say no. I say I'm not ready to say yes. Maybe another year, maybe two years I'll be ready."

"But why not now, Pa? Tell us why not now. You're too smart a businessman to pass up this deal without having reasons. If I presented this offer to the board of directors they'd snatch it up in a second. Marvin's got the whole thing ready for presentation, that's how sure I was you'd like it. Don't we always agree on everything? So why don't you let Marvin explain the details, let him present—"

"It's not necessary, Gary." Sam's patient smile requested time to be heard. Gary and Bruce moved back into their Eames-styled chairs. Marvin had never moved. "First, let's see something else. Our sportswear's doing good? Right?" They nodded. "Miss Greenstalk is fine? Nightstalks is moving? All the other divisions are in order? All going good? Right?" They nodded again. "All showing healthy profit?" Marvin built a steep-angled finger chapel over his mouth, his thumbs resting below his

189

jutting, narrow chin. The burps started. Loud ones, a series, growing in volume. No one was surprised. Sam waited solicitously. "It's bad again, Marvin?"

"The same, Sam." The finger chapel was dismantled. Wearily, Marvin slid lower in his chair, stretched his long legs beneath Sam's desk. His hands settled at his crotch, scratched stealthily for a tic-obsessed second, then stopped, abruptly.

"So then what I'm doing for you is a favor, Marvin. I'm saving you extra work. Your ulcers can rest up because I won't give you my go-ahead. Which you need, remember."

"Would we do anything behind your back if you said no, Pa?" Bruce looked to Gary and on to Marvin for support. Neither appeared as hurt by the implication as Bruce. "Come on, Pa. Don't take that attitude." The baby bear of the family at forty-two, Bruce heard everything his father said as a test of his love and loyalty.

"I know. I know you wouldn't, my son. I'm only trying to get all of you to concentrate on something else. A suggestion I've got. You'll do me a big favor if you'll think about it. Diversify here first, I'm saying. Then we'll talk about diversifying someone else." Serenely, he clasped his hands at the edge of his desk. "Right now you're talking to me about small companies that want to use us to grow with. And what I'm saying is that *we* should grow first. Greenstalks should grow bigger. The bigger we are, the bigger is going to have to be the company that wants to buy us out. Yankees we're not. Have some patience. Everything doesn't come overnight. Whatever offer you got now I'll guarantee in two years, three years you'll get a better one. Provided," Sam leaned forward, sliding his clasped hands toward them, his white head raised between hunched, pin-striped shoulders, his dark, liquid eyes looking out lovingly beneath bushy black eyebrows, "provided, of course, you keep building on what you have and what you get. Listen carefully to the last word. I said what you *get*." With fastidious concern for the effect, aware that six eyes were following his every movement, Sam pushed back suddenly, hands still clasped, but over his heart now. "So I'm suggesting, I'm advising that what we should do is to buy up companies *we* need. Companies to round out *our* picture. Good companies that are healthy. New companies that can grow. Companies with a higher price range than the ones we got already. All kinds."

Marvin slid higher in his chair, his chiseled, cadaverous face twisted into a grimace of thoughtfulness for Sam's suggestion, a grimace which others, fortunately, construed as ulcers—for the last ten of his thirty-eight years he had had a doctor-diagnosed case of ulcers—but which he knew grew out of a private, special kind of ecstasy. Sam's words excited him to pensiveness the way pictures of an orgy in progress excited others to heavy breathing.

Bruce smiled openly, clapped his hands. Whatever new companies they bought he would get to be stylist for. He would be the direct link. He liked that. The more people who worked under him, the more he had to do, the more he liked his life.

Even Gary seemed excited. His ingenuous, Cary Grant, who-me? expression, one that made every girl working at Greenstalks stammer, opened his full lips, rounded his rugged chin. "You're talking Seventh Avenue, Pa, aren't you? Isn't he, Marvin?"

Marvin nodded. Sam spoke. "I'm talking everything. Seventh Avenue is only part, Garele, but it's a big part. On Seventh Avenue those businesses, even the best of them, are having it hard right now. They put out a good line; they can't produce it properly. There's labor trouble. There's fabric trouble. They can't get enough. They have to substitute. Ends up they get resistance in the store. They don't deliver on time. And why? Because no matter how much capital they put in the business it's never enough. To make a big business you got to have big minds. It's a mentality you got to have. A business that starts big knows how to cope. It always looks like it has power. It can order all the fabric it needs to knock off any hot style Seventh Avenue puts out. It can make it look better than the original and sell it for half the price. That's a volume business for you. That's the way to grow. Right there. First take this step. Buy on Seventh Avenue and we'll have our own companies to knock off from. That's a step to take. That's the coming trend. One thing you all know is that I never, never in my whole life," Sam tapped the white formica desk with a blunt finger, "not once, stood in the way of healthy growth. I never will. I only believe that there's a right way and a right time to do everything. I'm not a jumper. I walk steady for my age and I don't look behind me. I walk and I look to see what's in front of me. When I was your age, Gary, I did it that way and I still do it that way. I walk and I watch and I listen and I hear what the news is. When I stop walking, that's when you'll know I'm ready to die, not before. Right now I'm not ready to stop so I'm not ready to die. The small-time offers can wait a few more years. Those are my feelings on it. If you'll take my advice, you won't be sorry. Whatever we built here so far we built for all of us and our loved ones to share. We'll keep it that way a while longer. We're fortunate we can.

Okay?"

Sam stood up, moved slowly, solemnly around his desk, stopped between Gary and Marvin, a hand on each one's shoulder as if for support. "One thing you can be certain of. I don't forget easily. I remember everything, from the way I began with nothing, until I got where I am now. I remember everything you did, Marvin, everything my good sons did to make what we have as solid as the Rock of Gibraltar. I'm thankful. I'm grateful. At seventy-four I got very few complaints. I got none, in fact. I'm surely not going to start complaining now like those old-time cockers on Seventh Avenue who go around blaming everyone but themselves for what happens to them. Nothing's ever their fault. A perfect example's my friend Alex Fleiss—you know him, from Mr. Jack, they just went bankrupt? So I meet him at our club to play gin and all I get from him is complaints. His son's no good. His production man's no good. His piece-goods man is a crook. The unions are ruining the whole industry.

"Everyone's cheating him. The other day he tried to buy back the name at a public auction and he tells me the judge cheated him too. Wouldn't let him talk. The man bids $15,000—all the money he's got left in the world—imagine, $15,000 for the name to a business that once grossed twelve million, Marvin? Anyway, someone who used to work in his showroom, a *gonif*, a Benedict Arnold, Alex called him, bid $15,500 and won. Imagine! Even the original Mr. Jack—I used to know him, another ego named Jack Farbstein—put in a bid. Jack tried to punch Alex, it got so bad. Alex thought he was going to have a heart attack. To me it looks like he did. Thirty years he's aged. I tell you it's pathetic. The only one he didn't complain about was his designer. His designer he loved like a son. Such a fool. A grown man with a rich wife and an ego so big he doesn't have enough sense to realize it's 1966, not 1946. And believe me, Alex Fleiss is just one. There's hundreds like him who don't know what's going on, who don't know how to change with the times. Who would ever think that such a famous company like Mr. Jack could go out of business!"

"Was it mismanagement, Pa?" Gary twisted around, stared up at his father proudly. The Greenstalks would never suffer from such a disease.

"Sure, mismanagement. Certainly. But it's a lot more. It's being dumb and stubborn for no reason except you want to stay rich and with power. Who doesn't want that? Everyone wants it. But when you start lying to yourself and everyone else why you deserve to have it, then you're a fool. When you start thinking that how it used to be is the way it has to be

192

now and in the future—that goes for all businesses—then you're beginning to die on your feet. Alex Fleiss is such an ego how could he stay in business in times like these?" Sam paused, embarrassed, sighed, laughed. "I guess I'm an ego too, but at least I'm an ego because I'm proud of what I did and what you did. I didn't lie to myself. I never had to go begging for help like Alex. I never called myself a cree-a-tore. That I left to the others. I'm not ashamed to say it. I made garments to be worn. I didn't cheat anybody. I was a worker so I worked. I worked hard and I made something sensible. I didn't make a show, a big splash. So who cares. I made a business. In America they like shows. They like everything should look like a show. But lots of shows flop. A good business lasts." His head raised, his eyes followed the view from the window behind his desk out onto Broadway. "Over there is Seventh Avenue. So one place we'll go is over there. You'll study it, Marvin. You'll investigate with Gary and Bruce. You'll look. You'll see. You'll buy. And remember it doesn't have to be just in the garment business. We'll diversify other places too, but you could look into lingerie. That we could have. It's going to be big again soon. And raincoats. Maybe furs. Anything you think is good and we don't have. Whatever you come up with I'll listen to. I'll be glad to look with you if you want, but you'll probably do better without me. You'll know better than me." He smoothed Gary's hair and, smiling, walked calmly over to the closet. "I talk too much, I think."

The others stood up, waited silently. When Sam turned, holding his gray fedora, his shoulders pushed back confidently, the others moved toward him. He was shorter than they but he seemed to spring higher. "It's time for me to go home. Four o'clock. Your mother will be waiting for her lover boy."

Down the white corridor, bending smartly toward each open office to call good afternoon to its occupants, Sam moved with a measured, comfortable stride. A bow to Olive, the receptionist. A genial scanning of the people crowding the benches on either side of the rotunda, their sample cases all in a row between their legs, at the ready. Another bow like an apology for the delay of their day. They acknowledged the greeting by standing respectfully.

The Thermopane doors swung open. Sam donned his hat, stepped onto the escalator, went down. His chauffeur opened the lobby door, held it open until Sam was well out on Broadway, then raced to open the door of the Lincoln Continental parked illegally between two trucks at the curb. Obviously content with what he had done this day, Sam lowered himself into the back of the car. The motor hummed. The power steering screeched. The sleek black car shot out into Broadway traffic.

Literally, by lifting a few fingers, without having to leave his office—it was an effort to leave his office during the day—Marvin Bernstein knew what was going on outside, on Broadway, on Seventh Avenue, on Wall Street. Even now, seated at his desk, he knew. A few telephone calls here, a few telephone calls there and pieces of information, vital pieces, could be fitted together to form a finished picture of the only scenes that interested him. It was all a matter of knowing exactly when to make the right call. Marvin knew, knew infallibly, as though he had a seventh sense; intuition, his sixth sense, had operated as a part of his essential equipment ever since he broke into this business. He had contacts, people whose job it was to walk around the streets and listen. At least once a week the contacts were called in for a meeting—everyone at Greenstalks liked meetings—and questioned. If the meeting yielded nothing important, it was because, that day, Marvin needed nothing more important than to reinforce his sense of total, permanent domination. As long as the stock closed higher: 5/8, 3/4, a whole point. It varied, but it kept going up. If it dropped, even a little bit, then he made other calls, right down onto the floor of the exchange. He knew whom to call. He had his own private book for those numbers. Even June Blechman, his secretary, never got to see inside that book. He wasn't sitting where he was behind this desk, a purposely small-scaled desk that made his lean, long body loom more formidable by contrast, without keeping some helpful secrets carefully hidden under a batch of precedent-making old reports in the bottom drawer of his desk, just like the marriage book his mother used to keep hidden under bras and corsets in her bedroom bureau in their Bronx apartment years ago.

He had *his* methods that fit the way *his* mind worked. Another person would do it differently. Fine. That's their business. Another person might not want his secretary working and typing in the same small office, for example. But Marvin liked it that way. He liked the sounds of her work as much as he liked the silence of his. June could hear everything that went on. She could watch everyone that dragged a white chair from a row of them along the side wall closer to his desk. And Marvin could watch her watch people during a meeting, could balance her simple, open-faced responses against his own cautious ones. Having her handy, he could tell her what he wanted done without having to call for her, without having to waste time.

Time was the one thing he valued above all else. Time used expeditiously was money made for Greenstalks and, therefore, for himself. He never wasted it willfully. When he was at work, he worked all day and some evenings. When he was home, in Larchmont, he worked too. Thinking about work was working. He didn't try to turn it off. He looked as if he were relaxed. He knew how to sit quietly and pretend he was listening. Fortunately or unfortunately—what was the use of judging it or fighting it?—that was the way he was built: for ulcers and success. He had both in abundance, and an ulcer or two were, according to Marvin's way of looking at life, not such a terrible price to pay—everyone had to pay some kind of price—for all the other things he had: a big, expensively decorated house that made his wife happy, a sleep-in cook, a sleep-in maid, a handy man for emergencies, two pretty daughters at a private high school in Massachusetts, vacations in Bermuda or Miami or Puerto Rico whenever he wanted them or the doctors told him he needed them. The doctors were paid plenty to keep tabs on his condition, to keep him going in the right direction. As long as he didn't smoke and drink, nothing would get out of hand. Screwing around? Well, that was his private business too. That was just once in a while, when he felt like it. That was organized too, exactly the way he wanted it. After all, he wasn't the type to go hunting for accidental adventures. He was too tall for that. He stood out in a crowd. Screwing around casually he had never been successful at, and he had learned early that what you don't do well you had better not try to do at all. Chance encounters happened to heroes on the make. For him it was better to pay for it, get exactly what he wanted and get it over with. A Romeo he wasn't and couldn't be.

Some people were equipped with the looks, had the talent for screwing around easily. Gary was one of those people. Buyers, saleswomen, models, secretaries took to him. His house in Great Neck, his wife were built for living that kind of noisy life. Perfect. Someone at Greenstalks, as Sam didn't say but knew, has to put on a show, has to project an appealing image to the people who count. That was Gary's job, just as staying in his office to work was Marvin's. Why complain about the role your constitution equips you to perform? The only important item on anyone's emotional agenda was to face the fact of what one was and never lie about it, ever, to oneself. If Gary liked good clothes, liked spending time having them fitted perfectly, liked going to the barber, liked plenty of lubrication, saunas, sunlamps, liked working out at a gym, then fine, let him have it. Marvin liked a column of figures to yield a net profit higher than they had the month before. That was that. One person's kicks were another person's sickness. Amen.

And Bruce? What was Bruce equipped to perform now that Sam had pointed them in this new direction? In the past, whenever Marvin worried about the company, it was always Bruce, finally, that he realized he was worrying about, not the whole company. Bruce wanted titles. Currently, he liked the title Style Coordinator. Okay. It worked out that what Bruce called stylish and fashionable sold, grossed, added volume. But now it was going to have to be different. Sam wanted it to be different. It wasn't going to be necessary for Bruce to send out his team of shoppers to the department stores to buy better merchandise they thought could be copied at a price. It wasn't going to be necessary to carry on the books hundreds of thousands of dollars' worth of rotting inventory, locked rooms filled with clothes the hired shoppers had bought and that Bruce and his sewers, tailors, fledgling designers had restyled. Part of that overhead they should be able to cut back on. Not all, but a substantial amount. The cheaper divisions were going to have to carry the new ventures for a while, until the Greenstalk system could make them show the kind of profit the shareholders were used to. What title would Bruce want when they did? What Marvin had in mind Bruce wasn't going to like: each company they bought up would have its own separately functioning staff, its own designer who made original clothes for a customer Bruce knew nothing about. So what then? Style coordinator of the empire? Designer-advisor? Never. Copier extraordinary, yes. But that he'd fight. That he'd go to his father about and say he could handle those fairy designers, whip them into shape, take care of them the way he took care of the Greenstalk sales force, by screaming them into submission, by threatening to cut them off from their 10 percent commissions. Screaming worked here, but it wouldn't work in the future. Classy types wouldn't stand for it, money or no money, and Greenstalks was going to be expanding into classy operations, trading up, not down, where they already had the market cornered. Bruce would have to be kept in his place every step of the way. If he wasn't, there'd be trouble, big trouble. Anyone with artistic pretensions was trouble, always. They never could admit they knew less than the authentic article. Maybe they couldn't because their deception was their way of life. Which is why Gary, on the other hand, was okay. Gary didn't fight what he was. Gary was the smiling face of Greenstalks. So, when the time came for it, he was going to have to smile his younger, stubborn brother right into line, or else. . . . Marvin surprised himself with a sudden series of loud burps. He lowered his head discreetly, reached for two Gelusils from the scattered supply in the knee-hole drawer of his desk.

At the other end of the office June Blechman stopped typing, waiting for the burps to end, the cellophane to stop rattling. "Some water, Mr. Bernstein? That's a fresh pitcher. I filled it just after I got in." She started to get up, but Marvin waved her back. "It's starting early today. You must have a big day planned. Always starts early when you've got a lot on your mind."

He snapped out of his slump, grimacing as the pain traveled its slow, slicing path lower, stretched his legs far out from under his desk to help its passage. "Sorry to bother you, June, but it caught me unprepared."

"Oh, I'm not bothered by things like that. You know better. My husband has the same thing, remember. So I'm used to it."

"Well, I don't mind if you don't mind."

"I really don't mind, Mr. Bernstein. Honestly." June's angular, forty-fivish face broke into smiling mounds of sincere, abundant solicitude, a cross between the universal mother's eternal suffering and a professional woman's sense of responsibility to her boss. In the next moment she was back to poking and patting the fringe of gray-blond hair on her forehead. The habits of the young girl linger on longer in a woman who goes to business every day.

Marvin laced his hands behind his neck, leaned far back. "I want you to set up a meeting for this afternoon. Two-thirty sharp. No refusals accepted. And don't tell the boys about it." His voice dropped in volume. June nodded, pencil poised over her steno pad. "I want any salesmen on our staff that used to handle Seventh Avenue lines. You can check which ones in personnel. I want my contact man from the bank. I want our P.R. lady, Esther what's her name?"

"Kaufman."

"Right. Kaufman. I want at least three—no, two's enough—fabric salesmen who sell us the most yardage per year and who also sell the Avenue. Gary's secretary can give you those names. Only make damn sure you don't tell what it's for. Also, I want our *yenta* guy from the exchange. Frankel. So when the meeting's over he can go back down there and start a rumor. When you call them, tell them you're from Sam Greenstalk's office but that the meeting's with me." Marvin stretched tautly, crumpled forward, his hands moving to cup his crotch, one finger secretly scratching. "Then, set up another meeting for four-thirty. Gary and Bruce. The heads of all our divisions, plus all the companies we're invested in. That'll be harder to arrange, but try to get what you can get. Don't worry about it. Just give them a hard time so they'll feel they're missing something by not being here." His mouth puffed, the hollows of his cheeks expanded around an upward surge of gas. He was prepared for it, fought it back down, twisting his head from side to side, won the battle. His mouth opened in what, for Marvin, was a smile, but what, for almost anyone else, would have been seen as a puckered, lemon-sucking frown. "Tomorrow I'll want to see some union people. I'll tell you who before you go. Just one more thing for today. A little detective work. See what you can scratch together about a firm called Mr. Jack. It's out—"

"It's out of business, Mr. Bernstein. I used to go there to get wholesale for my daughter. I just tried last weekend. Such beautiful clothes, but not well made. It's a shame they—"

"Yes. It's a shame. But don't waste your sympathy. Someone bought the name already. I want to know who. Don't spend too much time on it. Just see what you can come up with." He reached for the top folder on the pile of oak-tag-covered reports at the corner of his desk. "Hold the mail for a while, June. I've got to go through some of this stuff before Gary and Bruce begin with the interruptions." Tenderly his thin, asparagus-stick fingers smoothed back the cover of the folder. He bent lower to study the typewritten numbers, immediately settling to this task, concentrating as if one part of his mind's circuitry had been switched off and another switched on. His breathing deepened audibly. This was the real satisfaction of each day, the palpable proof of his accomplishment, a private fantasy of figures, an excitement he didn't have to share with anyone, like masturbation, studying the sales reports, the cost reports, wages, schedules for production, stock reports, capital gains, comparing totals without having to write down a thing, remembering from one week to another, one month to another; reading, interpreting, forecasting a trend, storing the information for future need.

That was his kind of pleasure. That was the way he was built. Some people played golf to relax, others read books, but City-College-trained accountants, even those who become vice-presidents like himself, remain faithful to figures. Everyone's different, thank God. One man's meat, as they say . . . the way some people couldn't stand to have sounds around them when they worked, hated distractions. Not Marvin. June's muffled murmur on the telephone, her typing, her presence in the room only served to amplify his pleasure. June Blechman's gray-blond Jewish head bobbing in the corner knew what he was doing and marveled at it. She made this hour every morning possible. She made sure no one interfered. He could trust her to do that. Thank God he had someone to trust.

They were all present and on time: seven faces spaced strategically around the white formica meeting-room table; frightened faces that smiled defensively, fearful that, perhaps, Marvin was dissatisfied with something, or, worse, that Mr. Sam was; faces whose only defense against attack from Marvin's inscrutable expression of familiar and chronic dyspepsia at the head of the table was a smile, a smile as fragile as a flower. They were all subject to his method and mood. Whether through choice or chance or both, they had no choice any more but to be here, to listen, to honor any and all requests. They were paid well for, were granted favors for, doing just that. Marvin began every meeting thinking that thought. His fingers beat an impatient, syncopated message on the table top. He waited through the silence that his presence alone had already won from them. He prolonged it, aware before he spoke that, damn it, this wasn't the kind of group to provide him with the information he wanted. The two salesmen? Cookies from the same cutter. Silver mohair suits. Money grabbers. Now that they handled, exclusively yet, the Greenstalk lines and had entrée into almost every budget shop in almost every department store in the country, what would they remember from the other world, the classy fashion world? *Bubkiss!* Beans. Borscht. And the fabric guys? Giants themselves, from the big mills, but stoopers who leaned over to please, hoping that this season Bruce and Gary Greenstalk were maybe going to buy up their entire lot of corduroy or cotton or ask to have a new synthetic made up special. Then they could stand up.

Marvin laced his fingers behind his neck and stretched back, suppressing some burps. For lunch he had had an appetizer of Gelusils followed by cottage cheese and sour cream. A perfect combination, as bland as the guy from the bank looked. Him you had to provide with the facts, with a prospectus, in order to see animation. No matter where he went, he was always guarding the vault for the Garment Center. That was his way of pleasing. A man to rely on, strictest confidence. Your balance is safe with me. Isn't that what the great Marvin Bernstein wanted? Reassurance? What a face! And Frankel was the opposite. A Wall Street runner.

Ready, willing, and able to talk, anxious to talk, but tongue-tied by anything other than ticker-tape quotations. So that left Esther Kaufman.
Now she was the one who might just know something about what was
hot on the Avenue. She was the one he had to make talk. She went everywhere, knew everyone, using her Greenstalk account as leverage, which
was all right, that was part of her job: to have dyed red hair; to have a
source of negotiable power that made you as appealing to as many people
as possible; to be a P.R. lady pimp. As long as her husband loved her.
The trouble was that as soon as she stepped onto the up escalator she became frightened for her life. Gary was really her contact at Greenstalks, so
being at one of Marvin's meetings numbed her. Her frozen smile was
about to crack the whole face to pieces. Well, might as well get this show
on the road. Marvin lunged forward, startling the group. "You can relax,
friends. I'm not going to bite you today."

Nervous laughs issued through the nervous smiles. There were the
sounds of wary readjustment around the table. Suit jackets were unbuttoned. Legs were recrossed. Chairs, pushed back from the table, squeaked
on the vinyl floor tiles.

"Greenstalks is about to embark on a new policy, something very big."
Pausing, Marvin studied the effect his first words had: intensified fear, as
if their lives, their jobs were held in jeopardy by the mystery that *new*
evoked. Esther pounced on her yellow pad, doodling furiously: S curves;
upside down U's. She wouldn't look up at him. "Mr. Greenstalk has always been interested in keeping abreast of new trends and changes taking
place in our industry. If you know him at all, you know that one thing he
dislikes is to see any procedure settle into a groove. When everything's
running too smoothly, he gets suspicious. He enjoys experimenting. For a
man his age, it's surprising how young he thinks. What he's after right
now is information, information that will help Greenstalks grow into a
bigger organization. For example, one area he'd like to investigate is Seventh Avenue and the fashion houses. He'd like to move in that direction.
Do you follow me so far?"

The puppet-string nods, the guarded, blank stares proved what Marvin
had surmised would be the case. Just what he was getting at was exactly
what they were wary of following. It threatened them. Any change threatened, no matter how gently he tried to put it to them. Only Frankel's
mind, at first, snapped at an idea. He began biting his nails. And then
Esther stopped doodling. She was following some sudden vision. Okay,
Esther baby, I'll get to you in a minute. "Each one of you has had,

some of you still have, contacts in the medium- and higher-priced markets. Mr. Frankel, I imagine you've got lots to say about pending deals between the big companies and the smaller, independent ones. That, of course, is what's happening today, and that's what we're after. And, Mr. Bailey, your bank handles financing for most of the Seventh Avenue firms, as well as Broadway, if I'm not mistaken. So I called you here today to ask your help. What we particularly want to know about is who's really hot, what kind of clothes they merchandise, which of the young designers have been doing a great job and look like they're going to make it to the big time. In that last category," he looked directly at Esther, singling her out as a lady with classified information, "I don't mean just the social ones, the climbers. I'm talking about the ones with real talent. The hard workers." Slowly, he scanned each face for signs of life. "That's the kind of information I'm after generally. Mr. Greenstalk doesn't want gossip. Gossip he can get from *Women's Wear*. He wants the straight poop. The facts. Do you follow my meaning?" Marvin's cheeks puffed. A hand shot up to cover his mouth, to let the air explode behind it.

"If you don't mind, Mr. Bernstein, I'd like to check out a few items." Frankel raised his hand. Marvin yielded the floor. "Of course I realize you're talking about long-range expansion, which means there's got to be an element of risk involved. Right now Greenstalk stock is solid stuff, very solid. I never hesitate to offer it to my best clients. Which is why I'd like to know, and it's something they're going to want to know before they buy, what kind of chances you're going to be willing to take? Like, do you think you'll want to speculate on potential, or will you play it safe right across the board?"

There it was. Good old reliable Frankel. He couldn't wait to get back downtown to start dealing, to start spreading the word around, to line up the buyers. Within a month he'd sell enough Greenstalk stock on the strength of a rumor for them to have enough new capital to buy up the world. "That depends, Mr. Frankel. We're not going to jump. We never do that. We'll have to sift through the offers when they start coming in. We'll balance everything. You can be certain of that. But if the combination of elements in a company looks right, I'm sure Mr. Greenstalk would want us to invest *something* in potential growth. A good company like ours has to experiment."

Frankel was content, his nervous hands locked together in temporary truce. Mr. Bailey from the bank revealed his excitement only through his eyes, whose gaze shifted from Frankel's hands to Marvin's face. The rest of him was still, unmoving, guarding the vault. Esther Kaufman's sudden vision of the role she could play had, finally, settled into insight. But she wasn't ready to speak yet. It was hard to be the only woman in a room filled with men. Marvin would have to approach her directly, but later. Afterward, when the others left. Then he'd be able to *schmooze* for a while. "Let me go back to my initial point. What we want is information. Authentic, verifiable facts. Of course we could find out all we need to know by doing some checking with Dun & Bradstreet, but, as I said, Mr. Greenstalk likes the human touch. Not just figures all the time. Like, for example, you gentlemen who sell us so much fabric each year, surely you must have some steady customers on the Avenue. Or you hear things from your friends. So, if you hear anything interesting, just give me a ring. Let me know. Mr. Greenstalk will appreciate it. That I can assure you. And you gentlemen who handle *our* lines . . . so well. I know you've got contacts with salesmen over there. Talk to them. Inquire. Find out what's what and who's who. Okay?" The smiling nods conveyed grateful relief more than they revealed growing comprehension. Which was all right, as far as Marvin was concerned. Better that way, to spell out a simple function to perform, to let them leave the building feeling necessary, still attached to the hot center of a growing business. Better that they could only guess at the fever that triggered the growth of the whole system. Much better. Like religion. Always leave 'em guessing and wondering! Just as long as *he* understood it all. "And, gentlemen, the last thing I want to do here is assure each one of you, and Mrs. Kaufman too, that personally none of you has a thing to worry about. Like I said, I didn't call you here today to complain. I happen to know what a good job you all do. But you've all been so quiet I thought I better make that point clear. What we're planning includes all of you. I promise that. And when I make a promise, you can count on it. It doesn't have to be in writing. My word is all you need." Which was true. They knew what his reputation was around the industry; anything he promised, he honored, eventually. So, here at the end, they relaxed. Even Mr. Bailey from the bank smoothed the spotless table, opened the vault a little bit. "If you'll just call when you hear something positive, I'll feel that I didn't waste your time this afternoon. Thank you all for coming."

Marvin motioned for Esther to remain seated. She did, but her smile, her certainty dissolved instantly, her pencil resumed its frantic doodling. She was really afraid of him. The others filed out of the room as if they were thankful for a last-minute stay of execution, with the exception of

Frankel, who waved, in a quiet, solemnly satisfied manner. June Blechman closed her steno pad, received silent permission to leave.

"I hope you can spare a few minutes more, Esther." Marvin lowered his voice. He had something confidential to relate, something meant for her ears only. "I'm aware of what a fine job you're doing for us. It's a great job. Gary keeps me well informed. But he doesn't have to because I can see the results. The kind of good image Greenstalks has, has a lot to do with your work."

Although her pencil continued to move in smaller and smaller circles, Esther did manage to look up at him and speak. "Thank you, Mr. Bernstein. I—"

"Marvin."

"Yes. Thank you, Mr. . . . Marvin. Thank you. I try my best. Greenstalks doesn't really need much publicity, though."

"Mr. Greenstalk, Sam I mean, doesn't like a big show, as you know. I suppose that makes it tough for you. But, nevertheless, whatever you do, you do well. You got us to the right kind of advertising agency. They understand the customer we want. Modest. Solid family. *New York Times* on Sunday. The *Daily News*. Perfect. We're all happy. But now—and I'm telling *you* this; I didn't want to tell it directly to the others—we've got our sights set on something quite a bit different, in *addition* to the way it is now. That *won't* change. I think, or rather I know, that you can really help us with the transformation."

"I'll be happy to try." Esther crossed, recrossed her heavy legs, forced herself to sit still. Marvin liked that, liked that she was impatient, nervous, and, finally, under control. He didn't have to soften up this kind of woman, to waste any more time. She wasn't a novice on the make. She ran a tight little operation, the kind that had to struggle for existence in the shadows of all the major businesses nowadays. Not parasitic. Not really. Unbalanced symbiosis was more accurate. And a hard way to make a buck. The host plant could chew you up any time it felt like it, get another one that was tastier. Marvin had checked Esther out when they gave her the Greenstalk account. A tough cookie who kept her private life private. Her husband the English teacher, her two sons, her camping trips every year, all of that separate and a surprise. For her, one kind of world had nothing to do with the other. Marvin never let on he knew. What was the point? Inside the private, hidden zone in every person was a human being waiting to be discovered. But once you let yourself into that zone, you were trapped by what you found out, what you had to spend time and energy understanding. Much better to travel along the circumference of people. Keep them out of your private world and stay out of theirs. All he had to know about Esther was that she stayed in P.R. work, apart from liking the money, because she was a smart *yenta*. The way some people craved pickles, she had to know what was going on and where and with whom. She went to all the fashion showings at the Hilton and the Waldorf, the Plaza, the Americana. She cultivated the magazine girls. She knew the ad execs. She got free-lance work for designers and she got paid well for her efforts. Marvin knew it all. It didn't really interest him. *She* didn't really interest him—red hair was not one of his things—but she could be made to help now. That's all that counted. His silence was beginning to worry her again.

"What I'd like from you, Esther, might be a little tricky. We're thinking of experimenting with some free-lance lines, on a trial basis. Well-designed lines. Not copies or knock offs. A higher-price thing. A lot classier than what we've got. Just to see what happens. One thing we don't want to do is jeopardize our bread-and-butter business."

"What kind of clothes are you going to want? Sportswear? Dresses? Suits?" Since the conversation had turned the corner into what she knew, Esther became animated, not relaxed. "There's lots of competition in better clothes, you know."

"That's exactly the problem. We're not quite sure where we want to end up. We'd rather try with a lot of things, in a small way, so the investment isn't too great. The designers would have to organize the setup. We'd supply the factories to make the clothes if we liked them. Our labor setup is no problem. The unions love us. So we're thinking almost anything. It's like we're shopping around, which is why I thought you could really help. You've got top connections. You know a lot of designers who might just fit the bill."

Before Esther could respond, Marvin was on his feet. That was all he wanted to say. The audience was concluded. When Marvin had to stand, he stood. Mouth hanging open dumbly, Esther watched his body unfold, straighten, in slow motion, going higher and higher, as if it would never stop. From on high, from the white ceiling, he spoke: "I appreciate your coming over. As soon as you have some ideas, call me directly. Whatever you come up with, I guarantee you'll be taken care of. I promise it. You also better close your mouth." She jumped up, closing her mouth, smoothed her wrinkled purple linen tent dress, followed Marvin out of the conference room. "We understand each other, Esther. So just get out there and circulate." Like a giraffe, he loped off down the corridor, leaving Esther to make her way back to the rotunda as best she could.

"Lousy meeting, June." Marvin poked through the pink telephone slips on his desk. "What the hell does my wife want! Three times she called?"

"Yes. The last time was a few minutes ago. I said you were in conference, but she wouldn't tell me what it was about."

"Get her for me." Sighing, he removed his wash-and-wear jacket, hung it on the rounded back of the Eames chair from which it slid to the floor as soon as he sat down. "Damn chairs!"

"Ready, Mr. Bernstein. She's on."

"Adele? . . . Yes, I got the messages. So what's so important you had to call me three times? . . . Yes, I remember about the dinner party. You reminded me this morning. I don't forget so soon." June retrieved his jacket, hung it in the combination closet-washroom. He nodded thank you. "If I'm not home on time just start without me. You can manage. You always manage. . . . Oh, what the hell do I know about Greek art anyway? You're the one taking the course, not me. You're the one who wants to go to Greece, not me. And an authentic Greek meal isn't exactly going to help my ulcers any. . . . It is not bland food, for Christ's sake! It's spicy. . . . All right, so I'm wrong. I'll be home when I get there. Your artist friends aren't going to miss me. That I'll take bets on. . . . Let's not go into that now, Adele. I'm too busy. . . . Goodbye, Adele. I'm going to hang up. . . ." The telephone was slammed onto its cradle. "Greek food," he mumbled. "Damn it, anyway."

"Did you want me, Mr. Bernstein?"

"Yes, June. Cancel the four-thirty meeting. Arrange it for tomorrow. Bring in the union guy at four today."

"But I already set everything up."

"Then you better *un*-set it."

"Yes, Mr. Bernstein. I'll do my best."

Marvin grabbed a folder from the diminished pile at the corner of the desk. He stroked the top onion-skin sheet lightly with the pads of his finger tips, folded it back, stared at the ordered columns of numbers, anxious for the marginal descriptions, their meanings, to overtake and silence the trivial flow of thought in his head, to have those facts claim his complete attention, to calm him before the rumble, the gas, the stabs of pain started up, spoiling the rest of the afternoon. Gross receipts. Net profit. Store checkout record of the Miss Greenstalk line in Alabama, Arizona, Arkansas, every state listed alphabetically; and in every state the net was up since the last report. So if that just continues to rise while this new crap gets under way . . . Marvin looked up. June was standing in front of his desk. "Yes? What now?"

"Mr. Gary would like to see you in his office as soon as you can make it. He says it's important."

"I'll bet it's important." He straightened the pages of the report, closed it carefully, slid it protectively to the side, and only then let his irritation explode. "Damn it! I can't seem to get a minute's peace around here."

Gary's office was white too, but with a characteristic difference: colored pillows—squares, circles, triangles of coral, blue, red, yellow, chartreuse— had been allowed as accents on the foam-rubber sofas; American beauty roses were on his desk; gold-dipped baroque metal-framed pictures, of his dark-haired wife, his children, a boy and two girls, as babies, his Georgian-style house in Great Neck, hung from the white walls, each picture tinted in rosy pastels. A personality established itself in Gary's office, made itself felt through your feet when you stepped onto the fluffy beige oval throw rug in front of his desk. He had persuaded his father that, at least in his office, a distinctive aura was necessary. That was his job: presenting a personality, and persuading people to do what he thought best. He had majored and minored in those courses at Dartmouth, had graduated without raising much of a sweat, except in the gym, where he was convinced, even now, he had excelled, telling everyone, when the subject of college Now versus Then was raised at any one of his parties, that he had been a three-letter man, that he was in as good condition now as he was then because of the healthy habit of exercise, that that was something the kooky kids of today just couldn't get through their dirty heads. They're repulsive, smart-ass freaks of nature.

In his circle of friends and acquaintances Gary was convincing. Good-looking people usually are, no matter what they say, no matter how sweetly they smile when they say it. People may not always listen to the words, but they almost always *look* at the speaker, especially when the coincidence of the speaker's having been born good-looking or having created a facsimile through surgery has been enhanced by the artfully tailored suit, by the correct silk tie, the correct matching silk handkerchief stuffed casually in a jacket pocket, by the unobtrusive but noticeable scent —manfully effeminate—by scrupulously trimmed and styled hair, a manicure and transparent polish, sun-lamp treatments or a week in the Islands, by expensive shoes polished to a high sheen. Gary was winsomely all these things and more. He was a *mensch:* a devoted, compassionate son, husband, and father. He was tall, big-boned, muscular, tapered at the waist to fit his waist-suppressed suit jackets.

All that Gary was, Bruce wasn't. Just the way he had of spreading himself like a big, soft lump across a sofa—he was in the process of doing that when Marvin entered the office—of tossing a red pillow, his security pillow, into the air, of catching it, crushing it between his huge hands, pressing it against his stomach, told the difference between the brothers. Gary had come to his style through exposure; Bruce had come to his by burying his need for anyone's good opinion. He had his work to worry about. That was more important than people. He wouldn't take the trouble to watch his weight. As tall as he was, he couldn't be bothered trying not to stoop. His suits and ties were determinedly unpressed and mismatched; his shoes were down at the heels and unshined. Casual and who-cares, that was the look he said he liked. If his hair was too thick and too curly, so what? that was the way he was born. Only when Gary coaxed him into getting it cut, getting an antidandruff treatment, at least once a month, would he do it. For two or three days he would try to maintain the appearance of a well-groomed executive of a well-financed corporation, but as his hair grew back, as the dandruff reappeared, so did the more familiar, determined sloppiness. He was a dedicated *schlump,* Gary said of him, grinning paternally, but a *schlump* with a heart of gold.

If it was a heart of gold, Marvin thought whenever he heard that description, it must be locked away in a deposit box somewhere because the only times he every saw it displayed was at bar-mitzvahs, weddings, and funerals, never at the office. The people who worked for Bruce thought his heart was made out of scrap iron. Screaming was his specialty, along with throwing things: dresses he didn't like; bolts of fabric that weren't printed properly; hangers, buttons, trays of straight pins whenever a sewer did a lousy job. Again, only Gary could coax him into temporary contrition. Not that Bruce ever apologized to anyone. He gave gifts, money, which he stripped from the wad he kept in his pocket, gifts which were never entered in the books and which made working for him bearable. Bruce didn't believe in any other kind of loyalty. No one was loyal unless you paid for it. He didn't listen to complaints. He sent complainers to Marvin because Marvin had to listen if Bruce sent them.

So Marvin learned how to listen and to make peace by saying very little. He had learned the role of peacemaker without really trying. He didn't care whether a complainer remained with Greenstalks or left. All he cared about was getting the clothes made, one way or another, and making damn sure that they sold, that the sales showed a profit. But he listened to the complaints, which were always the same, nodded when he was supposed to nod, lamented over what he was supposed to lament over: "Because underneath it all, Mr. Bernstein, I suppose he's really a fine person, only, between the two of us—and I'm saying what I'm going to say because I know you understand such things—he's not trained enough for his job. He's not a designer. College he went to, but a designer he's not. Maybe he's insecure. Maybe he's overshadowed by his brother. . . ." Then he asked the question he was supposed to ask, "Do you want to quit?" The answer was monotonously the same, as it had been for years now, give or take a few words, "Who said anything about quitting, Mr. Bernstein? Not me. I only wanted you should know how hard it is to work under such conditions and for such a man."

Bruce was somebody it was pointless for anyone to criticize. He was going to be just where he was until doomsday, which, at Greenstalks, would be never, as long as Marvin was where he was for every minute of every day of every week of every year. No contract said anything about having to like Bruce or Gary. They were Sam's sons and that was that. The hell with liking. All Marvin had to do was listen to them and then go ahead and do whatever he thought was *better* for the company. Which was why he was in Gary's office right now, prepared to listen, make peace, advise. So talk already, Gary. Stop playing with that junk on your desk.

"First you called a meeting and then you called it off. That's not like you, Marvin, so I thought I'd better find out what's going on inside your head. My father didn't come in today—he felt a little tired—but he called and I told him about the meeting and he wants me to call him later to let him know what's up." As he spoke Gary kept arranging and rearranging, into squares, circles, triangles, a set of colored bits of papers.

"Nu, Marvin? How come you called it off?" Lolling, Bruce squeezed his red pillow. "You're not feeling well? Is that it? What a funny coincidence if you were sick too because last night my father had indigestion the same way you get it."

"I'm all right. I wish all I had was indigestion when I get sick. What are those things, Gary?"

"These? Oh, they're just some idea I'm playing around with." He pushed them into a pile, scooped them to the side. "Sorry . . . Now what about that meeting?"

"Nothing really happened. I just decided to handle things a little differently. It takes time to develop an approach to what your father wants. Who gave you those?"

"Some paper salesman came up to see me. His boss wants to tie up with a dress manufacturer. I kind of like the idea. . . . What approach you thinking of taking?"

"As I said, I'm not certain yet, but by the next board meeting I'll have something firm to offer."

"That I'm sure of. I just—Bruce and I—just wanted to know a little of what your thinking was. We have to be prepared, you know, in terms of a lot of things. Like fabric commitment. Production schedules. Takes plenty of coordination to get a thing rolling."

Marvin's mouth shut. His cheeks puffed and popped. Too late. He stretched for comfort. They waited. "I won't forget your needs. I promise that. As a matter of fact, the direction my thinking's going might not interrupt anything we're doing here. I'm leaning toward something other than outright acquisition at first. Those companies your father's talking about could be risky investments. It"s possible to lose your shirts very fast." As he continued to talk, what had been, before he entered Gary's office, a vague, walking thought began now to take shape. His best ideas grew out of what he was forced to say. Sometimes he forgot that habit, got impatient with the service road detours his mind had to take in the course of a day. Yet even a meeting that failed, even this interruption sharpened his instinct, made him think on his feet. Inadvertently, Gary had done a good turn by calling him in here. "We don't want to be in the position of presenting half-baked projects to the board. If we haven't thought the whole thing through for them, they'll end up rejecting everything. Which, personally, they'd be right to do." A pause to make sure there was agreement. "So, what I plan for us is to make some small-time investments at first. Quiet things. Almost like consignment buying, where you finance free-lance deals that need limited capital over a specific period of time. Where you turn the responsibility over to a designer and the people he hires to work for him." They were following; they were content so far. "If it doesn't turn out then, if you don't like the clothes, Bruce, the worst thing that's happened is that we've got a legitimate tax-loss situation and a line to maybe copy from. But, on the other hand, if it *does* work out, we've got the nucleus of a new division which, contractually— I'll see to that—we control and guide into the big time." They loved that. "Meanwhile, we'll be strengthening our other investments. We'll get the principals to pump up production, little by little. We'll offer them new stock-option deals, all kinds of profit incentives, and when they begin to show us how good a job they can do, just at the point *before* their potential, the thing we invested in to begin with, becomes a reality, then we offer to buy them out, to make them part of the parent company, shareholders in the profits of all the subsidiaries. That way nothing gets interrupted and everything's kosher."

Marvin paced the beige fluffy rug in front of Gary's desk, his hands plunged deep into the pockets of his baggy pants. He was stalling now, his head raised, eyes searching the ceiling, waiting for inspiration, for new walking thoughts, new promises of capital gains and plenty of money for reinvestment. Practical plans. Not hot air.

"The major item is to get into the Seventh Avenue action before a lot of these small guys start forming their own organizations. My information is that the smart cookies are selling an idea whereby they tie up the few solid businesses left over there, then offer the whole thing as a package to companies like us. We want to prevent that from happening. We want to hit the small guy now with big money, hit his ego like your father said, get the personality guy who thinks he's running an art gallery instead of a business. They're the easy ones. They get crushed. Like that Fleiss man at Mr. Jack. They panic and lose everything."

Marvin marched to the sofa, squeezed in alongside Bruce. Internally, the machine was running smoothly. No gas, no sharp little pains. He felt loose for the first time that day, confident that the next thing he said or the next question he was asked to answer would prove all over again to himself, to Gary, later to Sam, that he was some kind of genius, that Greenstalks was in business to win all the prizes and that it could win them as long as he was around to keep everything bubbling. "We're in a position that's unique. We've got the healthiest growth pattern of any corporation in the industry. Those guys need us more than we need them, and we're going to keep it that way." Marvin glanced down in time to see Bruce's red pillow slide from his lap onto the rug.

"If you don't mind, Bruce!" Gary waited until Bruce had picked up the pillow, until he pressed it to his stomach protectively. "As you were saying, Marvin." The smile flashed back into place, but now Gary's fingers resumed a surreptitious shuffling of the pieces of colored paper at the side of his desk. His attention span had been reached and passed. Marvin directed his brain to keep those papers on file as a potential tool. Maybe Gary will want a new toy to play with too. Okay. If he can make it work, why not? Why not paper dresses?

"I was going to say that because we're in the position we're in we should feel free to experiment a little. We should throw out some feelers, start some rumors going, let the market know *part* of what we're up to. The small guys'll start smelling around. Then all we'll have to do—as they say—is select. We won't have to settle. We could try anything; even that paper idea might be worth looking into." Gary's smile spread into an O of surprised pleasure. "Find out some more about it. It could be a winner." That should take care of Gary. "And maybe," he had to honor Bruce's needs too, "you could hit on some idea for your sportswear line, something really novel. I understand sportswear's going to be the hot business. Separates, or whatever the hell they call it. Maybe there's a new trend you'd like to follow, something you think's going to catch on."

"How the hell did you find out what I'm doing? You never go in the back. You using spies or mindreading?"

"Neither one. I just use my instincts. You've been pretty quiet lately so I figured you were hatching a scheme. You want to talk about it now?"

Vitality and uncertainty, in equal parts, surged back into Bruce's slumping shape. Casually, he punched the sofa. "I think I'd rather show you instead of talk about it."

Gary, exasperated, sighed loudly, but Marvin, by suddenly standing up, concealed its sound. Patience, Gary baby, because one of these days, you never can tell, a Bruce idea might just catch on fire. It was always better, for everyone's sake, to see it or hear about it early. "You want to show us right now? I've got some time." Marvin checked his watch. Five o'clock. If he was going to make the train that would get him home for Adele's Greek gala, he should be leaving right now. He preferred being late. "Well? You want to?"

"Okay. Why the hell not. Gary?"

"Just for a few minutes. We've got to get home early tonight. That temple thing is at eight-thirty. Remember?"

"What thing?" At the door, Bruce braked suddenly, bumped against Marvin, who stepped back and bumped into Gary.

"The fund-raising meeting." Gary pushed out into the corridor.

"Tonight? It's tonight? Barbara didn't say anything this morning when I left."

"You and Barbara are coming to us for dinner. I was standing right next to you when Debby invited you both."

"That's funny because I don't remember it at all. I hope Barbara does.

She even had a meeting at the temple this afternoon. I remember her telling me that. Maybe I better call her right now."

"I think so. You can show us whatever it is first thing tomorrow morning." Gary started back into his office. Bruce ran off down the corridor at a pace reserved only for emergencies. Marvin remained at the doorway, leaning in. "My brother is not one of your orderly types."

"Maybe not, but he gets things done."

"That he does, Marv. . . . I'll call Dad. I get the pitch on what you're planning. Which is good enough. I'll also keep you posted on the paper thing, but it's got to firm up more first. So *ciao* for now."

Marvin moved back up the corridor to the rotunda. He stood behind Olive's empty desk, watching the girls leave. Day is done—for the stock clerks, the file and order clerks, the bookkeepers, Bruce's sewers and tailors, the secretaries. Some of them smiled cautiously; all of them waved goodnight. Marvin waved back, his gaze settling, however, on the swinging Thermopane doors instead of the people, his ear turned toward the hum of the rapidly descending escalator, the deadened sounds of distant traffic, the subway roar from deep down below the building. The tap-tap of high heels on marble and soon, very soon, silence, or its facsimile. A quieter time.

His favorite time, when the stillness of the corridors, the cubicles, the offices, the showroom, the workrooms was as complete as stillness could ever be inside the mazelike interior of a big business located in a big building in a big city. Then, even inside himself, the sensation of release, or the closest he ever came to such a sensation, had a chance to untie the tense muscles of his face. Then, alone in his office, he was freed from people and the need to service them. His mind could focus on his folders, on the order, clarity, sharpness of figured facts printed on onion-skin pages, figures that should prove he had chosen the correct method, that should indicate a new procedure to implement, a new plan for increase and plenty, another absolute formula for reasonable, successful action, provided, of course, that the people chosen to do the implementing functioned according to expectations. Figures and formulas won't lie. They predict what should happen, purely. It's people who misuse them, who lie about them. And all the time. Without even knowing that they are. Which was the chief problem, for him, for everyone in the world: having to push forward by using people. They were imperfect. They weren't as pure as numbers were. No equation could ever include the variable degree of their failure to perform the way they should. They came up that escalator, those people he needed to keep Greenstalks growing, ready to display one piece of themselves, and it was another one of his jobs, maybe the hardest one of all, to sort out all their other pieces, the unknown parts they hid, like the seven-eighths of an iceberg below water, to determine what their balance was, what the one surface quantity, carefully prepared in advance, weighed when compared to the unknown, ultimately unknowable quantities bubbling beneath their skin, quantities that made the person work or fail to work. He knew what the balance was in himself. His nervous tics, his gaunt unsmiling face were above water, available for anyone to see and be afraid of. And below the surface? What was the real Marvin? The essential Marvin Bernstein was . . . a compleat angler, determined, secretive, able, a scientist schooled by the facts of life as they are, as they will be, and not as others say they are and will be because they want them to be that way, need them to be that way. His genius was based on the fact that he knew how to use that common weakness in people: their longing to believe that in the end everything will turn out all right, that they, at least they, if not anyone else, will live happily ever after. . . .

"I'm going, Mr. Bernstein." June blocked his view of the glass doors. "Mr. Bernstein? Did you hear?"

"Yes, June. I heard." No one else was left in the rotunda. Gary and Bruce must have left without his seeing them. In a while the guard would lock the doors. They would stay locked until Marvin used his key to unlock them.

"I left the telephone messages on your desk along with a note on what I could find out about Mr. Jack. Remember you asked? Well, it's not much, but I'll do more tomorrow. Your wife called back again, I told her you were in conference so she said to tell you, in no uncertain terms—"

"Goodnight, June." He turned away, walked rapidly down the corridor to his office, closed the door behind him. Wincing with each sharp, brief stomach pain, he sat down at his desk. Most of all he was hungry, so, naturally, it was starting in. The doctor warned him all the time. Eat little, but eat often. And he didn't. A simple rule, one he didn't, wouldn't follow consistently. It took time to eat, even a little bit, time he grudged giving up. Stubborn. Add stubborn to your list of essential qualities, Mr. Bernstein. Very stubborn. The most stubborn. Which had to be bad, had to be another reason why the human equation would never check out 100 percent. Unpredictable when and why the hidden parts of a person all of a sudden force him to say, no, I can't, no, I won't. Stubborn was stupid, a devil, but, like everything else in life, at the same time stubborn could also be the best thing about a person, an angel in disguise, a beauty in the breast. Stubborn got him this job. Stubborn made him hold out with the accountancy firm he hated until Sam begged him to come to Greenstalks. Stubborn kept him on top, getting things done the way he wanted them done. And stubborn, if he didn't eat a little, might kill him, too.

The portable refrigerator at the bottom of the clothes closet had, thanks to God and June, a tub of cottage cheese. He brought it back to his desk, ate it slowly, a creamy plastic spoonful at a time. Tangy. Large curd. Bland. Monotonous. White and dull. Like his insides, by now. And his blood too, turned to chalk dust, what with barium tests and milk and sour cream and cottage cheese. When he could have been eating a Greek olive in his big beautiful house in Larchmont, the house his ulcers built, surrounded by a bunch of drunk, know-nothing-but-themselves intellectuals talking about the glories of Greek art. Yat-ta-ta. Yat-ta-ta. This museum. That museum. Charming. Gorgeous. Divine. The culture keepers' chorus. While the economy boomed and businesses grew bigger, while the stock market sputtered, up and down, up and down, and the action in Vietnam escalated toward a massive, money-making war, while his high-school daughters—private-school daughters yet—protested for civil rights and let their hair grow longer and longer.

He called home. "You're not going to like this, Adele, but I can't make it home until much later. I've got to meet with some people on something very big." He waited long enough for her outburst, then cut her off mid-sentence.

The cottage cheese finished, gradually his stomach pains subsided to more bearable discomfort, and now that he was alone, the gas had the freedom to choose its path, one way or another. No need to suppress either. No one to hear or care. A few more folders and he'd make plans for the rest of the evening. Without checking them, he threw away the telephone messages, read June's note on Mr. Jack: "When I bought wholesale at Mr. Jack I met their bookkeeper, who is now working at another firm where I buy wholesale. I called her but all she would say, because she was so angry about the whole business, was that the name now belongs to a young fellow named Michael Matthew Morgan and influential friends. They have big plans, which she was sorry to say might include the former designer whose name is Phil Hanssler. June. P.S. I *did not* mention your name or the Greenstalks even though she asked why I was calling. I lied and said I needed some buttons for an old Mr. Jack dress."

Marvin folded the paper, used the flattened edge to pick at his teeth. Nothing to think about on that score. It wouldn't pay to get involved there. With a bankrupt business. With a name that used to be known all over the country, that used to be powerful. What a label. Great customer identification. Even he could remember those big ads Mr. Jack took years ago when Adele bought only those clothes, before her battles with the bulges. Obviously, a lot must have gone wrong, very wrong, and over a long period of time. The advertisements stopped years ago. Probably the Mr. Jack customer was lost for good. If a company goes bankrupt, a lot more than a business is lost. Everything goes. Everything gets flushed down the drain. And all because the figures finally don't balance. That's how simple it all gets. What led up to it, that's an entirely different story. The complicated crap. The human failure story all over again. The weakness of the secret parts. If there was someone up there who knew what was happening, he must have gotten buried under tons of everyone else's failures.

But just for the hell of it, just to satisfy his own curiosity, maybe he'd look into the situation, for scientific reasons. Quietly, like a hobby. You never know what can grow out of a hobby. Maybe Esther knows that designer. If Sam mentioned Mr. Jack, he mentioned it for a reason. Sam Greenstalk didn't bother with idle talk.

Neither did Marvin Bernstein. He stayed on the safe side of the odds, stuck with the facts, let his instincts and hunches lead him. And if, suddenly, the odds dropped unfavorably, he beat a retreat, covered up his tracks. If you never commit yourself openly, you never get yourself nailed down. Just make believe you're following the leader when it counts. Like now. Only, as it turns out, Sam was right to reject being bought. Look what new possibilities were opening up, and at a time when the price per share—his fingers walked down the column of figures he was studying— continued to climb. Greenstalks was in the black, and with a rosy future. Not on top yet, but moving steadily toward the top, as high as the green neon signs on the roofs of their factories in New Jersey and Connecticut. Gaining, always gaining, always acquiring, piling one company on top of another, creating their own kind of customer identification. Like General Motors or Westinghouse or United States Steel. That's what capitalism is: a system of exchange as old as the Indians, as old as the world. A product in exchange for a fair price. Better and better products for fairer prices. Free enterprise. Incentive. Improvement. Competition. Supply.

Demand. And satisfaction, for those who make and those who buy.

Equality for all. That's the law of the land. The rule of the game. Everyone has to play in order to stay alive. One way or another, no one has any choice any more but to play. That's the system. But no one's free. No one's equal.

All his life, all around him, were the facts. Whether he was home in a Bronx apartment house surrounded by the Philco radio-toaster, floor-lamp economy package that his parents had cherished until the day they died, or in the subway going downtown to City College, or in his first job as an accountant, the facts of the system were everywhere. We live in order to keep getting more, and we keep getting more in order to live. We play the game even though the odds are against us, are always against our winning. Unless, somehow, we can work our way inside the counting house. Which takes know-how. Which is an art as genuine as any other art: to get inside, and stay inside, no matter what the consequences. Neither ulcers, nor chronic dyspepsia, nor the knowledge of an ultimate heart attack could stop him because that movement inside and upward, toward the top, was the only purely exhilarating thing being alive had to offer, and being alive was the most exhilarating just when that movement was challenged, when his artistry was most clearly and cleanly tested. Like today. And tomorrow. And the day after that. . . .

He closed the last of the folders, placed it on top of the neat pile of the others at the corner of his desk. He was satisfied that in spite of all interruptions the work he wanted to accomplish this day had been accomplished. The reports were read. One part of his head had digested them. Another part had come up with some good ideas for the future. And still another part had played with the twists and turns of free thoughts, thoughts no one could ever guess he indulged in. Not even Adele. Least of all Adele. Which led him to another indulgence no one could ever guess. He reached down to the bottom drawer, searched under a batch of old reports for his personal telephone book. Shouldn't really be kept there. But, if not there, where else? In his suit pocket? Where he might forget it one morning when he left the suit for Adele to send to the cleaners? Chances were that June wasn't going to be poking into that drawer. The odds were against it. And even if *she* did, what could she say about it? Telephone numbers don't mean anything by themselves. What they connect you to —well, that's something else again. That was his own private business. Night business as opposed to day business.

". . . Yes, Marvin Bernstein. The tall one. And what I want for tonight . . . about eight o'clock . . . is what you did the last time. Only not separately. Together. The guy and the girl. Both young. No rough stuff. Quiet and easy. Can you arrange it? . . . Good. See you later."

A little freshening up, some dinner, some relaxation, and tomorrow will go better than today. Greek Art, hell. I'll study my own Greek art.

He moved to the concealed cabinet washbasin next to the closet. The cold water felt good, the rough towel even better, but the face in the mirror over the sink, when he finally had to comb his thinning brown hair, was, and always would be, depressing. Long in the tooth, long in the nose, the forehead, the chin, the ears. Long in everything, including the deep creases zigzagging from temple to temple, the quotation marks at each corner of his mouth. Years of a sour stomach had put them there. Nothing, now, would ever remove them. The greatest service he could perform for himself was to avoid the mirror at all costs, even while shaving. He grabbed his jacket from the closet, and turned out the office lights.

The corridor was dark, but the glow of white walls and floor guided his slow steps. Even if he was blindfolded, instinct and habit could lead him to any and every corner of this space they called their loft, their castle. He knew the way everywhere.

The moons of pale light shone from the rotunda ceiling. The cleaning woman was somewhere nearby. He heard a pail being pushed along the vinyl tiles, then a mop sloshing with a heavy slap. Every night every floor had to be scrubbed. Sam's edict. That's a lot of white floor to clean.

He pressed the button on the box located at the side of the glass doors: one long buzz, one short, the electronic signal to the burglary control center that the final, important departure was at hand. The buzz was answered: one short, one long, the permission granted to unlock the doors. He passed through quickly, relocked them, tested them, began to descend the motionless escalator, stopping only to look back at the green neon label which remained lit through the night. He continued down into the darkness below.

The guard left his shadow-hidden chair to let Marvin out. "I heard you buzz out, Mr. Bernstein."

Marvin nodded. "The cleaning woman's up there, Joe."

"Yes, I know. I let her in and I'll check on her in a while. The other door's still open. It's a nice night out there, Mr. B."

Marvin stepped out onto Broadway, waited until the guard had locked the door behind him, started walking uptown. He didn't feel like hailing a cab. There was plenty of time to kill, and it was a nice night, with a breeze, a hot and dust-filled breeze, but it helped. Thanks to Daylight Saving, the sky—the building-bordered slice of it he could see—still held red-blue remnants of an artificial dusk. Unlit windows high up reflected the real western light. He imagined the view from there, imagined himself up there looking out alone, watching the sun curve down and out of his sight to become someone else's sunset, imagined how soon people would be able to travel faster than the speed of light, pass through sunlight, overtake it, move once more into darkness. A race against time—the ultimate race which everyone lost. And out of foreknowledge of that loss, that absurd fact, a private purpose sometimes grew. Incredible that it could, that it ever did.

At the corner of Thirty-ninth and Broadway he stopped, surveyed the hole that had once been the Metropolitan Opera House, that in a year or so would be filled in, would become the tallest office building in the area. Greenstalks should move there, to the top floors. He'd mention it to Sam. Be great for the company's new image.

He crossed the side street carelessly. So little traffic down here this hour of the evening. Even on Broadway. Only some speeding cabs sloshing against the sun-softened tar. But up ahead was the action, the flashing neon of Times Square, the Castro Convertible sign and Coca-Cola, the theatres, Duffy Square. A concrete park. He'd go to the dairy restaurant on Forty-ninth, eat something light and white, something that wouldn't start the gas line pumping. He wanted to enjoy tonight. He'd be paying plenty for his pleasure. No sense in running the risk of spoiling a second of it.

At Forty-second Street, his pace quickened automatically. He was leaving the quiet zone of his thoughts. Speed counted here. A green WALK. A red WAIT. And go again. Into it. The electric eyes. The heart of the Great White Way. Strings of bright bulbs flashing. Movies. The stars. Hookers and hustlers. Pizzas and frankfurters. Stalled faces looking up to the signs for a good time. Out of it. Going. Where he managed to matter. Marvin Bernstein. A mastermind, not just another face. A force. Controlling what was his to control. Always expanding the range of possibilities. And careful. Never caught. On top, looking down.

Chapter Eight

The best thing that could follow the kind of perfect evening he had had—a little bit of this, a little bit of that, mix together, lean back, let them do the work until you're ready—was a perfect morning after at work that worked out as well as the night before. Even Adele's silent anger at breakfast, instead of her yelling, was an unexpected prize. The offer of extra money for her to shop at Bonwit's, his promise to take her to lunch afterward, won her over. And the Greek evening had been a huge success anyway. Without his being there. By the time he was settled on the train for the city and smoothing back the pages of the *Wall Street Journal*, the odds on his having a good morning were good: Adele was pacified; he didn't feel guilty.

And then, at the office first thing, there was Kellerman, the union man, who was pleased to give Marvin—he wouldn't do it for anyone else—a list of businesses that might be willing to sell out. Good businesses. No *shlock* operations. And, while he made out the list, he talked, mostly about Mr. Jack. "Plenty they went out owing the union. More than plenty. Excuse me for talking, Mr. Bernstein, about something you don't ask me, but I just met with Fleiss so it's on my mind what he had to say to me."

"Talk, Kellerman. Talk. As long as it makes you feel better."

"Better it doesn't make me feel. Nothing makes me feel better in such a business. Every minute it's something else." Kellerman's lamb-chop hand cupped his double chin, caressed the heavy flesh. He rocked back and forth over Marvin's desk as if he were praying in a synagogue. "When a man who should know right from wrong tells me that *all* his trouble—not a half, mind you, not a quarter, but all his trouble—is because of the union, then what can help? I ask you, Mr. Bernstein? What? Of course nothing!"

"Of course. Nothing can help. You're absolutely right, Kellerman." *Oy,* how the union suffers. Like Job it suffers.

"Believe me, Fleiss is lucky we didn't sue altogether. Today everyone blames the union for everything. Right from the *schwartzes* to the bosses it's the same story. God forbid they should blame themselves once in a while! And why do they blame? Just because we learned how to take care of our own? We protected the workers. Certainly we did. It's a crime to do that? Not in my books. What Fleiss did was a bigger crime. Before he declared, he wanted we should extend him more time to pay up his debts. So we extended. You think we want a company to go out of business? A company goes out of business we lose too. So we cooperate. We extend. We extended and extended. We extended so much we ended up with nothing. What do they expect from the union, charity? Who makes the money? The bosses or the workers?"

"Let's not get into that, Kellerman. As long as you're satisfied with us, that's all that interests me."

"Satisfied? Every company should be generous like this one and we wouldn't need a union altogether. You give before we ask." Anxiously, his goiterish eyes shifted for a quick glance at June. "This is all confidential between us, Mr. Bernstein?"

"Of course it's confidential. Anything you tell me is confidential. And thank you for this, Kellerman." Marvin raised the list, half-raised himself. Understanding, Kellerman jumped up, ready to leave.

"A jewel of a man you are, Mr. Bernstein. A jewel. It's a pleasure to do business with you. And you'll, I hope, forgive my little outburst. I know I'm an old foolish man already, but still and all I like to like people and to trust them. Everyone has *tsouris.* If it's not one kind of trouble, it's another. What else can a person do but try to see good?" Kellerman leaned across the desk, extending his hand, whispered, "If you're maybe interested in Mr. Jack too—"

"You brought it up. I didn't." Marvin withdrew his hand.

"I realize. But just in case, I want you should know that Fleiss's union debt wouldn't be carried over. Also just in case, it happens I know who bought the name. It's a good name still, remember. If maybe you wanted to talk to someone, just in case, you should also know that a very good production man from up there is involved. Trebnitz. Morris Trebnitz. A very honest man. A personal friend. I could arrange . . ."

"We're not interested." Marvin's lowered head put an end to the meeting. "We don't buy dead businesses, only live ones. I told you that at the beginning. When you have more news, along *those* lines, give me a call. I'm sure my secretary will remember your voice."

Kellerman stepped backward, away from the desk. "It's a pleasure, Mr. Bernstein. When I have a chance to talk to someone who knows what he's doing, I'm happy to be of any service. Nothing is too much to do. Down in my office I always say to everyone how Bernstein from Greenstalks knows what he's doing."

"Thank you. Thank you very much." Marvin reached for a folder.

Kellerman bowed apologetically, stopped to shake June's hand. She led him out of the office before Marvin's anger had a chance to spill over and spoil what she recognized as one of his good moods.

The next perfect thing to happen was a perfectly timed call from Esther Kaufman: right on the heels of Kellerman's reluctant departure. "No, you're not interrupting a thing, Esther. Glad to hear from you so fast. I like speed."

Esther's idea was that he meet with a few designers she knew personally, ones she thought might be interested in free-lance work. "Of course they're all very talented, Mr. Bernstein. They all get top salaries."

"That's the only kind we want at Greenstalks. The top-salary kind. We always pay our people tops. Isn't that why you got to work on this project so fast, Esther?" Marvin waited for her response. Instead, what he got was silence. He was willing to wait. She was uncomfortable, not him.

"Whatever my reason is, Mr. Bernstein, *you* asked me to do something and I'm trying to comply. I've made a list of people and I'll send it over to you. They'll be expecting a call from you or Gary—I didn't know who would be handling this particular situation. Gary usually does."

"Send me the list. I'll pass it on to Gary. Also—hold on a second, Esther." Marvin found June's note in his kneehole drawer. "Esther? Is the name Hanssler on your list by any chance?"

"Yes, it is. He happens to be out of a job right now, but he's excellent. Very talented. He worked for—"

"Fine, Esther. You've done a great job. You'll be hearing from me soon."

And then it was Bruce's turn, as it worked out, to make things even brighter. He came in to remind Marvin of the promise made the night before. "Remember? I told you about the thing I was working on? Well, it's ready, and Gary's here and my father," a command performance, "so if you can come . . ." Of course he could come.

Bruce's crowded design room resembled the cramped insides of a closet more than it did the so-called creative heart of an expanding business. Originally, the space had been just another open section of the crescent-shaped workroom, but as the company grew bigger so did Bruce's estimation of his own importance.

He deserved private quarters too, like Gary's, only he needed to have easy access to his staff. What he devised was a narrow peninsula jutting out into the middle of the crescent with an entrance at the tip. The other sides had cutouts like kitchen serving counters in a diner. That way he had privacy as well as the privilege of peeking out on his workers whenever he felt like it. How he got anything done, how he kept tabs on what he was doing, mystified Marvin. Pieces of fabric dangled from shelves, from every available hook. The clothes he was copying were draped over chairs, across his desk, on his sketcher's table so that most of the time she had to work standing up. The two padded forms he used for fittings blocked the passageway from the entrance to the one wall window behind his desk. A mess. A pigsty of confusion. A man had to be part animal to stand it. Or an artist. Which Bruce claimed he was. And since he accomplished what he was supposed to accomplish, no one should spend time worrying about the procedure. This was his territory and he handled it his way.

Sam and Gary humored him. The artist in the family! Locked up in the back, out of sight, bothering nobody, except when he wanted to be appreciated. Like now. Sam leaned against the edge of a work table. Gary balanced his behind on the windowsill. Marvin could only hope that if he didn't move around too much the fabric piled behind his head wouldn't spill down and crush him.

"You see this form here?" Bruce wheeled it around so that each of them, especially his father, had a clear view of it. "Well, what's on it is my new idea."

Sam nodded, waiting patiently for the explanation. Bruce ran his hand through his hair, setting off a rain of dandruff which made Gary wince and turn briefly to look out at the sun shining down on Broadway. Marvin had a sudden desire for a half-dozen Gelusils.

"Anyway, it's what they call on Seventh Avenue a pantsuit." Inviting his father to come closer, to inspect the garment, Bruce stepped back from the form.

The habit of the old-time tailor took over. Sam rubbed the fabric, adjusted a button more securely in its hole, ran his index finger along the welted seam of a dangling pant's leg.

"Don't you like it, Pa?"

"Do I like it? Sure, I like it. But if such a thing becomes popular, they'll have to make forms that have legs. After all, how can you tell what's what if the pants hang from under the jacket?"

"That's true, but you can imagine what . . ."

"I can imagine all right. Can I imagine!" He smoothed the jacket's shawl collar. "I can imagine how history repeats itself. When I started out it was two pieces. Long skirts and blouses. So finally we put them together to make dresses and now they're going to take everything apart again. You think there's something new under the sun? There's nothing. Believe me. Everything goes round in a circle. But, still and all, I like it. What kind of fabric is this?"

"A synthetic, Pa. Like twill."

"Expensive?"

"This is, but we could get a knock-off, cheap. I checked it already. Anyway, what I thought . . . what I predict is that in a few years practically every girl, maybe even every woman, in America is going to need to have something like this in her closet. It's already a big item in England. That's where it really got started. With the Mods they call them. Even the big shots in Paris copied it. So naturally if Paris is doing it then the better market here is doing it. What I thought is we could get a jump in the cheap market. I believe in it, Pa. I really do. And it doesn't have to be seasonal either. You could do it in every kind of fabric. Double-breasted. Single. You could take the sleeves off. Make a long vest. Hey, Nita! . . . Give me those drawings you did." Dutifully, a nervous hand emerged from behind a hanging dress, offering a thick pile of sketches. Bruce grabbed them and passed them on to his father. Sam, satisfied by their weight, gave them to Gary, who riffled through them noisily before passing them on to Marvin. Marvin studied some of the drawings carefully. He liked the idea. Bruce paced impatiently.

"So what do you think, Pa?"

Shaking his head knowingly, remembering things past, resigning himself to things yet to come, Sam took hold of Bruce's arm and squeezed it affectionately. "What I think is that I'm glad you're my son. I like what you did. But I like most of all that you know what's going on. How you know is your business. As long as you know . . . Your mother I don't think will want such a thing in her closet but other women maybe will. I saw some already on Fifth Avenue this spring. It's very nice. It's practical too. Gary? You like it?"

"It's very chic. Very smart looking. What do you think, Marvin?"

"Me? You know I understand from nothing when it comes to fashion. But I like the idea. I also like these sketches." He handed them back to Bruce. "Lots of potential. Risky, I suppose. But what new thing isn't? If Bruce says it'll catch on, I'll take his word for it. He knows better than I do. The big question would be how we'd use it. You wouldn't want a separate division to manufacture them, would you?"

Sam moved past Marvin, anxious to get out of the cluttered room. "That you can decide with Bruce and Gary. You'll work it out. My only suggestion is that you keep it reasonable because you never know from one minute to the next how fast a fad comes and goes." He turned back. "You did very well, Bruce. Everything you do is good. Only maybe you could straighten up in here a little bit."

"Pa," Gary advanced on his father, "I've got something I want to discuss with you too. Can you have lunch with me?"

"With you I can have lunch any time. It's my pleasure, my son. We'll go to Al Cooper though, because my stomach is not up to itself. Some chicken soup would be good. I'm getting to be like Marvin in my old age."

"I don't wish it on you, Sam. Believe me."

They moved, single file, Sam leading, out of the office. When they reached the rotunda, Sam stopped the parade, surveyed the crowded benches, nodded greetings. Proudly, he fondled the white carnations on the corner of Olive's desk. Here everything was in order.

Just before Marvin stepped into his office the nonstop, piping sound of Adele's voice put an end to the morning's pleasure. Right on time. June was the captive audience. Adele was seated behind his desk in his chair. "It's about time. I've got a hairdresser's appointment in an hour." Marvin stood in front of the desk, looking down at the Bonwit Teller packages spread across the top, crushing his folders. "I'm very hungry, Marvin, so let's go to lunch right now." Discreetly, June moved off, returned to her typewriter. "Let's go to Al Cooper's. I'm in the mood for a lovely Jewish salad."

"No. Not Al Cooper's. Sam and Gary are going there."

"So? What's wrong with that? I haven't seen Gary in a long time."

"I said no. They've got business to discuss. Would you mind taking those goddamned packages off my desk!"

"I wanted to show you what I bought with your money. I got the most marvelous Bill Blass. I love his clothes. So elegant. And I got the most divine Gernreich bathing suits for the girls. I just hope they fit. Not that there's that much to them to fit into." She laughed loudly, picked at her auburn waves. Marvin was not amused. "You're not listening. That I can tell. And would you please try to control that . . . that disgusting noise. You sound like a pig."

"What noise?"

"I'm going to lunch, Mr. Bernstein."

Without turning, he nodded. Smart lady to get out fast.

"That burping! You could control it if you tried. Take some Gelusils. Do something. Don't just stand there gawking."

He moved a chair from along the wall to the side of the desk, settled noisily into it. He was going to have to endure her harangue for a while. Another part of the price for last night. But at least now she was going to have to rearrange herself to see him, to turn to him instead of his standing in front of her like some kind of bad boy about to be scolded. Position is everything in life. Which she knew too, but in a way that was much different from his knowing it. Even after seventeen years of marriage, almost seventeen; on July 4th, to be exact—his most active ulcer time and the Declaration of Independence never let him forget the anniversary—having to listen, as now, to her take-charge tone describe a new dress, a bathing suit, an expensive pocketbook, a new perfume—she'll talk so much she'll talk herself right out of lunch—or having to watch her diet-svelte, tennis-active body turn to vie with his impatience, or having to witness her healthy, rose-pale face redden with justified—yes, this time, remember, she's justified—anger as she purposely spread the tissue paper from her packages all over his desk, he was constantly reminded of, constantly saw proof of, constantly felt it like a kick in his sensitive gut just how different her knowing about position and its power was from his knowing it and just why that difference had made all the difference to him in his young life.

"I love lizard bags. I just couldn't resist it. Things like this never wear out. Don't you think it's beautiful? Marvin? You're not listening to me again!"

"I'm listening. I heard every word you said. And I'm going to suggest that you either clear up all that crap and go to lunch now, or we forget about it. What the hell did you come down here for anyway?"

"To make you miserable about what you did last night." First laughing, then lighting a cigarette, then searching for and not finding an ashtray—which, grudgingly, Marvin had to supply from his closet; otherwise, in her present mood, she would have set all his folders on fire—Adele began reassembling the packages, resumed a description, begun at breakfast after he had semi-apologized, of what he had missed—the guests, the food, the dancing—by not being at the Greek gala. It was the least she could do, she said, to fill him in on all the particulars. After all, he had probably been working very hard last night just so she could go on having all the parties she wanted to have. She was determined, as usual. And, just as usual, that also made him determined, to listen, to wait her out, to act unsurprised when she arrived at the punch line. Surely there was going to be a punch line, a command to go with the length of the performance, a special unrefusable—considering the circumstances of what he *had* done last night—request. More an order, an ultimatum it'll be. Such as a princess gives. Only this is a different kind of princess. This is a Jewish real-estate princess with a kingdom by the sea in Far Rockaway, a kingdom of new high-rise apartment houses her father made for her to play with, for her to inherit when he dies. That was the position she was born into, Adele Warshowski, now Bernstein. That was her marriage present to him: expectation. Along with a *zaftig* body and a medium-pretty face. All of which he had been glad to fall in love with. While he gave her . . . what for a present? What made her glad about him? Why did she choose or accept him? When she met him at a City–Brooklyn College dance what position did he have? What was he but a tall, thin, acned boy trying to hoist himself up from the Bronx? Trying to rise to her position? The only thing he could ever figure out was what her father said to her in front of him, what the old man was living to see happen. "Marvin? Don't worry about Marvin. A doctor he won't be, but I'll swear on the Torah he'll be something big enough to have from him anything you want." So that, plus she just liked tall men, no matter how they looked.

". . . and this one man . . . you met him. He's the art dealer from Greenwich, the one we bought the primitive from . . . well, he danced like a native Greek. Like he was born there. It was really something to see because he's a big man. Not big like you. He's also got some flesh on his bones and . . ."

"Excuse me for interrupting, Adele, but aren't you hungry? Because if you're not, I am. And if you want me to stop belching, I'm going to have to eat something right away or I'll spoil my whole afternoon. I've got a lot of work to do so you'll have to make up your mind right now."

"I made up my mind. I lost my appetite—for food, that is, not for other things. Must be the shopping and the heat—it's terribly hot outside

—and all that marvelous lamb I ate last night." One by one and with exaggerated, purposeful care she removed the packages from the desk, placed them on the tile floor alongside her chair, turned completely around to face him.

It was coming. She was ready to let him have it, just when she could see—he had straightened, moved to the edge of his chair—that he was balanced on the borderline between where impatience explodes into damn-the-consequences. What judgment she had! What a fine sense of timing.

"I've made up my mind that I'm going to Greece this summer. Maybe for the whole summer. With or without you. If the girls want to come, fine. If not, I'll go with my friends. That art dealer and his wife are going. So what do you think of that?" She lit another cigarette, recrossed her tanned legs into a new position of obvious comfort. "You don't need me around here. You've got plenty to do. That way you'll be able to stay here as late as you want without worrying about what I'm doing back at the ranch. I'm bored with going to Bermuda or St. Thomas for two weeks. You can go there—on your own—while I make a tour of the Greek islands. I need some cultural nourishment, not food." She lifted her packages effortlessly, stood up, started past him, stopped. "Incidentally, I called you here last night a few times and then gave up. You don't have to tell me where you really were. It doesn't matter because I'm sure it had something to do with business. You really work too hard, Marvin. Much too hard. But that's a quality I've always admired in you so don't worry about it. I'm not angry about last night either. I promise I'm not. I understand why you're so attached to this place and why you're so loyal to Sam and the boys. Only don't expect me to be. All right?" She continued moving calmly toward the door. "Try to get home earlier tonight for dinner. It's just the girls and us and I want to talk about going to Greece."

And then she was gone, leaving him at the side of *his* desk in *his* office. So let her go! Let her go to Greece. Let her go to hell. He was content to stay right where he was. . . . Nevertheless, tonight he would, he should go home earlier, for the girls' sake.

Chapter Nine

Since, ordinarily—as artistes in residence—Bruce and Gary would be the ones to interview designer hopefuls at Greenstalks, Marvin had to play his meeting with Phil Hanssler by ear. Eventually, Gary would get Esther's list. But for right now, Marvin wanted to satisfy his curiosity, play a hunch, do a little private investigation before the important part of his program was put into operation. Just testing the Bernstein iceberg principle—for Sam's potential benefit.

June brought in Phil Hanssler, who, looking up at Marvin, broke into self-confident laughter. "We must make quite a sight. You've got to be the tallest man I've ever seen." Surprised, Marvin continued to pump his hand. "Would you do me a favor, Mr. Bernstein, and sit down? My neck hurts."

Marvin laughed, frowned when June joined in, laughed again himself. It *was* a sight. David and Goliath. The long and short of it. Mutt and Jeff. He moved quickly around his desk, motioned for Phil to sit down.

"Esther told me you were big, but that's an understatement. You're a giant, Mr. Bernstein. An absolute giant." Phil hiked himself higher on the slippery Eames chair. "I hate these things. Even for me they're too small. I can imagine what you must suffer."

Marvin agreed. He also flashed another sour frown at June. This time he meant it, and she stopped laughing. Enough was enough. Openly, Marvin studied the smiling face across his desk. The smiling face studied him right back. "Do you have any sketches to show me, Mr. Hanssler?"

"Phil will do, and no, I don't have any sketches to show you. Only beginners do that. I'm not in the sketcher category any more. I'm a designer."

"How am I supposed to tell what you can do then?"

"I thought Esther would have told you that. But if she didn't, just talk to me. Ask me questions. You'll find out what you need to know." Phil folded his arms across his chest, prepared, it seemed to Marvin, for anything but winning friends.

"Esther told me about your talent. That's all."

Marvin, unsure of the correct interview procedure, stared at the folded arms, read Phil's nonchalant position as some kind of dare. But he certainly wasn't going to tell this guy to leave and come back with sketches. That would be like saying what wasn't the truth, that he couldn't do things any way but the ordinary way. So okay, Mr. Hanssler. You're on. If that's how you want to play it, fine with me. Perfect. A welcome relief from the nebs. A regular fifteen rounder with a real opponent who's got a breezy style. Great. But what kind of designer was this? Nothing about Phil Hanssler seemed to spell out designer: the stained linen summer suit, the polka-dot tie, the uneven fringe of hair, the nerveless, open-legged sprawl. Maybe the face did; it was childlike, but it was also virile, with searching, half-shut eyes that seemed to enjoy Marvin's scrutiny but were, nevertheless, innocent and honest. Marvin realized that what he saw was obviously just the top part. There was more, much more, going on underneath those good looks.

"Mr. Bernstein, I suppose you're deciding I come on pretty strong—that's just the way I am sometimes. But my information is that you're no slouch either. So I want to be prepared. And it wasn't Esther who told me. Don't turn on her if you don't like what I'm saying." Phil unfolded his arms, let them dangle over the sides of his chair. "You're the brain power behind the Greenstalk throne. That's common knowledge on the Avenue. Even *Women's Wear* reports it. You made this company, not the clothes. You're not the stylist. You're not the designer—I don't think Greenstalks has one—so what's the point of showing you sketches? What would they mean to you? If you end up being interested in me for whatever it is you have in mind—which, by the way, Esther wouldn't mention —it'll be because you dig me as a person. Then, if you want to know about my design ability, you can talk to people in the trade who know me, or you can call my last boss, or I'll even be glad to talk to the people here who know about such things. Like the Greenstalk boys. Maybe they're in a better position to judge, although, on the basis of the kind of clothes you make here, I doubt it."

"Hey, fella! Slow down." Marvin slapped the formica desk top. "Did you come up here to be interviewed or to make enemies?"

"Frankly, Mr. Bernstein, I don't know why I came up here. Esther just said go up and speak to you. So I came, with great reluctance. This company is too big for what I do. You're volume, and you're cheap. You dress most American women, which I'm not knocking. But I'm a *fashion* designer. I want to continue to be. Seventh Avenue's a different world, as I'm sure you've heard."

Marvin leaned over his desk, his eyes on a level with Phil's. "So I've heard, which is maybe why you're here." He paused, watching for some readjustment, some sign of interest to flicker somewhere on that handsome face. There was none. The grin stayed put, betraying nothing. "Whatever we have in mind here, I'll be glad to tell you about, after a while. When you stop being so critical."

"I'm not being critical. I'm just stating the facts. I respect your kind of company. *And* Jonathan Logan. *And* Russ Togs. You all make durable garments at a sensible price. Logan happens to give more fashion, but that's beside the point. What I'm trying to say is something very important to me, personally. Your kind of company doesn't really have any place for name designers. Where could I fit in? You sell a product like Dole sells pineapple. You don't need a creator. You need a packager. And if I'm a designer, I want to design, I want to be recognized, have my name on a label. When you work as hard as I do, you expect something more."

"How come if you work so hard Mr. Jack went out of business?" Marvin lifted his head higher, at an angle, as if he were listening for the bell that ended the first round.

Phil sighed, slid lower in his chair. "You must think I'm some kind of idiot. I come up here ready to tell you what's wrong with your company, without sketches, without a job. But one thing has nothing to do with another. Mr. Jack wasn't my fault. Obviously you know that or you wouldn't have me up here wasting your time. Besides, Mr. Jack is past history for me."

Marvin nodded, his expression, he hoped, admitting nothing. "Sam Greenstalk was telling me the story the other day. He's a good friend of Alex Fleiss, belongs to the same club or something."

"He must not have been a good enough friend to loan A. F. a million dollars."

"Only an enemy does that."

"Poor A.F. He had so many rich friends he didn't know what to do. No one wanted to treat him like an enemy. From such love and friendship spare me."

"In business only a fool expects help from a friend. The Garment Center's no social club. No one's giving anything away for nothing."

"That much I've learned, Mr. Bernstein. I don't expect help from any corner. I'd like it, but I don't *expect* it."

"That's the smartest way."

"I don't think it's smart, just realistic, unless you want to go join a revolution, which I'm too old to do."

"Too old? You can't be more than twenty-three, twenty-four. I feel like your father for Christ's sake."

"I'm older than that. How much, I won't say. It's bad for my career. And I've got a father of my own, thank you."

"You got a wife?"

"That I haven't got yet. Not that I'm supposed to have one. I'm a designer, remember."

"You're okay, Phil Hanssler. You're no designer I ever met. You're a *mensch*." Marvin wanted to reach out and pinch Phil's cheek. It was a crime for that face not to be smiling and laughing all the time, for that tapered body to contain even the slightest trace of bitterness. But it was. That was clear enough now; so were the secrets clear enough. Those were there in the squinting eyes, in the determined, tough-guy way Phil wanted to control the way this meeting went. So was the struggle, a kind of determined unwillingness to let the facts of present failure break his back. This guy was the genuine article. Someone to really talk straight to. No wind-up toy that answers yes to every question. "I'm curious about something. How come if you're as good as you say you are, you're still out of a job?"

"If that's all you're curious about, then I've got it made. I thought you were getting ready to kick me out of here." Phil glanced down at Marvin's big feet resting close to his own loafers. "You might change your mind when you hear my answer. Anyway, I just decided that it's got to be now or never for me. I'm tired of working so someone else can make money. I want to share the wealth my designs can pull in. But even before that happens I want to be able to design what I think is right, not what some pinky-ringed salesman tells me he's going to sell to his customers. I want to make sure the clothes I design are made the way I designed them. In order to do all that you've got to be the boss. That's exactly what I want to be. A boss and an owner. Someone who knows what the whole thing's about. Any other way is crap. Have you got that kind of offer for me, Mr. Bernstein?"

"Not exactly."

"I didn't think so. I told Esther not to waste my time and yours."

"How many times do I have to tell you to slow down? You lay every-thing on the line and you don't stop to take a breath. No beating around the bush with you, is there?"

"That's right. Not any more."

"Okay. But you don't happen to be wasting your time here. You're a little crazy, but I've listened to you. Now you listen to me for a minute. Relax. Sit back in your chair." Phil obeyed. "That's better. Don't get yourself in an uproar. If you're angry about something, don't make me your fall guy. I like you. I like your honesty. I don't know what's really eating you and you don't have to tell me. It's none of my business. All I've discovered so far is that you're a designer out of a job, that you've got plenty of ego, and that you're after something big. Great. So am I. So is Greenstalks. So you've come to the right place."

"Mr. Bernstein, I've gone through a lot recently. I'm tired, so don't kid me. It's not funny."

"Marvin's the name and I'm *not* kidding you. I know it's not funny." He stood up, moved quickly around the desk. "Why don't you come back here Monday afternoon? About three. I'll introduce you to the Green-stalks. Then we can talk some more. This afternoon I've got too much work to do so I'm going to have to kick you out now."

Phil remained seated, stunned for the moment. Marvin's hand, like a plumb line, fell on his shoulder, squeezed it. "You sure you know what you're doing?" Phil looked up at the pole-thin man beside his chair.

A smile, a twisted, meager smile that on someone else's face might have signified suffering, appeared at the corner of Marvin's mouth. "Get up already and let me worry about that. I don't do things I don't want to do. I can afford not to. You . . . I don't think you're up to that yet."

Confused, Phil shrugged, stood up. "Okay. If you say so. I don't know why, but I'll be here Monday."

For Monday, Marvin scheduled a tour of the Greenstalks first. He pa-raded Phil down each corridor, in and out of white-walled cubicles, back and forth through the white rotunda, and when the moment was right, when Phil seemed completely dizzied by the mazy movements in and out, then Marvin led him to Gary's office.

"Phil Hanssler?" Gary smiled his warmest and therefore most meaningless kind of smile. "I've heard of you. You get sketches in *Women's Wear*, don't you?"

"Occasionally."

"I read a comment of yours a while back. About paper dresses. Did you really mean what you said?"

"Truthfully, I don't remember what I said. It was ages ago, in another life somewhere."

'The reason I ask is because I've got a great idea about paper dresses. Have you ever thought about working in paper?"

"No thank you, Mr. Greenstalk. Before I design paper dresses I'll commit myself to an institution."

Gary's dimples disappeared.

Marvin nudged Phil in the small of the back. They walked off rapidly, Phil taking three steps to every one of Marvin's. "That's what I mean about not having wisdom. Just nod in the future. Gary's a good fellow. He means well."

"I'm sure. And so do I. Can't you tell that, Marvin?"

Bruce was back to his pantsuit idea when they came within earshot, telling his father how, now that everyone approved, the big decision was to pick the fabrics, settle on a price, meet with Marvin on how to merchandise it.

"Excuse me, gentlemen," Marvin parted hanging twists of printed cotton at the entrance, "but I've got someone here I want you to meet. Phil Hanssler . . . Where the hell are you?"

"I'm right behind you. If you'll just move inside. Meaning no disrespect, but what is this place, a rumpus room?"

"It's a design room." Bruce was not amused, but his father was. Shaking hands, he pulled Phil forward out of danger.

"You people are *all* giants, Mr. Greenstalk. I feel like Alice in Wonderland."

"Phil was the designer at Mr. Jack, Sam." Marvin's hand returned to Phil's shoulder, moved him another step forward, as if he were displaying a prize he had just won.

"Oh, so you're the young man. I heard a lot about you from Alex. Only the best things. It's a shame about Alex, no? If I could have helped him . . . But you know how it is with a sinking ship." Sam offered the palms of his hands up to heaven. "I'm glad, at least, Marvin saved *you*."

"It's not certain yet that he has."

Smiling paternally, Sam placed his hand on Phil's free shoulder. "If

Marvin shows you around, Marvin has an idea. That's Marvin. Listen to him. He knows. From me you won't hear too much. I'm the silent one. My sons and Marvin handle everything." He stepped back, turned, pointed at the form. "You're a designer, Philip, so what do you think about this that my son is doing? You can be frank. Don't be afraid to say."

"I'm not afraid." Phil approached the form, his eyes narrowing for professional perspective. As he did, a young girl appeared, materializing out of nowhere, it seemed. She smiled, spoke up in a great rush, brushing her long flaxen hair. "Remember me at all, Mr. Hanssler? Nita Neary? I was in one of your classes at Parsons when you taught there? I'm a friend of Pat Pearson's."

"Of course I remember you." Phil led her forward. "What are you hiding back there for? You were one of the most talented girls in that class." He turned on Bruce, whose anger was mounting. "She's a great talent. Why do you bury her back there under all that wool?" And then, to Nita, "How did you end up working here, of all places?"

"If you don't mind, Mr. Hanssler!"

"But I do mind, Mr. Greenstalk. It's a madhouse in here." Phil's hands came to rest at his hips, his head lifted to stare Bruce down to his size.

Quietly, Nita disappeared behind a bolt of fabric.

Marvin leaned his head against the edge of a shelf, unworried. Phil could take care of himself. No doubt about it.

Sam Greenstalk was less certain. "My son has an artist's temperament. You, of course, can understand that." He stepped between the two of them. "Bruce works in his own way. He styles our lines and he does a good job. Nita helps him and she's paid very well, so don't worry about that. It's no sweatshop here, I can assure you."

"You asked me about the pantsuit, Mr. Greenstalk, so I'll give you *my* artistic opinion."

Bruce stood protectively alongside the form. Now that his workmanship was about to be judged by a professional, an outsider that first Marvin and now his father had let into the inner sanctum, he wanted to set the record straight. "I'm no designer and I don't set myself up to be. I never went to school for it. I copy. That's all I do."

"Nothing wrong with that. As long as you copy the right things, it's great." Phil touched the sleeve where it joined the shoulder, ran his hand down the welted seam on the dangling trouser leg. "A beautifully made sample. Nice fabric. Right details on the jacket. An excellent copy of an expensive model. As good as they do it on the Avenue. You must have some expert tailors working for you."

"You see, Pa?" Bruce let go of the form. "I know what to copy."

"What do you plan to do with it now? That's a lot of fashion for the Greenstalks image."

But before Bruce or Sam could tell Phil, Marvin interrupted, recaptured his prize. His hand found its now familiar spot on Phil's shoulder, moved him toward the hidden entranceway. "You'll have another chance to talk about that, Bruce. I just wanted you all to meet this guy before I get down to offers." Marvin looked to Sam for a sign.

"Offer him, Marvin, whatever you want." Sam shook Phil's hand, but Phil's attention had shifted up to Marvin, who saw in those half-shut, searching eyes the same mixture of anger and relief he had seen in them on Friday. The guy liked and didn't like what was happening to him.

Marvin said nothing until they were back in his office and seated, facing each other. "Okay. So they were impressed with you. Now we can proceed."

Phil folded his arms across his chest. "Marvin, I'm going to have to tell you again. I just don't see myself working here."

"No problem, because you won't be working here exactly. What I've figured out so far is that you'll be on your own, you'll . . ." June stepped into the office; Marvin waved her away. "I'll call you when I need you. Go to the lounge for a while. Take a rest. . . . You'll do a free-lance line. A oneshot. If that works out, then we'll see. As soon as our fiscal year ends, which will be in a few weeks, I'll see things clearer. I'll be able to go to the board with something more. Meanwhile, you'll be on salary, you'll help Bruce, you'll consult with Gary, you'll get to know the organization."

"With Gary? On paper dresses? You've got to be kidding me!"

"Goddamn it, shut up and listen!" Phil sat up, unfolding his arms. "I'm putting myself out on a limb, remember, when I've got plenty of other safer bets to follow up. I expect a little sacrifice from you. You want money, right? Lots of it? You want to be a topnotch designer? Okay. What I'm telling you is that if you join Greenstalks now and you prove to be as good as you say you are, within five years' time you'll have everything you ever wanted."

"You're quite a man, Marvin. I'm impressed with you too. But I'm also skeptical. Couldn't you just tell me how and why you intend to make all my dreams come true? I mean, you're not exactly a fairy godmother type."

"And you're no Cinderella, but it's the same kind of story, without the magic." Marvin raised his hand, folded back all the fingers but one, pointed that at Phil, waved it back and forth. "When I came to this company, I promised Sam Greenstalk that he was going to become a multimillionaire. Very soon he will be. So will I." The finger was lowered. "This company's expanded to five times its original size. In a few months our stock will split again. In five more years it'll double that. I'm not talking bullshit. I can prove everything I say." He slapped the pile of folders on his desk. "But I don't have to prove it to you. You can take my word for it. And if I make you an offer, it's as good as gold. Eventually, you'll own stock. You'll be part of our biggest growth. That's the kind of chance you're getting. It's the chance of a lifetime so you better think it over seriously."

Phil's cheek muscles began twitching. Marvin watched the tiny tremor, saw the ruddy skin pale. So the boy's been rocked, hit hard right in the soft center of all his ambitions. Good. He needs that, and more. That's a legitimate part of the game. Offensive maneuvers. Bluffing. That's what the great Mr. Bernstein was doing. Because now that he'd said and done this much, what did he really plan to do next? How could he utilize this guy? Ever since Sam had turned down the idea of selling out, thoughts, like loose threads, had been blowing around in his head, refusing to tie together—until now. Now, and even while he was speaking, a form had been taking shape, a bright dot of a bigger, still vague pattern had been moving closer, a pattern that would require, when it was completely visible, Phil Hanssler as its center. Marvin felt sure of that now. A coincidence it should happen this way, from out of the blue, from Esther Kaufman, from Sam's casual hints.

"I really don't believe it, Marvin. You've got me hypnotized or something." As if it were being pulled by strings, Phil's head moved from side to side, was lowered, rested. "The other night I was sitting in my apartment trying to imagine just this kind of thing happening to me. Of course I didn't think it would. It couldn't happen. It just doesn't any more or, at least, not to me."

"Well, believe me, it's about to." Marvin was smiling, a real smile. He stood up. "Look, Phil, why don't you go home now—you look a little tired. Come back on Wednesday morning. Say about ten. I'll have a contract drawn up for you by then."

As if in a trance, Phil raised himself, his shoulder adjusting to Marvin's waiting hand. "Whatever you say. Ten o'clock's fine."

"Can you find your way out alone?"

"Yes. Sure. Thank you."

Marvin followed him to the corridor, watched his slow, stiff steps through the rotunda, waited until he disappeared beyond the Thermopane doors. Only when footsteps sounded behind him did he return to his desk. They were June's.

She held a stack of folders fresh from the Xerox room. "Mr. Bernstein, I'm sorry to bother you but I've got to."

"What's the trouble?"

"Well, I went to the lounge before like you suggested and I was sitting there talking to some of the other girls about . . . about girl things. Nothing important. I don't like to *yenta* when it comes to my work. I was only mentioning to the girls that Phil Hanssler was in with you that very minute because a lot of them used to buy wholesale up at Mr. Jack. They liked his clothes. Anyway, all of a sudden, Barney Susskind who's always complaining to you how he doesn't have a minute to sit down he's so overworked here . . ."

"Will you please get to the point already! What did Barney do?"

"It's not what he did but what he said that I thought I should tell you about. Barney said he had lunch with Kellerman from the union the other day and in the course of the conversation Kellerman mentioned a Morris Trebnitz who's going into the deal to reopen Mr. Jack along with Phil Hanssler."

"You sure he said that? You sure he wasn't just kidding about Hanssler?"

"Positive. I even made him repeat it. I know I shouldn't have opened my mouth, but naturally Phil Hanssler's name was on my mind because you just waved me out of the office and . . ."

"Will you please put that stuff down!" Marvin's head snapped back. He stared up at the pale moons in his white ceiling. "So that's what he's up to. That's what he's trying to pull on me. Well, we'll see about that."

Just then, Sam, on his way home, stepped into the office. He only wanted to let Marvin know that he liked the boy: "A very goodlooking chap too. You think he's talented the way Fleiss said?"

"From what I hear, yes. Esther Kaufman told me he was. My other contacts agree. But you can be sure I'm checking out all the facts, Sam."

"Fine. You go ahead then, Marvin. Do whatever you're planning. It'll be right." He started out, stopped at the doorway. "One thing not to do is to call Alex Fleiss. From him you'll get nothing worthwhile about the boy or anything else. A loser is a loser. Friend or not. The poor old fart . . . You should excuse my language, June." Sam bowed apologetically and was gone.

"Okay. Now we'll see. You get Kellerman on the phone. Tell him to send Trebnitz up to see me on Wednesday morning. Exactly ten-fifteen. Have him call you back to make sure Trebnitz can be here on time. Don't say anything else to him. Then tomorrow afternoon call Hanssler and remind him his appointment's for ten, ten sharp, because I've got a tight schedule. Understood?" He waved her away, then called her back, unsure himself for an instant why he had. Everything was happening so fast. "Before you go home tonight make sure you finish those contracts for the lingerie deal. Get started on the ones for the knit house. I'll need those by Thursday. I'll also need one for Phil Hanssler before Wednesday. You'll get that to type as soon as I check it out with our lawyer."

"I'll try to finish it all."

"Don't try, June. Do."

"I've only got two hands, Mr. Bernstein."

"So I've noticed. You know somebody who's got more?"

A flash fire erupted in his stomach. The sound of the telephone being dialed, June's polite voice only made it worse. Not even a million Gelusils would help now. But that's all he had to reach for. He bent sideways, chewing, waiting, as if he were on the pot, for a letup, for at least a temporary release, even though he knew that none would come. That's the whole hard story: facing the daily business facts of life and getting ulcers. There's never any letup. No release. In the beginning, in the middle . . . only at the end. Any other kind of story was just Mother Goose, manufactured by cowards to cover up the real truth.

And once you admit the real truth, you act from the winner-takes-all principle. You don't sit around on your ass hoping and praying for miracles to happen, for a golden chance to be dropped into your lap like Hanssler said he was doing. You fight for it. You do one thing in the beginning, and then another, and then you're on your way, changing directions sometimes, sometimes taking detours, but always moving further and further ahead toward whatever it is you're after, using every tool—including Gelusils—you can get your hands on.

The way Sam Greenstalk did when he opened a man's tailoring shop on the Lower East Side, which was the only thing he knew how to do when he came from Poland. And instead of men customers he gets ladies, so a whole lifetime is altered instead of a man's suit. And from his profits he buys a small sweatshop and makes shirtwaists. Then he makes skirts and blouses, finally joins the pieces together to make a dress, one piece, a ready-to-wear product that begins a new era, a New Deal for the American woman. Sam did the something he knew how to do, and he took advantage of a war when it came and just kept on going. That was the secret: not to look back and say *oy vay*, but always to look ahead to what's coming next and to be prepared to *make* the chances happen that can change your life. Use your brain—if you have one—not your heart. Look at the facts the way they exist, not the way you *wish* they were. If you get an ulcer, you get an ulcer. If you develop certain specialized appetites, certain protective outlets, you put them, keep them, in their place. You study a column of numbers and you have faith that the story of those numbers counts for more, in the long run, than all the stone columns in every church and monument in every city in every part of the world, regardless of what the guidebooks say. And, if you know that, then consider yourself lucky.

"Are you okay, Mr. Bernstein? You look . . . peculiar."

"What's so special about that? Don't I always look peculiar?"

June shrugged. "Anyway, it's all set with Trebnitz."

Eventually the contracts were typed and placed on his desk. Eventually she went to the ladies' room for her pre-going-home washup. Eventually Gary stepped into the office to give his okay on the kid, a lukewarm okay. "But you know what you're doing, Marvin. That's for sure. And Bruce likes him so you can use him there if you want. He's got class. Maybe too much class for us. If you could tone him down a little . . ." Eventually even Gary was gone.

The hum of silence grew stronger. He was alone for a while, the way he liked to be, with the written proof of new acquisitions in front of him to read through and feel good about. Something substantial to balance against the merging bits and pieces of deals yet to come, yet to be enjoyed. This was his kind of guidebook and told in the specialized language of his deepest understanding: stock-option clauses and capital gains; interest rates on loans and time-fixed repayments; leverage weapons and profit-sharing incentives dangled at the end of the fiscal rainbow. We loan and invest because we have faith in your potential growth. All you have to do is build your profits, pay back the loan. Meanwhile, we watch, we wait, we prod, and just before the potential becomes real, before the loan is paid back, we slip our offer to you: healthy, happy Greenstalk stock in exchange for 51 per cent of your business; the chance to grow up with us, to feel protected from the fickle finger of short-term reverses, to belong to something really big. A fair deal. The American way. The simple science of the honest-to-God screw. As honest as the next guy. Man to man—he checked his watch—or man to woman. Or both, for that matter.

I really am as honest as the next guy, Adele honey. You invested in me, I worked hard for you, you received your reward. No complaints. You demanded and I supplied. More money. More clothes. Two daughters. A house. Enough sex for our time of life. No shirking.

He did all he said he was going to do, for her and everyone else. Signed, sealed, and delivered. So he deserved his own little pleasures once in a while. Let her go to Greece. Let her get laid elsewhere. He'd do what he wanted to do. In his own harmless way. He only did what most people he knew didn't have the guts to do, what most people stopped themselves from doing. So what's so terrible about his way? All there are are men and women. So why not both together on occasion if that's what's needed to keep the body in working order? If Sam knew, he'd have a conniption. Or maybe he'd join in. Gary would. A sure thing. Not Bruce. And Adele? And what about Phil Hanssler? AC-DC? Handsome. Sophisticated New Yorker. We'll see what we shall see about him. One step at a time.

Because, of course, business comes first. Tuesday comes in between. Then, Wednesday morning. Hanssler and Morris Trebnitz meet by accident. A surprise party . . . And so Mr. Jack becomes part of Greenstalks, eventually.

For the last hour he had been deciding how to work it, how to get that name cheaply, how to test Hanssler's honesty and determine what way he could or should be used. And all for a name! Mr. Jack. What a thing to call a woman's dress company! The guy who thought that one up ought to have his head examined. Even so, that new blossom will be added to the old stalk.

He stood up, stretched—it's home for rest and relaxation. Not much fun, perhaps, but hard-working fathers and providers are not scheduled for too much fun. Those, Mr. Bernstein, are *your* facts of life, the columns on your balance sheet. So go to Larchmont already. Go get the train and shut up. Adele will probably expect that much, especially tonight. A family dinner. Amen. You're sad tonight, remember. You're disappointed. She's going away without you. For the whole summer. To Greece yet!

Chapter Ten

Phil Hanssler arrived at ten minutes after ten. Subdued, expectant, he sat at the edge of his chair, balancing himself. He wore the same linen suit he had worn on Monday but with a different polka-dot tie.

"Didn't you take your suit off all week?" Today Marvin would lead the band.

"Only to take a shower. I felt superstitious about wearing it again. Like if it's all a dream, I want to be dressed for the part."

"It's no dream. It's all real, as you'll see in a few minutes. You had a good week so far?"

"You're kidding? I couldn't sleep. I drank so much my ulcer hurts. Other than that, I'm fine. Ready for anything. So what's it going to be?"

"A good Jewish boy like you drinks so much? I pity your poor father. What else do you do too much of?"

"None of your business." Phil slid back in his chair.

Marvin pursued; he had the ball. He also had Phil's contract in his desk drawer. "Everything's my business."

"Not with me, sweetheart. Not until you own your small part of me."

"No one wants to own you. We're just going to pay for your talents. So don't get fresh now and spoil it. Everyone the other day liked you."

"Glad to hear it. That'll really help my career."

"You don't want people to like you?"

"Yes, I want people to like me. But *everyone* likes me. That can get to be a problem."

"It's not one of mine. I'm not exactly the likable type."

"Sure you are. You're obviously a king among men. And I'm just a knave, which is the first thing I'm determined to change about myself, if I can ever get you to start talking straight this morning. Do you have my contract or are you stalling?" Phil plunged his hands deep inside his jacket pockets, winced, leaned to the side. "Sorry, but my stomach is in a bad way."

Marvin extended a strip of Gelusils. "Chew these."

"No thanks. I hate them."

"Suffer then."

"I will, and do, all the time."

"That's because you don't live right. You don't think before you talk. You come in here asking to be thrown out instead of relaxing and listening to me." Marvin checked his watch, glanced across at June. If Trebnitz was on time, the curtain should rise in a few minutes. "The free-lance line and the consultant thing, remember, are only until I can square the big plans with Mr. Greenstalk. As chairman of the board, his approval comes first. When you're a public firm, you can't just go jumping into everything half-cocked. That's something you'll have to learn and understand about big business. The process is slow, but eventually everything gets done. According to all my information, you've got the talent so in the interim my plan is to get you going on the free-lance line. You'll get a straight fee—twenty-five thousand. You'll be in charge. No interference from anybody." Phil sat up; the tiny tremor was beating in his cheek. "Everything your way. You hire the workers you want, find the space you need—I can help with that. All we'd do is merchandise the line. Put it out under our label as a special designer group of clothes. Maybe we could even have your name on it. How does that grab you?"

The signs of struggle surfaced on Phil's face—Marvin was attentive to it, relished it—a struggle between satisfaction and doubt, between relief and anger with himself for feeling relieved. "What kind of line do you want? So far that's what you haven't mentioned and, as far as I'm concerned, that's the real problem. I can't design—I won't design cheap clothes for you."

"Will you just shut up with cheap already! We don't want you to design cheap. That's the whole point. We want better sportswear. Stuff that doesn't compete with what we have. We're not as dumb as you think we are. We want to offer our customers novelty, like a Greenstalks boutique, at a higher, but reasonable price. What you call medium."

A short, hat-turning man appeared in the doorway. Marvin stood up, and Phil, noticing for the first time the chair next to his, turned to see what was happening. Confused, he looked from Morris to Marvin and back to Morris. "What the hell is this? What are you doing here?"

"I know from nothing, Philly."

"You never met Mr. Bernstein before?"

"Never, Philly. I never had the pleasure." Morris bowed stiffly, sat down when Marvin pointed to the chair. "I'm happy to see you. For a whole week already I was calling you. You look tired." He squeezed Phil's shoulder.

Phil pushed his hand down. "Forget how I look. What I want to know is what you're doing here."

"Doing? I'm doing nothing. My friend Kellerman from the union told me I should come up to see this gentleman. So I came. I'm here. That's what I'm doing, Philly. And you? What are you doing here?"

Marvin intervened. "Glad you could come, Mr. Trebnitz. Phil and I were just deciding about his working for us."

"For you? He's taking a job with Greenstalks? It's the truth, Philly?"

"Why does that surprise you so much, Mr. Trebnitz?

"Surprise? Who's surprised? It's only that the last time I spoke to him on the phone . . . remember I told you, Phil? . . . I told him . . . something . . . about something else for him to . . ." He looked to Phil for help, turned his Panama hat in ever-faster circles.

So now both of them were nervous: Phil because he had concealed certain facts of his real situation, perhaps; Morris because he had let his secret slip out so quickly. Just the kind of development Marvin had hoped for. "I think you could safely tell me about it, Mr. Trebnitz. Phil didn't tell me all, but if it's about a better deal for him, better than my offer, I wouldn't want to spoil it. It's *his* future."

Morris chose silence.

Phil couldn't. "It's not important. Morris knows I'm not interested. I've told him over and over again I wasn't. It's not what I want. You wouldn't be interested either. It's a plan to refinance Mr. Jack." Phil stopped Morris's hands. "Don't take it so to heart. It's a crazy idea. Sweet, but crazy."

"Why is it so crazy?" Marvin was sure he sounded uninterested. "Maybe it is worthwhile. You're identified with the company, Phil. The buyers probably know that. It's only good business sense for whoever's behind the plan to try and get you to go with them. Who are the people anyway, Mr. Trebnitz?"

Anxious, still off balance, Morris looked up at Marvin, then at Phil, whose expression seemed to say, Do whatever you want, Morris. It's your turn. "To tell the truth, Mr. Bernstein, I don't think I should say another word." Morris's normally flushed face had gone pale and flaccid. "It wouldn't be kosher for me to say who. They're just people who don't know from the dress business. They want to invest a little—"

"You don't seem to trust me, Mr. Trebnitz. And that's not kosher either. Kellerman led me to believe you were a different kind of man. All I'm trying to do here is get at the facts. That's all. Maybe I know some of the people involved. It's a small world. Maybe I can help you." Marvin's fingers drummed a dull, waiting rhythm on his desk. Morris chose silence again. "Okay. Have it your way. I don't care. I asked you up here only to offer you some kind of job, as a favor to Kellerman, but if you—"

"Excuse me for interrupting, *Mr. Bernstein!*" Now Phil's face turned pale, last-straw pale. He was receiving the message. "Something shitty is going on here. You had your secretary call yesterday to make sure I'd arrive on time. You also asked Morris up here for the same time. You wanted us here together, didn't you, Mr. Bernstein? It's no coincidence it happened, so don't try to hand me any of that crap. Couldn't you realize that one thing I'm not is a dope? Come on! Level with me. What's *your* angle? What are you after? I didn't lie to you the other day *or* this morning. I'm not interested in being a part of any Mr. Jack deal. That's final. Before Morris got here you were ready to offer me the world. You were supposed to have a contract for me. Now I begin to see that maybe the world you're offering has conditions attached to it. I'm learning, Mr. Bernstein. I'm learning fast. And I can tell you frankly that I don't like what I'm learning." Phil was on his feet, circling his chair, yelling. "I happen to be out of a job, so don't fuck around with me."

"Watch your language first of all, there's a lady present. And then sit down. I don't like to be yelled at. Not by you. Not by anyone." Marvin's big hands clutched the farther edge of his desk. "Go ahead! Sit down! You're in my office so you'll do what I tell you to do." Phil's shoulders sagged, but he stood for a moment longer staring down at Marvin's upturned face. "That's better. Now get some control of yourself and don't look so miserable."

Phil sat grimly, arms folded, crushing his polka-dot tie. Morris was rigid, immobilized. His hat had fallen to the floor.

"I don't think I have to lecture either of you gentlemen on how things work in the business world. You've both been around enough, especially you, Mr. Trebnitz." Marvin frowned at the hat on the floor. Morris quickly picked it up. "Our company is always interested in what's going on. We're always interested in hearing about what's new in the market. That's how we keep growing. We don't sit still here. We keep expanding and we don't plan to stop. You don't know half the things we're into. Just take my word for it. Right now it's only important for you to know that no grass is growing under our feet. I've got a job to do here and I make damn sure I do it—and with the right people." He looked directly at Phil. "I don't care *bupkes,* not one lousy bean, for this Mr. Jack situation. But, if I thought it had potential as a Greenstalk investment, you can rest assured I'd want to listen to what anyone could tell me about it. Mr. Jack was once a very big name in fashion. Even I with my cheap *shmates* know that much. Maybe it could be again. Maybe if it opened with the right backing, with you as the designer *and* as a principal, it could be bigger than it ever was. Who the hell knows? All we're doing right now is talking about ifs. We're speculating. What did I know about your other deal until now? Your coming to work for us has nothing to do with this other thing. Make damn sure you understand that, once and for all!"

Phil was responding to Marvin's version of the truth, but the slant of his head, his eyes said that he was still testing it. So let him. He'll give in. He wants to.

"And you, Mr. Trebnitz." Morris jumped to attention. "What difference does it make to you who owns that name or who pays your salary? You're too old to be sentimental about such things. You're a production man. A very good production man, according to my information. If it wasn't for the two of you, that company would have died a long time ago. Okay. So all I've been trying to do is save what's worth saving from the wreck. Mr. Greenstalk wanted me to. And now, suddenly, I hear about another prospect, so I inquire. That's my job. To find out. Anyway *I* choose. And if I find out there's nothing in it for us, there's nothing in it. Finished. Over. On to something else." He pointed his Uncle Sam finger at Phil. "The only important item for you to remember, kiddo, is that around here *I'm* the one who decides what's for us and what's not. You don't decide *for* me. Understood?"

"*Oui, Mein Herr.* Understood. So what did you decide about Mr. Jack?"

"I'll let you know."

Morris, his hands at rest finally along the brim of his hat, sighed loudly, announcing by the depth of his sigh just how deeply he had understood Marvin's words and his own predicament. "You should excuse me, Mr. Bernstein, for saying, but one thing about me you got wrong. Sentimental I'm not. Old, yes. A good production man? That I'll agree.

Good enough. But about something else you said a minute ago you're mistaken. It matters to me who pays my salary. It matters if maybe I pay myself my own salary for once, because it's not written down anywhere in a book that a production man can't also become a boss." Smiling bitterly, resigned to this new play of fate, he looked over at Phil. "And Michael said to me, maybe he'll make me a partner if I'll put in a little money. So naturally I thought, sure, why not? At my age do I have to work so hard every day for the rest of my life? And for someone else? Why not once before I die I should be a boss? It wouldn't hurt anything. What would it hurt? Tell me, Philly, what?"

"Nothing, Morris. Not a thing."

"Sure, nothing. Except I can see already that it's not going to be. If you're not in it, I'm not in it too. Without you, what do they have, those kids? What do they know?"

"Don't make me the villain in the piece, Morris. It's not fair. I never promised I'd go in with the deal. I can't stand around and wait for those guys to get going. I have to live too. I need money to live. And who knows if they ever really will get started?"

"No one knows. No one knows nothing." Morris patted Phil's arm affectionately. "Anyway, Mr. Bernstein, I don't think I should talk about the people."

"Why you being so loyal? Those guys aren't giving you something for nothing. They need *you*. Apparently, they need Phil. Without the two of you what have they got? But you have it your way. Don't tell me anything. I know all I want to know now."

"So if that's the case, Mr. Bernstein, what do you want to start in with me for? I'm just a person. An old man. You said it yourself I should know better. All right, so I know better. I know what a little person is in a big business. I know plenty." He stood up so his back was to Marvin. "Philly darling, you should better listen to me. I know what I'm saying. Michael's backers have plenty of money. Money is no problem. You'll be an owner with me and Michael. You wouldn't have to put in a penny. You'll design. You'll own. You'll be whatever you want."

"Thank you, Morris. Thank you very much, but no thanks. I know what Michael's friends are like. All you have to do is talk to Michael to know. If you end up owning one percent of any business they back, you'll be lucky. Those guys know nothing about the dress business and they care even less. Michael knows maybe a little bit more. All they have are big plans with no idea how to make them work. They only talk a big game and talk is the cheapest commodity on the open market. They're going to do this, that, and the other, Michael told me. They'll corner everything. They'll buy up the world. It's crap, Morris. And, personally, I'm tired of crap. I've had it with the losers. I'm sorry to say it, but you'll have to do what you want to do, and I'll have to do what I want to do. That, sweetheart, is how I view my life from here on in."

Morris started walking out of the office, stopped when Marvin called to him.

"I think it would be best for everyone concerned, Mr. Trebnitz, if you didn't say anything about this meeting to this Michael character."

"I'll say what I'll say, Mr. Bernstein. Michael is my friend." Morris bowed to June, disappeared into the corridor.

"Well, that, as they say, is that. Mr. Jack comes to an end once more." Phil slapped his legs emphatically.

"You never can tell. Strange things happen in the dress business every day." Marvin did his best to smile convincingly, an action which, since the meeting had produced so far just what he had hoped it would, didn't tax his energy. Now Trebnitz would run and tell this Michael whoever that Greenstalks might be interested in Mr. Jack, that Phil was somehow involved with Greenstalks, and, if his hunch was right, this Michael guy would soon be sitting and doing just what Phil was doing now: picking at his nails. "Is this guy a friend of yours too?"

"Michael Matthew Morgan? A friend? I hardly know him. He worked in our showroom selling. He's young and with nothing much else than what he dreams about." Phil rubbed his stomach.

"It hurts? Take a Gelusil."

This time Phil accepted them, chewed, crunched, frowned.

Marvin waited, and then, as if nothing had happened since then, began once more to outline the free-lance plan, certain now of what it would lead to, careful not to reopen any Mr. Jack talk. That, for the time being, would bake in the oven. Right now the icing had to be prepared. ". . . And the twenty-five thousand will be your money to handle. You'll keep a record of how you spend it. Whatever you have to pay out comes from that. Whatever's left over is yours. You'll get a consultant's salary and if the one-shot plan works out, there'll be plenty more where that came from. We'll work out the production and the merchandising. I'll find space for you to work in, help you get whatever equipment you need. Tomorrow afternoon you can meet with Gary and Bruce and discuss the kind of sportswear you want to do. I'll expedite everything with Sam and the board. The rest will be up to you. You'll design and you'll supervise. That should make you happy."

"It does, but what about my contract?" The corners of Phil's mouth showed dabs of white from the Gelusils.

Marvin produced the contract, handed it across to Phil, and spotted, in the corner of the drawer, just before he closed it, the folded, tooth-marked piece of paper with the names that Esther Kaufman had sent him. No need to pass that on to Gary for a while. "You'll find it's all in order. Our lawyer checked it out."

"Well, it happens that I have an Uncle George, the accountant. I called him and he wants to see it before I sign."

"If you want to, sure."

"I notice that you haven't mentioned anything about my name being on the label. What about that?"

"I'm working on it, but it doesn't look too good for now. It's not a Greenstalk policy. In the future, after your first line's a success, then we can change the policy. So you better get to work in a hurry. By this afternoon I'll have something to tell you about the space. Meanwhile you can see about hiring workers and . . ."

"You're like a whirlwind, Marvin. Now it's your turn to slow down a minute."

"Never. You'll have to learn to keep up with me. You have no time to waste. The sportswear season is even earlier on Broadway than on Seventh Avenue. By this time in June, fall's almost dead in the stores. You'll start with spring. And maybe you could do something with Bruce's pantsuit idea. As a personal favor to me." He leaned back suddenly—but not because of any discomfort—he wanted to be in a better position to see and enjoy, while he went on speaking, the rise and fall of conflicting thoughts reflected openly on Phil's face.

This guy's confidence was not broken—no, it would take a lot more than losing a job to do that—but dented, weakened in spots. And why not? Mr. Jack had closed over a month ago and during that time he'd been shopping around, hoping something big would happen, getting offers probably, always the wrong kind and from the wrong people, having interview after interview probably, being tied to the telephone, rejecting everything while he waited for the right chance. And here it was, where he least imagined he would find it. As Marvin saw it—Phil couldn't be expected to see it as clearly yet—the richness of possibility was maybe too much for his stomach to take. An Achilles heel, that stomach. But a good sign too. Marvin felt it in his bones that it was all going to turn out happily ever after.

". . . so there's no telling where this can lead to, Phil. All I know, and this I can guarantee, barring the unexpected of course, is that it will lead someplace you've never been to before. It will lead to more money than you've ever had before. You told me you wouldn't mind that one bit. So, if you really meant it, then you're doing the right thing. . . . I can tell by how quiet you are you're not sure. I can understand that. It's only natural. It's not exactly what you had in mind. You're afraid you'll get lost in the shuffle, like your friend Trebnitz. My answer is you won't. You can't. Not your kind." Grateful for that, but anxious nevertheless, Phil sat poised at the front of his chair. "Don't forget, also, that we're taking a chance. A twenty-five-thousand-dollar chance to start with. Class we don't have yet, but good, solid gold we're willing to invest to get it. If everything works out with you, you'll get all the money and all the fame you ever wanted. I'll shake hands on that."

Phil jumped up, extending his hand. "It's a deal and I'm happy . . . I think. God or whoever help me, but for some reason I trust you, Marvin." He smiled down at the mound of squeezing fingers. "One thing more. I'll say it even if it sounds silly. Don't treat me like a little boy or like a son. I'm a grown man, almost your age, no matter how I look." Phil stepped back as if to give Marvin a chance to look. "What time this afternoon? Set a time because I've got a lot of calls to make between now and then."

"Be here about three. I'll set up the meeting with Gary and Bruce for two-thirty tomorrow. So get snapping and don't lose your contract."

June stopped Phil to shake his hand, to extend her good wishes, her warmest good wishes, her absolute feeling that from listening to him talk—she couldn't help but hear—she knew he was going to be very successful. He was definitely going to like working for Greenstalks because everyone in the company was so nice. Just everyone . . .

June approached Marvin's desk. "He's in a state of shock, Mr. Bernstein. Also, he's very happy. That I can definitely tell. And he's such a doll."

"Happy-schmappy. He just got the break of his lifetime. He's a lucky kid."

"I suppose that's true enough. But he's got something special about him, nevertheless. Not everyone has such a quality, Mr. Bernstein. I've watched plenty of people come into this office who didn't have such . . . what can I call it? . . . Appeal? Also, if you don't mind my saying so, you're not exactly handing him charity. If I know you, Mr. Bernstein—"

"Which you do, June. You know me very well. Like a book."

"Could I just say one thing more that's on my mind?"

"One thing more you can say."

"Well, it's about Mr. Trebnitz. I can't help feeling sorry for him. It broke my heart how he walked out of here."

"That, June, is why you have your job and I have mine."

June heaved a heavy, mother's-body sigh. "I suppose if you put it that way, it's true, but I can't help it, Mr. Bernstein. That's just the way I'm built. I'm not a businesswoman type really. I'm not very well-educated, but I know enough to know that certain kinds of people, especially old people, always get hurt in the end. Even intelligent people get hurt. It's a hopeless situation today because human beings don't care what they do to one another. They go right on murdering and fighting wars and . . . there's no finish to it. And what do you think my husband says when I tell him how I feel? My husband, mind you, who's suffered so many years with his stomach and his kidneys, you know what he says to me? He tells me not to act like such a child. That's life he says, my wise husband, and snaps his fingers. Just like this." June's attempt failed to produce a sound. She looked down at her hand, smiled sadly. "If I live to be a hundred, I'll still see the picture of that old man's face. It was tragic. Absolutely tragic."

"It's not so tragic. The man did well enough. He had his chance. Now it's someone else's turn. Businesses have to be run differently today. That's the simple fact of it."

"It's not so simple, Mr. Bernstein. An older person has pride too, you know."

"Everyone has pride, even when it's not justified. Trebnitz is a good man, but he's not good enough for now. Phil Hanssler is. That's what counts."

At three that afternoon, Phil called in to say he was tied up trying to get some of his workers notified; he just couldn't make it back to Marvin's office. That being the case, would Marvin please tell him where the space was he'd found? Marvin would. It was in a Greenstalk subsidiary on Thirty-eighth Street, right off the Avenue. Sewing machines were there already, and whatever other junk he needed he should ask for. Phil promised to go up there first thing in the morning.

The next day Phil called in again, just before lunch, to say that he was up at the place. Everyone was being very helpful, thanks to Marvin, he was sure. The place itself was all right. Not great. Not a fashion image. It had to be fixed up a little, which was what he was doing already with Pat Pearson, his assistant, so he couldn't make the meeting with Bruce and Gary. Marvin would understand how anxious he was to get started. Marvin did. Marvin wasn't annoyed, which he didn't tell Phil, because he had a meeting scheduled very shortly with Sam to discuss plans for a Mr. Jack deal. Bruce and Gary were not invited.

But, when Friday afternoon rolled around with still no appearance from Phil, Marvin was annoyed. He had June call *him*. Phil was at the new place.

"He's on the wire, Mr. Bernstein, and he says to tell you he can't come over this afternoon either."

"What do you mean *can't!*" Marvin's head shot up. "Let me talk to him." He swooped down on his telephone. "What do you mean you can't come over here? . . . So you'll go away tomorrow morning instead. . . . Who doesn't have things to do? You're working so hard and you haven't even signed your contract yet. I want you to have dinner with me tonight to talk about something you'll like. . . . Well, where the hell are you going that it's more important than your future? . . . Bucks County? For Christ's sake come up to our house for the weekend if that's all you're doing. You'll enjoy my wife more than Pennsylvania. . . . What other people are involved? Your girl friend . . ." They argued back and forth, but Marvin did not win. Phil insisted. He was tired. It had been a long, hard week. He'd see Marvin first thing Monday morning. Marvin slammed down the receiver so hard that June jumped.

"Sorry . . . Put down on my calendar that Phil will be here at ten on Monday morning or else. Keep all of Tuesday morning free too, because that's when you're to tell Michael Matthew Morgan and friends I can meet with them. He called *me*, and he'll suit my convenience. I've wasted too much time on this goddamn thing already."

The little prick. That contract is going to be signed before the meeting with Morgan come hell or high water. Bucks County! Fire Island is probably more like the truth. With a girl friend yet!

He steadied himself with work on the annual stockholders' report, and before he knew it, June was standing in front of his desk wishing him a good weekend. He pushed the papers aside, nodded. Another Friday night and Adele wasn't even expecting him home for dinner. That's how sure he had been that Phil would be eating with him. Damn him anyway! He'd pay for it all right.

Listening first to make sure there were no steps in the corridor, he reached down to the lower drawer of his desk, found his telephone book. He dialed, barked out his request, the same as last time, the same two, if possible. It was possible. It was arranged. Marvin slammed the receiver down, replaced his telephone book, slammed the drawer closed. Why not? What the hell. Better this way. A certainty instead of a game. Less wear and tear on the old machine that's only patched together with cottage cheese. Goddamn it. And goddamn that kid. He realized that for all his thirty-eight, almost thirty-nine years, this was the first time someone had really gotten to him, someone he could, maybe, talk to, open up to.

He leaned over his desk, let his head come to rest on the cool, white formica top, listened to the whirr of the air-conditioner, felt his stomach tighten as if it had a mind of its own and its message was that coolness and quiet were not for him. Not even for five minutes. Not even one minute. He'd settle for thirty seconds relaxed and calm, without something else, something more, gnawing at his insides. It would be a heaven on earth. . . . But it'd never happen. He wasn't built that way. He was already thinking of what he would say to Morgan, how he would handle that whole thing. He would have to be ready for Tuesday, at the top of his form. He held his head between the palms of his big hands, shook it, squeezed it as if that way he could rearrange the pieces that had slipped, temporarily—that's all it was—out of place.

Phil did sign his contract on the following Monday, but the meeting between Michael Matthew Morgan and Marvin did not take place on Tuesday. June reported that Mr. Morgan said he was going to be out of town all that day. She thought he was lying, but that's what he said. Marvin's frustration with people, people, people was greater than usual. So now it was Morgan's team that had decided to play hard to get. Or maybe they weren't interested in being gotten. A possibility, of course, but not one that Marvin, after so much preparation, was going to take lying down. There had to be another angle, another approach they were planning to take. No one who knew the industry would be so dumb they'd pay no attention to a Greenstalks feeler. First they call, and now they're stalling for some reason, waiting for something else to happen.

What that something else was Marvin couldn't be sure of until later on that week when Phil, after a visit to Bruce, stopped in. Marvin slowly brought the subject around to Mr. Jack and kept it there.

"Well, I really don't know for sure what the hell they're doing, except for one thing. Michael still wants to get me to go with them. He's got Morris Trebnitz calling me every two minutes to tell me how big it's going to be. A corporation. Expansion right away. And there's plenty of money behind them. Piles of it. I know some of the guys. They're not dress people, but they're into everything else."

"What more can they offer you than I did? Your name on the label?"

"That, yes, plus a full partnership, if I make a token investment. It's appealing only because of how young they all are. They know just what's going on now." Standing, Phil pushed back and forth against the edge of Marvin's desk, folded his arms across his chest. "One of the guys is a real smoothie, maybe too smooth. But he's a big-time talker. You know the kind."

"That's all it is is talk. Words. Hot air!" Marvin frowned, poked the air between them, punctuating his contempt. "By the time they get an operation going—remember they're going to have to start from scratch— they'll be so far in the red it'll take them years to show a profit. And already they're talking expansion. They have to be nuts! My advice to you, kiddo, is be careful. You make the wrong move now and you'll live to regret it. Listen to me. I know what I'm talking about."

"Funny, that's what my friends tell me. And my father too."

"Then you've got some smart friends and an even smarter father."

"Some of them are smart. My father? He's just acting like a father acts. He's happy I'm with Greenstalks. It's security, etc. You know the routine. One in the hand is worth two in the bush. That kind of crap."

"Listen to me for one more second, Phil. I'm not going to *tell* you what to do, but believe me when I say your future's better off here. You like what you're doing for right now, don't you? And Bruce tells me you gave him all the colors and ideas for his whole next line already. He's crazy about you. Even Gary doesn't care how you screwed up his paper idea, and Sam loves you, so don't be so quick to throw all that away. If you really think those guys have something good to offer, why don't you get them to come talk to me? I'd like to hear what's so good about it. Ask them—"

"Come on, Marvin. Don't fool with me. I asked you before not to do that. You should know better than that by now. Michael told me he's been in contact with you. Morris told me. So what are you talking this way for? As if you didn't care about anything but *my* future?" By then, Phil was leaning over Marvin's desk, close to his face. "You had to realize I'd find out. I'm no dope. I remember our meeting with Morris."

Marvin grabbed Phil's arm. "Okay. So you found me out. After so many years of dealing with phonies, I forget who to level with sometimes. That's all it was." He let go. Phil did not move back.

"You really are something, Marvin. What a mind."

"Believe me, it's not easy to live with it. You should know, because I see that you've got the same kind of mind."

"*Touché*, as they say." Phil laughed.

"It's no joking matter. I don't want you to make a mistake. Especially now. Just arrange for me to talk to these guys. It can't hurt. You can even be in on the meeting. Maybe nothing will come from it, but at least we'll both be able to see what there might be in the deal for you or for us."

"If you want it. Why the hell not? I'll call Michael, but I'm going to tell him it's for you, not for me. I really don't want any part of it, Marvin, honestly, no matter what happens after I finish my line for you."

"Whatever you say. Just don't you worry about a thing."

The meeting did take place the following week in Marvin's office. Phil was there and so was Michael Matthew Morgan; also an accountant named Seymour Feinstein, who carried a lizard attché case; a lawyer, Arnold Robbins, who carried a shiny, bulging, black-leather briefcase; and a Stanley Elias who carried nothing—Phil whispered as they entered that Elias was the smoothie—whose exact category Marvin couldn't define, unless it was *macher* extraordinary, of the new, beautiful-people variety, golden locks and perfectly turned out in a double-breasted, monogrammed summer blazer: the crest of the House of Elias. All of them were underthirties—Marvin would swear to that much—but the scrubbed, clean underthirty type.

They fanned out in a semicircle in front of Marvin's desk with Elias in the middle, Phil at one end, and Morgan, who throughout the meeting smoked an enormous cigar, at the other.

After being introduced and refusing, firmly refusing, a cigar, Marvin settled back to listen. To begin with, he'd let them carry the ball. He was just going to stretch out, lace up, do some fancy, quiet burping while Stanley Elias told him the whole story of what the group's plans were for the Mr. Jack venture, how they envisioned a whole empire of Mr. Jack clothes, first dresses, then sportswear, leather things; Mr. Jack lingerie, perfume, costume jewelry; even, eventually Mr. Jack home furnishings, a total designer look for sofas, chairs, sheets, pillowcases, matching sets, the works. "Quite naturally, Mr. Bernstein, we don't expect to do all this immediately, but it's all being considered, carefully and imaginatively. We can certainly foresee, for instance, and in the very near future, a Mr. Jack men's-wear division and men's cosmetics. That's coming very soon— if it isn't here already. It's going to be a big item. Very big."

Occasionally Marvin nodded, just to be polite, but his expression was inscrutable, admitting nothing, noncommittal. Only when he glanced over at Phil did he permit a flicker of judgment to register in his eyes, something that he hoped looked like "See! Didn't I tell you so! Aren't you glad you said no to them?" Marvin felt secure. He would be in control very shortly. He got the picture, loud and clear. This Stanley Elias could go on for as long as he wanted to in that flat, Boston-English, fancy, educated, bullshit artist's accent, but in the end Marvin was going to squeeze his balls. The guy would holler uncle all right. Who the hell was he trying to con? What was he building this mound of shit so high for if it wasn't for Marvin's benefit? To get Greenstalks interested, of course. So Marvin had only to listen and nod at either Elias's grand ideas or Michael Morgan's corroborative, cigar-pointing interruptions and can-you-top-this grins.

What an act. It reminded Marvin of that old Borscht Circuit–Catskill Mountains routine. Saturday night in the casino. At Laurel in the Pines or the Flagler or Tamarack Lodge, where he was a busboy for a few summers. One of the comics is out to marry some girl. He's talking to her father, trying to convince him what a great husband he'll make. He tells the father things like he owns a little furniture business, not much, and a little house, very small. And every time he mentions what he's got, his friend, who came along for moral support, breaks in: "A little business? What do you mean little? It's the biggest store on the East Side. A little house? Small? It's a mansion." Finally the would-be-wooer coughs, the father asks what's wrong, the wooer says he's got a little cold, and the friend pipes up with "A cold he's got? Consumption he's got!" End of skit. Blackout . . . So Marvin sat there comfortably, doing his private stretching isometrics, listening to Stanley Elias weave his dreams and Michael Morgan embroider them, waiting for the inevitable consumption line which came, in a few minutes, like this, in reverse, from Morgan, very modest and coy, "It's just the beginning Stanley's sketching in, Mr. Bernstein. You understand, I'm sure."

"Yes. Sure I understand that. Also I understand that the beginning is the hardest." Marvin remained laced and nodding. "So I'm wondering if maybe you have any of this planning down in writing yet? Like in a prospectus or a report, something I could show to the Greenstalks board of directors?"

Elias fell against the back of his chair, not nervous, just annoyed by such a request. He even coughed, then buttoned and unbuttoned his blazer, grinning derisively all the while.

"Mr. Bernstein, you just don't know our Stanley here very well. Stanley doesn't need to put these things in writing." The end of Michael's cigar glowed a bright red. The smoke curled lazily up the front of his carefully curled hair. "Stanley's like a genius when it comes to ideas and figures. He's been doing this kind of business all his life."

"You don't say." Marvin looked out from under.

Seymour Feinstein, the accountant, who, up until that moment, had remained reverentially silent, uncrossed his fat legs. "I've known Stanley a long time, Mr. Bernstein, and I can tell you quite frankly that I've never met anyone who could beat him when it comes to carrying complicated figures around in his head. It's really amazing. He never has to write down a thing. All in his head." He pointed to Elias's glistening, lowered head. So did Arnold Robbins, the lawyer, who, in addition, kept nodding like a needle caught in a scratched record groove. Michael puffed proudly. The team was well rehearsed.

Phil grabbed the edge of Marvin's desk, turned his gaze on the musketeers. "Are you guys for real? That's the way you came up here? With nothing to show him? I can't believe it. You must be a bunch of idiots or something. You're talking millions of dollars. You're talking about an empire. You've been talking that way to me for weeks and that's all you've got to show? Talk? Words?"

"You've forgotten one little item, Phil," Michael lowered his cigar dramatically, "which is that we *own* the name Mr. Jack. Lots of people would like to get it. We even know someone in this room. Morris told us about that little interview you had here." The cigar shot up.

"Big deal! That fact wouldn't even get you into the subway, baby. You'll still need a token."

"I don't ride the subway."

"You will if you keep this stuff up." Phil looked away, disgusted, waving Morgan down.

Which Marvin read as his entrance cue. He lunged. "You gentlemen have convinced me of one thing. You're wasting my time and I don't like it. I've listened to your bullshit for a half hour, waiting for you to say something sensible. So far I haven't heard anything. If I went to the board with your plans, they'd laugh me out of the room. This is no merry-go-round, boys. You're all supposed to be professional men. How the hell do you have the nerve to come up here and try to play with me? So you own a name! The best thing you can do with that is shove it up your collective asses. In a few months—because it'll take you easily that long, even longer, to get started—that name's going to be buried like everything else that dies. When Mr. Jack dresses don't show up in the stores for the new season, the romance is over. I kid you not!" Marvin laced up once more, supremely confident, enjoying the nervous movement in front of his desk, the turning of chairs, the uncrossing of legs, the lighting of new cigarettes.

"Just one little moment, Mr. Bernstein." Stanley got slowly to his feet, leaned over the desk. "You are not exactly talking to a novice, you know. It just so happens that we are ready to roll. We have offers from companies bigger than yours and—"

"How old are you, Elias?"

"Twenty-eight."

"Would you mind just sitting back down again?" Marvin waited until he did so. "Now *you* can hold on for one little moment while *I* tell you something. I'm only thirty-eight, but I've moved this corporation from small potatoes to the big time, to a public firm, in seven years. We show a gross profit of forty million dollars a year, and you and your friends are trying to tell *me* that *you're* an expert? Come down off that mountain you're living on, pisser. This is 1966. It's not 1905. A Horatio Alger you're not. So you've got plenty of money. Fine, I'm glad for you. But *you* didn't make it. I checked that one out, believe me. So now, what I want from you are a few facts. Like what the hell are you offering a potential investor? Just answer that for starters."

Indifferently, Stanley smoothed his hair, brushed his jacket front, straightened the crease in his gray, silky-worsted trousers, glanced at his friends in turn, as if to say, "See what you forced me into, what I have to go through." He spoke up, finally, his voice cold, flat, controlled. "I've been around much more money in my *short* life, Mr. Bernstein, so forty million dollars doesn't cow me. In answer to your question, an answer you should have understood already if you were listening carefully earlier, we are offering a *name* to an investor. Just that. And it isn't anything to belittle. In America it means everything. It comes equipped with a guarantee. A ready-made customer. All we have to do is build an advertising program the way Mr. Jack used to do it and the name will be more powerful than it ever was. Today we've got television to work with. But I won't bore you with that kind of detail. Marshall McLuhan is obviously not your speed. Our plan is to lease out the name to established manufacturers, ones that have proven their classmanship in each of the categories I listed earlier. We would provide the design know-how and supervise the finished product. Phil would be in charge of all the design—"

"That's the first sensible thing you've said since you arrived. Now how do you propose to get these classy manufacturers interested? Why would they want to tie up with you?"

"The name, Mr. Bernstein. Don't you understand! The name's the thing!"

Marvin maintained his position without flinching. Silently, not trusting himself to speak yet, stonily his gaze traveled from one face to the next, ended up at Phil's. "This guy is crazy, Phil. An egomaniac." He jerked his head around to Stanley, stared him straight in the eyes. "You don't stand a chance in the world, buster. You'll never get off the ground. I say that with all these witnesses present. I say it with certainty. I don't care how many contacts you have, I don't care how many wealthy men you know, Elias, you'll never convince enough of them. You're offering hot air. That's all. And to tell you the truth, you're not even offering that much. Those ideas aren't the story. You don't want that. You just made it all up as you went along. I know what you really want, and I'll tell you straight from the shoulder that you won't get it here. We're not giving money away for nothing."

Marvin stood up, towering above the seated figures. Even when they rose to meet the challenge of his size, no one came near the shoulder he was shooting from. "Thank you all for coming up here anyway. It was instructive, if nothing else. I'll tell Mr. Greenstalk about it, although I'm sure he won't be interested in getting us involved."

There was no handshaking. Seymour Feinstein and attaché case, Arnold Robbins and briefcase lined up behind Stanley Elias. Only Michael failed to fall into place. Disappointed, confused by the rapid dismissal, he seemed to want to say something else. "Mr. Bernstein," he tilted his head back bravely, "I wish you'd not be so final. I mean, let's not take this thing personally. Stanley doesn't mean to be rude. It's . . . it's just a way he has." Stanley turned, bumped into Seymour Feinstein, who pulled him by the jacket, stopped him from leaving Michael stranded. "I do think there's something worthwhile in the name and not just the fifteen-thousand-odd bucks we paid to get it. Phil's been associated with Mr. Jack too, remember. We can offer that association, which is worth millions, as well."

"I don't believe you can, Mr. Morgan." Marvin's hand on Phil's shoulder restrained him from movement or speech. "You don't have him to offer at all. You know that from Trebnitz *and* from him. He's on our side so you can't give me what I already have. He didn't sign anything with you. He has a working contract with us and only a sentimental attachment to you and that name. From the way this meeting went, I don't think even that's left. I know what you've been up to. You were trying to catch him first, make him the bait for the deal. That's why you stalled with me. Well, you've lost the race, so I advise you not to go around offering him to anyone else. He's not the kind of guy who lets himself be sacrificed or taken in by people like your friend Elias here."

Michael, without his cigar now, looked forlorn. "Stanley bought the name with his own money. He bought it for me because I don't have any, and he bought the chance that goes with it. I call that a friend. A good friend. The best. He wants me to make the grade too, and I appreciate that." Stanley started out of the office. "He's not a selfish guy, no matter what it looks like." The others followed.

"So be it. It's your life to handle the way you want. But *you* better start handling it. You're a decent fellow, Morgan. At least you're honest. You'll hear from me."

"Thank you for that much." Michael shook Phil's hand. Phil seemed not to be aware of it. "I'll keep in touch anyway. Take care."

"Stay, Phil, for another minute." Marvin forced him into the chair that Elias had sat in, then sat down next to him, both of them facing the empty space behind the desk. "I want that name. I'll admit it to you. I want you to be in control of a company with that name. That's the combination it needs. And I promise you, you will be, if you do what I tell you. Morgan is going to have to get his friend Elias to sell out his claim, in writing. Greenstalks will be interested if no one but you, and Morgan —he'll have to be a part of it unfortunately—have the name. Then we'll set you up in business—are you listening, Phil?"

"I'm listening. That's what I always do. I listen." Phil escaped from

Marvin's reassuring hand on his shoulder. "But why I listen so much I don't know. All I ever hear is how great everyone thinks they are. If it isn't an Alex Fleiss dreaming about the past, then it's a Stanley Elias describing how he's going to use all his money to buy up the whole future —for himself. Some new breed they are. Some beautiful people. The showboys of the Western world they are. And *schmucks!* They're all *schmucks*—not you, Marvin; that's one thing you're not—and so am I. I'm the biggest *schmuck* of all. For a while I even let myself be conned into thinking they knew what they were talking about. Anyone can do that to me. Even you. And the saddest part of all is I know none of it's worth the trouble. It's all a bunch of shit, no matter how hard I try to make the grade. But I keep on trying anyway, along with the rest of them."

"Of course you do. But you're equipped for the game. Some people aren't and they're the ones who find it a very hard thing to admit about themselves."

"It's the hardest thing. Because wanting is like a disease today, and once you have the disease, it's incurable. It blinds you. It stays in your blood all your life. You have it too, Marvin, and Elias has it and Morgan and myself, all of us. We all have different styles, but it amounts to the same thing in the end. We don't have any choice in the matter. And how it got there, who put it there, who the hell knows. What made Dorothy follow the yellow brick road? It's the same thing. So that being the case," he was at the door, "you can do whatever you want with those guys and their lousy name, but I'm going to follow, as they say, my own star."

As Phil left, June's typing started up quickly. Marvin felt comforted by its monotonous rhythm. Nothing was breaking apart. Nothing would, no matter what he did next. And what he would do next would be to call Morgan, meet with him, alone. Morgan could be persuaded. He was hungry. He'd find a way to get rid of Elias, because if Elias was such a good friend he'd bow out of the picture. Morgan would be a partner with Phil in a Greenstalks-backed business.

Phil would be persuaded too. Sure he would. The system would work the way it was supposed to. That's just the way things are and always will be, given the constant of a forever dependable, imperfect human nature. It's simple arithmetic. How can it be otherwise? It's in the blood—right you are, Phil—to want, to connive, to play the game by the dirty-rule book, the whole *schmier*, and all done in the name of getting ahead, rising above what you were and where you were when you took charge of your own life. Well, some people have to rise by defying gravity, like himself; others, like Phil, have to be goosed; and still others, a Stanley Elias for example, are born flying. And we're all reaching into the human grab bag for the prize. Best. Better. Bestest. Bingo.

Before Labor Day, Marvin had worked out the final resolution of the Mr. Jack question. It was all settled just the way he planned it would be. Sam Greenstalk, Gary, Bruce, all the members of the board were pleased by the transaction. After all, a prestige label for such a cheap price is a happy event in any family. The Greenstalk family was accustomed to being made happy by Marvin, but to gain such a classy addition without a major capital outlay, that was something out of the ordinary. Sam called it a milestone, told Marvin and his sons how now they could really begin to trade up a little, put on a richer face for the public. See, he reminded them, this never would have happened if he had let them sell out months before. Patience, he told them. Patience, and in a while they'd be the biggest in the industry. Then they could sell out.

So, once more, Marvin won a round. The only hard part was convincing Phil to do what Marvin insisted was the best thing for him to do. The free-lance sportswear line that Phil designed that summer for Greenstalks turned out to be another unexpected bonus for the company. Bruce had enough ideas to copy from it to last for years, and when the clothes were duplicated, produced, sent to the stores, they sold everywhere. Greenstalks didn't make much profit from them, but that was only because their factories weren't equipped to reproduce fashion clothes cheaply enough. That wasn't Phil's fault. The styling was there. The taste was there. No one blamed Phil for that. It was only simple proof that Greenstalks just wasn't ready yet, not yet, to handle real fashion, but neither were they about to let Phil go. Never. Marvin reassured Sam and the others, reassured Phil that there was no thought of that.

There was another problem. Phil didn't see himself in the same league with Michael Morgan. Morgan was in the Minors. He knew beans about the inside working of a business. He had no experience. He was too young. He couldn't be trusted to order large amounts of fabric for production, to work out delivery schedules, to keep records of style numbers sold, shipped, reordered, plus a hundred other details, to say nothing of hiring the right staff. The guy knew so few people on the Avenue. It would be too much for him. All he was good for was to be smooth with a few buyers. He'd have to learn the rest on the job, and who needs a partner to do that? That's pointless altogether. It would never work out. They'd be lost before they ever had a chance to be rediscovered.

Marvin agreed with everything Phil said. It was a risk. No question about that. But the one thing Marvin couldn't do was to ease Morgan out of the picture. Impossible. Morgan was part of the deal. That was the single hard condition that Elias was smart enough to force Marvin to accept: no Morgan in the new business, then no name. So Marvin had yielded, just as Phil would have to yield on that one point. The opportunity was too great for Phil to refuse. Mr. Jack *was* Phil, to the buyers. If Greenstalks was willing to take the chance, Phil would have to. After all, he wasn't being asked to put anything into the business but his talent. And just think what that investment would bring him within five years' time. Everything he wanted. Money. Fame. Plenty of Greenstalks stock each year. His name on the label: Mr. Jack by Phil Hanssler. His name on the label of any other division they opened up.

When Marvin swore that he would write that last item into the final contracts, Phil promised to sign them, but only if Marvin would go along with one more of his suggestions, one that wouldn't affect Greenstalks in any way. As a matter of fact, it would be like an extra added insurance on their initial investment, a guarantee for them and for Phil. He swore he was determined to have it even if it meant jeopardizing the whole thing. He insisted on finding a third partner to do all that work that Morgan couldn't and that Phil wouldn't have time to do. He was willing to give up a part of his percentage in the business—Morgan was going to have to do the same—to get the right man. That was fine with Marvin. Why should he object to that? But his advice to Phil, his sincere advice, was that Phil shouldn't be so free with the potential profits before they started coming in. Phil was convinced that there wouldn't be any profit at all if they didn't do this one thing.

So okay. Marvin said yes, as long as he, in the name of Greenstalks, had approval rights. That would be his element of control. Morgan said yes. No conditions attached. He admitted how little he knew, an admission that made him rise in Phil's estimation, and one that only confirmed Marvin's previous hunch, repeated to Phil, that Morgan was, after all was said and done, a good kid, a well-intentioned guy.

Late in August the search was on for the third man. Michael suggested Morris Trebnitz, who was still willing to invest some money if only they would let him join. The no came from Marvin. Money they didn't need.

Greenstalks would provide enough of that, all that was required, just so long as the monthly payments kept coming back. Marvin was the only one to laugh at that joke. Also, Trebnitz might be a swinging production man, but he wasn't a businessman. That Marvin could tell for certain. He'd make a business too much a question of the people he liked or didn't like, which was no way to run a business at all. One around like that was enough, the one he meant being Phil, who was going to have to watch that kind of stuff, now that he was a boss.

When rumors of the in-the-offing Greenstalks purchase appeared in *Women's Wear Daily*, the tempo of the search accelerated. Road salesmen from the old Mr. Jack tried to buy in, and Andrew Berns, who at the end had run the showroom for Alex Fleiss, was the most persistent. He approached Phil, called him daily for news. Phil liked him well enough. He was fortyish, had had plenty of experience, although before he was with Alex Fleiss he had run his own business, which, unfortunately, had failed. Maybe he was a loser, two strikes in a row, and the third would be fatal for all of them. And, besides, Phil was in total agreement with Michael on this point, they should have fresh blood, no reminders of the past. Marvin suggested someone from the Greenstalks organization. Phil flatly refused. No strings. No umbilical cords. No hot breath of an informer blowing down his neck every day of his life. "So let's have that settled permanently, Marvin. You people agreed to be silent partners in the deal, remember. Like a bank. That's all. That's the way you said you wanted it to be, so we'll just try and keep it that way."

"You'll never learn, will you? You don't trust anyone. Not even me. Who has time to waste spying on you? Calm down. Find your own man, but find him already, because there's no green light until you do and until we approve. You're the one who wanted it that way."

Michael's cigar glowed red, then brown, and red again, punctuating his stop-and-go excitement. "Don't worry, Marvin. We will. The most important thing is that we get going. We've missed resort and spring already. If we can start with a summer line, we can really get some volume sales fast, build up a reserve. We need to concentrate on getting a loft and equipment, that kind of thing, so you can begin designing, Phil."

"Don't *you* worry about a thing, Mr. Morgan. We'll manage. Mr. Moneybags Bernstein here will make sure we manage. Right, Moneybags?"

"Correct, lover boy. I'll be goosing both of you every step of the way. I want to see profits."

Morgan laughed, expanded the laugh into a sitting swagger that followed the movement of his cigar into the ashtray on Marvin's desk. "No sweat about that, not with Phil designing. He knows how." The ash knocked off, the cigar was snapped back to his mouth; he chewed the end. "My best guess is that in a year we'll be a four-, maybe five-million-dollar operation."

"Not if you don't stop smoking those cigars. You'll scare the customers away with the smell alone." Phil waved the smoke from his eyes. "Also, sweetheart, four million's too big for the first year. We're not—I repeat *not*—going to oversell, because that's a sure way to kill the whole thing. I want it small. I want it to grow bigger gradually. I want it to stand for something. For fashion. And at a price. For a good product. That's the most important part of it, making a good product, so don't start in with the figures. Don't hand me the Stanley Elias line of bull shit. I know the Mr. Jack label still draws a customer. I know it better than anyone because I'm the one who's been doing the road shows. I've met that customer and she's not a kid any more. She still wears a junior dress, but she grew up and got married. She lives in the suburbs. She's got *some* money. Not piles of it, just some, and she knows what she wants. If we don't give it to her, somebody else will."

"You're right, Phil. A hundred percent right. I was only thinking about the future. That's all."

"Well, don't. Think about right now because that's what counts. I personally have waited too long for this chance to come along to see it squeezed to death in one season. We'll take it slow. Very slow. Do we agree?"

Michael nodded.

Marvin nodded too, not that he was really listening to what Phil said; he was, instead, approving of the way he said it, was hearing the energy, the assurance, clicking on spontaneously. Alone with Marvin throughout the summer, at lunch or dinner or at a meeting, Phil had been different, quieter, more of a listener, attentive, flaring up only when Marvin tried to sell him on an item that Phil knew more about: a design idea that would cut down on labor costs or a color change or fabric change in one of the outfits on the free-lance line. Then he had burned, and he was right to burn. Marvin knew what his own taste was like. Bronx Provincial. Broadway, not Seventh Avenue. Adele told him the same thing, and wait until she came back from Greece, then she'd never stop telling him how this he didn't know and that he didn't know. Phil, at least, said it once and it was finished. Marvin, you've got no taste when it comes to clothes. Period. A friend talks to someone that way. Friends they certainly were. But business friends. Maybe a little more than that, but not much more, and now not much chance to make it more. Phil would stop dropping into the office every day once Mr. Jack was officially opened. He'd have plenty to do to keep himself busy for a long time to come, and Marvin would have to leave him alone so he could do it. Business was business. That was the first thing. And business friends were business friends, a combination, true, but a forced combination usually, of trust and distrust, of wariness and challenge and cunning.

They ended up choosing Andrew Berns. At least he knew about how a business, an old-style business, should be run. Michael tried to fight the choice. Andrew Berns had been his showroom boss at the other Mr. Jack. That was the kind of competition Michael Matthew Morgan didn't want to face, that was what *he*—Marvin read it that way—was determined to rise above in himself. But Andrew Berns was an honest, known quantity. Marvin decided to like him. Having done that, he convinced Phil to accept Berns, and, therefore, simple arithmetic forced Morgan to accept him too, because if they didn't get started soon—it was almost October; spring business was lost—they'd never get the summer line finished.

They found a loft in 498 Seventh Avenue. Phil wanted to be in 530 or 550 with the American couture designers, but nothing was available. Marvin ventured off Broadway long enough to check out what they were being forced to accept. He admitted to Phil that sure it was small, but they could always move later on, and if the loft was small, Phil could at least control the way the business grew. Right? Right. So the loft was rented, the key money, Seventh Avenue's fancy word for paying off the landlord, was supplied by Greenstalks, and the three bears—Marvin's joke: they could decide who the Mama bear was—took possession.

The papers were drawn up and signed in Marvin's office. June, beaming at Phil all the while, handed them around. Sam, Gary, and Bruce looked on. Greenstalks owned 55 percent, for which they had paid $15,500 plus a loan of $150,000, the total amount to be paid back in monthly installments spread out over eighteen months. Payments were to begin as soon as there was an accounts-receivable department in operation. Phil, Michael, and Andrew, stunned by his sudden good fortune, each owned 15 percent of the new business. Details of staff, equipment, production procedures, all of that, were strictly up to the boys, except for the bookkeeper. Marvin would pick her personally. Phil's name would appear on the label beneath the old logo. All advertisements would include a replica of the label. The contracts bound all parties for five years. Renegotiation was possible whenever Greenstalks determined, but the three partners had the right to refuse any new offer, a two-out-of-three vote was the only requirement. Slips of paper were drawn to determine who would be president. Michael won.

If Phil had any lingering misgivings before or after he signed the contracts, Marvin did not hear them that afternoon. Marvin was satisfied that everyone else seemed satisfied. Seated behind his desk, feeling only minor gas pain, he watched Sam first, then Gary and Bruce embrace Phil while Michael and Andrew smiled nervously, embarrassed, out of it for the moment, but safe enough, hopefully, for the next few years anyway. That morning they had had the pleasure of seeing the little white letters being returned to the lobby directory of 498 and hearing Morris Trebnitz, their first staff member, tell them, right in front of the revolving doors, how if he couldn't be their partner, then he was at least content to work for such good bosses.

And now June was handing the signed papers across to Marvin. It was all kosher, a fact: the new Mr. Jack was officially in business. Marvin waved the papers high in the air. Sam Greenstalk, his arm draped behind Phil's neck, raised his champagne glass. "Good luck to all of us!" Everyone but Marvin sipped. "I'm happy how it turned out. Alex Fleiss, you can be sure, is not. But that, my friends, is life. Somebody wins, so somebody else has to lose. It's all scientific in the modern age."

When everyone else cleared out of Marvin's office Phil made a point of remaining. He had just a few more things he wanted to say to Marvin alone, nothing important, personal things, he assured his partners, but things, he told Marvin, that the champagne, maybe, made it possible for him to say, about how it really *would be* a new company, no matter how many people in it were carryovers from the old one, and how it was going to be run differently, how it was going to project a new personality. It was going to be a healthy company. No phony ego shit. No prima donnas . . .

"Whatever you say. You're the boss, Phil, so do it whatever way you want. As long as you're happy too. You are happy, aren't you?"

Phil poured more champagne. "Happy? Such a funny word to hear coming out of your mouth. Me? Happy? You? Happy? What's that got to do with anything?" He set his glass down, abruptly pushed the fringe of hair across his forehead. "Happy is not my *shtik*. I don't expect what I don't see much evidence of. Not for people like me. Or you, for that matter. But at least my father'll be happy. Maybe he'll even believe I could grow up to be a boss." Laughing, he picked up his glass once more. "It's even hard for me to believe it. Me? A boss? . . . The one person I've got to do something special for is Esther Kaufman. She's the one, the only one of all the people I know, who was willing to do a damn thing for me. And I hardly knew her."

"She'll be taken care of. Don't you worry about that. I'll see to it personally."

"And then there's you, Marvin. Why you did all this, why you went to so much trouble and took so much time, I'll never be able to figure out."

"There's no figuring. I just played my hunches, so do a good job, otherwise *I'll* end up being the *schmuck*." Marvin reached over suddenly, his face twisted into a smile, squeezed Phil's shoulder, left his hand there. Phil didn't move away. "Just remember one thing. If I didn't think you had the stuff, I wouldn't have lifted a finger. A business deal isn't a personal matter, except in the most selfish way. Either it makes sense or it doesn't. That's all that counts."

"That I know from way back. What happens, happens. One coincidence leads to another. That's the way my life always moves, so I'm used to that part of it. All I'm really trying to do here now is thank you. Is that such a terrible thing?"

Marvin's hand slid from Phil's shoulder. Slowly he moved back in his chair, stretched his legs, laced his hands behind his neck. "No. It's not such a terrible thing. Only you don't have to thank me for anything. As you put it, it's coincidence. That's all. You were at the right place at the right time." He began searching through a pile of folders at the corner of his desk. "So get the hell out of here now. Get to work. And remember that I'll be checking up on all of you, kiddo. That you can be sure of."

"I hope you will. I'll be counting on you for that."

Part Three

The Enchanted Harpies

Chapter Eleven

What'll be'll be. The one thing first of all, like I always say, you should only live and be well. You should let well enough alone. So who needed such a big loft like the old place? The showroom alone was Radio City. It's too big to start out, Philly. Even the ones who bought it they broke it into two pieces. One'll be for cheap knits. *Dreck.* Garbage like I never saw on a line. For the other they make beaded sweaters with fur collars. The whole thing they painted pink. Maybe salmon. With gold fixtures. So that's that. I wouldn't miss it, but my only worry about here is that we're two floors lower than in the other place." Morris pinched Phil's cheek and laughed. "I'm an old man so naturally I'm superstitious. It's bad luck to move lower in the same building."

"My father told me what to do about that. You just take a chair downstairs and you sit right out in front of 498 for five or ten minutes. Maybe you'll do it for an hour, Morris. To make sure. That way it's like you moved out and then you moved back in. How does that sound?"

"Exactly what I was going to tell you. Your father knows the right things. A smart man. And such a good man. All the fabric we got left I'll guarantee I'll sell to him, no matter who offers more for it. That you can be sure of. But I'll also bet that now you're a boss you wouldn't buy so many sample cuts to waste money on what you'll never use. To be a boss is a difference, Philly. A big difference. Wait and you'll see."

"Morris, will you get off my back already with that crap!" For the tenth time, Phil paced the imitation brick tile runway, leaned against the door frame to the bathroom-size office that Michael and Andy were going to have to squeeze into. "It's too small, I tell you. My living room's bigger. And that green carpet'll make every buyer throw up. You can't show clothes next to that green. It's an abomination." The sculptured green carpet on either side of the runway was supposed to be the perfect touch

271

to show off the Early American tables of brown and black oak formica, the tufted black vinyl captain's chairs, the stained-pine partitions with their copper rods that divided the room into ridiculous cubicles for buyers who didn't want other buyers to see how big or small their orders were. "It's no wonder the guys before us folded. Not an ounce of taste in the whole place. The whole room's a phony. And my personal philosopher here keeps telling me to live and be well. How can I live and be well when I can't stand the idea of showing my clothes in a shit house like this? And those lights! Look at those lights for Christ's sake. Pink and green."

Wearily Morris retreated to a cubicle where Michael and Andrew were seated. Andrew Berns, pencil poised over a list of carefully calculated budget figures, every one of which Phil had attacked, rushed a trembling finger down the list of items, certain that there was, in fact, an allowance for the changing of fluorescent bulbs. "Whoa, Phil. Easy does it. We'll be changing the bulbs. It's in my budget."

"Bulbs shit! The whole place has to be redecorated. The bulbs, those lousy copper fixtures, everything. It's a phony. And I warned you. I told you I didn't want to be in this building in the first place. I wanted 530. I wanted some class around here."

"Look, Phil. I don't disagree with you. All I'm suggesting is you have to be a little reasonable too. This was the only place available in our price range, and we don't want to be asking the Greenstalks for more money right at the beginning. After a while, when there's some coming in, then we can think of expanding." Andy stared down at his pad. That's where the sense was and not in talking, not in words. Never in words. That habit of his, of always pointing to the figures, of tapping the list with the sharp point of his pencil as if that was the ultimate proof of what was possible and what was not, frustrated Phil, worried him, so that whatever faith he had in his own ability to lead the three of them out of that narrow path where the money was piled up but where pride and joy surely weren't, seemed puny, always faltering. It was his own old weakness, the free-fall symptom surfacing. That's what really worried him, that sensation of not really caring enough when it counted, that feeling that none of what he would attempt here mattered in the great, grand scheme of things. That's what stopped him now as he looked down, waiting, undecided, at Andy's balding, sandy, perfectly cut hair. Maybe Andy was being sensible, but he was also being dull. He was dull. Without an ounce of imagination. "In any case, we only signed a year's lease and Michael's going to keep his eye peeled for something bigger. Aren't you, Mike?"

"Of course. I've already got my friends working on it. They understand exactly what we need. They have plenty of real-estate connections. You can be sure they'll come up with something before very long." Michael had no cigar, so his idle fingers occupied themselves with curling the edges of the blank pad that rested before him on the table. Michael had no calculations to make. What was there for him to calculate now? He was president. A flip of a coin. A short straw. The underlings could do that kind of thing.

"Better we should pay attention to the other things. We're here already. So let it be. Bigger you're not ready for yet. First it'll be the dresses. Then you'll sell and then we'll maybe move. Come. Let's go to the back and see what's what." Morris started for the door that led from the showroom to the long back room where the cutting tables were. Andy held the door for everyone.

For Phil, the behind-the-scenes space story was even gloomier. His office was no bigger than a walk-in closet with a window. It was meant for dwarfs and it was too far away from Michael and Andy. They'd be screwing him right and left, making dumb deals with the cheap fabric houses, switching the quality goods of his sample dresses for shit. That he'd definitely have to prevent somehow. That would kill the business sooner than anything else. And the sample room. A hole. The most it could take would be four machines, if no one breathed. Dorothy Krakauer wasn't going to stand for that. The shipping area might be adequate for a Madison Avenue boutique, but for a new business, never. Only the cutting area had possibilities. On the surface, that was, because there was no room for storage below. The cutters would have to suspend the bolts of fabric from the ceiling and the walls—like inside a smokehouse. And where would they put the duplicate makers? Out in the hall? "It's no good, I tell you. How can I fit a dress in my room? If I take one giant step back to check on a proportion I'll be outside. You guys want to build a big business in a chicken coop and it can't be done. It's impossible."

"You went along with it, remember." Michael pressed up against the wall, trying to get out of the way of the others as if that way he could prove there really was more than enough room. "You said go ahead. You said take it."

"I did. You're right. I'm not blaming anyone. I'm as much to blame as the next guy. I wanted to get started already."

"Don't worry so much, Philly. You'll get started. You'll forget how small it is here." Morris palmed Phil's chin, raised it. "We'll all make do. One thing you shouldn't forget at least is that it's your own business. You should at least enjoy that part. No?"

"I should at least. And I will. When the sign goes up in the hall with my name on it, then maybe I'll believe it happened. Then maybe I'll enjoy it more."

"About the sign, Phil," Andy quickly found the figure for the sign's price. "Apart from the fact that it costs too much, the man who does all the signs in 498 says that it's not building policy to have the designer's name appear anywhere outside in the hall."

"Well, sweetheart, they're just going to have to change the building policy. My name *will* appear that way on our label—you better make damn sure about that. And our sign is going to look like our label, so, therefore, my name is going to be on it or else. I promise you I'll pull out of the whole deal otherwise. That's final. If necessary, I'll go see Marvin and tear up my contract. Maybe I should anyway, because you guys don't seem to understand one very important item, which is that in addition to being the designer I'm also an owner. You might tell the building man that little fact. And while you're at it, tell him we need a telephone here that works. When the hell is the guy coming to turn it on, or do we have to pay under the table to get that done too?"

"According to the information I have, he's supposed to come today."

"He better. Why don't *you* handle that problem, Mike? Andy's got enough to do. I need that phone. I've got to call my girls. I've got to hire a new assistant. I've got to contact some fabric men and buy supplies. I can't do everything from my apartment."

"That's why I'm convinced we should go slow about the showroom for a while." Andy turned back to the page with the estimates. "Redecorating would really set back the budget. Later, when the first checks come in, then you can play around with changes."

Phil sighed. "Okay. I give in. First things first. Let's go back to your office. What we need is an executive meeting to settle certain matters like Marvin would. You can come too, Morris. You can play the part of advisor. You'll be Nestor."

"Nestor? It's Marvin Bernstein's friend?"

"Never mind. Just come."

Two desks, back to back, so that each time Andy looked up from his pad and Michael poked his cigar importantly through the air, they would have to face the fact that they were all in this thing together; two chairs pushed against the side wall to leave a few inches for passing, and between the chairs the console refrigerator-bar that Mr. Hanssler had sent as a gift for his son and which just couldn't fit into Phil's office; that was the executive office of the new Mr. Jack. Jack Farbstein should see what his name meant now. Alex Fleiss would be hysterical, not after, but before he killed Benedict Arnold Michael Morgan. "Gentlemen! Our first meeting." Phil sat on the bar, swinging his legs, waiting for the president to officiate.

Michael searched the pockets of his crestless blue blazer. "I must have forgotten to take a supply of cigars this morning, damn it."

"Our luck."

"Come on, Phil. Be nice to me. You're the one who said let's have a meeting so why don't you say what you want to say and we'll listen?"

"Don't cop out now, baby. You're president, and you're not even thirty yet. You're full of vitality, aren't you? You're exploding with great ideas."

"What my ideas are no one wants to hear. I wanted to have an initial advertising campaign. A big splash. Announcements in all the media. Even television. Things like that. But Andy has already put a nix on that idea."

"That's the first I heard of it. So, okay. That'll be the first high-level policy decision. On any issue like that we're going to have a vote. Two out of three. If you forget to ask me, then you can forget I'm your partner. Understood?"

"Well, in that case let's discuss the idea, because I think it has merit and Andy just said no, Phil. We didn't vote. Do you like the idea? Don't you think it's a good concept?"

"No. Not yet. We don't have anything to advertise. Not one dress."

"It's the name we'll advertise. Mr. Jack comes back. Something like that."

"That kind of something, sweetheart, is exactly what we're not going to advertise." Phil stood, folded his arms. "It's not Mr. Jack that's returning. I thought I made that point clear before. It's Mr. Jack by Phil Hanssler that's beginning fresh. I'm not interested in advertising Jack Farbstein's name. It's bad enough that people all over the country really think there is a Mr. Jack, a big-man-in-the-sky designer who does everything singlehanded."

"That isn't exactly what they have in mind over at Greenstalks." Andy spoke so quietly that Phil had to lean closer to hear. "I spoke to Mr. Bernstein this morning about that and he seemed to feel that at the outset we should stress the fact of Mr. Jack and not your name. I'm only repeating what he said to me, so don't get angry. The sign business is a case in point."

Hoo ha! Nothing would surprise Phil any more. So Andy was another one that would have to be watched. A last-minute choice yet, who knew that he was. He must have called Marvin to squeal about the sign business, and Marvin probably said something like do whatever you want, settle it between yourselves, it's your company to run. Or he might have said, sure, Andy, you're right—but you'll have to handle Phil, not me. Anything was possible. Even Michael's convincing him that Andy should be made to feel he was a favored man, that an honor had been bestowed upon him when he was taken on as an equal partner without having to invest a cent. First Howie and then Wilma had warned him that was no way to open a new business. Either you're in it with people you treat as equals or you're out of it, Howie said. Wilma was more cautious. Her approach was that as long as he could control the others nothing else mattered. That's all he had to be sure of. And be assertive, which was another way for her to say, well, Philip darling, now that you're launched, when the hell are we going to get married? Soon. Very soon. As soon as I can be more assertive with you and Michael and Andy, the sneak thief who knows something about running a business—maybe running it right into the ground. "Frankly, the experience of losing a business taught me a lot. I don't claim to know everything, but I do know how to prevent this business from failing. Spending money foolishly on frills that may or may not pay off is one thing to avoid. I'll always be against that. I can really be a miser when I have to be."

"I'll bet you always are."

"Have it your way, Phil. But in the future you'll thank me for it."

"I doubt it. I'll never thank anyone for doing what comes naturally to them. But let's skip that for now. It's not relevant. The sign and what it means are."

"Agreed, and so is the system of operation we're going to follow. It's got to be something we're all willing to agree on, something that's solid enough to stand up when things get hectic around here, because before you know it they will get hectic. Once you start doing duplicates with Morris we've all got to know exactly what we're expected to do and do it." Andy paused long enough to make sure Michael was listening. Michael understood the implication. His gaze shifted to the only clean spot on the dirty wall above Phil's head where once a painting had been hung and where now there was only the tracing of the frame. "And as far as the sign is concerned, I think you better take that up with Mr. Bernstein, Phil."

"I intend to."

"Not without us." Michael's attention was re-routed. "We all have to be present. That's the deal."

"You want to be present when I take a shit too? And when I get laid?"

"Come on, Phil. You know what I mean. I asked you once already to be nice."

"I'm being nice. But neither one of you guys trusts me is what I'm just beginning to understand. I'm also wondering why you don't. Let's all try to remember that if I hadn't been working for Greenstalks you wouldn't be here today. So, I repeat, I'll talk to Marvin—alone."

"Gentlemen, please already. I'm sitting here listening and to me, personally, if you'll take the opinion of an older man, to me you sound like a bunch of ladies from a union meeting instead of partners in a business. Time you're wasting. It's precious, time. Philly, please, be a good boy so we can go ahead already. Please?"

Phil nodded. To a man of Morris's age and nature all this talk was beside the point. He had to see some good in everyone. In spite of all the evidence to the contrary, in spite of the way Marvin had treated him, Morris just went right on believing everyone was good underneath. That was one of the reasons six million Jews died. "You're absolutely correct, Morris. Time is precious. It's golden. So let's just concentrate on Andy's point about our system of operation. I know what *my* jobs are. The clothes will be done the best way I know how. I'll always be willing to listen to your suggestions about what fabrics the salesmen want and what colors. Not that I'll always go along with it. The clothes are my responsibility, and if they're not good it'll be my failure."

"They'll be good, Philly. That much I know. And you'll work with the duplicates like before?"

"Not like before, Morris. Like now. This time I'll check every duplicate *while* it's being made. We'll fit them on Cindy. And I'll personally okay the finished product. This time, also, there's not, I repeat it for everyone concerned, there's not going to be any switching of fabric in the garments unless I say so. Got it?"

"Cross my heart. Better you should tell Andy because if he'll be ordering the goods for the contractors to make up, then he's the one to tell. Me, I'll do whatever you'll tell me now."

"All right, so I'm telling him too. You heard, Andy?"

"I heard and I'll do. Morris and I will work on ordering fabric and settling with the contractors. We'll organize the whole production schedule with you so our delivery will always be on time. I want to set up a strict returns policy and keep to it no matter who the customer is. A big account or a small account, the same policy applies. If they get the merchandise on time, they can't return a thing unless it's damaged. I'll keep all those records and I'll also keep the stock records and the piece goods. Which leads me to a very major item. I think we should decide it today. Do you want to have a big reorder business and keep running dresses on the line until they're absolutely dead, or do you want to move from one line to another very quickly? I have to know that in advance because of how I order the fabric. If a dress is hot, I want to have the fabric available and ready to cut. But also it means you have to predict what *might* be hot. It's risky. One thing I definitely don't want to do is overbuy. If you start buying big, you're doing too much hoping and all your capital gets tied up in a worthless inventory, which is the biggest part of what happened to Alex Fleiss." Andy halted his lecture as if for a moment of respectful silence. No one interrupted, but Michael fidgeted in his captain's chair. "All I mean—and I'm not trying to tell you what to do—is that I'd like to see some kind of policy established. It's the most important item to me if we're going to try and get extra shares of stock from Greenstalks. What our net profit is per year will determine that."

"I don't see why we can't play that by ear. Do both things if the situation warrants it." Michael looked seriously at each face, searching for some approbation.

Morris's sigh sounded the sentiment. "You must decide before. You hire contractors to make a certain number garments. Everything they can't put together at once. If the sewers there start one dress, they can't every minute stop to cut more of an older one. It costs plenty every time they stop. And then, if they stop to cut, then they got to have the fabric. You understand?"

"*My* plan," Phil disregarded Michael and Morris, "is to work not so much by lines as by groups. Each month we'll produce maybe twenty, twenty-five dresses. We'll get the big-store buyers up here somehow each time we've got a few groups ready. That'll be your major job, Michael. You're going to be the public-relations expert, that and running the showroom and shipping. So you'll get the buyers up here. We'll see how they react and order fabric in advance that way. We'll have a strong enough indication, and we can also pretty much predict what dresses will reorder. I want a reorder business. Sure I do. As many reorders as possible. That's how a business grows big and that's how my ego gets rewarded. But, on the other hand, I don't want to overextend ourselves at the beginning. I don't want to be a pig about the money. The business should be kept purposely small until I can work out a proper fit with Morris and until each department is running smoothly. That way if a dress doesn't reorder, we won't have to worry. We'll always have new ones ready to show. There won't be any serious dry spells. I guarantee you'll always have clothes to sell to someone."

"It's going to be very hard to do it that way, Phil. Especially hard on you. You'll never have a breather and it's going to make a real guesswork thing out of my ordering." Andy consulted a page of figures; the plan didn't exactly fill him with enthusiasm.

"If I'm willing to make it hard for myself at first, Andy, then you can work a little harder too."

"I'm willing. It's not that. You'll always find me willing. It's only that I don't want to be the one that's blamed if we fail. I don't want to fail at all and I'm not expecting that we will. Don't get me wrong. This is *my* chance too, you know. Probably my last chance. I'm forty-five, remember. Some items there's just no time to redo."

"Let's not worry about that now, Andy." Michael was beaming. "Because there's absolutely not going to be any failure around here. I predict that by the end of the year we'll be the hottest house on the Avenue. We can't possibly miss. We have the best young designer in the business. We have an old pro for a production man. We have a great name to work with and ready-made customers. So now all we need are the clothes. Let's all stop being gloomy and get down to work." With that said, Michael reached into his pocket and produced a cigar. "I really did have one but I didn't want any of you to yell so I waited until the end to light it."

With hair even longer and wilder, now that simply everyone in New York City in November, 1966, was wearing it that way, Pat was absolutely thrillola to return to work. She had held out—"in total poverty, I might add, but I just couldn't stand the idea of working for anyone else on this planet as long as you were alive." At first, all she had to do was paint Phil's office, put up a curtain on their tiny window, buy sketch pads and Pentels, arrange a white formica slab on top of some filing cabinets that would have to be used as their sumptuous desk.

The girl that Phil had salvaged from obscurity in Bruce Greenstalk's room was willing to do anything just to work for Mr. Hanssler. Since Anita Mangiapane had decided to retire—"Better I to stay home with my son he shouldn't get into any more trouble"—Phil hired Nita Neary— "You can't resist a girl with that kind of name, can you, Pat?" "Absolutely never. I'm devoted to it"—as a sample hand and as someone to train for bigger things. Dorothy Krakauer was available and anxious to come back to Phil even though it meant exchanging a job in a nice, airy sample room for the cramped quarters at Mr. Jack. If anyone trips over something here, she said, she'd have to report it to the union because this was like a sweatshop. How can someone do good work when they can't breathe? Carmen Ruiz, cha-cha-cha, came back gladly. Evelyn Washington said she was beginning to think that Phil turned prejudiced, she hadn't heard from him in so long. Mildred Berkowitz was a problem. The budget didn't call for a finisher—each sample hand would do her own finishing—and besides, there just wasn't an unused corner of the room for her. Mildred was hurt—"I could work in even a closet." Fortunately, she too had another job. "I'll be all right, Mr. Phil. I'll get over it. But if it should ever come a time you could use me, you should only call. For you I'll work for nothing even."

The biggest problem was finding an assistant. Ginny was married and content to be just that, for the time being and as long as the money held out. Although Nita had the touch and taste for the job, she didn't have the experience. The girls wouldn't like taking orders from a mere child. They'd step all over her. Not having an assistant held up the works. Phil couldn't really start production until he had someone to cut the patterns. The sample hands could do it, but they hated having to. They weren't paid enough for that kind of responsibility. They would do it just in the beginning, Dorothy the spokesman told Phil, because they wanted to help out. So there he was with hundreds of ideas and hundreds of sketches scattered everywhere on the formica slab and no assistant. Pat was willing to try, but when the moment of truth arrived, she faltered. "It's one thing to cut a muslin pattern, but to cut into the fabric itself panics me, Phil. I'll ruin everything. I'll waste time. The business will fail outright. I can't do it. I wasn't trained for it. I hate it. Ab-so-lute-ly hate it. I'm . . . I'm . . ."

"You're insane is what you are. Forget it. Just sketch. That's all. Sketch. Be a designer. Think prints for summer. Contact some of the magazines. Get the editors up here. Let them know we're around again. Call Lovey Gray at *Women's Wear*. Get some free publicity because one of your bosses won't pay for any. No names, please. Only do something besides decorate this room. You've got us swimming in paisley already."

"I feel paisley."

"Stop feeling so much. And maybe you should cut your hair so I can see you."

"Never! Can't. Refuse. Ab-so-lute-ly refuse. Ask for anything else and it's yours, but not that."

"Knock it off. Also call Cindy. Tell her to come up. I want to see what she looks like these days. I hope her breasts aren't hanging too low. I want to bring back the breast."

Phil contacted Sandy and then Aram, called the State Employment Service looking for an assistant. They sent some women over, but none of them had hands like Ginny's. He was spoiled. These ladies were all too nervous, pulled at their clothes as if they were embarrassed, talked about how they really could have been designers. And time was passing. They were into November. The cutting room, the duplicate maker were waiting. Morris had made his rounds of the contractors and spoken with the union representative about their labor setup and their pricing. He and Phil had settled on the fit they were going to use for duplicates, measuring the proportions throughout the size range, a junior range, 3–13, a 15 once in a while, if the dress was right for a matron, but the fit was going to be zippy, always youthful. Phil wasn't trying to win every customer, just enough. The dummies, with their wire bottoms and their bronze metal knobs for heads, waited, languishing, unused, but padded according to the new Mr. Jack fit. The sewing machines in the duplicate makers' cubicle behind the dummies were switched off. The steam irons on the pressing tables gave off no hissing sounds of work in progress. It was maddening. And every day Michael poked his anxious, sweaty palms through piles of sketches, muttering, "Great. Beautiful. *That* we can sell. In the thousands. We can run it like a Ford. Only get started already, Phil. Will you, Phil? Please." Phil had stopped responding. What was the use of trying to explain? Silence was all he could manage with Michael because one word only led to another and the result was Michael's contrition and instant flattery.

Even the bookkeeper arrived to set up her office procedures, her books, her files, her billing methods, methods she had been trained to perform by the Greenstalks' efficiency experts. Mrs. Dubester, equipped with a streaked platinum beehive hairdo, perfect for pencil holding, the kind that looks as though it lives its own unattended life between bleaching and setting appointments, was the mother of two very successful college graduates, mind you, ". . . and they are almost professors, full professors, already, Mr. Hanssler. I know I look to be too young as a mother of a twenty-three and twenty-five-year-old son, respectively. But as you'll see I'm very capable of doing many things at once. Anything which I decide to do, I do. I'm both a mother and a bookkeeper as well as a wife. I have a lovely home on Pelham Parkway in the Bronx. I've worked all over for the biggest concerns, and I don't think it would be talking out of turn if I tell you that in my entire career I was never fired from a job. Anything which I do, I do to perfection, otherwise I don't try. It's not idle boasting, mind you. I just want you to know who is working for you so you can rest easy. It behooves me to tell my bosses that I'm a capable woman."

"Behooves?"

"Yes, Mr. Hanssler. It's something . . ."

"Phil."

"All right then, Phil. It's something I believe in doing immediately. That way you'll know, and Mr. Berns and Mr. Morgan will know that I'm not just any kind of woman who needs the money and who's afraid to stay home in her place. My husband, thank God, is able. He's a very capable breadwinner too. My sons are both geniuses, which is not boasting because it's the truth. All their instructors said so, and I'm therefore just going to set the record straight right from the beginning that I believe in doing things my way because I know what the right way is to do. My training was excellent."

"I'm glad to hear that. And do you know how to work a small switchboard, because there's one being installed today?"

"Of course I know. I've worked the biggest with so many trunk lines like a plate of spaghetti. I never disconnect. Only I don't believe that's something for me to be called upon to do. I'm a bookkeeper, Mr. . . . Phil. My first name, by the way, is Glenda. Glenda Dubester. And, as I started to say, I'm a bookkeeper. A professional person."

"You mean like Dr. Kildare or something?"

But she could laugh too, in addition to working a switchboard. She laughed then. "All right. This once I'll give in, but only temporary, just until you hire a kid. I told Mr. Berns already that I will need a kid to help me in the office. Once you get started it's entirely too much for one person with only two hands to do. I know that from all my other jobs.

You're too young to know about that, but Mr. Berns understands. He told me in a while he would hire a kid. He's such a lovely man, believe me I know."

"Thank you for that information, Glenda. Just remember, however, that you have three bosses."

"Of course, I wouldn't forget it. I should forget that? Never! I wouldn't offend a flea. I strongly believe in the proper things to do. I'm from the old-fashioned school. I only meant that since Mr. Berns is the one I shall be working closest with, it behooves me to find out what kind of man he is exactly. After all, I can't be disturbing you all the time you're designing. I know how temperamental artists are. I used to be friendly in my youth years ago with a group of artists in Greenwich Village. Lovely people. Don't get me wrong. I love artists because they understand so much about life. They have such feeling for people it's heartbreaking sometimes how they suffer."

A pencil fell out of her hair and while she leaned over to retrieve it Phil left the office, raced back to his own room holding his forehead. "That woman! She's unbelievable. Did you speak to her yet, Pat?" Pat was once more redraping the folds of the oversized paisley curtains.

"Courage, *mon vieux*. She's absolutely the most ghastly addition to any business on the face of the earth."

"She might just be, but you better learn to like Mrs. Glenda Dubester because she's here to stay. She's a Greenstalks baby."

"Oh! In that case I love her. Mrs. Dubester, I love you!" Pat screamed.

Mrs. Dubester, situated out front, clear across the showroom, was too busy with her new files to hear. But she did hear Cindy Rubin enter. She turned and stopped her. "Whom shall I say is calling for Mr. Hanssler, please?"

"Miss Rubin. I'm his model."

"Oh, you'll excuse me, Miss Rubin, but as you can see I'm new here. Before you know it, however, I'll catch on to whomever belongs. I'm very fast at names. I'm Glenda Dubester, the bookkeeper." Ceremoniously she led Cindy back to Phil's room, where she announced from the doorway, "Miss Rubin to see you, Mr. Hanssler."

"I don't believe it! You don't have to do this kind of thing, Glenda. You're too busy. Cindy is family." Phil managed not to laugh. Pat was unsuccessful. Glenda bowed and left, embarrassed.

Cindy enjoyed the formality. "It's dreadful of you to laugh, Pat. Good manners do help." With grace, with what she thought was elegance, slowly she removed her long leather gloves. One finger caught on the raised setting of her ruby ring. "Damn it."

"Manners, Cindy. Manners." Phil studied Cindy's new hairdo disapprovingly. "You've got so many attachments I don't know where you stop and the fake part begins."

"That's the whole point, Phil. I need falls. My hair's too short and everyone's using them now. Don't you like it either, Pat?"

"Divine. Devoted to it. Would you like to buy some of my hair for Christmas? It's guaranteed."

"You don't like it either. Well, if you *insist*, Phil, I'll try to arrange it another way." She removed her thrift-shop skunk, studied her burgundy knit tent dress in the recently installed full-length mirror, squashed it to her waist. "I'm so tired of tents." She poked at her hair, unwilling to disturb it really. "Your showroom's a horror, by the way. You *must* redecorate, Phil. I'll be glad to help for a nominal fee. You simply can't open a new business with that color carpeting. It's unprofessional."

"Let's not start in on that. I tried to fight that battle and lost, but I did get my sign up in the hall."

"It's gorgeous. Strikes your eye as soon as you step off the elevator."

"I don't know how gorgeous it is, but it'll do for now. . . . You've gained weight, Miss Rubin."

"I did not." She squashed her dress to her waist again as proof.

"Well, then you must be developing a middle-age spread." Phil circled her, squinting.

"You're so cruel to me. Why is he so cruel, Pat?"

"He hates women. Don't you know that all designers hate women?"

"Phil doesn't. Do you, Phil?"

"No. I don't hate women. I love women. Especially dykes. Have you been working the market lately, Cind'?"

"A little. Some fittings for that new dreamboat Carlos Casalla. He does very elegant clothes, but they're so overpriced. I hate couture clothes. They're never worth the money, especially that friend of yours. I did some fittings for him, too. What's his name?"

"Sandy White?"

"No. Better known than that. One of the top names."

"LeGeis?"

"That's right. Monsieur LeGeis."

"*He* used *you?*"

"You really are cruel. Some people think I'm a good model, you know. He booked me once, gave me a big line about my becoming a high-fashion model and then he never called me back. He is a prissy bastard, I must say."

"If you must, you must. He is. Don't let him bother you. You didn't happen to hear of a top-notch assistant floating around the Avenue, did you?"

"As a matter of fact, yes, I did. But isn't Ginny coming back?"

"Would I ask you if she were?"

"You really are beginning to sound more and more like a boss. But I'll forgive you because you're so handsome. Anyway, the one I know is working now for Mix 'n' Match. Sportswear house. In 498. I could call her for you. She's a divine worker. Just like Ginny."

"Call her! Instantly. And when you're through with that go out and buy yourself a new bra that'll pick you up. Our fit's going to start out bustier. Women are bustier since they're taking the pill."

And that's how the first summer line was born at the new Mr. Jack. Mary Lyon stepped into the sample room that first day on the job only slightly inebriated, not enough for Phil to discover the awful truth immediately. All he saw then was a savior, a plumpish, fortyish, moon-faced, water-spaniel-eyed madonna whose color seemed to redden as the day progressed, especially after lunch, when tiny networks of sky-blue veins rose to the surface of her sharp, narrow nose. Give or take an ounce, depending on the particular degree of daily tragedy she was living through or was expecting to live through, she remained partially drunk each day thereafter, except on those days when she promised Phil to reform. But so what! Let her be drunk. Her work was even better than Ginny's. Her fingers never seemed to impose themselves on the texture of any fabric she touched. They skimmed across each surface like a seaplane over the water before it landed gently. Every pattern she cut—she could cut more patterns than five assistants when she was forced to stick to her own job —was a demonstration of total affection for the dress, for Phil, for everyone that worked at Mr. Jack.

La Lyon—Pat dubbed her that and the nickname took root at once with the salesmen in the showroom, with the two underpaid black shipping boys, with Link, with the cutters, the sample hands, who were the first to complain about her drinking, with Andy and Michael, with Barbara Perkins, Glenda Dubester's kid, and with Glenda Dubester, who loved the sound of La—La Lyon had a giving nature. She was, and not just by virtue of her intimate acquaintance with Jack Daniels—it went deeper than that—a free, sympathetic, available ear for anybody's problems. She was equipped for tears: such watery eyes. And since she knew everybody else's skills, cutting, pattern making, duplicating, grading sizes, even production—she could save a penny here on stitchings, a penny there on linings—she managed to move around plenty in the course of a day, offering her services to one and all in return for just a little love, a little kiss. Morris especially clung to her as if to a rediscovered lover. Pinching her bottom while she whispered advice to him was not off limits, married though she was to someone ten years her junior and, therefore, a better drinker. It was all part of a joyous day's work, and a day's work for La Lyon might mean anything, the least part of which was running the sample room, Phil soon learned in exasperation. Vacuuming the showroom carpet if she saw dirt there was just as possible as cutting a pattern for one of Dorothy Krakauer's dresses, a fact about which Dorothy complained bitterly, but which Phil wouldn't honor because when the sample clothes were finished they looked as if she had personally supervised each stitch. They were clean, snappy, never fussed over. Phil's only criticism was that he couldn't be sure where he might find her when he was ready for a fitting.

"She's on safari, love, looking for new problems to solve." Pat's appreciation for La Lyon was professionally high, personally low.

"Never mind, Miss Hardhearted Hannah. The work gets done, doesn't it? It's beautiful, isn't it?"

"It is. There's absolutely no gainsaying that. But at what cost, *cher maître*? What cost? The woman needs to be protected from herself. She's like a roller coaster out of control. And when she's not rolling she's on the telephone crying with her husband or mother-in-law, the invalid, or just plain smelling out another wake to attend. I mean that woman just literally dotes on tragedy. Since she's been here, Phil, she's taken more time off to go to church and light more candles and say more novenas than the entire combined population of the Catholic Church. It's no wonder she's at the brew all the time. You know that plain little medicine bottle she keeps above her work table? Well, sweetheart, that ain't no elixir of paregoric for a nasty tummy. It's the stuff, honey. The purest bourbon known to man. Of course when *I* want to spend an extra hour at Bendel's you blow your top."

"I need *someone* to stick close by me. And what she keeps in her bottle is all right with me just as long as she accomplishes what she has to accomplish."

"Philip, you are the ultimate joy of my life. If you don't marry me after you make your first million I simply don't know what I'll do. Why don't you get rid of that Wilma woman and fly away with me to the

Mexican border? By the way, I've been neglecting to tell you that she called only sixteen times today. Do *me* a favor and call her back, please."

"I will. But did you hire the models for the preview?"

"I did and I made an appointment for *Mademoiselle* tomorrow morning at ten. *Glamour* at eleven-thirty. *Women's Wear* at two-thirty. *Cosmopolitan* the following morning and *Harper's* thereafter. *Look*, *Life*, and the Marines I haven't contacted yet."

"Beautiful. Keep after the Marines. Did the rhinestone buttons come in for the print group?"

"The buttons came in. The linen arrived. As did the voile and the satin. I've sketched some fabulous ideas if you'll only stop running long enough to look at them. Please remember that I want to end up being a designer, not a telephone operator. Capeesh? Cindy will be in right after lunch for fittings, so why don't you take me to a feedbag right now? After all, it's almost Christmas and I'm very sentimental."

"All right already. I'll take you to lunch, but first scratch my back."

"Will do, as long as La Lyon doesn't catch me at it. She'd stab me as soon as watch my fingers run down your shirt, which, by the way, has a rip under the sleeve. You're going to have to marry *someone*. That's all there is to it. As long as it isn't La Lyon, I'm satisfied." She scratched Phil.

"How can you be jealous of a middle-aged Joan of Arc?"

"Me? Jealous? The only one I'm jealous of is you. I want what you've got. And I don't mean your body—at the moment."

"You'll have a career, eventually, and then you'll leave me. They all do. Not that I ever blame them. Train 'em and let 'em go. That's life. There's no reason to be jealous of me."

"Oh, I'm not *really* jealous, Phil. I'm impatient."

"Don't be. You're not ready yet for the big time." Phil picked his nose, collapsed into the director's chair which Pat had bought him as a reminder that he was her boss and leader, on the day they completed the fittings on their first dress for the new line: a djellabah, the African influence, a wavy black, tan, white print that no one other than Pat, Cindy, and himself appreciated. Michael said: "Sure it's nice. But you won't get a cutting ticket on it. Maybe five of our customers will touch it." Andy said: "It's very pretty," which meant that the fabric was too expensive. Morris said: "All right. If you like it. But it's too much wastage because I got to match the print along the seams, you know." Even Glenda Dubester thought it wouldn't be right for her future daughter-in-law. Such were the challenges of a new firm, as Phil viewed it when he relaxed long enough to be philosophical: to satisfy everyone, including the salesmen and the magazine editors, who wanted only the avant-garde, the newest silhouette, the fashion news; the buyers who wanted the safe and the familiar but with just a touch of the new so they could make their figures each month, and his partners who wanted whatever the salesmen told them their customers were asking for. Last of all, he wanted to satisfy himself, which could only happen if everyone else's taste and temperament were satisfied. Impossible to achieve that goal. And, if he did, what would he want next? Better to concentrate on the fact that here he was and here he would have to stay for a while, a long while longer, five years longer, among the harpies who kept right on picking him to pieces. "You do think the clothes so far are good, don't you?"

Pat stood before him, smiled. "You always ask me and everyone else the same question when you know better than anyone else that they're good. Why do you do that?"

"I'm insecure, Wilma tells me. I'm blocked. I'm an idiot."

"You're a love. You're one of the sweetest human beings I've ever met. Certainly there's no one close to you on Seventh Avenue, which I suppose is not exactly a compliment. Just don't worry so much. The clothes are fabulous. Everyone who knows thinks they are."

"We're on the right track?"

"We're on the express track. Don't even doubt it for a second."

Phil stood up abruptly, posed before the mirror, flattened his silky hair into place. "I've aged ten years in a month. That's why I doubt it."

"Well, isn't that the occupational hazard? I mean, don't you think it's worth a few age lines if you can get some recognition out of this preposterous profession? I'm being serious now because it is preposterous what we do, isn't it?"

"I suppose it is. But I also suppose that everything people do to get themselves recognized is preposterous. That's why I work so hard. I don't have any time left over to think about what I'm doing."

"I refuse to feel that way at my age. Doesn't the sign in the hall mean anything to you?" Pat held Phil's six-button blazer for him to slip into. "You even bought a new jacket. A French one yet! So you must feel proud about something. If you don't, then what's the point of . . . I mean, then why bother at all? Why try?"

His jacket was on, but she wasn't budging. Her mood, her expression had suddenly changed. Banter and play were being shelved so that his holy statement of some simple truth, whenever it came, could be heard. She was waiting for some kind of alphabet-soup answer like See Dick

Run, Jane Can Run Too. That had been the answer his generation got when they asked, Why, Daddy? Now she was asking him. She was standing behind him, her face reflected in the mirror, her hair falling freely. The new generation! Her eyes were etched with eye-liner, her mouth was glistening with white lipstick—the new *in* shade this year. Only she wasn't any hippie revolutionary about to forge a new life style. She was just as much a hangover from the old world as he was. She cared about clothes and cleanliness as if they were the eleventh and twelfth commandments. She was a once-upon-a-time baby too. She was told that there were absolute answers to every question and she still believed it. Not every young girl with long hair was a free-love bunny. "The way you're staring at me you must think I've got something important to tell you, something prophetic, like purple's going to be the next hot color on the Avenue."

"Of course I do. You always tell me what I need to know."

"Well, this time I can't. I can only tell you about dresses. I don't know why I try to do what I'm doing. I'll bet you even believe in God."

"Really, Philip. What's God got to do with it?"

"Nothing. It's just shorthand for the idea that if devoting yourself to a career, with a capital C, isn't going to get you what you're after, you'd rather find a husband and raise a family. I don't exactly see you as a mother, but I do see you as a designer. You need to be, for the same reason I do."

"Which is what?"

"We're back to where we started. Let's go to lunch." He got his coat from the rack, but Pat remained in front of the mirror.

"Why won't you talk to me about anything but dresses? Sometimes you're so busy doing your own thing I doubt if you ever think about me at all."

"I've been accused of that before, so don't take it personally. I never tell anyone what I'm really thinking. I don't know how."

"Then I guess I'll just have to take my troubles to La Lyon. She can light a candle for me."

"Come! To lunch!" He grabbed her hand, tugged her out of the room and down the corridor to the delivery entrance. Out in the hall he stopped to study his sign. The curved silhouette stretched her arm out like a Statue of Liberty above Mr. Jack, above Phil Hanssler. "It *is* pretty."

"See! I was right."

Chapter Twelve

Between the death of the old Mr. Jack and the emergence of the new, money had been a tight item for Phil. The free-lance work for Greenstalks had helped some. At least it eased the panic of being totally without an income at thirty-five and eliminated the need to turn to his father. No checks bounced at the Chemical Bank. But those summer months were minus the usual beach weekends in the Hamptons or Fire Island or the frequent evenings out for dinner. He and Wilma spent a few days at Howie's Bucks County place, but those were nerve-racking events. Howie had rented with a gay, married couple, each of whom tried, secretly each thought, to get Phil into bed. When the second visit proved too much for Phil, Howie stopped going, willing to lose his share of the rent rather than lose his never very secure peace of mind. In August the three of them fought—just twice, that was all they could take—the bumper-to-bumper battle of the Long Island Expressway out to Jones Beach. Once, Aram summoned Phil, alone—Wilma had to take her mother and father to a wedding—to his Easthampton castle on the ocean. Again there was someone who followed Phil around all the time, even as far as the bathroom door. Not one hour of his two days there was peaceful. He was even deprived—a deprivation not experienced since his army days—of that pleasant moment when the bowels are allowed to loosen as they will. He badly missed being able to rent his own house and to choose his own companions, but renting and choosing were exactly the kinds of extra luxuries he couldn't afford just then.

So he and Wilma spent most of their summer in New York, including a warm Labor Day weekend when they made believe they owned the city: its quiet streets, its cool movies, its empty restaurants. Even Howie was gone, willing to be coaxed back to Bucks County because he had to begin teaching again the following Tuesday.

And then the contracts were signed. He was in business and it was just work, work, work. Every day of that autumn was tiring, but the fatigue was exhilarating. It had nothing to do with apathy. It kept him out of danger and in Wilma's bed. He was glad to be there. Their sex was the best it had ever been. No strain. No forcing. Just easy and simple, in the storybook way. Admittedly, by December, when he was knee deep in pulling the line together, he ached for a trip to Mexico with Sandy or for a few days in St. Thomas without Wilma, but that was out of the question for the new Phil Hanssler image. For Sandy White maybe, for all the almost-made-it Sandy Whites all over the world running away might be the best thing to do. But no more of that crap for him. For him it was Pikes Peak or bust. Perhaps in another year he could think about stopping and resting and spending money again. Deferring a few pleasures for a while was not so terrible.

Actually, Wilma helped with that part the most. Accustomed to waiting for what she wanted without complaining, like all law-abiding Americans, she could afford, especially now, to wait a little longer. So far, she had overcome. So she soothed. She reassured. She was certain the struggle was worthwhile. "If you didn't do it, you'd never be content. You're the one who wouldn't settle for anything but your own business. So just keep on smiling and make us all believe you're enjoying the sweat, which you really are. Especially tonight, smile. For your father's sake. And for mine too. We're bringing him good tidings, remember."

They were on their way to Teaneck—Wilma, Phil, Howie, Liffey—for what would have to be called a historic Friday night, a pre-Christmas, post-Chanukah celebration of an announcement—an in-between-holidays announcement—that Phil hoped would bring some belated joy to his father. His own sense of joy was not yet—maybe it would never be—one hundred percent. "Didn't I ever tell you that as a psychiatrist you're a better secretary?"

"You told me. But I insist on my talent. Talent will out, you know."

"No fights, children, please. My head! And we're in New Jersey already. You doesn't raise your voice." Howie's chin rested on the top of Wilma's bucket seat. "Why are you driving so slowly, Philip?"

"Because I'm not very anxious to get home."

"Why are we going then?"

"Wilma insisted on it."

"I *insisted?* Me? Turn the car around this instant. Take me back to the city where at least I can dwell among honest folk."

"I can't. U turns on major arteries are punishable by death. You're stuck and you're glad. I'd know that glad expression anywhere."

"How come I was asked to tonight's performance?" Howie moved Liffey from one window to the other so he could rest next on the top of Phil's seat.

"I told them I wanted to bring you. My mother was delighted."

"That's flattering. She loves me for my mind, for my formidable accomplishments, and you, you love me for my yellow hair."

Phil glanced up at the rear-view mirror. Howie was not smiling. "I wanted you here for . . . for support."

"Support? You know better than to count on that. I'm an outsider. Jewish families don't like to share their bliss, or sorrows, with outsiders. It's a law from the Torah."

Phil peered intently ahead at the line of traffic. "My mother loves you. She loves teachers. She thinks they're the smartest people in the world, next to upholsterers. And also you're an orphan, don't forget. A Jewish mother and an orphan! That's the greatest blessing you can give her. To feed you."

"Look at all the Christmas lights." Wilma pressed her button nose against the window. "They must have a lot of Gentiles in New Jersey. It's so pretty. Isn't it pretty, Howie? I mean in a superior aesthetic way?"

"Bee-you-tee-full! Aren't you sorry you weren't born a Catholic, Wilma?"

"No. I'm very happy to be what I am, thank you."

Phil pressed down on the accelerator. They were approaching Teaneck and there was no way to delay the encounter any longer. This evening would have to happen and take its place alongside all those other memorable events in the Hanssler history of memorable events.

Wilma moved as close to Phil as she could without slipping into the crack between the two seats. She played with fugitive strands of Howie's long hair. The three of them bent toward each other, smiling. "Say what you will, this *is* a lovely time of year, especially in the suburbs. They certainly know how to string lights out here."

Howie placed one hand on Wilma's fur-trimmed collar, the other behind Phil's neck. "I'm very glad to be with the two of you tonight."

"Let's not get sticky, Howie." But, even so, Phil felt the tribute of the moment. He sighed, a heaving sigh for old thoughts in a new world, for flickering Christmas lights on a darkened ranch house, for snow patches on a well-tended winter lawn, for the moon and broken street lamps, for his cold hands on the steering wheel and the loud chugging of the rear-engine Corvair—America's answer to those Jews who wouldn't, just couldn't, buy a Volkswagen—for Howie's simple sentiment, spoken, as they say, from an open heart, reminding Phil of affection he was trying, every day, to forget, that work and time and Wilma would, he hoped, help him to forget. And even Howie, straight-arrow Howie, would, after the shock waves had settled deeper, have to admit that what Phil was going to do was worth all the trouble it might begin. Everyone makes his way by stepping across the rapids from rock to rock anyhow, so this would be just his rock to rest on. For a while? For the rest of his life? Who knows and who cares? What else was there to do in this make-believe, stock-exchange world but to try and smile and shut your mouth and cope with this night and the hundreds of other nights to come, for his father's sake, for the Pasternacks' sake, for Wilma's and his own. Because, in a little while, when they fell to their food, everyone staring dumbly at each other, what difference would anything make? No one could look up into that unsmudged crystal-chandelier world over the dining-room table and be glad of anything for long, certainly not the heir apparent. Clean crystal had cost him too much.

And then there they were, parked, the front door of the house opening before they had a chance to get out of the car, his mother waving them in out of the cold, Liffey scampering onto the lawn to pee quickly, car doors slamming, Wilma extending the bouquet of yellow mums to Mrs. Hanssler, brushing cheeks with her and calling that a kiss instead of what it really was, armed neutrality; and Howie hanging back, tying his shoelace, waiting for Phil to go before him up the steps and into the gold damask foyer, into the dining room, where everyone was seated, ready to begin, as soon as the hellos and how-are-yous were over with and Glenn got his kiss from Phil and Mr. Hanssler his, and Paul, nodding his greetings impatiently, put the coats away. Betty and Andrea, the precious pair, immobilized by habit and their mother-in-law, stared Wilma down into her seat between Phil and Howie, checking out her pink silk tent dress and her hidden weight, her short, loose-curled hair, her bright, white, prepared-for-all-emergencies teeth.

They were nine for dinner, Mr. Hanssler in his patriarch's place; Phil, Wilma, Howie down the left side; Paul, Andrea, Betty, and Glenn down the right; Mrs. Hanssler, when she sat at all, at the foot of the table, at the end of the straight row of pickle plates and sour tomatoes, of sauerkraut and cranberry sauce and the challah: the line of scrimmage; the border between two worlds, one of light and one of dark; the sacred, never-changing order of the field. And Mr. Hanssler, good, graying Herman Hanssler would be the referee.

"Herman? No drinks for our guests? Phil, darling, don't you want a drink of Scotch? It's all out in the kitchen, Herman."

Sure Phil wanted a Scotch, so did Howie, probably, for courage; but, as usual, Phil declined and so did everybody else. If a Friday-night meal began later than seven, his father got nervous. The Messiah's arrival would be delayed another thousand years.

Mr. Hanssler speared his fish. The meal began. Betty, as usual, frowned and scraped the roe away. The others ooh-ed and ah-ed as was expected, dipped their golden challah in the horseradish, gulped, wheezed, red-dened, reached for water.

"It's very strong tonight, the horseradish. Be careful everyone." Mr. Hanssler spread it thickly on his fish.

Mrs. Hanssler was up and running, refilling water glasses, bending, shuffling around the table in her gray felt Indian moccasins, her daugh-ters-in-law steadfastly still, refusing to collect a plate. Wilma tried to help, half-rose, was pulled back down by Phil. "My mother doesn't allow that in her house. Not even relatives are allowed to help."

And between each course—the chicken noodle soup, the roast chicken and the dried-up pot roast with the hard potatoes and the Jello mold—the conversation sputtered, went out, began again about easy things like cars, the weather, flu, the fact that Glenn had bought some Greenstalks stock because now that Phil was in it it had to be a safe investment. Top-ics meant for semi-strangers' ears to warm to. Wilma and Howie had been "home" for dinner before, but still and all, Mr. Hanssler had been known to say, they were guests, not relatives. They were to be wined and dined, not shocked. Tonight, Phil was glad for that slice of Jewish wisdom: whoever heard of a family's problems being discussed in public? What's ours is ours; it's nobody else's business. At times like these it's a lot more sociable to shut up and eat. Besides, Wilma and Howie didn't seem to care. Whether they liked the food or not, they ate it. No need for him to criticize the pot roast. Just eat the chicken instead and make his mother and father deliriously and totally happy. So he smiled at everything and everyone, even at Betty when she asked, inevitably, if he noticed anything different about her.

"You've got a new wig on."

"No, I don't! Be serious." She poked Glenn's ribs with her elbow.

"Your brother remembers everything. He's really something. . . . No, it's an entirely different thing."

"Well, then, I'm afraid I don't, unless it's that . . ." he proceeded cautiously, "you've gained a little weight."

Instead of frowning or pouting, which is what he expected, Betty's mouth opened cheerfully. "You really are something." She shifted heavily in her chair, said nothing further, but glanced at Andrea proudly. Andrea did not change her expression of trancelike indifference. Silence reigned for a while longer, until just before the tea and cake and nuts and fruit, when everyone moved their chairs back from the table. Phil picked Liffey up, settled her between his legs, fed her some grapes. Wilma smoked. Howie watched Mrs. Hanssler stacking dishes. And so now was the time for desultory talk to ripen into give and take, show and tell. Politeness would be put away and, with it, reason.

First it was, naturally, Mr. Hanssler's turn to question his sonny boy about the business. "I hope you're making sure you're getting everything that's coming to you. Your partners look to be good men, which I'm glad for, thank God, but you, you have a tendency to look the other way too much."

"I'm not looking the other way. I'm looking straight ahead, Dad. No one's going to be cheating me."

"Cheating? Who said anything about cheating? Of course no one's going to be cheating. The Greenstalks people are honest. Your partners are honest—"

"So then what's the problem?"

"There's no problem. It's only that I know you, my sonny boy, from way back. I know how you were never interested in how a business works." He covered Phil's hand with his and squeezed. "I don't mean it as an insult because you're smart enough to understand that I'm talking for your own good."

"Then you don't have to worry about a thing. I've changed, Dad. I really have. I know what my own good is. I know how to make good clothes."

"They are beautiful." Wilma moved her chair closer to Phil's. "I've seen some of them."

"I'm glad they're beautiful. I also hope they sell because if they don't sell, what good is being beautiful? Correct, Phil?"

"Not correct." Without his wanting it to, anger began a rapid boil in his stomach. "The most beautiful dresses never sell. You have to force

295

them on buyers to get enough for a cutting ticket, but I'd rather be dead than stop making them."

"Dead? Don't talk like that, Phil. Of course, make them. All I mean to say is that at the beginning maybe you should concentrate on the other kind more, just so the business can build up some capital, so it'll have what to fall back on in case you should do one or two bad lines. Because you never can tell. Even the best can't do it perfect all the time. True?"

"That's a nice positive attitude. It's very reassuring when your own father has such faith in you."

Mr. Hanssler indicated, by a quick movement of his index finger, not once, but twice, that there were strangers present.

"Just say what you want to say, Dad. Wilma and Howie are friends. They're not enemies you have to be afraid of. They know all they need to know about our family. And what they don't know yet, they'll find out soon enough."

Embarrassed, caught in the act, his face flushing, but smiling anyway, Mr. Hanssler began his familiar struggle for peace and harmony. "All right then. I'm sorry. I didn't mean for you to think I didn't have faith in you. Of course, I have faith in you. I always did."

"Fine. I'm glad. So try and relax and just enjoy the fact that I, alone, accomplished something and that I'll accomplish more. Doesn't that please you? Why must all the dumbest things bother you?"

"Shah! sonny boy. No need to get excited. We're only sitting and we're talking. And, after all, is it such a dumb thing for me to be concerned about your future?"

"And, after all, I'm just telling you not to be. I'm a grown man. My future is my own business. My past, unfortunately, was yours."

Beaten back, Mr. Hanssler lowered his head, turned his napkin nervously. Phil watched him, sorry for what he had said, but his father had heard much worse and gotten over it.

"Do you think that kind of remark helps matters any?" Paul charged onto the field.

"No, I don't. But I think Dad knows I didn't mean to hurt him just like he didn't mean to hurt me by what he said."

"One thing you're not, Phil, is a very compassionate person."

"And you, of course, are?"

"I hope so."

"Well, hoping won't make it so. Let me be the first to clue you in. You're not."

Paul slapped his palms down on the table. The gun was aimed, but before the trigger was squeezed, Wilma interceded on behalf of Mr. Hanssler's pleading expression. "We live in very troubled, anxious times, don't you think, Paul?"

"Very troubled," Howie echoed.

Startled by the non-sequitur, Paul let go of the trigger.

"Besides," Wilma continued, "your mother is ready to serve the tea. . . . What a beautiful cake, Mrs. Hanssler. Don't tell me you bake too?"

First Glenn, followed by Betty, Phil, Mr. Hanssler, Andrea, even Paul, in that order, broke into laughter. Wilma grinned. Howie reached for a piece of the cake.

Mrs. Hanssler, a filled teacup in each hand, froze. "I don't see what's so very funny that you're all laughing at me."

Once more Wilma assisted. "They're laughing at me, Mrs. Hanssler, not you. Something I said before. People are always laughing at me."

Looking as if she believed what Wilma said, Mrs. Hanssler laughed too, then settled the teacups in front of her husband and Phil, the Jewish order of things: men first, starting with the oldest.

"Don't you have any chocolate cake, Mom?" Betty fidgeted, looking with disgust at the slices of honey cake nearby.

"It's coming right out. I can't bring everything at once, you know." Annoyed, but at herself, not her daughter-in-law, she shuffled off into the kitchen.

"She should have a tray, as long as she won't allow anyone to help her." Howie's suggestion provoked another round of laughter, but Howie was not as happy to accept the role of social patsy. "Is there something humorous in that idea? Something I'm missing?"

"Don't pay any attention to them, Howie. It's just that somehow the picture of my wife carrying a tray . . . Please, Paul. Control yourself a little. Must a grown man behave foolishly?"

"Don't you like people to laugh, Dad? I thought you wanted us to laugh so we wouldn't fight?"

"I don't like foolishness at someone else's expense."

"It's all right, Mr. Hanssler." But it wasn't all right, Phil saw. Howie was turning the other cheek too soon and toward Mrs. Hanssler, who was finally returning to her seat to try and finish dinner. "It was my fault."

"Yes. It *was* your fault. You're a little too—what shall I call it? Sen-si-tive?" Whistling the s's, Paul stretched the syllables, raised one eyebrow.

During the silence that followed, Phil lifted Liffey from his lap, leaned forward, his anger at a bubble, waiting for Howie to say something, because if Howie wasn't going to out of respect for the occasion, Phil would. In 1966, yet, this is happening, and his brother, his very own little mixed-up brother, was doing it.

Andrea broke the spell. "Drink your tea, Paul." Even she was embarrassed.

"I'm waiting for it to cool off." Paul kept his gaze locked on Howie.

"Your brother was quite correct, Paul. You don't have a compassionate nature. He does, however. Although if he didn't, I could certainly understand why he didn't." Howie's voice sounded calm. He spoke slowly, deliberately leaning toward the center of the table so everyone would be sure to see and hear him. He was prepared for a counterattack, but Wilma's hand pulled him back.

"What exactly do you do on Madison Avenue, Phil?" But before Paul could shift gears and answer—his concentration on Howie was so intense—Wilma went on to Glenn, asked him the same question. Glenn was allowed to answer.

"I don't work on Madison Avenue. I work with my father."

"Of course. How nice you can be with your father. In fabrics together. Phil told me it's called piece goods. What exactly does that mean, Mr. Hanssler?" Her diversionary action stopped the advance cold.

"I buy up remnants from dress companies, pieces that are left over when they finish making up the garments. Then I sell the pieces to stores." Mr. Hanssler's smile overflowed with grateful appreciation for Wilma's peace-keeping effort.

"So you're actually like a middleman who comes at the end. It must be very hard work. Keeps you on your toes, I'll bet. As you know, my father owns a little grocery store in Brooklyn. . . ." Effectively, without even having to stir her tea for attention—Paul, marking time, began to do that—Wilma managed to effect a lull, a cessation of hostilities, some semblance of people actively engaged in finding out about each other just because they enjoy the game of knowing, for its own sake. She went on in her winning way about her father and mother and their store. She told new stories about old facts. Mr. and Mrs. Hanssler, Glenn, and Betty were enjoying it. Andrea wouldn't join the party. But at least there was some good feeling in the room. Wilma smiled triumphantly at Phil. He leaned over, kissed her cheek.

But Phil knew, as Wilma couldn't, that Paul was a long way from giving up. His next target would be the little big shot, the star. So the only thing to do was to deprive him of the moment, to make the announcement right now. He'd never have another chance, maybe not even for the rest of his life, and Wilma would like it now. Her information-please strategy had had method in it, apart from silencing Paul. She wanted an atmosphere and she had gotten it. Her eyes said, they're all listening and quiet. So why not now? "I've got something to say—"

"So do we," Betty interrupted, excited in a way she seldom was. Glenn blushed, gazed off at the wallpaper above his father's head.

"Do you want to go first?"

"Not necessarily. You could, Phil. You're first anyway."

"Why don't you both speak at the same time?" Paul struck his spoon against the gold-rimmed teacup, "and that way no one gets *star* billing."

"Are you always this nasty or is it just reserved for your family and their friends?" Howie was not calm now.

"I don't think that comment was called for. No one asked *you* for an opinion." Paul braced his palms against the table edge, his handsome face, its smooth tan skin suddenly turning a brilliant red. He was an almost perfect replica—strange that at such a moment Phil would be reminded—of their own mother's kinder beauty. But her face had been reddened by sunburn, hardly ever by anger.

"Herman!" Frightened, without knowing about what, Mrs. Hanssler yelled across the table.

"All right, Ethel, I hear. Paul, I want you to stop that kind of talking right now." He pointed his impotent finger.

"Let him talk, Dad. I told you my friend Howie knows what's what. He knows what a good, solid Jewish family's capable of."

"Your sarcasm doesn't help, big shot." Paul's chin jutted forward. "What the hell do you know about Jewish families anyway? You and your friends arrive late, like potentates from the big city, sophisticated you think, lording it over everyone else."

"Doesn't your psychiatrist tell you you're very sick, Paul?" It was call to quarters and Phil was ready. What the hell.

"If he does, it's none of your business. As long as you're not sick. As long as you've got a girl friend *and* a boy friend to display! Do you think I'm some kind of fool who doesn't know the score? I know New York too, you know." Andrea tugged at her husband's arm, but he shook it free, continued to stare across at Phil, waiting, blinking, tears beginning to form in his eyes, which heightened the brilliance of their blue. But he didn't cry. The strongest instinct of survival seemed to stop that from happening, seemed to silence everyone. And Mr. Hanssler muttered, "Please, please, please," not understanding what Paul meant or Phil meant or anyone meant, just wanting peace and his cup of tea and his faith in the belief that, no matter how it looked, everything was all right, fine, just fine.

And how odd it was that during that challenging silence Phil felt the racing boil in his stomach subside. He waited. A calm, a sense of relief settled slowly. Maybe he was even smiling because he was certain that when he spoke again he wouldn't yell. He was free, home and free finally. That's what it was, freedom, a moment's peace, a rest before the need to move, a freedom from any obligation to anyone in his family, to anything he had ever done to Paul, to anything he had ever shared with Paul in the past. Over. Finished, if not altogether then, if not all at once, then soon, very soon. He knew it. Paul's hatred, love—it was probably both—would never let him alone unless he took a chance and let it explode into clear, clean accusation. So here it was. The perfect time. Okay. Good. He thinks I'm queer. Either/or. He has reason to think so. And if it makes him feel superior, if it helps him, then all right. It doesn't change a thing that didn't need changing anyway. "No, you're not *some* kind of fool. You're just a fool. A pathetic fool, and the score, as far as I'm concerned, is even-steven now." Phil's quiet tone, almost a whisper, shocked everyone, including Paul. "The only thing that bothers me is that you had to take it out on my friend. Because Howie *is* my friend. He doesn't deserve the way you treated him before. No one deserves that. He didn't offend you. He only protected himself. That fact even you should have understood. The other fact, the one I came home to tell everyone tonight, so I could feel warmed and satisfied by the happy, loving hearts of a loving family, is that Wilma and I are going to get married."

Mr. Hanssler jumped to his feet, smiling, tears springing up instantly, moving to kiss Phil, then Wilma, allowing his wife at them next, shaking Howie's hand in confusion. "Thank God. Now I can die happy. Now maybe I'll have a grandchild."

"*Mazel tov.*" Glenn pumped Phil's hand over the line of scrimmage.

"Congratulations." Betty remained seated, forgotten for the moment.

Paul and Andrea said nothing. Paul, in defeat, was as uncharitable as he would have been if he had been the victor. His attention was for Howie, for his smile that seemed to struggle to stay put. "I guess you knew all about this, didn't you?"

"Yes."

"And I suppose you're happy about it, aren't you?"

"Of course he's happy. Who wouldn't be happy?" Seated once more, crying freely, Mrs. Hanssler reached for an apple, offered it to Howie, who declined. "He's Phil's best friend. Of course he's happy. What a question! . . . When will you have the affair, Wilma?"

"It depends. We haven't decided. A few months maybe."

"I still have something to say." Betty sat up, silent until every head turned toward her. Glenn stood behind her chair, his gaze wandering to its favorite spot on the wallpaper. "I'm expecting. The end of June the doctor thinks."

And once more Mr. and Mrs. Hanssler were out of their seats, crying now beyond ecstasy, kissing Glenn and Betty, looking up at the crystal chandelier, where God was stationed and ready to accept their thanks for such blessings to happen all at once.

"This calls for a real celebration." Mr. Hanssler clapped, then rubbed his hands together. "Ethel, how about opening that bottle of champagne you're keeping in the closet!"

Before she could hear Phil tell her that champagne kept in a closet wasn't going to be cold enough to drink, Mrs. Hanssler was off and running to the master bedroom, to the kitchen, her felt moccasins slapping hard against linoleum, back into the dining room with an ice bucket, a tray of glasses, a bottle of Piper Heidsieck, 1937. She set the tray down in front of Phil.

"Mother, you can't put ice in champagne. It has to get cold in a refrigerator."

"What's the difference? On such a night I don't mind drinking it warm. It's the happiest night of my entire life. My son is going to have a baby. We're going to be grandparents, Herman!" She scanned the table, clapping her hands, suddenly remembering the other great announcement. "And Phil's going to be married. It's too much to take."

While everyone watched, waiting for the pop, Phil undid the gold foil, unwound the wire from around the cork. It didn't budge. He pulled at it, twisted it slowly. There was no fizz in the bottle. When the cork came out, there was no sound but a squeak. "It's flat. It's turned sour."

"What do you mean flat?" Mrs. Hanssler leaned down to look into the top of the bottle. "It can't be. It's champagne."

"You're not supposed to keep champagne forever, Mother. You're supposed to drink it, not save it for special occasions." He laughed, reached for her hand, held it. "It doesn't matter. We don't need champagne to celebrate. Everyone's happy enough as it is, aren't we? A new business. A birth. A marriage. A new life. A new world. What else do we need?"

A light snow had begun to fall by the time they started back for New York. The roads were slick, the bridge slippery, and Phil had to concentrate on his driving. That was as good an excuse for his continuing silence as anything else was. Conversation just yet seemed impossible, maybe even superfluous. Wilma, staring ahead, beyond the slapping windshield wipers, had placed her arm behind Phil's neck and left it there, as a touching reminder of her determined presence, her patience, her victory. Occasionally she turned to smile affectionately at Howie, but each time she did he peered more intently out the clouded side window, as if his life depended on what he would see there.

Phil, watching him from the rear-view mirror, could tell that Howie knew that his answers, if he could find any, had to be outside, not inside this skidding car. Most of what had happened to Phil inside himself for a long time, especially that calm, free moment of understanding earlier, had happened because of, sometimes in spite of, Howie's talking, urging, doing, loving. And Phil had asked him to come tonight. So Howie had a right to sulk, brood, or say nothing. What Paul had said and done had to hurt, no matter how much he denied it. Howie didn't have to take that kind of crap from anyone. Usually he didn't. Hadn't he said often enough that as long as he had to live alone, as long as he didn't have anyone to answer to, he might as well enjoy the opportunity of saying whatever he wanted whenever someone gave him a hard time? But tonight he hadn't. Tonight telling the truth would have hurt other people, not himself, and so Howie had held back, had let Paul ridicule him right up until the end, when they were just about to step out of the house and Paul, shaking Howie's hand and telling him he hoped there were no bad feelings, had added, "You're next," had raised his eyebrow again, had hung on maliciously to Howie's hand. The look of disbelief on Howie's thin, sad-eyed face, the whitening ridge of his lips then, that ridge of restraint, that was his gift to Phil and Wilma, to Mr. and Mrs. Hanssler and their bliss. Howie wouldn't spoil the joyous scene with a screaming exit. He wasn't like that. When he stepped out of the house and walked slowly to the car, that was the end of Paul as far as he was concerned, like Wotan saying to Hunding as he killed him: "Geh! Geh!"

Sometimes Howie's apparent weakness was his greatest strength: his ability to gauge an adversary; to know that with some people it was just a waste of time and energy to argue; to let them think they've won and not to care. That was one kind of Howie, and what he was doing now with Wilma was another kind. Now he was the appreciator, the respecter of the rules of the game when the people playing care about each other. Then there really *are* winners and losers and also-rans. That's the human condition, baby, Howie would have said. *Finally*, everybody loses. That was Howie the teacher, the professional, the man with a black view of life who wanted to live, nevertheless, as if it could be better, as if by everyone's being made aware of how dread and fear and finitude are everybody's lot, the future could be made better. How do you feel about them eggrolls tonight, Howie? And then, as if Howie had been reading Phil's thoughts in the clouded window, reacting to Wilma's consoling smile, he spoke up without turning from the window, "Don't feel sorry for me. Neither one of you. I can't stand that. I'm perfectly fine, or will be. A little bloody, but unbowed."

When they left the West Side Drive at Nineteenth Street and headed east, Wilma suggested that Phil drop her off first and then whispered, "Maybe you should have a talk with Howie. Call me later." He nodded gratefully.

Regardless of snow and sleet, Howie didn't want to stay at Phil's apartment, nor did he want to go to his own. So, after Liffey had been walked and taken upstairs, they drove around, finally headed uptown to an East Side gay bar that Howie knew. He insisted on going there. "It'll be crowded. It's late and it's Friday night, but the way I feel it'll be easier to talk with a crowd around."

Phil maneuvered through the Village side streets, turned north on the Fourth Avenue of another era. They passed Fourteenth Street, Klein's, a wet, white, deserted Union Square Park. Up Park Avenue South. Ahead was the Pan Am Building, soaring above Grand Central in ugly domination of an ugly avenue, acting like a barricade, an aluminum shield protecting the legends of upper Park Avenue, the real Park Avenue, from the sight of the death throes of its older, grayer stepsister to the south.

The car moved slowly through the dark, curving road beneath the building, emerged in a different world, faced a richer, more pretentious vista: the sudden, rushing stretch of tree-lined islands between the traffic as if they and not the cars were in motion; the trees strung with Christmas lights; the setback, well-lit, reflecting glass façades of new buildings decorated with huge Nutcracker wreaths, these buildings that had appeared as if by magic, overnight, it seemed to Phil, during the money boom of the Korean War and after, when Eisenhower stuttered through his good, gray years of heart attacks and Richard Nixon smiled patiently, waiting for his turn; all of this, the entire avenue from here to Ninety-sixth Street where the ghetto started, an enclave of hard-sell, soft-smile power and lock-step taste, a tiny provincial outpost of posh restaurants and night clubs, of old hotels and new apartment houses, the city's diamond in a dungheap that many, too many, aspired to reach, like El Dorado, to live and die within, without the worry of a black neighbor, inside the promised land, protected by the Pepsi generation and Chase Manhattan, by the Lever Brothers and Seagram's VO. To travel from Teaneck to the Carlyle Hotel, however short the distance, could take a whole lifetime. If that's what you wanted. If that's what making money meant: the choice of this or Scarsdale or Great Neck—or Greenwich Village and Howie's kind of life that banged the gong for values and ended up as valueless, as finished, as anybody's life.

Howie wasn't looking at anything except, maybe, the landscape inside himself. He remained silent even after they arrived near the bar over on First Avenue in the Fifties, even after the car was parked.

The bar *was* crowded, the air thick with smoke and sibilance and staring eyes. Frank Sinatra from the juke box sang about the winter of his life. They weaved through the dim glow from blue lights overhead, an X-ray light that bleached the skin, passed between rows of well-dressed men drinking at the long bar and leaning against the wall. The small back room was empty. Tables were pushed up tight against tufted leatherette banquettes.

"Will they serve back here? It doesn't look as if anyone ever makes it this far." Phil removed his raincoat, folded it over the back of his chair, prepared himself to face Howie's hunched question-mark body.

"I think a waiter will get here eventually."

Eventually a waiter did appear, pushing through the last layer of men being forced back, against their will, into the empty back room, and eventually, after the first Scotch and the order of another, they did talk, Howie starting off because he knew better than anyone that Phil wouldn't, didn't know how to, begin. Most of what he said at first was ancient history, a précis of the past: their meeting, the army, Germany, Phil's trips to Venice and Capri, Carl Kalb and Aram and Sandy. Paul was disposed of quickly, and then there was Wilma. Perspective was what he wanted, he said. A balance of the parts. Connections. A way to understand why Phil was, after all, making the choice of marrying Wilma—"Not that I don't like her. I love her. You know that"—and why it was necessary to make a choice at all. "That's what I don't understand. Why do you have to?"

"You think I should have chosen someone like you, for instance? Is that what you mean?"

"No, I don't think that at all. That idea I gave up on a long time ago when I went upstate to teach."

"You sure?"

"No. I'm not sure . . . about that . . . or anything, except what *I* am. The rest of it, what I feel, is beside the point, though. It's academic now."

"And you want me to be the same way you are. That's been decided. As far as you're concerned I'm supposed to be. All the facts seem to point to that. It's all figured out scientifically. . . . Howie? Do we have to stay *here* and talk? Can't we go home? I hate having those guys looking back here all the time and that damn juke box . . ."

"As well here as any other place. We started out on your home court so we might as well play this set on mine. I'm not embarrassed by it and I'm not going to get sticky."

"I knew you didn't like me saying that before." Phil gulped from his drink, looked away, above the crowd, at the blue lights, at the strands of cigarette smoke stilled by the still air around the bulbs, wanting to leave, but wearily willing, also, to let Howie have his way. That's his right. That's only a small part of what he deserves from this—what could he call it?—this friendship, this contact that was, even at this moment, the most intimate, the most honest, most important one he had ever had in his life, certainly more honest than the one he had established with Wilma, which was the point, the reason for being here or anywhere with Howie. Why was he going to marry Wilma? And, as always happened between them, their telepathic shorthand, developed without their knowing how or why, continued to operate. Howie's first question was repeated: why?

Slowly, Phil's eyes turned back to Howie, lingered on the long, nervous fingers that were spinning a matchbook on the slippery table, impatient fingers, anxious for Phil to find the words, to gather them together in a bunch, to say out loud what was in his mind, words and thoughts that began in fumbling determination but always ended in a silly logic which

305

was not the truth at all. More than anything else, that's what speaking was for himself, for most people he knew: a chance to show how logical and wise and smart they were; a protective sifting through imperfect truths, confusing clichés, for words that wouldn't prove how vulnerable they were, that wouldn't lose them the advantage, wouldn't reveal too much, just enough to maintain the cherished edge, the hold over others. Phil did it that way, had to do it—that's the way his mind worked automatically—with everyone except Howie, most recently with Marvin Bernstein, and that caution mixed with candor had earned for him a part of a business. How wrong could it be then to operate as if everyone was out to screw you? Including Howie. Wasn't it, after all, Howie who had suggested he face up to Carl Kalb? When Carl was removed from the picture, hadn't that moved him closer to Wilma? "I have to marry her. She expects it."

"Expects it? What kind of reason is that? Expects? I expect things too, but that doesn't mean I'm ever going to get them. It doesn't work that way. You can do better than 'have to,' Phil. You can even say you *care* for her. That would be more convincing than 'expects'. *Do* you care? I'm afraid to say 'love'."

"Of course I care. I wouldn't do it if I didn't. But let's also remember Wilma's side of the deal. She's no kid any more. She wants to be over the waiting-around period. It's time already. You can't blame her for that. She even wants to have children and a house and she wants to stop working and—"

"And you want those things too? Like children and a house?"

"Maybe. Why shouldn't I?"

"Because I think—and it's just my opinion—that you really don't feel that way, certainly not where it counts. You don't ache for them. You want other things much more. The rest of it is secondary, a lot further removed from the real target."

"What's the real target? *You* tell *me*. I want to hear you say it."

Then it was Howie's turn to draw into himself, to light another cigarette, to piece together an answer that sketched, if not the clearest picture of "much more," then at least its outline. Howie's face reflected the effort it was to get at that picture; nothing he said was easy for him to say. He pulled at his hair; his eyes closed, his head tilted against the silent hurricane force of his thinking, trying to grab and save as it passed one item, then another, that would be substantial, hard, true: an impossible task. And, finally, he spoke, letting the words out reluctantly, as if each one might suddenly be recalled, rejected. It was the teacher in him, weighing, always weighing affect and effect, and gaining time, not stalling, but hoping that at the last moment the idea would, mysteriously, connect, become a part of a larger order of things, become, at least, something worth saying. That was the Howie paradox: saying there was no larger order of things, yet searching for it anyway. "When I was a kid in elementary school I would come home for lunch every day. And every day my mother would be listening to soap operas. So I would listen too. Things like *Helen Trent* and *Our Gal Sunday* and *Big Sister*. You know the kind. . . . Well, anyway, those programs were nothing like my mother. Nothing at all. My mother was an authentic *shtarkeh*, strong and small. Like you, Phil. . . . So anyway, I'd always ask her why she listened to them. What did she have in common with those people? Nothing, she'd say. Nothing except suffering, only—and this was the part that got me, when she'd say, only I never get amnesia like they get every week. I remember everything. I can't get rid of a single thing that ever happened to me."

"Why do you have to bring your mother into this right now? You always do that, you know. Can't you forget her for once?"

"No!" A luminous smile broke out on Howie's face. He lunged forward. "That's precisely the point I'm trying to make, that for certain unknowable reasons I can't forget her. Something won't let me. I can't forget a single thing that ever happened to me. And I'm glad. It helps. It doesn't trap me. It frees me. I try to face what I think it means and then I try to move ahead. Life, for me, is all about losing one thing or one person to memory and gaining something else in reality that reminds me of it and that can take its place. What surprises me, what has always surprised me about you, is that you *can* forget, that you really want to." He leaned back, stamped out his cigarette. "You seem to be able to slip out of your memory book entire experiences as if they were pages in a loose-leaf notebook that didn't have reinforcements. And once you do that without noticing first what was on them, then only what's ahead counts, not people and not places, not even Wilma or me. . . . So the reason I'm trying to answer your question this way and the reason I wanted to come to this place is to remind you that sooner or later I think you're going to remember everything. Your mind isn't really locked up. Sooner or later it's going to throw the past up right between your eyes. Getting married right now is going to turn you into another Carl Kalb eventually, and I don't think you'd like that."

"You know what, Howie? You give me a pain in the ass. You talk too much and I don't understand half of what you say."

"Yes, you do."

"No. I really don't. Just tonight, with my brother, I thought I'd gotten somewhere, made some progress, as they say. And then you started talking and got me all confused again. But this time, my friend, I'm not going to stay confused. I'm going to do what *I* want to do. . . . You want to isolate the black and white all the time when you know damn well you can't. All there are are shades of gray. Which is all right by me. I'm not made like you, Howie. Can't you tell that by now? I don't need to live my life by your rules. I don't want to be the wave of the future. I can't be. I'm not built for it. I'm living for right now, and right now they use labels. I'm an end product, a result, not a goddam cause. You saw my family. You know what they're like. That's what *I'm* like inside. My father all over again, with only slight improvements. I'm in a business. I'll make money. I'll get married to someone who loves me. Maybe I'll even be a father. And then I'll die. What the hell more do you want from me?"

"Nothing." Howie spoke so softly Phil had to lean forward to hear. "Not a thing. Except that it will never be that easy and you ought to be prepared." He finished his drink, got up, squeezed through to the bar to get two more. When he returned Phil had put on his raincoat. "I got you another drink."

"I don't want any more."

"Don't be angry, Phil. I don't mean to be a pain in the ass."

"I'm not angry, for Christ's sake, but I am tired of this kind of crap, and talking to you makes me more tired. You suffocate me. You push me up against a wall and it's hard to take. When I look up at those guys over there I wonder what the hell you think you're offering me. You want me to be like Sandy White? Because that's what I'd end up being if I listened to you. I'd be nothing but a queer designer. I'm not criticizing, mind you—far be it from me to criticize. I'm just observing the facts as I see them and trying to tell the truth for once. I do want much more and I won't find it getting drunk in a gay bar or any kind of bar. Neither will you. I may not find it anywhere else either, but I'm certainly going to try. So come on. I'll drive you home."

"I'm going to stay."

"Okay. Suit yourself." Phil moved rapidly away, through the knots of men, zigzagging to avoid more contact than was necessary. When he reached the door, he turned. Howie was behind him. He raised the two glasses of Scotch. "So long, Phil. Take care. And thank you for everything."

"Thank *you.*"

"Okay. Let's thank each other. Just make sure you invite me to the wedding."

Phil opened the door and stepped out of the blue light. Next there would be Wilma to face. He welcomed that tonight. All she wanted to do was get married. To hell with the truth about anything. Thank God for her infinite wisdom. Without that what would anything he had earned so far be worth?

Chapter Thirteen

When it comes to working with the fashion magazine editors, a designer puts more than his artistic ability in the poker pot. His heart, his nervous system, sometimes his liver, if the editor drinks, go with it. The result can be a rich kitty or a bust hand, and how he operates depends on what he can never know in advance: what their "stories" are, what their colors are going to be in issues that won't be published for three or four months from the day he meets with them. All he can do is present the clothes he has made, the dresses the sample hands are working on, show the fabric and sketches of the ones he plans to make—if he knows what they are—and hope that one group, even one dress, will fit into their plans, their stories. "I feel pink and beige for summer." "I feel lilac and rust." "I'm mad for silk chiffon in African prints. We'll be photographing in Tangier." "Why Tangier?" "Well, I've never been and my husband wants to go and the magazine will pay so I just dreamed up a Tangier story. Don't you have a Tangier dress, something Moorish and exotic?" "As a matter of fact I don't, but . . ." It's the handling of what comes after the "but" that squeezes the blood from the heart.

". . . But I can do one for you, if you'll only promise to use it." Or ". . . but of course you know I don't design that way." Or ". . . but I also think your colors are old hat. I used them last year. Don't you remember? For your own sake, you had better change your story and go to Tangier next year." The designers who can influence an editor to change her story are the ones who have arrived, the couture stars from the higher-priced market, the guys who win the Coty Awards, and not the ones from the Mr. Jack by Phil Hanssler price range. No one tells the stars what to do. No one offers them the bait of free editorial publicity. They don't need it. They can afford to advertise on their own, and the more they advertise in *Bazaar* and *Vogue*, the better the odds are they can get an editor to do whatever they want. That's just simple economic pressure, the same kind in operation behind every closed office door in every major industry on every level of our free-enterprise system. That's just elementary arithmetic.

And there are some designers who build their lines on the basis of what magazine girls leak to them and what powerful volume buyers tell them they want. Phil Hanssler, in spite of what he was after and especially since the business was untested, was *not* one of those. He never had been. Sure he wanted the publicity, but he had his own brand of artistic integrity—a quality in scant supply on the Avenue or anywhere else. He knew how to persuade and coax diplomatically. He had confidence, a brash, refreshingly masculine, positive point of view. The editors liked to look at him and listen. They always came when he called. "Well, if there's nothing here for you, then maybe the next time we'll be on the same wave length. I believe in what I'm doing. I think it's the right direction. I also think you're going to miss out on something big but . . . maybe you know better. You see everyone's clothes. If I'm ahead of the trend, that's all right too. I just happen to feel the movement in to the waist. If every woman in America's dieting or is going on a diet, then she's going to want to show what she's accomplished. That's why I'm taking the plunge. We'll see what we shall see. I want to be a designer, not a copier. So far the buyers seem to love it."

"I love it too. How could you not! You *are* a designer. I never doubted that for an instant. . . . Maybe what I should do is a little linen story. Uncovered linens." Lanky, long in the tooth, Peg Masters from *Mademoiselle* bent back from the pink linen sleeveless wrap dress that Phil held before her. She herself was dressed for winter in the total look, all black today, high black fitted boots, shapeless black knit dress that buttoned down the front, long black hair parted in the middle wisping around her pensive face, and, draped around her shoulders, a black caracul coat. "What might be smashing to do is a story on diet dresses. The American woman takes her diet abroad to Cairo." She put some strands of hair in her mouth and sucked, still studying. Then she straightened, stole a glance in the full-length mirror. "I know where I can get three others that will go with yours. They're not nearly as good, but they'll do. I'm putting a hold on this and the printed voile. We'll be shooting in three weeks. Can you spare it for a while?"

Phil handed the dress to Pat, who handed it on to La Lyon, who returned it to the sample-room closet where all the new styles were kept.

"That's going to be a problem. It's not like at the old company. We plan to *sell* clothes here, not just get them placed in magazines. Right now we have to do both. So I'll have to keep the sample to show to buyers but I promise I'll have a duplicate made up for you."

"Marvelous, Phil. I'm really excited by the dress. I agree with you. I think it will start a whole new trend, and I think I'll start a whole new trend on myself while I'm at it. Just look at me. Did you ever see anything so impossible in your whole life?" Her caracul slithered to the floor. She posed before the mirror, tall, flat-chested, unchangeably boyish. "It's a major overhaul job. I'm not exactly endowed with fine points like Patricia here." She accepted her coat from Phil, checked her wrist-sized wristwatch with its wide black band. "I must dash. The clothes are smashing, Phil. Remember about the duplicates." She kissed his cheek and was gone, her head refusing to be buried inside the turned-up caracul collar.

The first dress that Alice Cristabel of *Glamour* wanted, absolutely insisted on having, she loved it so much, was the pink linen. Phil showed it to her right off. "Fits right into our big linen promotion. I must have it. I won't look at another dress until you say yes. Just remember I've always been your friend. Believed in you from the first minute I laid eyes on you. You're a great talent. You must do this one itsy-bitsy thing for me. Please? Pretty please?" Alice never sat when she was shown clothes. She liked to pace. Perhaps, because she was so short, shorter than Phil, sitting to look at a dress further diminished her sense of power, or maybe it reminded her too painfully of the fact that almost all the clothes she looked at she could never wear. The Mr. Jack fit was not, nor would it ever be, junior petite. It was closer to Peg Masters, with breasts, if it was anything.

No matter what Phil showed Alice—she liked everything: the voile group, the dotted-swiss groups, printed and in solids, the shirts, the lace, the ottoman silks—she kept going back to, insisted on having, at least two from the linen group. Phil told her it was a hold for *Mademoiselle* too many times for it to have any but the reverse effect. "I've always been your champion. Right from the beginning. Peg's just catching up. How could you do that to me, love? How could you!"

"If you had come up here when I wanted you to—I called you first, didn't I, Pat?—it would have been the other way around. How would you have felt about it then? I can't make a promise to someone and then break it. Some success I'll be. Be cooperative, Alice sweetheart, love of my life." Phil hugged her, moved her away from the mirror, walked her around in a circle. "It's a new business. Give us a chance. Be a doll and take something else."

She returned to the mirror. "I could take all of them. They're all good. The line is going to be sensational. But this dress is news. It'll be a scoop. I guarantee it will *make* your summer business and put Mr. Jack back on the map, to say nothing of Phil Hanssler. And just remember one other little item. *Glamour* has the biggest circulation of any fashion magazine in the country, maybe even in the whole world. I rest my case."

Genuinely pleased then, Phil stopped in front of Alice. "That's the sweetest thing anyone's said to me since we returned to 498. Just for that I want to show you the next group going into work. You'll be the first to see them. . . . Pat? Get me those new sketches we did."

Pat's face was all open mouth and wide eyes. "Which sketches do you mean exactly? We've done so many lately I don't—"

"The ones we did this morning. You're getting punch drunk from overwork. I'll have to send you for a cure."

With all deliberate speed, Pat pushed through the mounds of sketches on their desk. "I don't seem to be able to find them."

"Did we give them to La Lyon already? Excuse me, Alice. Just for a minute." He started for the sample room. "Pat."

She followed him to the other room, where the noise of the sewing machines was loud enough to drown out their voices.

"You must be losing your marbles, Phil. You know we haven't even planned that group yet."

"Shah! Not so loud. I'll sketch them new, right in front of her as if La Lyon misplaced them."

"I didn't lose anything, Phil." La Lyon had stopped cutting a pattern and now wedged herself between the two of them. "I never lose anything."

"I know you don't, Mary baby. Don't fret. It'll be okay, Pat. Just don't panic. I've been sketching them in my head for a month."

Alice accepted the story. "Did your assistant *lose* them?"

"It seems that way. She's in there panicked." Phil seated himself at the desk, Alice at one hand, Pat at the other. The palm of his left hand smoothing the blank sketch paper, Pentel poised in his right, eyes blinking, narrowed, squinting, upper lip nibbling at his lower lip. The Pentel came down, swept up to the top of the page, moved to form the profile of an eyeless face, then a neck, and, without stopping once, he completed the silhouette of a new dress. He went back to the face to give the sketch some eyes and hair, jumped down to draw a single line reaching to the bottom of the page that meant a leg. It was a sleeveless dress with a halter top done like a bib, a skimmer that moved over the breasts, suggesting fullness there, then eased out slightly in a narrow A-line skirt. The woman who wore it could show off her body without being obvious, and, over the front of the dress, the final detail, like an insert that would function to control its entire movement, was a panel, the dress's chic, not a gimmick but a necessary part. "And along the seam, on each side of the panel, just where the fingers reach, about here, will be two pockets. It'll just tie in a bow behind the neck and the tie will be self fabric that comes right from the top of the halter, like a high apron. I'll do three in the group and I'll do them in linen."

"I'll take it. It's a natural. Not as good as the other one, but very chic. Why don't you do it in lilac?"

"I will, just because you asked me to."

"It's a pleasure to do business with you." A tiny high priestess of fashion news, junior division, Alice put a hold on four other dresses before she had to dash off to another appointment. And so Mr. Jack by Phil Hanssler had its magazine baptism, its first free publicity. And if the *Mademoiselle* and *Glamour* editors came up, the others were certain to follow. Every new resource had to be tapped for oil. You never could tell where the next Norell was hiding.

They did come to look at the clothes. And each one had a specific story in mind for a specific readership. *Ladies' Home Journal* needed one kind of dress: for a housewife on a strict budget. *McCall's* wanted medium-priced fashion, never kooky or avant-garde, just plain, old-fashioned, good-taste dressmaking to fill the few fashion pages squeezed between the oversized pictures of roasts and vegetables and prize-winning cakes. *Family Circle*, with a circulation surpassed only by *Woman's Day*, didn't care about stories, just decency. A good dress was as good as the next new recipe for a tuna casserole, but if one of their editors requested something, the picture they ran in washed-out color without concern for exciting photography usually turned a slow-booking garment into a hot reorder item. They didn't bother with the high-priced designers. What was the point? Phil's price range was even stretching it a bit, but they liked him, so they came and they took what their readers might wear: the dresses that actually sold most in the stores. So did *Redbook* and *Good Housekeeping*. *Cosmopolitan* had a different kind of seed to sow. The *Cosmo* girl might end up the *McCall's* lady but she was going to have a good time before she did. She wanted to be a swinger, to be *in*, to have sex and have fun and be unmarried for a while longer. And she could and would. The editors spent their time convincing her of that. But the *Cosmo* girl couldn't afford to buy the expensive dresses that the *Vogue* girl or the *Harper's Bazaar* girl could.

What the Lincoln Continental and the Cadillac were to the automobile industry, *Vogue* and *Bazaar* were to the ladies' fashion industry. Their editors were slower in making an appearance at Mr. Jack. It wasn't their fault. The price wasn't right. It was too low. They handled the stars, the permanents, not the comets, not at first, usually, not unless they were allowed by the highest priestesses of all, their editors-in-chief, to pick an unknown and push him to the top. The dresses featured on the glossy pages of their magazines were not expected to entice a mass market. But, eventually, transformed by the copiers, vulgarized, they would. A second coming was always at hand in the world of fashion, and the new god for American women with taste and money was sure to be found among the native talent and French couturier designers introduced and lionized by them each month. These editors stood at the head of the stairs looking down at the anxious candidates for elevation. They could afford to choose their moments for descent. They could make appointments, cancel them, and then appear unannounced. Mylene Maillot from *Bazaar* did it that way. She arrived at Mr. Jack after having phoned in that she was running dreadfully behind schedule. She was surprised she could make it at all, but she was awfully glad she had. The clothes were lovely. She selected one of the prints for editorial comment, an omen suggesting very good days to come for Phil, for Andrew Berns, for Michael Matthew Morgan. Michael turned the omen into prophecy. "What we are going to have here is a class operation. I always said you were a chic designer, Phil. A. F. just didn't understand that, but we do. Right, boys?"

The boys were the road salesmen, three of them, crowded into the front office, along with their three bosses, for a meeting. Andy, his head bent low over the style cards he was preparing for the orders when they came, was skeptical. "We don't want to be too chic. We want to sell clothes first of all, which is what I thought this meeting was about. . . . Maybe you could douse that cigar for a while? It's pretty stuffy in here with the door closed."

Michael obliged, but, substituting one symbol of his rank for another, pushed back his chair, raised his feet onto the desk.

Phil was perched on top of his father's gift, the bar-refrigerator. "All right. Let's forget about magazine credits, Mike, and get on with this meeting you called. You're in charge of sales, so talk already. I've got work to do in the back."

"Well, all I really wanted to do was familiarize everyone with some new ideas I've been kicking around. I've given it a lot of thought—"

"You're kidding me!" Charley Tunick, red-faced Charley whose boutonnière, a white carnation, was as famous along the Avenue as the rose in Carmen's teeth, spoke with the voice of authority and almost always put his excitability where his mind should be. "You had to get me away from my other accounts—Mr. Jack is not my whole life, you know—to inform me about that? You're going to tell me?" Legend on the Avenue had it that Charley was the richest, best-dressed salesman in the whole country. His sales record supported the legend, spread it deep into his territory on the West Coast and neighboring states. "What were you doing at the old Mr. Jack when I was trying to save it? And you're going to tell me! Hell'll freeze over first. When you were in diapers, Michael, I was selling already." Charley's pudgy hand with its diamond pinky ring, the pinky always separated from the rest of the fingers as if he were waiting to receive a teacup, beat the smoky air in disgust, amiable disgust. He never beat too hard any hand that fed him.

"Look, Charley, as far as you're concerned, from this day forward, I'm not any longer the schmucky kid who worked for you in the showroom at the old Mr. Jack. I'm one of your *bosses* now. A little respect wouldn't hurt."

"Ah-hah! So you're going to play the boss routine. A. F. should see you now."

"Let's forget A. F. And that's exactly why I wanted this meeting: just to make sure all of you understood that whatever A. F. did is what we're not going to do. Stanley here didn't work for A. F. and that's all to the good, but Alan did and I want to make a few things plain to them and to you, Mr. Tunick. What position I held in the old company is beside the point."

"Why is it beside the point?" Alan Finkelstein who, unlike Charley Tunick, only sold the Mr. Jack line and who, therefore, had been unemployed recently, spoke up as if he expected, momentarily, to be slapped down. He thought that a college education, however misused, gave him a right to be curious, but no one ever let him be for long. "I mean, after all, I understand Phil's clothes. I've sold them before on the road, and to sell in the South is another thing altogether, something which I think I understand pretty well, better than you do. What do you know about the

South? You were in the showroom all the time."

"Who's trying to say I know *more* than anyone! I realize what I don't know and I realize what I do know. All I'm trying to get across to you people is that this business is not going to be run like Alex Fleiss did."

"When I see it I'll believe it, not before." Charley patted Phil's knee. "You, darling, I'm not criticizing. It's not your fault what went wrong upstairs, but you know better than anyone, Phil, that between the time the sample's duplicated and manufactured and shipped, nine million things go wrong. You can't prevent it. I know because I've seen it happen over and over again."

"Some things we *can* and we will prevent." Andy's sharp tone seemed to be directed to a list of items on his ever-ready pad rather than to the salesmen.

"Like what can you prevent?" Charley clasped his hands securely over his swelling corporation.

"For one thing, we're going to stick to our production and shipping schedules. Your accounts will get what they ordered and for when they ordered it even if you gentlemen have to come here on Saturdays to do the billing and shipping. If you want your fat seven and a half percent commission checks on time, you'll have to service your accounts. Once I project a shipping figure for the month to the Greenstalks, we're going to meet it. Each year you make a fortune, Charley, from all the lines you sell, so now I'm just suggesting—we're suggesting—that you work a little harder to earn it."

"You know something? You don't frighten me. I'll work as hard as the next guy. I believe in this company. I'm behind Phil two hundred percent. He's a genius." Once more Charley patted Phil's leg. "This boy has class. No one has to tell me that. I know."

"Thank you, Mr. Tunick, but flattery will get you nowhere. I'm spoken for."

"I heard. Congratulations." Phil's hand had to be shaken, his cheek had to be kissed. "A designer gets married. They should put a headline in *Women's Wear*."

Stanley Shapiro, the Midwest representative and the only one not connected to the old Mr. Jack, recrossed his legs carefully. "I can't see what all the fuss is about. All I know is that if you give me clothes to take to the Chicago market, I'll sell them. I assume it's the same for Charley in L.A. and for Alan in Dallas. I've got my accounts solid. They'll buy. As long as the styling is right, they'll buy." He buttoned his silver mohair suit, brushed, ever so gently, the side of his slicked-down red hair.

"The *designing* will be right, sweetheart. We don't do styling here." Phil stood up, began turning on a dime's worth of space in front of the salesmen. "Just do me one favor. When you take the clothes on the road, don't treat them like a piece of shit. Even if *you* don't like them all, remember that I do. Especially sell the ones you don't like because they'll probably be the best."

Charley Tunick slapped his own short leg this time. "That's the spirit. That's confidence for you."

"And let's also cut out that jazz. Don't butter me up and don't paw me like I'm your favorite faggot designer. I'm tired of being pinched and petted. We're in a business. We're not fooling around any more. We're out to sell clothes. Not to every store in the country, just to some of them. If one of your accounts passes up the line this time, maybe they'll buy it next season. If they don't buy it next season, then maybe the buyer doesn't need our kind of clothes. It's all right with me. Don't worry about it. You can't please all of the people all of the time. End of quote. Get my point, gentlemen?"

The three monkeys, in their different ways, felt, saw, and, maybe, understood.

"And now kids you can go on with your meeting. Without fights, Michael. I've got *work* to do."

Lovelady Gray from *Women's Wear Daily* was waiting in his office examining the sketches of dresses that would complete the line.

"You like?" Phil played with the gold spear that pierced Lovey's neat bun.

"Beautiful clothes. The best I've seen anywhere in the junior market."

"Every time I see you, Lovey, I love you more. No man with an incipient ulcer could have a better friend." Phil sprawled in his director's chair.

"Well, you know I know whereof I speak. I don't have to tell you that, so you know I'm telling you the truth."

"Thank you. I appreciate it. I need it. What a job it is to get this thing started. All kinds of petty crap. Hundreds of details which have nothing to do with designing that I have to do because one of my partners is retarded and the salesmen don't have the faintest idea what fashion's all about. They never will. No one here, outside of Pat and myself, knows or cares about it. Sometimes I wonder if I do. Sometimes I wonder if it can possibly be worth it. By the time I get home at night my motor's going so fast it takes hours and a pint of Scotch before I begin to feel human again."

"You always *look* human. That's the greatest thing about you. You're a realist. A designer who's a realist and isn't all ego is a rare commodity. I hope you can maintain that balance." Lovey opened her notebook to a fresh page. "I'm going to be doing a feature article on the accessories market. I'm using four designers from different price ranges. One of them is going to be you. Pictures and everything. The works. It's cleared the editorial department so it's definite. Basically I'll want predictions on what things are coming back in: jewelry, belts, hats, bags, whatever you think. From the look of your line you're obviously expecting big changes. The hippie influence is personally what I think is going to change everything in fashion. So is men's wear. It's impossible to ever know, but you'll try, darling, because the spread will come at a perfect time for you. You're going to have a formal showing, aren't you?"

"I've been fighting that out with my partner who thinks everything is too much money to spend. But I'll win that battle. . . . We'll have a preview *and* a showing, probably the last week in January if we can ever get everything done in time. Which reminds me, I'll have to list it in the Fashion Calendar and I'll have to get invitations sent out. Pat make a note of that please." She went to the cork bulletin board over their desk, entered those items below a list of twenty others that had to be attended to before the showing. "You see what I mean, Lovey? It's endless."

"Stop complaining. You wouldn't have it any other way. The spread will be in the paper the third week of January. That'll be perfect timing. Also I'm going to run a sketch of this linen." She held up a Pat-perfect drawing of the pink dress. "It'll be the hottest number on the Avenue. That's not a prediction; it's a fact."

"You've helped me every step of the way up to this . . . this . . . whatever the hell it is. If it wasn't for you and some of the magazine girls I don't know where I'd be. In an insane asylum, I suppose."

"Don't thank us, Phil. As a newspaperwoman who enjoys what she does, I swear to you I wouldn't do anything if I didn't believe in you. There are lots of designers who have found that out. With you it's the easiest thing for me to help. Within a year you'll be a star. Within two you'll win the Coty Award. Then we'll see how sane you are." She checked her Timex. "I must be up and doing right now. I'll be in contact with you about the article, but the pictures will be next week for sure so get a tan somewhere. You look pale. Take care of him, Pat. We need him for all kinds of reasons." Her notebook slapped shut and she was off to visit the next lucky designer on her list.

"Were there any calls, Patricia?"

"Were there any calls, he asks. From your mother, your brother Glenn about a dress for his wife and his mother-in-law. From Wilma, of course. And Howie Goldstein. Sandy White just wanted you to know he was back from Mexico. Peg Masters called to say two out of the four dresses she took will definitely be in May *Mademoiselle*. Mr. Bernstein said never mind, but he was angry anyway. Also, we are scheduled for three fabric appointments for tomorrow morning. La Lyon booked Cindy for tomorrow at two-thirty. Scads of dresses to fit so don't take a long lunch hour. While all that was going on I even sketched a whole pile of good ideas just like I promised. I'm a good girl I am."

"You're the best little girl in the world. You may take four giant steps, but don't take a drink yet. It's not five."

At five o'clock the exodus began. The time clock rang. The sample hands leaned into Phil's room, waved goodnight. La Lyon appeared. She could legally join Phil and Pat then, but tonight she couldn't stay. "I'd love to have a drink with you, not that anyone asked me, but I can't because I'm going to a wake in Staten Island and I'll be late if—"

"Staten Island? You're kidding?"

"No, Phil, honestly. One of my old sample hands. Her husband died and she asked me to come for old time's sake. I feel so sorry for her. It's the least I can do for the poor soul." Ignored, Mary Lyon waited behind the sketching, bent bodies of Phil and Pat. "You know it's sad when people are left alone that way. With no children and all. Just like me. It's very sad. So when Carmella called, what could I say but yes."

Phil looked up at her, smiling. "Now don't start crying. Why are you crying? It's not your wake."

"I always cry. It's a habit." Now that Phil was paying attention, the tears stopped. "You're so good to me. I love working for you." She planted a wet kiss full on his lips. "You're satisfied with me, aren't you, Phil?"

"Absolutely satisfied. Go to your wake. Have a good time, but please don't come to work tomorrow with a hangover. That's my only request because we have lots of fittings."

"I promise . . . Phil?" She lowered her eyes demurely, a little girl dreaming again. "Am I as good an assistant as Ginny? I only ask because the girls talk about her as if she was a saint. So I want to make sure you're pleased with my work and all. Am I as good? Do you like me as

320

much?"

Phil sighed loudly. He tried not to, but he couldn't help it. This too. On top of everything else. He cupped her chin. It didn't cost anything to give her that much. "Yes. You're as good, if not better."

Once more she kissed him. "Thank you, Phil. Thank you for everything. You're so understanding." She skipped out of the room, humming. A great brain, no, he thought, watching her, but she certainly is light on her feet for a heavy woman.

"You're not only the best designer in the business, you're also the world's greatest liar."

"Just shut up and sketch. I like what I've done here. Look, Pat."

But Pat refused to sketch any more. She was tired. She had a date. She had a yoga class. She began her hairbrushing ritual.

Before she left, she bent over Phil, kissed his neck. "One thing more. I hate asking and all, but just tell me if I'm as good a worker as your other girls? If you say no I'll just kill myself on the spot."

"That's good because then we can have the wake right here. La Lyon can cater it."

He stopped sketching too. He was tired too. But he wasn't ready to leave yet. He stepped into the littered sample room to look once more at the work in progress. A padded dummy had half a pattern pinned to it, one half of what would end up being a basic white piqué dress, understated, no gewgaws, salable. Its construction had troubled him for days but he was determined not to throw it out of work. Then, suddenly, during the second fitting when La Lyon was removing some pins, she gathered the excess fabric together behind Cindy. The troubling fullness fell into place. A pleat was what he wanted. An inverted pleat in the back. The dress made sense then, looked fresher, newer, younger, not so basic. To his eye, at least. Maybe not to another designer's. A matter of taste for which there was no measuring rod. Good taste could be found at $45 retail as often as at $1000. Oftener, if he had anything to do with it. Except for the fact that at his price range women wanted beads and sequins for bar-mitzvahs, weddings, confirmations, cruises, sodality breakfasts. They wanted their breasts to point to heaven and their asses to be squeezed so tightly the side seams of every dress looked as if they would split. And why the hell not? If they had the equipment they might as well show it to the world.

Taste-shmaste! This year's good taste would be next year's gaucherie, faux pas, goof, tack. That's *out*. This, my dear, is what's coming in. Campari and culottes. Pajamas and pantsuits. Wine with dinner. Two cars in every garage: foreign and American. Andy Warhol and Breughel. Campbell soup and a codpiece. Hate for one thing and love for another. Do one thing with one person and another thing with another person. That's just the *smart* thing to do! Go to the opera. Go to work. Go to bed. And don't worry about a thing. The designers, interior and exterior, of America and France, all the culture boys will always be on hand to tell you what's what, to lead you by the hand. They're the small guys with all the power in this big, big world.

Phil hoisted himself onto La Lyon's work table, dangled his short legs, stared down at the snips of colored fabric on the floor, the hundreds of straight pins ready to be swept into oblivion by Link's broom. Before the night was over the room would be back in order, prepared for tomorrow's disorder. The hissing steam iron, the fluorescent lights would be shut off and the stillness, the darkness would entertain this wire dummy until morning. He could hear Link's broom out in the shipping area moving closer. It was time to get the hell out of here and over to Wilma's. Or it was time to go back to his desk and sketch some more until another idea ended up being a dress, a picture to tack on the wall alongside La Lyon's work table.

He stood up, retrieved a snippet of dotted swiss from the floor, brushed the dirt from it, and then let it float down again, studying its descent. Energy wasted. A piece of useles fabric. . . .

"What the hell are you doing in here when there's a meeting going on up front?"

Expecting Link's voice, Phil was startled to see Marvin Bernstein in the doorway. "It's still going on?"

"Who are those idiots in there?"

"Those aren't idiots, Marvin, those are our road salesmen." Phil hoisted himself back onto the work table. Marvin was standing in front of him and that way his neck wouldn't develop lockjaw from looking up.

"I called you today. You weren't here."

"I know. Pat told me."

Solemnly, Marvin stared at Phil, then smiled, as if he were embarrassed by the stare. "I just wanted to check on things. See how you were progressing."

"The clothes are great. We even got some magazine credits already. You want me to show you some of them?"

"What for? What the hell do I know about clothes? If you made them, I'll take your word for it they're good. As long as they sell. That's all I'm interested in." Slowly, Marvin's gaze shifted around the room, ended up where it began. "It looks like a shithouse in here. How a person can work in dirt is beyond me. You work in dirt, you end up with dirt."

"Not necessarily true. Sometimes dirt is inspirational. This is normal dirt. Just like Bruce's room. It'll be cleaned up soon, but by tomorrow night it'll look the same way all over again. Wait'll you see my room if you think this is bad." Phil had to climb over Marvin's legs to get by. He stumbled and Marvin reached for his arm to steady him. He held on to it as they stepped next door. "See what I mean?" Phil pointed with his trapped arm. Only then did Marvin let go.

"Well, this I can understand. You need some shelves in here, that's all. But maybe you like it this way. You're a creator, I shouldn't forget. You like a little chaos, don't you?"

"That's all I know. Take a seat, why don't you? When you stand up that way, you make me nervous."

"Why should I make *you* nervous?"

Phil began gathering up pencils, sketches, buttons, fabric swatches, buckles, all the odds and ends that Pat and he had thrown over the formica desk. Marvin did sit down, stretched his legs so that it seemed they took up all the walking space in the narrow room. "So? Tell me why I make you nervous? I make a lot of people nervous because I want to. But with you it's different. It's not intentional. I thought you had guts. You're a cool cucumber, I thought."

Phil stopped his cleaning, leaned against his desk. "Guts I have, but cool I'm not. A lot of things bother me. Someday maybe we'll talk about them."

"Someday! Everything with you is someday. When, for Christ's sake? Have dinner with me tonight. I have an appointment later, but dinner we can have."

"I can't, Marvin. I have a date. But another time. Just as soon as the showing's over and I can think straight."

"It's a deal. I'll take you out to celebrate that night after the showing. How about that?"

"We'll see."

"What is this see crap! Either you will or you won't. What do you have to do, clear it with your girl friend?"

"As a matter of fact, I do. Since we're going to be married, I think—"

"I heard about that. They told me up front. Congratulations."

"Thank you. I'll invite you to the wedding."

"You better." Marvin stretched his legs further until they touched Phil's loafers, yawned, smiled, dropped his hands onto his lap.

Link's broom was heard in the sample room banging against the sewing machines. Phil and Marvin stared away from each other, each absorbed, excessively absorbed, it seemed to Phil, in listening. He, at least, was grateful for the banging, sliding sound moving nearer. He shifted his weight, trying as he did to inch his loafers back from Marvin's feet, trying to avoid any contact with this giant he both trusted and distrusted, respected and feared. This thing Marvin was doing now, that's what made Phil nervous. Could he tell him *that?* Could he say, Marvin, you make me nervous because you're queer and I don't think you even know you are? Never. Impossible. He'd kill me, and Marvin Bernstein could really kill. Marvin Bernstein was unlike anyone he had ever known.

And it wasn't just a question of size, although of course that had something to do with it. Maybe it had *all* to do with it. Size was a lot more than just a physical thing with Marvin. It was the way he used it, the way he controlled people by it. It meant, it symbolized, Howie would say, everything Phil wasn't but wanted to be. And, right from the beginning, right from the minute they had met, Marvin had seemed to insist that they get to know each other better and in a way that, as far as Phil could figure out, had nothing much to do with the fact that they were tied together in a new business. It was more than that, but what the more was Phil didn't have a convenient label for. It couldn't be like Carl Kalb. Marvin didn't have that kind of style. Marvin didn't know from clever innuendoes and bitchery. What he wanted to say he said. What Phil didn't know about business he explained without being patronizing. That was almost his most appealing trait, the way he would stop a meeting, no matter who was there, no matter how naïve Phil's question, and explain every complicated twist and turn of corporate procedure, never letting up, no matter how long it took, until he was convinced that Phil understood. "You can't be a millionaire unless you understand what I'm talking about," like a loving father explaining the mystery of life. Which was probably what the whole attraction was about. Gee, Ma, I won another father. The only difference this time was that Marvin was different. He was thirty-eight, not sixty, even if he did look ninety. . . . "How's your ulcer, Marvin?"

"For December it's all right, but it's coming into season. How's yours?"

"Status quo. Quiet." Their heads jerked away, back toward the direction of the approaching broom. That's no Alex Fleiss sitting there. Or Morris Trebnitz or his own genuine father. No siree. That's a demander, a getter-of-what-he-wants, and that's the frightening part of the whole situation. If he doesn't know yet what he wants from me, if he suddenly finds out, if he stops squeezing my arm and my shoulder unself-consciously in front of people and wants to squeeze my leg under the table at dinner somewhere, then watch out, Philip baby, watch out. That's when the shit'll hit the fan. That'll be the end of everything, maybe. He'll explode. He'll belch himself to death and take me with him.

First Link's broom, then his body bending over it, appeared in the doorway. Marvin drew up his legs, looked annoyed. "So you can't come to dinner tonight and you won't let me take you out to celebrate after the showing."

"I didn't say that, Marvin. I just said we'll see."

"Okay. Have it your way. But one of these nights you're going to have to have dinner with me because I've got an idea to discuss with you about a franchise deal. Something very big, for the future, but I want you to start thinking about it now. Also, my wife and daughters want to meet you so you're going to have to come up to Larchmont. You can bring your girl friend. Sometime after the showing, very soon after, because my wife is driving me crazy about meeting you. I can't figure out why."

"Because I'm a designer. Women always want to meet a designer so they can tell him what good taste *they* have. . . . You want us out of here, Link. I can see we're in your way."

"Stay where you are, Phil. I'll come back when you're finished." Link started to leave, but Marvin called him back. "I have to go anyway." He stood up, all seventy-five feet of him, waited for Phil to escort him back to the showroom. "So you'll come up to Larchmont?"

"Sure. Be happy to if it'll make your wife happy."

"To hell with my wife. It'll make me happy." Marvin glanced into the front office. Andy and Michael were there. They waved, started to stand up. Marvin motioned them down. He kept walking, faster then, pulling Phil with him. "You better watch those two guys. Like everyone else, they'll screw you if they can."

"You can protect me."

"Sure I can and will. You're my investment. But you better learn how to protect yourself too." Marvin brushed his hand thoughtfully across Phil's hair, then messed it up. "I'll speak to you soon. Don't mention the franchise thing to them. I'll tell them myself when I'm ready."

Phil waited in his room long enough for Marvin to make a certain getaway, then combed his hair, straightened his tie, put on his jacket and camel's hair coat, wound his wool muffler, poet style, around his neck. The guy wants to tell me something too, but he's afraid, like I get afraid. He's afraid to talk to little Philly. Imagine that.

There was only one elevator after six-thirty and it took a long time coming, but when it did, it was empty, thank God. Enough people for one day. He was tired but exhilarated, and the cold night air, the gusty wind when he met it full in the face beyond the revolving door, made him shiver with a delight you only feel when things are most decidedly, irreversibly tipping the scales in your favor. You don't just walk then, you rise right off the dirty sidewalk, you race across Seventh Avenue. This time of night, even if you're not feeling good, you can do that. There's nothing to stop you. No people. No traffic. No rolling racks. No loiterers in front of any building.

The candy stores at all the corners were closed, and Dubrow's was almost closed or might as well have been at this hour, and beyond that, to the north, the Metropolitan Opera House was no more, an empty space beneath the December night sky, a little breather between buildings for a half year, before the next one started up.

He decided to walk east on Thirty-sixth Street for a while. He had told Wilma seven, but fifteen minutes late wouldn't matter. Even an hour wouldn't matter these days. She'd wait forever now without a whimper. The Garment Center hooker joints he passed were crowded, hotboxes of too much forced laughter these cold winter nights between seasons, after the spring lines which did or didn't sell, the samples hanging limp, lifeless now in showroom closets, before the summer lines, which have to sell or else, are shown. The trimmings stores, their colored ribbon windows darkened, dulled by old dust, the buildings up above them dark, their long, narrow Gothic windows framed by gray, patterned stone. Buildings with character, not like the dirty brown hunks of nothing on the Avenue. Even the garages, homes during the day for the Cadillacs, Lincolns, Rolls-Royces of the Alex Fleisses, were pointless now at night, just ugly dugouts with flashing, broken neon signs. PAR ING, RAT S.

He stopped at Al Cooper's restaurant, stepped inside for no reason but the smells he knew were there, the super-duper relish trays and good sour pickles, the sauerkraut and chicken soup, and the decor, burnished, bright, rococo, modern *belle époque*. The hat-check girl wanted his coat.

Without a word he left again, warmer, hungry for a drink and food, especially drink.

At Broadway, on the edge of his world, he looked south, nodded his greeting to the Greenstalks building, and hailed a cab for home and Liffey, first of all, then Wilma Pasternack and rest.

No. It wasn't new or unexpected, but familiarity had a power too, sometimes, and this night, this night after such a good day, was one of those sometimes, was going to have a power more than newness. Watching Wilma get undressed, the bedside lamp left on, himself naked on the bed, on display, knowing what he would see when she was naked too, and how her hands would feel on his skin, how her lips, moistened first, would feel on his, that could be exciting too, could be more exciting than a darkened room might be when you didn't know what would happen next, didn't even know the person it would happen with. That could be as undependable as he might be on a different kind of night when he didn't feel aroused and Wilma did.

But he was aroused and Wilma, stretching now beside him on the bed, was too. And the day had done him wonders, had given him the chance to show his talents to his world, his small world of big tastemakers; the day had made him feel that maybe, maybe, he could get all he wanted if he just closed his eyes and wished hard enough before he fell asleep, before his mind began to ask again what *all he wanted* was all about. The day had made him feel he wanted Wilma now, wanted her almost as strongly, almost as keenly as he wanted everything else, that he could handle her body almost as well as he would be able to handle other kinds of power when it came to him. Because he wanted that other power too, that invisible power that fame gives you for a while, and that everybody wishes they could have, a power that makes you feel big enough to get on top of your life, to control it, direct it beyond dying and death, a power that lets you forget you're powerless, that lets you think you're not a servant in another power person's nightmare.

"Wilma . . . don't worry."

"I won't. I love you."

Your fingers say that, squeezing my skin and digging, digging deeper for some joy. Your body says it, moving slowly, slowly back and forth beneath me. And I . . . I want to say it too. I want to move us both to pleasure in our skins and heads, to move us both beyond our thoughts of

327

time, tomorrow, dying, of other people losing, lost beneath the weight of always having lost, to remove, as easily as you remove your bracelets, my knowledge of another kind of need, for a few minutes, one minute, while this thing goes on, this sex goes on, giving you pleasure and joy and me —what? Not that. Not really. Not lost in it like you. And why not? Why? Why almost but not all? Why? . . . Because! That's just the way I'm made. That's just the way I've always been and always will be. So live and let live. Let me do the best I can and get on top and push and pull, push and pull, in and out, in and out, and up, finally, up, up, up. . . .

"Phil! Phil! Oh, God! Phil!"

And together then they throbbed and sighed and laughed and fell apart, aware of what they were and where they were in the lamplight, and how they were different even now, even now when they were most alike, trying, trying to feel the same things in the same way.

And they would get married because . . . because why not? Wilma wanted it. And he loved her and wouldn't hurt her. No, he wouldn't hurt her. Which is all he meant by saying love. Which is all he had to give her.

Chapter Fourteen

One week before the showing! And if he lived through it without cracking up, without his ulcer turning on him now, demanding blood, then the odds were better than even he could get through the rest of his life unaided, without falling into the arms of a psychiatrist. The two lists that Pat prepared, one of things still to be done before the preview, the other relating to the showing two days later, were tacked to the bulletin board, but the more he did, the more the lists seemed to grow. They helped, though, in the way a packing list helps when you're leaving on a long vacation. They kept him steady, on his feet, at least, reminded him that it was all real and really happening. Pat helped too. She kept order in the classroom. She forced him to check off each item, one thing at a time. But no other help was going to arrive in the nick of time. Michael was next to useless, an obstacle to sidestep. Andy was hidden behind his style cards, sorting them, checking them each day and all day, it seemed to Phil, now that orders were actually being posted on their network of tiny squares. Admittedly, there were things, too many things, that only he could do, tricky, sticky, wheedling things, like conning the sample hands into working overtime each night so all the clothes would be finished; like making sure, by telephoning back and forth, back and forth, that the samples were returned to the showroom from the magazine girls so they could be sold and not just photographed; like convincing a buyer to buy a style he believed in and that she said she didn't understand; and like just plain keeping the peace among the soldiers on the battle line. Michael did his I'm-the-boss routine with the staff. No love blossomed there. Andy screamed at them and smiled, screamed and smiled. Hate was growing there. So Philly, little Philly, had to bring goodness and light and Scotch everywhere.

And he had another list, one he carried in his head, including calls he had to make, to Carl Kalb and Aram and Sandy and Marvin, inviting them personally to the showing, calls that were a pain in the ass, but that he'd make. None of that putting-off crap. His conscience would be clear. If Carl was bitchy, screw him. He wanted Carl there, but he wouldn't beg him. According to Sandy, Carl was in no condition to be proud. Carl Kalb, Inc., was about to fold. *Women's Wear*, which Phil barely had time to skim through in the bathroom, had done one of those nostalgic pieces on the old-name, used-to-be-famous firms that were losing out, losing their customers. Carl's business had been mentioned prominently. Mr. Jack by Phil Hanssler, on the other hand, Sandy said, was listed as an example of how, with backing from the giant Greenstalks complex, a new vitality, a new approach was gaining momentum on Seventh Avenue. Lovey Gray, that sweetheart, had done what she promised once again. Love Lovey . . . As for Aram, his business was all right too. And he will or he won't come to the show. Who cares!

The list! Models had been booked for the preview and for the showing. A check mark. Just seven. He would have liked ten, but the seven were a compromise he was forced to reach, for the sake of harmony, with Andy. Andy didn't want anything—not a preview, especially—because, he said, brandishing his style cards as proof, we don't need to waste the money. The clothes were selling without it. Michael, fortunately, had cast the winning vote, and Phil said, all right, seven instead of ten. So seven for sixty-six pieces. It would be tight: lots of quick changes. But he knew the girls well, had used them before. They'd cooperate. For $40 an hour at the preview and $40 an hour at the showing they'd better cooperate. The preview was essential. Because he wanted it. He wanted the show to look professional, no matter what. And the accessories—the stockings, textured ones; the hats, just a few for summer, which would make Andy happy; the jewelry, Pat's duty; the shoes . . . He flipped through his appointment book. "When's the Capezio time, Pat?" He dropped his Pentel, sipped from his second container of tea that morning.

"Eleven-thirty. Who was that you were just talking to?"

"You've got some nerve listening to my private conversations. It was Aram LeGeis."

"Is that a fact? Well, I just want to sit here and tell you that nothing's private in this zoo."

"No temper tantrums today, please. I don't have the time."

"Fear not. Patricia won't flip her wig. Patricia's pliable, like steel. She'll be a good little girl. She'll answer the telephone politely. She'll laugh through her tears when Wilma checks in. . . . I've got an appointment for the jewelry after lunch."

"Don't spend too much."

"Really, Philip! You're turning into as big a chintz as Andy. Rest assured I've been warned to stay within the budget."

"What is that you're doing right now, sweetheart?"

"I'm following your orders. I'm making a sketch of every damn dress on this damn line so that when we have the damn preview the damn order of the damn showing will have been arranged in damn advance. You wanted it that way and I'm damn well doing it."

"You're a damn good girl. You know that?" He fluffed the back of her hair. "You're also gorgeous. How come some film tycoon hasn't forced you before the cameras?"

"I can't act and I don't like tycoons, only magnates."

"No! Really? You can't act? You can't dance? I thought you were out swinging every night?"

"Since your banns were posted, I've gone into seclusion." She turned back to her miniature sketches, her face hidden inside the circle of falling hair. "Just let me work. It's the only thing that helps."

"Work! Go ahead. Who's stopping you." Phil hiked up his hip-huggers, smoothed his four-inch, blue moiré tie under the long pointed collar of his blue shirt, posed for a three-quarter profile shot at the mirror before starting off on his morning round. "If you need me, just whistle. You know how to whistle, don't you?"

A "Good morning, ladies" for the sample hands from the doorway. A hug from La Lyon. No way to avoid that and her leftover bourbon breath. "How you doing, love?"

"Fine, Phil. Just fine," but her eyes were glazed, their lids flecked with caked sleep. She followed him out into the shipping area. "I'm not really fine, but I didn't want the ladies to hear. They don't like me. It's my stomach." She rubbed it. "Must be the flu coming on. My husband's got it, you know."

"I didn't know. You didn't tell me before."

"He's been terribly sick. High fever, vomiting, diarrhea—"

"Lyon, baby, let's skip the details."

She smiled bravely, her full lips quivering, her puffed cheeks all aglow. "You do like me, don't you Phil?"

"I love you, so get back in that room and start working."

It is a zoo. Pat's right. The whole world's a zoo and at Mr. Jack I'm the trainer-caretaker-tamer-feeder. So who's next? Advance out of shipping, you sweet black boys, and let me have it. I'm ready. What they did was smile and wave. He returned the compliment.

In the cutting room it was Morris who cornered him. "Philly, you see what I told you how much wastage is on this print? We laid out the goods and the lines we got to match. The buyers they like it, this dress? You were able to get enough for a cutting ticket?"

"Would you be cutting it if we didn't? They did. They liked it, the buyers. Enough of them anyway. It's our signature print, Morris. Be loyal." Phil pointed to the end of the long room where Tessie and Sheila, the duplicate workers, were busy at their machines. "The duplicates for the road salesmen?"

"They're doing. As fast as they can, they're doing. Don't worry. If I say it'll be done, it'll be done. Even this print. But you can see for yourself how hard it is." Sam and Arnie, the cutters, looked up, nodding, agreeing. "Still in all, it'll be done. My word." Morris placed his hand over his heart, solemnly smiling. "It's me, Philly, who's promising. You saw the work my contractors did, no? You like the stock. It's a hundred percent garment. So don't worry a minute. When the shipping dates are going to come, everything'll be ready." He wagged his finger under Phil's nose, pinched his cheek for good measure. "Such a boy! I love you as if you was my own son."

In the reception-room-office, where, finally, the switchboard was working properly after weeks of everyone being disconnected by Hettie, the Negro girl that Phil insisted they hire no matter what the Southern buyers thought, there was the semblance now of sanity and order, an atmosphere of business going on as usual. Glenda Dubester's blond beehive bobbed menacingly over her newly organized books. Hettie, between phone calls and typing letters, was alphabetizing the orders for Glenda to enter. Phil made the mistake of saying, "Everything fine in here, I can see." Hettie rolled her eyes in the direction of Glenda, who looked up and out from over her glasses, stuck her ball-point in her hair. "Philip. Good. Just whom I wanted to see about a certain matter." She turned around in her swivel chair a few times, making her dilemma graphic. "You know that I've worked in many companies in my day so I'm experienced about what I am about to say. I am a bookkeeper, not a secretary, Philip. I'm swamped with work just checking on the credit ratings of your customers. That's an absolutely essential part of my job." Phil's head, as if set off by a special automatic, concealed button that only Glenda knew how to operate, began a rhythmic rolling. "And of course it must be done very carefully. Let me tell you, I've seen company after company go right down the drain because they sold to bad credit risks. I have been specifically warned by the Greenstalks accountants that only I can do that job, so naturally I'm trying to do it as best I can. But your salesmen don't seem to understand what I have been instructed to perform. They want I should allow every customer to buy, which, believe me, I'm not against—don't I want you to be successful? Of course I do. No one wants it more than I do. I can assure you of that much. You're all such lovely people here. It's a pleasure to work for you. But I must insist on what's right, mustn't I?"

"Yes. You must. Whatever you say, I'll tell them." He tried to move off, but she grabbed his wrist, held on to it like a wrestler.

"That's not, however, what I wanted to talk to you about. The real thing is concerning what Mr. Morgan asked me to do. Now you shouldn't get me wrong because he's a darling young man, but between the two of us," she pulled Phil closer so Hettie wouldn't hear, "he's got a lot to learn about this business, believe me. He comes in here this morning, first thing, mind you, with the list for the invitations to the showing, and then he says these must go out today, just like that. Can you imagine? With all the work I'm swamped with?"

"Can't Hettie help you?"

"Philip darling, the kid tries. She really tries. But I can't trust her yet with my work. She's just learning."

"What is this business with *kid*?" He shook his wrist free.

"Hettie, I mean. Excuse me, Hettie. She tries very hard, which I'm very appreciative of."

"I'll talk to Mr. Morgan about it."

"That's all I ask. A little thoughtfulness on the part of all concerned would be highly appreciated, so thank you." Glenda returned to her books, immediately absorbed.

The best part of his tour was the showroom, not its physical presence —no amount of squinting was going to blur the color of that carpet and the phony brick runway, the black vinyl chairs—but the fact that all the tables were occupied by satisfied buyers approving the clothes they were being shown. Everyone was smiling: the three salesmen, their three assistants, their customers. Charley Tunick's round face glowed like a Delicious apple. "Phil, my boy. I want you to meet Miss Sharp and Miss Carleton. They're from Joseph Magnin, from the Coast. They love the clothes. Absolutely love them."

Miss Sharp in a fur-trimmed hat that hid her hair, Miss Carleton in a miniskirt and long amber fall told the story of that store and where it was going, where fashion generally was going. Phil bowed graciously, shook hands. "They're not bad clothes."

"Bad? They're great. Don't tell me." Charley spoke before the ladies had a chance to breathe. "This boy's an artist. I've known him for years. Always knew he was an artist."

Miss Carleton examined Phil. Miss Sharp spoke. "They are lovely." She pointed her Mr. Jack pencil at him prophetically. "The linen group is the best I've seen in the market. It's sensational. I don't often say things like that, so consider yourself fortunate." The pencil was lowered to her order pad. "They're perfect for California."

"Then I consider myself fortunate." An ingenuous smile, an oh-you-shouldn't-have-done-it expression on his face, another bow, and Phil moved to his partners' office.

"Michael. I need a few minutes of your precious time."

Michael, who was busy doing nothing but watching Andy and turning a Mr. Jack matchbook over and over in his palm, snapped to attention. At that moment, at any moment since the reaction to the clothes seemed certain to lead to a big season, if Phil had asked Michael to sweep out his office, he wouldn't have done it, no, not that, but he would have stood over the someone else he made do it. For Michael, that was the same thing. He lived by the law of let John do it for you, or Link or Morris or Andy or Phil. Today's example of that law in operation was one that Phil was not going to let go by unnoticed. His own future might depend on making those fingers active. "Glenda's bitching again."

"About what now?"

"The invitations. And goddamn it, she's right." Phil leaned into the wind. Michael tried to back away from him but there was no place to hide. Andy stopped working, looked up, preoccupied, but attentive enough, and always glad to be a witness to any attempt on Michael's life. "If I live to be a hundred I'll never understand you. You can't be *that* dumb, can you? No one could. You're the one who said you'd handle the invitations and here it is a week before the showing and they're still not done. You'll never get the press up here now. They don't sit around on their asses like you do waiting to be asked. Do I have to do everything myself around here? I'll bet you haven't even called about the champagne you said you were going to get us for nothing. This shit has to stop. You can't run a business on promises you don't keep."

"Just a minute," Michael's hand shot up authoritatively as if he had re-membered suddenly that he too was a boss. "Don't get so excited. The champagne is taken care of. My friend up at Piper Heidsieck guaranteed it. You don't have a thing to worry about. And the caterer you were sup-posed to do. As far as the invitations are concerned, I figured that's what I have a secretary for."

"Who's *your* secretary?" Andy joined Phil at the lectern now. "Glenda Dubester is not your secretary. Neither is Hettie. Everyone's his own sec-retary for the time being. You have to stop acting like a big-time execu-tive and do what you're supposed to do. We laid out enough money for this affair as it is without your screwing it up."

"Listen, Andy, don't both of you gang up on me. I do my share around here."

"You do? That's news to me. Did you get that impression, Phil?"

Michael was searching frantically in his inside suit pocket for a cigar which, when he found it and lit it and puffed it, he used as a protective smoke screen. "I realize . . . there are . . . things . . . I don't do . . . perfectly . . . yet." He coughed, cleared his throat, disappeared from view and had to clear a path in front of his face to be seen. "But I'll catch on. Rest assured of that."

Since it was only another function of the zoo master to keep himself as well as the animals calm, Phil stepped away from his simulated anger. He had to. It was just a waste of time to go on with this performance. Mi-chael was never going to learn the ropes, so the best thing to do was to humor him, neutralize him, get him out of the way of danger. "No one's saying you won't catch on, but if you don't take care of simple things, what's going to happen when the stock really starts piling in back there and the shipping has to be done. What then, Mike? Also, how come the two of you are in here when the showroom's filled with customers?"

Andy's pencil said: Who? Me? I'm busy. Michael rolled his cigar.

"I think what we're going to have to do is sit down and have a meet-ing. Some things better get straightened out around here or I'm going to be off to see the Wizard of Oz, kiddies. We're not a success yet, remem-ber, and at this rate . . ." Always leave 'em a little frightened.

In the showroom Phil lingered to straighten the tangled sample gar-ments hanging from the copper rods at each booth, to collect compli-ments from some more buyers, to bow—not scrape—and smile. The sam-ples looked like shit already. Soft summer fabric, voile, dotted swiss, lace, has such a short life when salesmen get their greedy paws on it. And yet, what the hell, as long as they sell. He heard Michael's maple-syrup voice raised in greetings to the customers. It worked, but he had better take care of the invitations himself. Rudolph Valentino's too busy making love. So move out of here already because this is your life, Phil Hanssler, and the way it's likely to remain. You have to hang in there and keep punching. You signed the contract. You let yourself be linked to Michael Matthew Morgan and Andrew Berns. Maybe not forever, but for now. You told the truth so you'll have to pay the consequences. You'll have to take what you get because you can't leave it alone. Like it or not, you'll have to like it. Some classy operation. And you'll also have to take the time to find the time to sit down and do the thing you're most of all supposed to do: design clothes.

When he entered the room, Pat was deep into her drawing. She didn't even stir. Quietly he sat down next to her, began to doodle, starting from a point at the center of his sketch pad, a series of concentric circles going nowhere but around. He squinted, drew some more circles. Design clothes. Design clothes that were good. Design clothes that were good and that sold, that were booked by the buyers, that checked out in the stores, that reordered, that Andy awarded another cutting ticket to. Design clothes for cutting tickets. A hundred pieces per. So Andy would order more fabric, so the duplicate makers would make duplicates, so the grader would grade the sizes, so Morris would lay out the goods on the cutting table, so the cutters would cut the patterns, so the sewers at the contractors' would stitch the pieces of the patterns together to make dresses. . . . It was like the song he used to sing at Passover: "One only kid, one only kid, which my father sold for three zuzim." Or like "Old MacDonald had a farm, eee, i, eee, i, o!" . . . And then the union representative would come and represent and Morris and Andy and himself would fight and argue and bargain with the man for a fair price to sell the dress and make a profit, allowing for the fabric cost at so and so a yard and the labor cost for each stitch, each buttonhole, each zipper, each dart, seam, hem, sleeve, each bow and bead. . . . "Maybe you'll be able to use one less row stitches on the tucking, Philly? Maybe one pocket's enough? I wouldn't want you should spoil the dress. If it's no, it's no. But the price'll have to be higher. It's no way to change that, unless, maybe, you'll find a cheaper goods to substitute. The price of the garment is in the goods you used. You can't maybe find a cheaper? A knock-off maybe? Because in our price range . . ."

Pat was resting between strokes, studying, disappointed with what her good right hand had produced.

And then the clothes would come back from the contractors, would be inspected, pulled for orders, charged out on the billing machine, packed inside Mr. Jack corrugated boxes, that were picked up by the truckers, shipped out on time, or were returned because of late delivery, or checked out, reordered, earned more cutting tickets so the same thing could start all over again. So try and design. Go ahead. Try and create fashion news and chic at a moderate price, clothes that don't end up on a sale rack in a department store. Clothes that you like, are proud of, that stand for some idea you have of beauty instead of being innovations for innovation's sake, like feathers stitched somehow to welded steel or battery-operated breast lights, innovations that some smart-ass social scientist writing for the Sunday *New York Times* will offer as further proof that male designers are what they are, do what they do because they really hate women. Bullshit, and more bullshit! Women have to hate themselves, otherwise they wouldn't wrap their bodies in stuff that passes for fashion greatness at $1,000 a shot, stuff they're told to like and wear for a while, just for a while, by the ladies of the press. Maybe what he should do was smear silk crepe with his mother's chicken fat. That would help his career, win him a Coty Award. He could call them organic dresses. Just the things for when you're marooned on a desert island without your three favorite books and three favorite recordings. Chicken-fat clothes would never be discarded from the line, never be relegated to a rack in the back behind the basic stock that sold. . . . "What I want from you, Miss Pearson," she jumped, startled by the bitter, bass sound of his voice, "is something ab-so-lute-ly new and di-*vine*. Something that will sell in the thousands. It'll be the finale group for the show. Got it?"

"Got just the thing right here." She poked through her pile of sketches, offered it for approval. "Isn't it smashing? It's a pantsuit made out of organza."

"What happens if the lady sweats a lot in her behind? This *is* a summer line we're finishing, remember. It gets hot in the summer, baby."

"Who cares? Let them wear sweat pads. But isn't it the most heavenly look you've ever seen in your life?"

"No. That's the kind of outfit you do when you're a student at Parsons. You win the Rudi Gernreich award with it, but you don't make our kind of dresses out of it. We need fat cutting tickets, sweetheart. We're in business. We're not running a museum."

"How odd. I thought that's what you wanted to do. You're a beast. You never want to put *my* things in work."

"I always want to put your things in work—when I like them. That's what my job is around here. That's why my name's on the label. Mr. Jack by Phil Hanssler for Pat Pearson. Would that make you happy?"

"Nothing short of fame will make me happy." She was smiling, joking with him and herself as usual, but just as Phil meant exactly what he had said too, she did too. "I think what I'll have to do is open a nifty little boutique on Madison in the Sixties. I don't see myself on Seventh Avenue nohow."

"A Parsons graduate and admitting defeat so soon? I don't believe it. It's un-American. Come on. Let's go up to Capezio. That'll cheer you up. And then we'll have lunch and then we'll go look at a fabric line where we'll find exactly the right fabric for our finale. Then we'll come back here and design it and live happily ever after. Okay?"

Phil's preview learning experiences came from his Carl Kalb, Inc., days. There, Carl, personally, would pick out the model to wear each dress, would accessorize it while she had it on, would instruct her on how she was to move with it on the runway, what he wanted and expected the audience at the showing to react to. "A model must never overwhelm a dress with the presence of her personality and style. She must act like she feels comfortable in it, like she actually owns it, but she must also remember that she wants to make the buyers feel as if she would really prefer giving it to them as a gift. Her job, in short, is to present an idea." When Carl was finished with one model and one dress and was completely satisfied, he went on to the next and the one after that, very slowly, until he reached the end of the line. He never allowed the salesmen who were ordered to be present to say a word. They watched, on white antique-velvet-covered chairs that lined the white, gold, beige showroom wall. He was in charge. He was the designer, the nominal designer, since he always had sketchers, like Phil, who did a lot of the designing. He was the boss and the owner. The line was lined up; it came alive just as he said he expected it would. Everything was order, sequence, serenity. If there were last-minute alterations to be made, new hem lengths to be taken, buttons or pockets to be reset, he ordered his assistant, who stood near him throughout, to make notations of those needs in her notebook and have the sample hands do them the following day. When Phil was

338

given his own line to do for Carl, Carl presided at the preview too. A dress business was ultimately a question of the owner-designer's responsible good taste. That was the only way it could be as far as Carl was concerned. And a preview run by Carl was, at least, never a traumatic experience.

At the old Mr. Jack every preview was traumatic. Alex Fleiss, out of panic, especially during the last few years, reversed Carl's procedure. A preview was run like a contest between Phil and all the salesmen, road and showroom, to see who could scream the loudest. All A. F. ever did was stay near a telephone in case he had to call for a doctor in a hurry. The salesmen used the preview as an occasion to discard dresses. A. F. insisted on having a big line produced in the frantic hope that there would be something on it for everyone. Phil never expected, nor did ne want, all the samples to be put into production, but it was one thing to discard and another thing to kill a dress. Charley Tunick, the world's star salesman, yelled the most. He knew this and he knew that and in California this wouldn't sell and that sample was a piece of shit and he would grab it, sometimes throw it on the floor, step on it, while Phil, with A. F. trying to calm him down, yelled and pushed and fought to save it. In those days, if he didn't save at least 55 percent of the line, he went home, after two or three hours of screaming, hating himself, his profession, Alex Fleiss and every perfumed, oily, silver-suited, pinkie-ringed illiterate salesman in every dumb dress company in the Garment Center. The one thing that never had a chance to surface at a preview there was exhilaration, the thrill that comes from seeing all the clothes together for the first time, all of them real, suddenly, something more than just an idea which was sketched, something flowing with the life that a good model could bring to a dress and that a hanger never could.

Now, since he knew what could happen, he had made it an unarguable point with Andy, Michael and the salesmen that nothing would be discarded from the line before the showing unless he, and he alone, decided it. None of the salesmen were to be present at the preview—they were specifically asked to stay away.

The seven models were to arrive at five-thirty. The whole thing would take an hour. Phil promised Andy that that was all the time it would take because he and Pat had already lined up the small sketches of each dress he had asked her to make. Each sketch had a model's name on it. Pat had even made up cross-reference lists of all the dresses that each model would wear and noted the accessories that went with each piece. The

Scotch, ice, glasses were arranged neatly on the table next to the lists. All was ready. The sample dresses, including the ones the sample hands were still working on, were brought out to the showroom, separated for each model, and hung from the copper rods on the partitions. The doors to the front office, the executive office, the back, the main hallway entrance were to be locked so the models could change right in the showroom. So, fine. Excellent. Order and calm.

The first thing to spoil the dough was that La Lyon neglected to tell Phil she couldn't stay. Her husband was sicker, or sick again, it was unclear to Phil, and she, although it was pointless for her to deny what Phil accused her of—her smell alone was strong enough to drop him on the spot—swore on her rosary she wasn't drunk. "All right. Get out of here. But if you're drunk on the day of the showing that's the end. Remember I told you that. I'm not kidding. Enough is enough already."

Complaining that she wasn't paid a living wage for all she had to do already, Pat was given the added task of listing all the alterations.

"You'll be getting a raise as of the end of the week. It's definite. I had a fight with Andy. I won."

She wasn't overjoyed, just pleased. It could never be enough, never restore her sanity—Phil agreed—but she thanked him anyway, and fixed them both a glass of Scotch.

The models, all except Cindy, arrived on time. Phil knew each one of them well enough to be kissed, congratulated, told how happy they were for him, and what good things they'd been hearing about the clothes from everyone, just everyone, on the Avenue; they couldn't wait to see them for themselves. The nicest part of it all was that it was true: what they said and how they said it. It was always a shock for him to be told by designers how they might fit their clothes on so and so and show on her but would never think of socializing with her. Phil liked his models, but maybe it was because of the way he chose them, by disposition and not always their look. They had to seem human, not kooky. He didn't have anything against kooky good looks—live and let live. But the clothes he designed weren't like that. They were feminine and fun, serious too when they had to be but in a way that congratulated the wearer and not the maker. His models had to reflect that philosophy. If it was diluted Carl Kalbism, at least the application was different. He didn't strut. He paced the runway, sipping Scotch, apologizing for the showroom—the girls agreed it was ugly—explaining how he felt about the line and that all he wanted from them was to put the dresses on and do whatever they felt like doing in them. They were stripping for action down to their bras and panties, applying fresh make-up, brushing their hair, talking among themselves, laughing, concentrating on their mirrors, being professionals: attentive, eager human beings who plied their trade just like the next guy. Their instruments were themselves, and if they wanted to be kept on by their agencies, if they wanted to be called by designers for showings and fittings, they had to take the time to care for their bodies, to train them as athletes do and have the same kind of healthy unself-consciousness about how their bodies worked. To be almost naked half the time, to be poked and pinned, pushed and turned, to spin and settle to a pose required training, and just like athletes and any other kind of professional, some were better at it than others; some were naturals and some would never be; some, like his dark-haired Petey and his blonde Mimi, hated outsiders standing around and gawking at them as if they were freaks; some, like Ella, the ivory-skinned Austrian, and Betty, push-button, more-bounce-to-the-ounce Betty, could have undressed in the waiting room of Grand Central Station without a qualm. Not Dahlia, his Eurasian girl. She opened slowly, never all at once. Her performance was a joy, a mysterious ritual, a poem that had to be read over and over again to find its heart. Reena, his black beauty, had her share of problems. Just breaking into the trade was one that made her look tough on a runway. A smile was a gift, saved for special moments.

Cindy, all contrition, arrived exactly at five-thirty. Five minutes later she was in her first dress, ready to be adorned along with Petey and Mimi. Five minutes after that was when the dough didn't rise.

Pat was all lists and Scotch and sketches and hands dipping into the jewels. The first group was the print one. Phil wanted nothing but earrings. Pat wanted earrings, bracelets, pearls. Cindy wanted whatever they wanted. She was nervous, out of character, concerned about more than herself suddenly, but not surprisingly. The fitting model of a collection is under the greatest pressure at a preview, almost as if she is responsible for its existence. She knows all the dresses, knows exactly what *she* expects to wear at the showing. The others have to take what's handed to them. She's the queen bee. The other models are attendants to the throne then, but just until they get the lay of the land, until they decide that one dress is not right for them, that it would look so much better on one of the other girls. Phil didn't like the way Cindy looked in the print. She did. So did Pat. He didn't like the way her hair looked. Instructions had been given to the girls about how he wanted their hair to be done for the showing. Close to the head. Curls, if possible. No falls. He wanted the dress switched to Dahlia. Pat said that would completely botch up the whole line-up because then Dahlia would have too quick a change and everybody else would have to be moved around and the whole point of what she'd organized would be a shambles. It wasn't fair. He knew he was being stubborn. Phil insisted, reached for the Scotch bottle. Pat declined. Phil ordered. Calm fled before the crossfire of innuendo and raised voices. The models caught fire; the blaze spread rapidly. They loved the clothes, adored them. Couldn't this one wear that dress? Shouldn't Reena wear the long white lace? Why not switch Ella into the plunging linen? Her skin tone was perfect for it. Pat raised her hand from the jewel box and refused to lower it until Phil apologized. Cindy cried off and on. The doors which were supposed to be closed began opening. Glenda Dubester had something to say about the printed voiles. They weren't right for her future daughter-in-law. Phil screamed her out of existence. Petey wouldn't change unless those men, the salesmen, got the hell out of the showroom. Ella told her to stop being such a priss. Petey told her to stop being such a pisser. Betty brushed and rebrushed her hair, indifferent to the commotion, telling everyone that Phil was the designer. What he said went, as far as she was concerned. The clothes were just too beautiful to fight over. Andy, roused by the noise, looked in to complain that at this rate the preview would last for three hours and Phil ought to think about how much money it was costing them. Phil told him that Andy ought to just shut up, go back to his style cards and count out his cutting tickets. Michael blew smoke back on the fire. The shipping boys peeked in for a free show, which started Petey and Mimi in all over again.

By seven-forty-five, Pat's lists in pieces, jewelry strewn on captain's chairs, on the floor, on every table, stockings and shoes kicked into corners, the samples twisted into unrecognizable shapes, the last dress was reached. Pat had a notebook filled with alterations Phil wanted done. The models began to pack up silently and steal off, each stopping to kiss Phil, to promise him that all would go well at the showing, it always did, that there was nothing to worry about, not a thing because those clothes, well, those clothes were just the most gorgeous things being done anywhere on the Avenue at any price. Phil was too drunk and disgusted to care. It was his fault it had happened the way it did. He was responsible, no one else. Pat was sullen and just as certain that it was her fault. If she hadn't been so damned organized she could have been more flexible. That's why she wasn't a good cook. She always followed the recipes too exactly. Couldn't they just leave everything the way it was until tomorrow? She didn't have the heart for cleaning up now. No. It was now or never. The two of them bent to the task forlornly. At no point during the preview had Phil felt any exhilaration, any thrill. The one thing he couldn't remember at all was the way the clothes looked on anyone. He hated them anyway, all of them. They were *shmattes*, not dresses. Send them to Klein's on the Square. Get them out of his sight. Let him die in peace. Oh, Wilma. Where are you now that I need you? Phil Hanssler's his same old *schmucky* self. Out of control. Underneath it all. A failure. Some boss! Some designer! Some winner!

"But after all, Rhett, tomorrow is another day. I'll make new sensible lists. I promise. First thing in the morning." Pat pulled him by the tie back to the Scotch bottle. "One drink for the road."

"One more drink for the road and I'll never stop walking."

"You will. You know you will. It's bigger than both of us."

They drank. They cleaned up the mess. Andy watched, glaring his I-told-you-sos. Michael wondered why there was such a big fuss about nothing. Previews are always like this. The show would be a smash. Not a thing to worry about.

Andy went around turning out all the lights, motioned them out into the hallway while he rang in the signal to the Holmes protection service, waited for the answering ring, then locked up.

When they hit the air in front of 498, they stood in a silent, prayerful circle, until the fact that it was snowing washed away their sins. Phil smiled, laughed, kissed Pat. "Tomorrow, Scarlet, honey, we'll try again." The circle broke up. Arm in arm Pat and Phil, the artists, walked off toward Thirty-fourth Street doubled over with laughter.

Andy put a hand beside his temple, moved it around and around. "You know what, Mike? They're nuts."

Although Phil would have liked the Hotel Delmonico or the Plaza, the first showing of the new Mr. Jack by Phil Hanssler clothes, summer, 1967, was held in their vest-pocket showroom. If nothing else, at least the affair was catered. Phil's mother hadn't made chopped liver, it only seemed to him as if she had. The occasion had that old-fashioned, furnished-basement feel to it: not enough chairs, not enough dishes, but plenty of good, wholesome food. Everyone behind the scenes, from Glenda Dubester to each sample hand, felt personally responsible for seeing to it that the show was a success. So if it wasn't Aram LeGeis elegance, it was more than enough Phil Hanssler, my-son-the-designer, down-to-earth, heart and style nonsense.

The caterer had to have a place to arrange his platters, check on his chafing dishes, instruct his servers. The long cutting table in the back was ideal. The cutters and duplicators were dispossessed. The bolts of fabric were moved from one cluttered spot to another while Morris howled they should be careful, they shouldn't disturb the markings from the patterns. The champagne man was given one end of the cutting table to set his bottles icing, a small piece of territory, according to Michael's thinking, for such an important company.

The seven models were going to have to have places to change. Two went into Phil's room. Three went into the sample room. Two would have to be in Morris's partitioned-off cubicle. Sample hands were assigned to help the models with their changes and with each one went a rack to hang the dresses on. Pat had new lists for everyone, detailing what shoes, what stockings, what jewels, what hat, if any, went with which dress. The lists were final now. It was all down on paper. Nothing could go wrong. She kept assuring Phil of that all morning.

"Something will. I know something will. No one will come. The invitations were mailed out too late. No one will check the Fashion Calendar for the time. I'll go out into the showroom at four o'clock and it'll be empty. That's my nightmare. It kept me up all last night." He sipped from a paper cup repeatedly filled with Scotch. He began sipping at eleven when he heard Michael on the telephone still arguing with his big-time friend about the champagne, telling him that the showing was scheduled for four so could the champagne get there at five? Okay, so there wouldn't be champagne. Let them drink water if they're thirsty. Only keep cool.

By one-thirty, with Phil screaming all the way, the tables, the captain's chairs, the partitions had been moved out of the showroom, and the fading red velvet bridge chairs were set up neatly, row upon squeezed-together row with pads and pencils placed on each, ashtrays on the carpet. The Mr. Jack logo stared up from everywhere.

At two-thirty La Lyon returned from two and a half hours of lunch teetering on the edge of total drunkenness and clutching her rosary. "Phil sweetheart. Phil, you love of my life." He steered her into his office, past Pat's hair-combing hands. "All I did was go to church. I had to pray for you. Everything's all right now. You'll see. God's ready."

"Only you're not. Some help you'll be. How many fingers do you see for Christ's sake? Will you put those beads away. You're supposed to be at the door to the showroom to check on the girls. How the hell will you know if they're even dressed, let alone in the right dress? You wanted to get my attention? Is that it? Well, you got it and you're also going to get a boot in the behind if you don't get in there and finish those hems. You better pray to God to sober you up by four o'clock."

She cried quietly, her rosary dangling from the fingers of the hand that stroked Phil's arm. "Don't be angry with me, please, Phil. I can't take it for anyone to be angry with me. It's so hard. I've got so many problems to face. My husband's sick and I'm sick and . . ." she leaned her head on Phil's jacket, "I just have to turn to God. Be kind, Phil. Be understanding, please. You like me, don't you? Don't you like me for myself?" Tears dropped everywhere, on the floor, on Phil's jacket, on his sleeves as he tried to straighten her before she fell into a heap at his feet.

"I love you, sweetheart, but only when you're not drunk. Then you're the best assistant there is. Now you're drunk and you're no help to me when I need you the most and I hate it."

She raised her head unaided, slid the rosary into a sweater pocket. She was actually smiling, as if she were happy to be scolded for being a bad girl. "I'll be okay. You'll see. God bless you, Phil, and don't worry about a thing. Whatever needs to be done I'll do." She managed to get to her feet, to set them apart and remain standing. Maybe God *was* everywhere. "I'll be a good girl from now on. Cross my heart and—"

"Get the hell out of here before I puke." He turned her, pushed her, and she went obediently, a middle-aged Marguerite on her way to a painted paradise.

"I don't see how you can stand that!" Pat shook her head. "Absolutely do not see how. That woman is dangerous. She's liable to kill someone at any given moment. A quick swing to the eyes with those beads and you're blinded for life. An invalid. A charity case."

"Calm down yourself. We'll save her yet, doctor. There's still a ray of hope left, so let's sit down, take stock and have some more Scotch."

"Not while you're operating, Doctor Kildare. It's against all the principles you've struggled all your life to uphold."

At three-forty the models began to arrive and a few spectators entered the showroom. Phil went out there to entertain them. At three-forty-five the duo of hairdressers, who were supposed to check the models and fix a wig for Cindy, appeared. Cindy herself arrived at three-fifty, a long fall attached to her Sassoon haircut, looking the exact opposite of what Phil had asked for, which was why, knowing that she would, he had hired the hairdressers. Three minutes later she emerged from her dressing area in Phil's office in her first dress and in tears. "How could you let him do this to me, Pat? You're a traitor. I had my own hair done. It's better than a wig. Call Phil back here, please, Pat."

The hairdressers, young, long-haired baby boys, oblivious of Cindy's cries for help, pushed her into a chair before a make-shift mirror in the shipping area and set to work. Silently, the other models, all done up in their first outfits, formed a semicircle behind the mirror, watching and horrified. The sample hands, Pat, the duplicate makers, the cutters, out of work for the time being anyway, gathered behind them, all of them mesmerized by the unfolding horror-pantomime. The noise coming from the cutting room, where the caterer and his crew, the champagne man and his crew banged buckets and ice and silver salvers were the sound effects for the drama.

Meanwhile, out in the showroom, only the sound effects were heard; Phil would learn of the accompanying drama shortly. Just then he had his hands full coping with the melodrama underfoot. The time was four; the guests were met. A shrill, sibilant, impatient din rose around him near the microphone, along with the smoke rising from the cigarettes of buyers who had other shows to go to after this one. The noise from the back swelled, crashed against unsuspecting eardrums like a brass band. The anxious eyes of family and friends who were joined together in the bonds of love pleaded with Phil to go back there, to tell them to quiet down a little. Michael had tried; Andy had tried. It didn't help. So Phil would have to go, sweating, trapped, nauseated Phil would have to do that too. It was some kind of smell that was making him nauseated, not the Scotch. It too was drifting in from the cutting room, a smell of fish, fish hors d'oeuvres being heated back there. And then, there was Pat's hand from the side door at the other end of the showroom, motioning frantically for him to come quick, to hurry.

It wasn't easy to hurry down that gantlet of a runway, past quizzical, irritated, sympathetic eyes. It wasn't easy to avoid Marvin Bernstein's front-row legs. He didn't. He tripped. Gary, Bruce, and Sam Greenstalk caught him. Everyone was laughing, everyone but Phil. As if he were going down for the third and last time, his life flashed in front of his eyes. Wilma was smiling encouragement from the other side of the room. Howie next to her—he had played hooky from school—was waving.

Sandy next to him was biting his corrugated nails. Carl Kalb, his arms folded, found it all repulsive. Aram was doing his oh-my-dear-but-you're-gauche scene from a Noel Coward play. Mr. Hanssler in a far corner was checking his watch, holding up ten fingers to tell Phil they were ten minutes late already. Mrs. Hanssler's hair was falling from her tortoise-shell combs. Perhaps it was the swaddling Scotch, perhaps it was the showman in Phil, perhaps it was instinct that allowed him the time between his fall and recovery to see that carousel of faces and gestures, the love and the scorn, but whatever it was, when he rose he found himself safe and sound, floating on a wave. He smiled, he mugged, he swaggered boyishly and yelled, "Be right back. Please don't anyone leave." He was applauded as he left the room.

When he reached the circle of hushed people around Cindy, he was totally in control. Cindy was crying bitterly; Cindy was refusing to look at herself in the mirror. Phil took command. "That's horrible." The hairdressers fell against each other. "I give you two minutes to get that disease off her head. I asked for ringlets, not dead snakes. Send me a bill, but scram. Get out of here." As he whirled away, the models ganged up on him, threw him to La Lyon and then to Pat. "Let's get lined up, kids. It's time. It's time."

Then he was into the cutting room, sipping a glass of champagne, telling the caterer to turn on the Airwick. "It smells out there. Open a window at least." He waited for that to be done. "That's too wide. You'll blow every marker for every dress out onto Seventh Avenue. Let's get with it. I've got a show to do. You're not on until after me." The caterer snapped to attention. Thrust! Attack! Lead them on to victory. They love life that way. Make them want what you want, as if their lives depended on giving you what you asked for. Poor people on the periphery everywhere, unite. You have nothing to lose but the power of your attachments.

Phil walked slowly back down the fake brick runway to his microphone, conscious now of the following eyes. These were the poeple he had to convince about his future. He knew exactly where he was and exactly why he was there. In spite of everything he was not and never could be, didn't want to be, he was going to get by and keep on going in his own way, at his own speed, Aram LeGeis and Carl Kalb notwithstanding. So stop checking your watch, Bonwit Teller, and don't light another cigarette, Lord & Taylor. Relax and have a good time. "Ladies and gentlemen, now that we've conquered the kitchen, maybe we can get on with the reason you've all been asked to come up here. You'll only be uncomfortable for forty-five minutes or so." Muted, bitchy, relieved applause. Who cares? He moved with the microphone down the runway à la Judy Garland. "We scheduled this first showing of the new Mr. Jack for four o'clock so that for most of you it would be the last thing you had to do today. Afterward I hope you can stay for some champagne and food. So do my partners hope you can stay. After all, we went to a great expense —that's what the smell is all about—to bring you the very finest available at a moderate price. Even my mother's chopped liver . . ." General laughter. That was what he always tried for at the beginning: laughter at his own expense or a joke about the clothes if he could think of one. At the old Mr. Jack commentating a show brought out the realist in him. It had to. What else could he do to save himself but become just another member of the tribe, an observer too, like a buyer who has sales figures to meet each month, who looks at a collection and says, really, my dear, you're only showing me dresses, not the goddamn crown jewels. This wasn't haute couture where a directress announces the dress's number and the rest is reverential silence. This was medium-price ready-to-wear and you had to offer more, as an emcee in the Borscht Belt tries to do, otherwise the paying guests will go somewhere else. It has to be socko, homey, earthy, the way a woman feels when she takes off her corset or a man feels when he takes his newspaper into the bathroom. A.F. hated it. It was cheapening. Just give them the clothes and that's all, he used to say. Well, your way was wrong, A.F. sweetheart. Now, wherever you are in sunny Florida with the old folk, you don't have anything to give. "But seriously, friends—you have to be friends because only a friend would suffer through this kind of thing with you—the clothes you're going to see in a minute represent the hopes of everyone here at the *new* Mr. Jack. We know we have a bad reputation to live down. Why deny it? But when I look around the room and see the faces of buyers who haven't bought Mr. Jack clothes for years, I feel encouraged. It's crowded in here and that's got to mean something. You want good clothes to sell and you want a good, dependable product with a label that used to be a force in American medium-price fashion. We hope to make it that again. That's why you came here today, to see if we could and—"

"We came here because we love you!" The voice was clear and unashamed. It belonged to Sally Diamond, a resident office buyer who had followed Phil's career right from the beginning at Carl Kalb's. She was sitting next to Carl now. Phil's grateful smile was beamed through the rows of people at Sally's powder-caked, serious face. Sally didn't crap around. Fashion-shmashion. It's a business and it's people you like or you don't like. He touched his fingers to his lips, blew her a kiss. "Thank you, Sally . . . And," he turned in a circle, "that's not my mother either." Full-throated laughter, applause.

"No more talk. The clothes. The first summer collection, 1967, of Mr. Jack begins with . . ." he looked toward the doorway, signaled to La Lyon who, through prayer, was prepared, walked up the runway to the other end of the room, "Cindy, my love, in a silk signature-print djellabah, a print we loved in a dress that no one will buy. We don't mind. It's too hard to produce anyway. Morris Trebnitz, our production man, told me so. In any case we liked it so we decided to show it. . . . I won't quote prices with each dress but the range is from $19 to $39. This one, wouldn't you know it, is $39." Cindy made her tour of the runway, disappeared into Glenda Dubester's office on her way to the back, where her next dress was being readied. Pat, lists waving, directed traffic, handed jewelry to the models before they lined up at the showroom entrance to be checked and sent out once more to the customers, and Phil's commentary.

"Ella . . . Don't you just love Ella's skin? . . . Ella is in the first of a linen group that we hope will be prophetic. A simple wrap, sleeveless, lots of bust showing, a plunge right to the waist." The applause that greeted the dress had a different quality to it, not the we-love-you-Phil-no-matter-what sound, but the solid slap bang of approval.

When Ella got to the back and into the hands of Evelyn Washington, Pat was crying. "They loved it, Ella. Ab-so-lute-ly loved it."

"They're loving everything. I never heard so much applause."

Cindy and Dahlia brushed past. "It's a smasheroo."

It was Pat's first real showing. She didn't know what to expect, but she hadn't expected what was happening. Midway through the show when the movement of the models through the back was settling into a rhythm of ordered frenzy, when breathing was possible, Cindy stopped to put the experience into precise perspective. "It's got to be a hit when models care about the clothes they're putting on. They put so many on each day."

The reaction in the showroom to each dress, to each group became a constant buzz, an excited murmur. Even the tough buyers, the ones with the inscrutable, bored expressions, seemed to melt in the heat of the success. The Greenstalk trio craned their necks forward to smile at Phil, to turn and stare at the crowd. Marvin Bernstein, Esther Kaufman behind

349

him, leaned toward the trio to make sure they remembered who had given them this moment, and Marvin's glance, from them to Phil, was one which Phil was forced to see, receive, return, even as he went on speaking —as if he were two people, one doing, the other judging what was being done. Marvin's eyes demanded it; the pointing finger resting at his knee said, here I am, I made it happen, I own you.

"Now this dress I love. I love the look of the waist again. It's right. I think the tent has had it finally. . . . Thank you, Mimi . . . Let's slow things down for a minute . . . just stand there, Reena. Yes, right in the runway . . . One of the things that makes me particularly happy this afternoon is the presence of some of my—what's the word they use if you're a Senator?—colleagues? Yes. That's it. Sandy White, a designer and a friend who helped me to get my first job on the Avenue. Don't stand up, Sandy. Just smile. And there's Carl Kalb, another friend who taught me whatever I know about this business and a lot of what I know about life." Phil led the applause. Carl blushed. The steel was almost all gone from his hair now. It was white. Apart from the closing of Carl Kalb, Inc., which everyone knew about, Aram had whispered that Carl was also on the point of losing still another lover. Carl didn't look as certain as he used to look about everything. The applause that mounted and sank made him look worse. "As long as I'm presenting, I'd like to introduce another friend, a fashion leader, Aram LeGeis." The applause splattered dully. Aram stood up just the same. The wave of silky fawn hair, its cute, studied curve across his forehead seemed to say he could stand anything that *these* people had to hand out. You never have to live on lumps, do you, Aaron baby?

"Okay. My mother and father will have to wait until later. . . . To resume. Reena is in a peasanty dotted swiss. There's the waist again, but higher. A romantic way to look for summer."

On it went, the parade of dresses, and what he had missed at the preview he got now. He felt proud of what he saw, proud that there were people watching with him. He was glad to be standing where he was and where he would be standing for a while, for five years, his contract said. It was good to know that some kind of success could come at $50 retail, but it would be a lie to think he'd never want the chance to win a Coty Award, to get what Aram's $1,000 dresses could get.

Then the last group of clothes. Three pieces. Ottoman silk for summer. Betty. Dahlia. Cindy. He thought of introducing Wilma, changed his mind—she'd hate it—handed the microphone to Michael, who had stood behind him faithfully during the entire show.

"Betty," Phil met her on the runway, "is in the first of a group we call the hope chest, dresses that re-emphasize the bust. A cocktail look, but simple. . . . Let's have Dahlia and Cindy out here together." They appeared, posed along with Betty. "Cindy's in my favorite. I love that high-waisted plum satin top against the white. Dahlia's in the long. The criss-crossed straps end up in the back with two rhinestone buttons." There was applause, sustained applause, during which Phil returned to the microphone. The models started back down the runway. "I'm glad you like them because with these dresses we end our first show at the new Mr. Jack." The applause continued. Some people stood up, raised their arms, yelled, "Bravo." "Don't forget the champagne."

Even as the two packing boys and Link rushed in to start folding up the bridge chairs, the trays of champagne appeared. Phil was encircled on the runway, shunted from one embrace to another like a bride, pulled from one handshake to the next, pushed from the runway to the green carpet and back again, past chafing dishes and cigarettes and champagne glasses. It was an orgy of expanding, rising noise, of contracting space. Faces swirled around him. Arms stretched, grabbed him. Buyers, editors, merchandise managers, Wilma, Howie, his stepmother, his father had their way with him. And then Pat was there, screaming in his ear, and La Lyon stumbling, and Cindy, followed by the other models.

It was fully five minutes before the Greenstalks and Esther Kaufman, the one responsible for everything, reached him. And behind them Marvin's hollow cheeks puffed out with pleasure, his head higher than the rest, his twisted smile a beacon beckoning. Phil's double vision of himself-watching-himself dissolved. He tugged at the vest of his new suit. Hidden in the crush of people, Marvin's hand moved down Phil's arm. The frozen-tableau quality of the moment sustained itself while Marvin leaned close to Phil's ear, "You're some actor. Some kid. We're having lunch together soon and talk. Remember!" Marvin moved away. Wilma was holding on, like an anchor. She and Phil moved together down the runway.

Carl was there, smiling, nodding at Wilma, his eyes remembering everything. "I'm proud of you. You've got more talent than I thought." Mr. Hanssler surfaced, kissed Phil, disappeared. Sandy hugged him, whispered, "Relax. This is the world of fashion. Anything goes."

Aram was the last to reach him. "I must go, Phil. An excellent beginning. Keep it up. You'll do well at this price range." He started off.

Phil held his jacket, pulled him back again. "In case you don't know it, you're a first-class fuck."

"As long as it's first class, I'm content." This time Aram got away.

"Never match stingers with a queen bee," Sandy giggled, "because you don't know how. You're a king."

In the midst of a group of buyers nearby, he saw Michael forcing champagne on everyone. Andy, as far as he could tell, was nowhere.

And soon the buyers who had to go were gone. The food was eaten, all the champagne was drunk. The editors who didn't want to go were going. The caterer's crew were cleaning up. The crowd thinned out. The noise died down. His friends, the staff were left. Sandy had disappeared. Carl was drunk and about to leave. He looked susceptible, lost, without a business and a lover, but with a wife and children somewhere. Phil walked him to the elevator, accepted the kiss Carl gave because he was drunk. "Why don't you call me, Phil? We could have dinner, go to the theatre . . ."

"You'll come to my wedding, Carl, won't you?"

"No!" He was himself again. "Your showing, yes. Your wedding never. I hate that girl and that . . . that Howie." He stepped into the waiting elevator and was gone, for good, perhaps.

Mr. Hanssler was watching. "What's happened to that man? He looks terrible. You should remember to be nice to him, Philly. After all, he helped you get your start."

"Sure he did, Dad. He helped me get my start. But he didn't help me get that." He pointed to the sign above their heads.

"That, everyone helped you to get, including yourself. It's a beautiful collection. I only hope you'll be able to keep it up."

Phil laughed, grabbed his father's shoulders. "Worry, worry, worry. That's all you ever do."

"If only your mother were alive today to see you, she would have been so happy. And Paul? Why didn't Paul come?"

"I don't know and I don't care. I invited him. That's all I know."

Mrs. Hanssler joined them. She'd been looking for them. What were they doing out in the hallway, she wanted to know, when there were people still inside? "Those were some gorgeous clothes. I'll bet Betty could wear every one of them." She checked her tiny diamond wristwatch. "We have to go, Herman. We're going to hit plenty of traffic as it is, and Glenn's coming for dinner tonight. Betty's beginning to show already, Phil. Maybe you'll come home soon and see—"

"Soon, Mother. I'm glad she's showing. Let me know when she begins to feel life. Then maybe I'll come home."

They kissed and then that departure was accomplished.

He looked up at the sign again, at the curving silhouette of a woman's body, at his name. From Jack Farbstein to Alex Fleiss to Phil Hanssler. Tinker to Evers to Chance. The next thing would be to get rid of the Mr. Jack part. But not today. Not now. Now he had some other things to do. Now he'd just like to stop climbing for a minute and enjoy the fact that he was officially in business.

He and Wilma and Howie went to their steak restaurant. They hadn't been there together for a long time and Wilma thought it would be a nice place to celebrate in, a place they knew, that they had fought in and laughed in and that was close to her apartment. The dim lights, the wrought iron, the fake flowers were still perfect, she thought. Didn't they think so? They thought so.

When they were seated, like back in the good old days of less than a year ago, before the new Mr. Jack and the new wedding plans, Wilma gathered the big menu cards together, prepared herself to order for them, bracelets jangling the same old gold tune but in a different key, capped white teeth aglow in the light from the overhead sunburst fixtures.

Phil took the menus from her, placed them alongside him on the leather banquette. "I'm not ready to eat yet. I want some more to drink. I might even get drunk."

"Don't get drunk, love. You know what that does to you." Wilma took up his hand, squeezed it, moved it back and forth toward Howie, as if it were a prize she had won and wanted to make sure that Howie and everyone else in the restaurant, saw. Phil didn't object, didn't object to her doing whatever she wanted with his hand. He was too tired and softened by the sense of everything being all right now, now that the show was over and apparently a success. Besides, Wilma had her rights, her claim to it. Howie had never had, never would have in the way he wanted, those rights. The south and north pole of Phil's planet, the light and dark side of his moon were being separated at the center because they had to be, and he wouldn't blow apart either, wouldn't stop circling in the orbit he had fixed for himself. No one else had to keep him afloat any more. No one else had to paddle while he rested on his oars. Wilma could help, but he'd do his own rowing. And Howie? What would happen to Howie now that he had been relieved of his official duties as chief advisor to the Hanssler throne? He'd drink too much, read too much, teach too much, be alone too much. He'd be his own unit of one. Wilma and King Hanssler would, hopefully, be another.

When the drinks arrived, Howie proposed a toast. "To the new order of things everywhere. In business, in the home, and on the farm."

"What do you mean 'on the farm'?" Wilma leaned her head on Phil's shoulder, stared across at Howie. "What do you care about farms?"

"Nothing. I don't mean farms exactly. I mean country, trees, quiet. I mean that I'm going to move out of New York."

"You're kidding, Howie. You can't." Phil waved the thought out of existence.

"I'm not kidding and I can. Very easily."

"You're not quitting your job, are you? You're not going to be that dumb?" Flustered, Phil freed himself from Wilma. He knew he was responsible for whatever Howie was going to do, but there was a limit. He couldn't go through the rest of his life worrying about Howie. That would be the last thing Howie would want.

"No. I'm not going to be that dumb. I'd like to level with you and with Wilma. I'd like to try and tell you what's in my mind, why I'm going to do what I'm going to do. But I'm not sure it's necessary, that it makes any difference. Certainly tonight is not the time to do it either. I don't want to spoil the day. You always tell me I talk too much anyway, both of you do. So maybe I should just shut up and get drunk and tell you another time."

"Now you are being dumb. Spoil the day? What day? I'm not celebrating anything. All I am is temporarily relieved. Tomorrow I'll be starting on the next line." Phil clinked Howie's empty glass. "Just like you'll have another drink. So talk. No one wants you to shut up."

Howie's solemn gaze shifted as Wilma linked her hand to Phil's once more. He nodded to himself, as if he was deciding to make public what should be kept private. "Okay. You asked for it. I'll try to say what I have to say as simply as I can. I don't want to make a Greek tragedy out of it, although it is my fate that's being played out along with everyone else's. We know what the end will be. That's the only fact. The rest of the story is just coincidence. That's all it is, no matter how much the happy humanists try to convince people it isn't. Life isn't full of order and reason. People can't just plan things, work hard, and reach goals. That's bullshit, a myth manufactured by historians. At least it is to me. People do what

354

circumstances within themselves and on the outside force them to do and then someone comes along and says, well, isn't that great. People have guts and fortitude and strong wills. They endure. They get by. They accept what they have to accept. As if they had a choice in the matter! They take what chance throws up to them and they try to like it or they try to change what they don't like even though they know they're going to fail. For some people that's the only excitement life has to offer, that trying to change their chances. That was my excitement for a while. I met you by chance, Phil, and I took my chances because I had to. I lost. I knew I would. But you don't owe *me* anything, and I don't owe *you* anything. We're even. You're not responsible for whatever happens to me in the future. Even if you think you are, you're not and if . . ." Howie hesitated for the first time since he had started speaking, as if he had suddenly reached the end of the carefully prepared, memorized portion of his thought. From here until whatever end he had in mind, it would be the searching-for-a-word Howie speaking, the Howie that Phil was used to, the hurt, honest Howie that observed, registered, cried, fought and accepted, finally, what had to be accepted. ". . . and if you think I'm kidding, I'm here to tell you that I'm not. Painful or otherwise, I think those are the facts in the case. I think I . . I think . . ."

"I think you're right." Wilma raised her free arm, shook her bracelets, clanging them like a coda to the chorus, an amen. "I also think you're marvelous, whether you like it or not. But I don't see why we have to talk ourselves into the glooms like we'll never see each other again. Where are you going anyway, to Siberia? And also you're not going anywhere until you're best man or whatever the hell else you'll have to be at the wedding."

"I think you're right too." Phil ordered two more drinks, for Howie and himself. Wilma had struck ice in hers, but one was still her limit. "So tell us where you're going to already. If you can't be best man, you're not going."

"Well, since you're so insistent, both of you, I accept the call, but your brother Paul is going to have a gas over that one. Best man, indeed!" He raised his eyebrow, hung his wrist limply under his chin. "All I'm going to do is move my hi-fi set and records and books up to Westchester near school. Another teacher told me about a house I could be the caretaker for. It's in Croton. A lot of bachelor teachers, if you know what I mean, have lived in it before, so it's probably haunted. But it's on a hill and it has a great view of the Hudson and it's what I want to do so I'll do it.

I'll be able to see you and if the two of you want to go away or anything I can take Liffey. She'll love it."

"She'll love it, but will you?" Phil handed Wilma the menus.

"Listen, I'm just thirty-five, going on ninety, so of course I'll love it. I'll have nature and I'll be a sleep-in teacher and I'll . . . commune. I'll live alone . . . and I'll like it. And if I should happen to . . ." he laughed suddenly, the sound too loud too quickly for it to be real, ". . . maybe . . . I'll be able . . . to meet . . . a nice . . . Jewish man a . . . teacher. My mother would like that."

Wilma waved the menus at the waiter. Howie lifted his head, pushed back his hair, smiled across at Phil, laughed and then began to cry. "I *will be* . . . all right. Let's eat."

Chapter Fifteen

Lovey Gray's review of the collection in *Women's Wear Daily*, the accompanying picture of the linen dress, the word of mouth, big mouths and little mouths, spread the success story down the side streets and onto the Avenue from 498 to 512 to 530 and even 550. The Mr. Jack summer line became one that no buyer could afford to pass up. They had to spend on it. They had to write orders on that line and forget about others. They had to have those clothes in their junior departments because if they didn't and their merchandise managers found out that the clothes were checking out in another store in town they were in trouble, they weren't with it, they were out of touch with the new trends. Bonwit Teller's, Bergdorf's, Bendel's, Bloomingdale's, Best's, the big bees, Saks', Altman's, De Pinna's were up to the showroom and bought big, even vying for the chance to work out window stories and bringing their window display men with them to prove they meant it. The Lord & Taylor buyer thought the clothes were the best in the market at any price. They were fresh, new, full of ideas, "As long as the product is good and you keep to your delivery dates, you're all set. Mr. Jack will be back where it used to be and stronger than ever." The word from the out-of-town stores and specialty shops, from Rich's in Atlanta, Harzfeld's in Kansas City, Marshall Field's in Chicago, Nieman-Marcus in Dallas, Sakowitz's in Houston, Godchaux's in New Orleans, Goldwater's in Phoenix, Higbee's in Cleveland, Jordan Marsh, Filene's, Wanamaker's, Jenny's, Magnin, I. & J., and Bulloch's on the West Coast, was the same. Each day after the showing during Market Week, when the out-of-town buyers flood the Garment Center to buy or not to buy, the Mr. Jack showroom packed them in and still overflowed. Tables and chairs had to be set up in the hall. Appointments had to be made in advance. What Phil, never a relaxed optimist, had called an apparent success was a total, genuine, 90 percent success.

The orders were big enough so that even Andy was caught smiling occasionally. Michael was almost overcome by cigar smoke and switched to a pipe. Phil was both gratified and worried by the volume sales. They weren't equipped to handle it. They didn't have the staff. "Hire another shipping boy, at least. Get another girl for the showroom, Andy. We can afford *that* much. You can't keep using Charley's girl and Alan's girl. We only pay *part* of their salaries, remember. And, for Christ's sake, get someone to clean this place up once in a while. It's a ghetto. Pat found two mice in our room yesterday." "That's because you leave your Scotch glasses everywhere." Andy wouldn't budge an inch, and Michael was too busy trying to create new systems for the shipping room—systems *he* had dreamed up but couldn't control—to pay any attention to fights between partners. "If you want to fight with Andy, Phil, do it on your own time. I can't waste mine in meetings like that." Andy just kept adding to the black man's burden. Link, who had come to work at the new Mr. Jack out of loyalty to the past and because he couldn't find another job, earned less and worked harder and longer than he had at the old place. Phil had a battle over that and lost. "He's willing. We're doing him a favor." Andy, Phil decided for eternity and told him so, was not only a bastard without a touch of taste in his blood, he was also a narrow-minded, thoughtless, *dumb* bastard who went around looking meek and thankful but who was, underneath it all, a cool, calculating fiend with an adding machine where his heart should be. Without saying a word to Michael or Phil, he fired the two black shipping boys because they wouldn't work on Saturday and because they were too slow and then hired two more for less money. Phil won a raise for Hettie, Glenda Dubester's kid, to make up the difference. Even Morris complained how he couldn't work with that man. "How can I know what's what, Philly, when he comes to the back and takes from Tessie and Sheila dresses you told me to duplicate already. He's crazy, that man. One minute he wants and the next minute he don't want. If a dress'll be ordered ninety times he wouldn't give me a cutting ticket. Right away he discards. With him it's only one thing. A hundred. Not ninety-nine, but a hundred."

Phil screamed and called another meeting. "We have to sit down and get this thing straightened out once and for all."

"There's nothing to straighten out. I'm only doing what we agreed to do. I'm not going to buy extra yardage unless there's a cutting ticket. The style cards don't lie, and I'm not going to send a report over to Marvin Bernstein with an inventory of useless goods. As it is you buy too many sample cuts that you never make into a dress."

"For the next line I'm going to buy even more."

"Okay. Suit yourself. But it's your business too I'm trying to run efficiently. We set a budget, we projected our sales figures for each month, and that's the picture we'll give to the Greenstalks. If you want to keep our profit percentage high so we can make extra stock this year, then you won't interfere."

"I'll interfere. I'll interfere plenty because you're not going to squeeze me to death. The way you've got it rigged every dress I design has to be a Ford. The best dresses you discard, and you don't even ask me. You switch to a cheaper fabric and I don't know it unless Morris tells me. So I'm telling you right now that I want Bendel for a customer too. If you get a fifty-piece order from three fashion stores or if there's a credit in *Vogue* or the *New York Times,* I want a cutting ticket for that dress. I want us to stand for something besides bread-and-butter clothes. This isn't Jerry Silverman. It's a business, yes, but it can be a fashion business too. The trouble is the both of you have taste in your ass."

"No. I won't do it. Not now. Not at the beginning. An agreement's an agreement."

"I'm on Andy's side in this. First you'll make one exception and before you know it everything's going to be an exception." Michael's mind might always sound like it was at a tennis match, but he never forgot that the players were using his ball.

They argued, day after day, in and out of the office, in the showroom, in shipping, in the cutting room, all over and about everything; and as they did, the clothes continued to order and reorder; the stock came in, was checked by Phil, and shipped out; the duplicates for the next dress to go into production and the one after that were fitted on Cindy and handed to Morris; Phil began work on the fall line.

He had closed the sample room down for two weeks after the showing, Dorothy Krakauer reminding him, as if he could ever forget, that the girls were tired and that he always did that at the old place. She and Nita would come in the third week to start work on whatever was ready. La Lyon was given two weeks to nurse her husband and herself back to health and to have as many lost weekends as she wanted. "But if you get drunk once more like you did at the showing, it's curtains for you, and I don't mean lace curtains either." During those two weeks Pat and he shopped the fall fabric market looking for something new that wasn't too expensive and the other designers hadn't found yet. They sampled, they sketched, they dreamed of new silhouettes, a new look that, come August and September, would be exactly what a woman wanted to put on her back for $50 a throw. Mindreaders they had to be on top of everything else.

And, while he was doing all the things he had to do every day, the checking, fighting, thinking, looking, planning, and, when the sample room started up again, creating, he was also trying to make himself feel good about it all, trying to enjoy the flattery he received from the buyers and the people who stopped him on the Avenue to tell him how they always knew he'd make it, the same people who when he was out of a job passed him by without so much as a nod. Now the manufacturers stopped him, pumped his hand, and said, "If only I had listened to you." But he was democratic. He could afford to be a sport. Why the hell not? They were only human beings. He supposed he felt as good as it was possible to feel when one line you designed became the hottest junior resource in the market but you couldn't stand your partners; when you knew you were in the spotlight but the light could be switched off if the next line failed; when the fit of the clothes was good, for now, good enough for the buyers to tell you that once a woman tried a dress on in the store she almost always bought it and, most important of all, seldom returned it; when you were planning to get married and gain a wife but lose the only important friend you ever had.

Yes, he supposed he felt better than he used to feel; he was off dead center anyway, and no matter what the weather, even in a March sleet storm, he walked slower when he passed 530 and 550 on his way to Ted's for lunch. Just time, a few more years, and those big boys up there would have to let Phil Hanssler in, without the solid-gold Greenstalks behind him, with only what his talent and know-how had earned for him. His own business, alone, no partners, just the people he chose. Five more years. A five-year plan. If his ulcer could stand five more years of Andrew Berns and Marvin Bernstein trying to tell him the facts of life. Marvin had tried to do it that morning when he surprised Phil in Bruce's room and made Phil go back to his office and sit down and listen to him burp and tell him to cut out the crap about avoiding him because Marvin had heard about the arguments with Andy, he had his spies, and Phil hadn't called about going up to Larchmont or anything else since the showing, which was over a month and a half already, what the hell was he pulling off? What kind of crap was that? Marvin wanted to get to the bottom of the Andy situation and he wanted to discuss that other big plan he had in mind. "So you're going to dinner with me tonight. You're not tellimg me some other time again. Tonight! For once you're going to do *me*, me, one stinking, lousy, goddamn favor. One!" Phil had had to say yes then. He was afraid of what would happen to Marvin if he said no.

He stepped into a frozen puddle of water at the corner of Thirty-ninth and Seventh, had to race across and under the candy-store awning because the light had changed and the long line-up of trucks was bearing down on him. No rubbers on. No umbrella. No hat. Nothing. Pneumonia he'd get.

The same puddle that got him got two rolling racks. They converged, collided, fell on their sides, the string tied around the tarpaulin protective covers breaking, a mound of cotton dresses spilling into the puddle. The walkers, hunched up against the driving, icy rain, stepped around the pile of color: the blazing red, the royal blue, the turquoise and fuchsia quickly being darkened by the rain. The rackmen, one Puerto Rican, the other black, stared down, immobilized. Phil crossed back to try to help, but when he reached them, he stopped instead to stare down too, immobilized by what he saw, anguished too but for a different reason. The dress was his, a knock-off of the linen, the biggest-booking dress on the line. How could it be? How could it be so soon? What buyer who also bought cheap clothes was being paid off by what manufacturer for information? He wasn't going to help these guys. To hell with that. They didn't need his help anyway. What they needed was a bomb to blow the world up. They looked at him as if he was some kind of nut for standing there getting wet when he didn't have to.

He dashed back beneath the candy-store awning, stood there watching, as if, out of all the people passing by, that's what he had to do, just watch this scene from the wings. The rackmen looked up at the dark gray sky, down at the pile of wet dresses, at each other. They broke their stance. No knives or teeth flashed. They straightened up the racks, bent, scooped, stuffed the dresses beneath the tarpaulin, bent again, disgusted, mute. Each armful told them they were fired, finished, done, get out of here, you lazy-good-for-nothings before I call the cops.

Phil ran the rest of the way to Ted's. Now when he entered the restaurant he was greeted by Ted himself. Now there was always a table immediately available. Now he was a small star getting bigger in a dark gray sky. Now his clothes were copied before the originals ever got into the stores. Now two more men lost their jobs. Shit on it. Shit on everything, except on the day of a storm when you can afford to step in out of the cold, stay for as long as you want, be greeted with a heartwarming hello, a heartwarming, phony hello.

They met at Keen's Chop House, just across the border from the Garment Center. Marvin wanted to go farther uptown, away from business and dresses for a while, but Phil said no. Keen's or nothing. It was easier, the weather was bad, it was close by for both of them, the silver-suiters never went there anyway; the perfect atmosphere, as far as Phil was concerned, for battle: a man's restaurant of scuffed and weathered dark wood, well lit, with old vaudeville playbills in simple frames on every wall, and long-stemmed, small-bowled clay pipes the patrons sometimes smoked dangling from wires stretched across the ceiling. And the food was right for ulcers of any size: a baked potato with sour cream, a lamb chop, a toasted roll. Marvin let Phil have his way. He had won the first round that morning. Now it was Phil's turn.

Phil ordered a Scotch sour. Marvin wouldn't drink, not even one. He couldn't. If he did, he'd spend the rest of the night regretting it. He opened his linen napkin, spread it on his lap, moved closer to the table, his legs shifting, stretching, contracting, settling very close to Phil's beneath the cover of the long tablecloth. Above the table, all around them, were attentive waiters, the ripe strong smell of mutton, the sounds of man laughter and, at first, their own dull words about the weather and the healthy state of the stock market.

Phil sipped his drink, flicked his nails against the glass, felt himself losing ground before he even started. Marvin leaned closer to Phil, placed his hand along the armrest of his chair. Phil ripped a stalk of celery from the relish tray, chewed it loudly, snipped pieces of roll out of the bread basket. "I always eat too much of this stuff and then I can't finish the meal. My stomach's shrinking, I think, the older I get."

"My stomach shrank a long time ago. I have to eat five, maybe six small meals a day. But you, you don't have to worry about a thing. You've got a perfect weight and build for being short." Marvin concentrated, deliberating about whatever it was he was going to say or do, nursing his intention with a glass of ice water, flushing out of its hiding place his mood of that morning, reviving it slowly for this evening's . . . what? pleasure? pain? performance? What? Phil wondered, but wouldn't ask. That was Marvin's obligation. He asked for one stinking, lousy favor. He got it. He got his one wish. That's all he was going to get. So now what was he going to offer in return? And what was he going to expect in return for his offer? Parry and thrust. Parry and thrust. How long was this kind of crap going to go on? Throughout my five-year plan? For the rest of my life? Even after I'm married? I should have hung up on Esther Kaufman when she called to set up that first appointment. So ask me already what you want to ask, Marvin, and get it over with? What are you afraid of? Of me? A giant? Afraid of me? Or doesn't he know what he wants to ask? Is that what the trouble is? He doesn't and I do? Or do we both know and because we both know what's going on we can't say? We have to protect our business interest, our mutual investment in each other. But come on, Marvin. At least say something.

Marvin's knee pressed lightly against Phil's and remained there. He knows what he's doing. Phil couldn't move his away. It was up against the table leg. He couldn't move it away without spilling the beans. He would be all right, though. He knew how to play this kind of game better than Marvin. He had the equipment for it. Marvin didn't. He had one thing. Marvin had something else. It balanced out. It made them even.

Phil motioned to the waiter, ordered another drink. They both ordered their meals, then went on to talk about the right diet for an ulcer and for a bad heart and about low cholesterol foods and high blood pressure, which Marvin said he had in addition to everything else he had—Phil didn't; his was low if it was anything—and about smoking and lung cancer and if a person with a serious heart condition could really enjoy sex and if all women stopped wanting sex after menopause, and Marvin asked if Phil was looking forward to getting married, yes, and what kind of girl Wilma was, Marvin wanted to meet her, and his wife, Adele, kept nagging him about bringing Phil and Wilma up for dinner so would Phil make a date already, and while they went on talking Marvin's leg underneath the tablecloth wavered back and forth, back and forth, beating out a message all its own.

They ate the lamb chops, freed for a while from the need for any talk. The uninterested sounds, the uninterested eyes around them, the indifferent waiters waiting to be called, the coughs, the laughs, the disconnected phrases, the clinks of silver and of glass conveyed the sense that no one was concerned with watching them. Marvin checked his watch. Phil asked if Marvin had another appointment. Marvin said maybe, then no, and that he only had to consider the train schedule for later. About when? Phil wanted to know because he had to call Wilma at his apartment because Wilma was there walking the dog, and Marvin said that *when* depended—and asked what kind of dog it was.

"A poodle."

"A poodle? You've got a poodle?"

"You're surprised?"

"Yes. I thought you'd have a German shepherd or something?"

"Why?"

"Because you're such a tough number. I like to see the right kind of dog with the right person. A poodle's for a . . . a lady."

"Don't you think it's about time you started talking like the whizbang businessman you are, Marvin, instead of like some silly kid?"

"You know, if someone told me I'd be sitting here letting someone talk to me that way, I'd say they were crazy. But you I take anything from. Why is that? Can you tell me?"

"Because you love me." Phil laughed easily, continued eating. Marvin laughed too. He had finished eating. His legs began to swing beneath the table. "Sure, I love you. You're a beautiful designer and you're under contract for five years. That's what I call a perfect relationship."

Phil ordered tea and ice cream, pistachio. Marvin ordered tea and poundcake, and when they were finished, he leaned closer to Phil. He was ready to get down to serious things, the first serious thing being Andy.

"It's not just Andy. They're both *schmucks*."

"You're in business less than six months and you know that already?"

"I knew it before the business ever started."

"So why did you do it then? Why did you let it happen?"

"You're kidding me, Marvin. You're playing games with me. Don't do that. It's still not funny. I didn't let anything happen. You did. Michael you had to have because of the name. Andy you decided we should have because you wouldn't give us time to find anyone else."

"All right. Let's assume that's the way it happened. What can you do about it now? What do you want to do about it now?"

"What *can* I do? Complain. That's all I can do until my contract runs out. Andy will never run the kind of business I want, and, by chance, Michael's the president. If Andy does what makes you and Mr. Greenstalk and the board happy, then that's that. From your point of view the business is a success."

"And from your point of view it's not?" Marvin's fingers, like pointed spears, jabbed Phil's arm. "What I say is that Andy's right. For now, he's right." Phil moved his arm away. That was permissible. "I talked to Andy too, you know. I'm not sitting around in my office waiting for you to get off your high horse and come see me, you know. I find out what I have to find out about everyone and everything. Even about you."

"Who told you about me?" Phil was smiling and that's how he would stay, smiling, no matter what. Marvin wasn't going to knock him out.

"Esther Kaufman. Esther's a good girl. She knows her stuff. She explained the situation. You want to be an *artiste*. You want to win awards. Fine with me. As long as you make money too. That's what Andy's for." The indifferent eyes nearby were not so indifferent now. Marvin had raised his voice. "As long as he keeps your profit figure where it is now, you guys will be very wealthy *schmucks* by the end of five years, even by the end of this one because what I'm planning to do is ask the board to bring you into the family, which means that you'll become stockholders, that we buy out Mr. Jack entirely, convert the percentage of the business you own into stock and that you share the profit of all of the companies we have. Do you understand? Tell me the truth. Do you?" Marvin was suddenly at a meeting ready to explain whatever Phil wanted explained and for however long it took.

"I understand, Marvin." Phil pushed back from the table, crossed his legs. "I understand everything." His smile didn't fade. If anything, it brightened. "Sure, I understand."

"Good. So what do you think?"

"It sounds great to me. But it's not up to me alone. You'll have to speak to the boys. We'll have to vote on it."

"You okay? You don't look so good. What are you squinting about?"

"I always squint when I'm thinking."

"So what are you thinking about? You like the offer . . . you're sure you understand it?" Phil nodded. "Well, then, what is it?"

"Nothing. I feel fine. I trust you. If you say it's good, it's good. I'm sure Andy will like it. Michael's going to hate to have you own all of that name though." Phil moved his legs under the table. Almost instantly he could feel Marvin's knees.

"You're taking all this too quietly. Something's wrong. I can see your mind working. I hope you're not thinking about trying to break your contract because I'll tell you right now you can't. I won't let you get away. Your name is on that label and it's going to stay on it. Even if those guys won't accept the deal when the time comes—it won't be until the end of the fiscal year anyway, beginning of July, after the fall showing maybe—

even if they don't, your name's still on that label. You wanted it there and that's where it went. So you're hooked one way or another."

"I'm not hooked, Marvin." He applied his own pressure beneath the table. "I'm just where I want to be. You promised me money and I'm making it. You promised me a business and I have it. You're promising me more money and I'm sure you'll keep your promise. So I promise you I don't feel hooked. You're the one who's hooked. You're the one who's being taken, not me." Phil laughed. Marvin didn't. "But we're both going to get something out of it, I think. Aren't we?"

Now Marvin pushed back from the table. Hunched over, bent forward, he looked much smaller to Phil than he ever had before. On that great balance in the sky they *were* even right now. Marvin straightened, stretched, and spoke quietly, "As long as you're happy, I'm happy. Now if you'll do me one more favor, I'll be happier still."

"What's that, Marvin?"

"I do have another appointment. It's uptown and I'd like you to come with me."

"What kind of appointment is it?"

"A sex appointment." Marvin stared directly at Phil, watching carefully. "You work too hard. You need some relaxation. I'll pay for it. You'll enjoy it."

Phil returned Marvin's stare. He wasn't going to look shocked or act coy, but he wasn't going to go, no matter what. "I can't tonight. Maybe some other time."

Marvin didn't seem to want to press the point. "Have it your way. That's a promise, and I'm going to make sure you keep it, even if I have to wait until after you're married."

"You don't have to threaten me, Marvin. I'm a big boy now."

"You certainly are. No question about that. And I always knew you would be." Marvin motioned for the waiter. "My treat."

"Thank you."

"Don't mention it, big boy."

Outside, the rain had stopped. They walked the short distance up to Broadway. Marvin bent down, squeezed Phil's shoulders, looked at him for a long moment without saying anything but goodnight.

Phil, waiting for a cab, watched Marvin stride away. He headed north toward Times Square, jumped a puddle, turned and waved back at Phil. No giant then off to conquer frightened tribes of defenseless people. No. Just another tall man dwarfed by the taller, dark, empty buildings along this stretch of Broadway, bearing whatever inside burden he had to bear to whatever appointment he had to keep. Just like everyone else and different from everyone else, preserving himself first in the only way he could with whatever special weapons he found available. Phil had his own special weapons, and tonight he had won, and that was, for right now, all he could expect.

After that night, Phil saw Marvin at least once a week. Whenever he went to the Greenstalk Building to do some busy work that Bruce conned him into doing—"I'm no designer, Phil. So just this once more. Help me out"—he made a point of stopping to talk with Marvin. If he couldn't get there in person, he called. The strategy seemed to work. If Marvin was disarmed for the moment, who could be certain his mood would last. At least, he had nothing to be angry about. Phil was making himself available. He wasn't playing hard to get, and because he wasn't, Marvin didn't have to grab so hard and so fast every time they were together. Marvin was never what anyone would call relaxed in Phil's company, he never was that any time with anyone, but at least he had something to do with his hands. Phil was Marvin's fetish and as long as Marvin could reach out and squeeze an arm, a knee, a hand, he was soothed. If Marvin wanted to have lunch or dinner and rest his leg for an hour or so, Phil went. Phil even went up to Larchmont with Wilma, and then Adele Bernstein was satisfied. The one thing he didn't do was join Marvin for one of those appointments uptown. Marvin kept asking and Phil kept refusing. His excuse was one that Marvin had to honor for the time being: Wilma. "Sometime soon, Marvin, but not now. It wouldn't be right."

More than anything else, his campaign in the Greenstalk theatre of operations on Broadway strengthened his position in 498. Andy and Michael were neutralized, forced to battle each other. Phil didn't stop fighting with Andy. He would never stop that: a mock battle is necessary for troop morale, all the manuals tell you. But now the arguments were planned and productive. Phil had Marvin's attentive ear tuned to his frequency as well as to the stock market. His partners knew it. Phil made them know it. He went on designing exactly the way he wanted: something to keep Andy happy, something to keep himself and Pat happy. He bought more sample cuts than he needed. He fought for raises, for a cleaning woman, for a coffeepot, for an extra cutter, for an experienced shipping clerk to work with the packers, for the right to decide any artistic issue pertaining to the clothes before, while, and after they were produced. Marvin didn't have to convince Andy and Michael of the need for anything Phil wanted. He just had to call them and say he agreed with it and that was that. In return for what he gained, Phil gave up only one thing of value: his recently discovered spontaneity. It was still there inside, waiting for the day when it could more profitably be called back into active duty. But all that counted now was that the clothes were good, that the magazine girls came up without being asked—to pick, to haggle, to help him gain the kind of free publicity that would, perhaps at a slower pace than he wished, push his career to the top.

The fall showing the first week in June was an even greater success than the summer one had been. This time the buyers were prepared in advance for what they were going to get, and they were prepared to spend money. When the orders began piling in faster than Glenda Dubester could process them, it behooved her to ask for more help. She got it. At a meeting conducted by Marvin to which Sam, Gary, and Bruce Greenstalk were invited, the deal to buy out Mr. Jack was formally proposed and formally, gratefully, proudly accepted by Andy Berns. Michael balked at first, felt that it was too soon to do it, that the Mr. Jack name was too powerful to give up before they had had a chance to exploit it more, that if they waited a while longer the Greenstalks would have to offer more. Marvin didn't push him. He only explained what selling out meant in dollars and cents, what it would mean in five years: they would all be halfway maybe to becoming millionaires. Sam Greenstalk told Michael what the name Mr. Jack meant: "*Bubkes*, beans, in case you don't understand Yiddish, Michael. You're Jewish, no? With a name like Morgan? So anyway, without the name Phil Hanssler, Mr. Jack is nothing. Phil Hanssler is what counts. Mark my words well because I know." For the first time since the company opened, the three votes were the same.

During the two weeks following the fall showing, Phil closed down the sample room. Wilma and he were married and Aram LeGeis won the Coty Award as designer of the year. The two events had nothing to do with each other—Aram, although invited to the wedding, didn't attend —but in Phil's mind they did have some connection: they were both the products of determination, different kinds, of course, but determination nevertheless and just another proof of how a lot of people can play make-believe in a lot of different ways and maybe go on to live happily ever after. Phil, at least, was more prepared to try than at any other time in his life.

The affair, in spite of Wilma's and Phil's wishes, grew from an immediate-family-and-friends gesture into an extravaganza held at the Chanticleer Arms in Montclair, New Jersey, a long way from the grocery store but not from Teaneck. Mr. and Mrs. Pasternack, who, as parents of the bride and as custom dictated, would be paying for the wedding, wanted a big one. They didn't care where it was held just so long as it was big enough to include all their relatives and friends. Through the month of January Mrs. Pasternack cried her heart out into the butcher's apron she wore at the store and at home while cooking. During February she cried behind the ring finger of the one suffering hand she raised, unnecessarily, to cover her square shield of a face. In March, very close to victory, she spoke up, out in the open. "An only child? And a girl yet? What else did we stay in the store for for all these years? To die rich? No, my darling daughter, a marriage you're having and so a real wedding you're going to have. I didn't think any more I would live to see it happen at your age. So thank God it's happening and in order to repay God what He deserves it'll happen in the right way." That, with a few variations, was the substance of her argument, and, like a chorus of two at a Greek tragedy being performed at the Wailing Wall instead of an open-air theatre, Wilma's mother and father, each time she took a taxi to Brooklyn, with or without Phil, recited responsively, "What else is our money for? Wealthy we're not, but for this there's plenty." Mr. Pasternack didn't wear his apron at home. He used the *Jewish Daily Forward* as his weapon, waving it, folded neatly, at his daughter and Phil, sitting erect and thin at the edge of his club chair in the parlor. "For what is it, our money? A bar-mitzvah we didn't have to make for you. College you got. A wedding you're going to deprive us of? Never, my darling daughter. On a stack of Torahs never!"

Then, Mrs. Pasternack would pull wads of crumpled Kleenex from her apron pocket. "A whole family we've got to invite. A whole family and the friends from the store we've got to pay back for all the affairs we went to. Before I'll die, just once, I'll do—we'll do—this one thing for them. Any place you'll pick we'll hold it. No matter how much it'll cost it'll be worth it. You'll do this one last favor for me, darling, please? Phil? After that I wouldn't ask another thing. A promise I'm making."

When they went to Teaneck, the words were different but the story was the same.

The two families met in March for the first time at the Steak Joint on Greenwich Avenue in the Village. Throughout dinner tall Mrs. Hanssler, her hair falling out of her combs, and stubby Mrs. Pasternack, a gray-brown braid twirled tightly around the back of her head, bent together, determined to have their way. Their husbands sighed, echoing support. Afterward, when they all went back to Phil's apartment to see where the bride and groom were going to begin their married lives together and where Mrs. Hanssler immediately went into the kitchen to put on a pot of coffee, the argument was resumed and intensified.

"Why not?" Phil asked Wilma that night in bed.

"Yes, why not?" Wilma had to push Liffey away but she got her head placed just where she wanted it on Phil's pillow. "That dog is going to have to get used to me."

"Tell her you love me. That's all you have to do. . . . As long as we're having a wedding we might as well go all the way. They won't stop until we give in anyway."

"Whatever you say, Mr. Hanssler, just as long as you tell *me* you love me."

Two hundred and fifty people at $12 a head, 125 for each side, were invited to a June wedding done in mauve and white. For the money they got smorgasbord and drinks, a double-ring ceremony including a cantor, a roast-beef dinner—boiled chicken for the old folks—more drinks, champagne, a cake, lots of crying and dancing and mazel-tovs.

Women's Wear Daily reported the event because Lovey Gray was both a guest and a roving reporter. Howie, in a rented tuxedo, was best man. Paul was angry and told Phil so. Phil told Paul to kiss his ass. Until the day of the wedding, right up until the pictures were being taken at the Hanssler home—moving pictures of both families before, during, and after the ceremony was Mrs. Hanssler's last request—Paul said he sure as hell would not attend. Mr. Hanssler coaxed, begged, all but got down on his hands and knees, told Paul please to come if only for his dead mother's sake. Paul finally yielded. It took him five minutes to get drunk. Andrea had to remove him to an anteroom for safekeeping. He missed the ceremony. Howie appeared to be under control throughout. His hands trembled a lot, but as far as Phil could remember his hands always trembled. Just the effort it took Howie to get by each day was reason enough for that. Along with Sandy White, he got reasonably drunk at dinner. Not as drunk as Paul, but enough so that he could do a lot of frugging and twisting whenever the five-piece band obliged by switching from Cole Porter, Irving Berlin, or Rodgers and Hammerstein to something groovy.

The matron of honor was a last-minute choice. Wilma had many female acquaintances, but not one who mattered enough—most of her days

and evenings for so many years had been spent whittling away at Phil's resistance—nor was she particularly sentimental about who should have the
honor. Both she and Phil were noticeably unsentimental about the entire
affair once it swelled to monstrous proportions. They did what they were
asked to do and they did it as graciously as possible, a graciousness which
settled Wilma's choice on Betty, Glenn's very pregnant wife. Phil suggested Pat Pearson, present in Phil's long ottoman silk with the plum-col-
ored top, but Wilma preferred not. Reasons were not given. The buzz,
the not so successfully suppressed laughter that rose in the chapel when
Betty walked down the aisle, was about which would finish first, the wedding ceremony or Betty's pregnancy. The cantor embellished his sad,
high-rising trills with such eye-rolling art for so long a time that even the
rabbi began to shift his weight from foot to foot. Betty wavered, but she
never toppled. The assembled weeping, moaning, laughing audience were
praying for her.

Wilma's gown, which La Lyon, crying and kissing Phil all the way,
stitched up herself, was the simplest white silk jersey with self strings that
crisscrossed to a loose tie beneath the bust and full sleeves that opened
into accordion pleats. She was a little too old at thirty-three and a little
too heavy—no matter how much she dieted in preparation, 128 pounds
was where she landed—to look like a Juliet, but that was Phil's idea for
the gown. White teeth flashing as her veil was lifted, brown ringlets all
aquiver, Wilma accepted the wine chalice from the rabbi with the kind of
magically radiant, relieved smile that makes rabbis, priests, ministers of all
Protestant faiths seem necessary, because who but a specialist can a person call upon to interpret a miracle?

Phil was nervous, that much he was willing to admit to himself, but no
more nervous than he was at one of his showings. He acted like a happy
professional doing the best job he knows how, and because he was he felt
a little bit of peace, a little bit of joy. The surface was as smooth as
whipped cream; the inside doors were locked up for the night. He carried
off the ring ceremony with flourish. He broke the sacred glass as if he
were stamping out a fire. He kissed Wilma with all the passion he felt capable of feeling for her or anyone, and then he led her back down the
aisle of the chapel, guiding her, holding her elbow, smiling at her and the
250 guests as if as a husband now he was experiencing the happiest moment of his life. If it wasn't the happiest moment of his life, it was certainly close to it. That was good enough. As long as Wilma was as content as she seemed to be, who else's business was it?

The post-ceremony reception line produced the only moment of *un*-happiness, a second of instantly rising, instantly falling panic. Marvin Bernstein, preceded by his wife, who was preceded by Glenn, did what Glenn and before him Mr. Hanssler, crying, had done and Mr. Pasternack had done: he hugged and kissed Phil. There was no preventing it. Marvin acted as if it were the most natural thing in the world to do to someone you genuinely liked, and, of course, it was. But its passion was something only Phil could gauge and Marvin know. Adele Bernstein laughed, pleased with her husband's performance. Sam, Gary, and Bruce Greenstalk followed the leader, but those kisses were forehead kisses, not lip kisses. Phil's confusion was so brief, his recovery so fast that only the keenest observer could have noticed. Howie, standing behind and to the side of Phil, saw. He whispered in Phil's ear, "What's *he* up to?" so quietly that the laughter, the words of congratulations, the shuffling feet absorbed the faint trace of sound. Wilma never turned to question what was going on. Phil made believe he hadn't heard what Howie said. Howie didn't repeat his message. Once, he must have realized, was more than sufficient.

The mauve color in the dining room on all the tables, the cloths, the deep pink peonies, the matchbooks and menus matched nothing but Wilma's eye shadow and make-up; which is why, true to her matchless style, she had selected it. What did she know about color? she told Phil. That was his department. She and Phil danced the first dance together, a waltz version of Wilma's favorite Bob Dylan song, "*Sweet Lady of the Lowlands*," while the guests stood, applauded, cheered, yelled how they thought the pair made a storybook couple.

The storybook wedding—that phrase became everyone's theme for the rest of the night—ended when the storybook couple left the Chanticleer Arms for a storybook trip on BOAC to storybook London and Paris for one storybook week.

For being such a good boy, Howie got to take care of Liffey while the newlyweds were away.

Chapter Sixteen

Phil Hanssler liked and disliked some things, some people fiercely, and if asked, he said so, but he was not, nor would he ever tell anyone he was, a connoisseur of anything in particular, except maybe a good dress. Even that was, when you got right down to it, a question-mark item. When he was at Syracuse University he had heard and read a lot about standards of excellence and beauty, standards of taste and how to get it, aesthetic absolutes, the eternal search for the perfect this and the perfect that, perfect love and perfect sex. And then he was in the army, met Howie, afterward met Wilma, Carl Kalb, and Sandy, designed his first dress, met Marvin Bernstein, got married and learned the only perfect truth there was, that everything for everyone was less than perfect. So live and let live. If a tasteful, well-designed, moderately priced dress was a good seller for one season, that was perfection enough. An expert he wasn't; an appreciator of many things he hoped he was. He knew how to stand in awe as well as the next guy. He knew his cathedrals and his Parthenons, his Picassos and his Poussins, his Willie Mayses and Bob Couseys, his Laurence Oliviers, Joan Sutherlands, Marilyn Monroes, Tennessee Williams, Bob Dylans and T. S. Eliots. He knew his architecture and he knew his Art, capital A Art, the serious stuff, respected-from-one-generation-to-the-next-until-the-sixties stuff. He knew his museums, where capital A Art was kept, had done a lot of awe-standing in them, especially in the Metropolitan Museum of Art, where the Coty Awards ceremonies were held and where he and Wilma, Marvin and Adele Bernstein had come that night in September, in the year of our Lord 1967, to stand in awe of Art and Aram LeGeis. The other thing he thought he knew was how the Coty Awards committee selected its winners—in theory and in practice—and why they selected, and were allowed to have, the Metropolitan for the night.

He swore to the others over drinks at the Hotel Stanhope before they crossed the street to go to the museum that it wasn't sour grapes, that he wasn't beating a dead horse to death all over again. It was just one of those funny paradoxes, ha-ha-ha, that's all, just another one to add to all the others in an already paradox-stuffed civilization. Fashion was, as Marvin well knew, big business, the biggest in New York City, one of the biggest in the country and maybe even in the whole Western world, to say nothing of how it was beginning to grow behind the Iron Curtain. Now even the Russians show designer clothes. Fashion was also supposed to be an art form. It depended on who you asked for an opinion: the Coty cosmetic company, the director of the museum, and Aram LeGeis, or himself. You can argue it either way, like everything else, he supposed. But, no matter how much you argued it, a few facts you have to start with. The Coty people must have figured they were contributing something to the world's harmony when they tied commerce to Art, sales promotion of new products to the best, most artistic, elegantly creative—that was the rub for him, that elegant crap—minds in the country. That's what they say they're doing, raising the fashion taste level of the country by recognizing designers of hats, shoes, lingerie, dresses, coats, make-up, everything, who have influenced the look and outlook of the American woman. Do you believe it? Don't, because who wins the awards? The stars from the couture market. Not that he was knocking them. They were all talented. That he wasn't arguing. But the real question was who did the influencing? Once, only once, did the committee give a joint award to eight young medium-priced designers who dress more American women in a year than all those guys do in ten years.

Getting a ticket to the Coty Awards was the kind of feat to inspire awe too. The guest list was restricted to former winners, the *Women's Wear Daily* editorial board, fashion-page editors of the New York and big-city press, fashion-magazine editors, no matter what price range they reported, women's news reporters from *Look, Life, Time,* sometimes the Mayor of New York, sometimes one of the Senators from New York, always, of course, the new winners and their friends, plus anyone, like Marvin, who had enough power to apply enough pressure to the right people at the Coty cosmetic company. The reason Marvin wanted to go was that Phil wanted to go. The last time Phil and Marvin had had dinner, Phil had talked about Aram and his career, about how they had started out together in the business, as friends, but how now you might say they were enemies, speaking enemies who hadn't spoken to each other since before

Phil's wedding. Not that Phil missed him or anything—he and Aram never saw anything eye to eye, especially about how to get ahead, how sex could help. Marvin had jumped for that bait, had somehow managed to get four tickets, had arranged the agenda for the entire evening: the drinks before and the night club afterward. Marvin wanted to have a good time. "So stop being so serious and let's go there already. Someday you'll win the Coty Award. I promise you. If anybody can, you can." A friendly squeeze of Phil's knee in full view of Adele and Wilma and they were off to the races.

The Metropolitan Museum by day is not a sight for sore eyes to rest on very long. In a city built to reach the sky, it is low-slung and long, stretching, like a Léger nude sprayed gray, in a series of massive rectangles and squares from Seventy-ninth to Eighty-forth streets. Its face and arms face Fifth Avenue menacingly. Its huge backside nudges the thinning foliage of Central Park. Its geometric torso presses heavily on the eroding soil there. It wasn't built for comfort but for Calvin, to overwhelm, to put a person in his place, once and for all, to make him know forever that Art is long and life is short, so why try to fight it? If you want to have a good time go up the avenue to the Guggenheim Museum, don't hang around here. At night it's different. Bright globes of light directed on its face soften the cruel, hard lines. It comes alive, is transformed into something a person might even love for a few hours.

But the possibility of love ends once one is inside. . . . Nevertheless, the two couples stopped to gawk for a few moments. The straining, washed-out light, the dappled marble floor of the circular entrance area, the distant, frosted-glass dome high overhead, the dirty gold-leaf arches, the filthy fluted columns stunned their senses. With awe, perhaps, but not the kind that swelled the spirit. Opposite them, on the bottom steps of the wide stone staircase that led up to the museum's prized Renaissance and Flemish galleries, Aram was being interviewed by CBS, NBC, and ABC television and being photographed by the press. The four of them scanned the dazzling crowd, heard the hollow, rising roar of talk and laughter in that vast space. They froze like statues all in a row: Phil, Wilma, Adele, Marvin; one, two, a leap to Adele, a giant step up to Marvin's head. They joined the general movement to the right, toward the Egyptian wing, past the lioness-ready-to-spring Sphinx of Queen Hat Shepsut, the wall of the tomb of Peri-Nebi, down a corridor lined with showcases of rare Egyptian jewels, to the Grace Rainey Rogers Auditorium whose entrance was guarded on the right by a statuette of Ha'py, a

Nile River god, and on the left by the head of an unknown official from who knows where, both pieces brushed against, ignored by chiffon, satin, and silk dresses, and black worsted evening suits.

The party of four had to split up inside. Tough luck, Marvin, Phil's shrug seemed to say to Marvin's departing hand, but what he really felt was relief, a wave of ease that could not be ruffled by the polite shouting around him, the cascades of elegant laughter, the zipper-mouthed, murdering "Darlings," "My dears," "Thrilling," "Divine gown." Wilma had told him he was tense when they left the apartment. He looked nervous, she said. He was, but he didn't tell that to Wilma. He had an intuition about the night. He was talking too much and Marvin was listening too much. They found seats down front.

"Love her, hate him." Wilma had to rest her head close to his ear to be heard.

"Don't hate the hand that feeds you." He craned his head from side to side, studying the notables, the powers, the ones he'd have to get to look his way if he was ever going to end up on that stage. They were all there, that committee of how many magazine editors? Wilma held on to his arm just as she'd been doing ever since they were married. So far, so good. She pulled him back. She steadied him. They were having a good time being married. They were eating home a lot more, going to the theatre a lot more, having sex a lot more and liking it. No sweat, no great strain, except for Marvin. Marvin made him nervous. Marvin made him tense. Marvin made him feel, not all the time, but now and then, how tough it was and what a toll it took to hide inside a lie. Marvin had told him one night in August about his appointments, had told him part, there was more he intimated, of what he did, had stopped an inch away from again asking Phil to do it too. "You've been around. You know the score. You've got a lot of designer friends. So if you're really a man of the world . . ." "Who said I was?" "You. You act like you know about everything." "Not everything, Marvin. Almost everything." "In that case you need to bring your education up to date very soon, my boy." And that's where he had stopped that night. But the rest was coming. All right, only not in front of Wilma. No monkey business in front of Wilma and Adele.

The mistress of ceremonies, Clara McDowd, fashion editor of *Look* magazine, emerged from behind the curtains at a corner of the stage and stepped up to a lectern. The packed house hushed respectfully. Good taste and good manners go together like museums and awe, like life and death in old English movies. The lights were lowered. Spotlights picked highlights in Miss McDowd's platinum Sassoon, flashed across, then steadied on the faces of the seated stars of the evening: Senator Jacob Javits, grinning, embarrassed; Aram LeGeis, his Edwardian tuxedo buttoned high beneath his double chin; Kobi, a naturalized male Japanese fur designer, thin, small, and scrutable; Patrick Proussé, award winner for creating a new series of luminous eye-liners which Coty produced; Alo Astrid Hecke, as cool, as tall, as thin and blonde as her Finnish name sounded, a shoe designer. A former winner, Rudi Gernreich, was receiving a return award, but he wasn't there.

Clara McDowd spoke of her pride, the thrill of being there with such illustrious people for such a marvelous reason in such a legendary place as the Metropolitan Museum, but it wasn't her pride alone, no, representing as she did all the editors on the committee who had worked so hard to arrive at a verdict—she giggled, alone—to arrive at an impartial judgment about this year's fashion leaders. . . . But she didn't want to take up precious time talking about that. The proof of that they would shortly see, and now, without further ado, they were honored to have with them . . . Senator Jacob Javits spoke for ten minutes about the role of design in American life, about style and life, about how good style produced a good life and how a good life made good style a desirable, a potent, peaceful weapon in the defense of the democratic system and how he hoped there would always be a Coty Award, just as he hoped there would always be Academy Awards, to honor these brilliant people—he pointed to them—who contributed so much to the realization of the American dream of peace and plenty for each and every American regardless of race or religion. Swelling applause, quiet, then he said he was sorry but he had to leave, he wished he could stay, another engagement, he was the loser, this time, because he knew how beautiful the show that followed would be. He rushed off the stage, bowing to everyone, smiling like anything but a loser.

The plaques, inscribed with year, name, category, Coty Fashion Award over a bronze cast of a curvaceous nude, were handed out, in ascending order of importance, by Clara. Aram was last. Aram was demure, self-effacing, said simply, accepting his award, thank you, one and all, for letting him know that what he tried to do meant something to someone else. Then there was a ten-minute film displaying Patrick Proussé applying eye-liner to Greta Garbo eyes, over and over, in brilliant color, which was followed by another ten-minute film of feet, a screen filled

377

with walking feet, wearing Alo Astrid Hecke's sandals and shoes that were called ugly shoes. Applause was the comma while the screen was raised, and then the curtain opened on a fur tableau and frozen, posing models in Kobi originals. The models, eight of them, moved in interweaving patterns, like the skins they wore, across the stage, removed the coats and jackets while the lights changed color, draped them on their shoulders, dragged them along the floor, returned to their frozen posing; the pieces of the tableau fell back into place, and then there was a blackout.

Aram had twenty minutes all his own. Sparkling, beaded gowns with pointed petal hems, tulip scalloped hems, and crushed chrysanthemums. A rose turned upside down and right side up in turquoise tulle. Murmured ah's and then a sigh for so much fantasy. Ten minutes of Rudi Gernreich's ladies' underwear, ten minutes of his knits, and that was that for 1967.

Applause was warmer now, here at the end, resounded, echoing from the warm blond- and brown-stained wooden walls of the auditorium. The audience rose, bursting to talk, decide, declare, to begin the polite, impatient pushing out of rows, to join the caterpillar movement up the aisle —Marvin and Adele were waiting for Phil and Wilma at the back—and out past the guarding Nile god statuette, to mill about and show themselves, their gorgeous gowns and jewels and falls and coils of imported Italian hair, before they were forced out of Egypt and Oriental tapestries into the center marble circle and the washed-out, straining light where they milled some more, waited for a sign from friends that they were right, that they should keep on going into the Greek and Roman wing. They started up again, heels tapping hurriedly now, voices hushed in the high-ceilinged corridor between sarcophagi. And Adele just had to stop and study them because when she was in Greece she had such an indescribably perfect time visiting the ruins. The ruins were everywhere there, they knew, and she met this young Greek artist and flew to Crete, with her daughters, what a place, beyond belief, and that's where Wilma and Phil must go on their next trip, to Athens, and those islands. Phil said no, he didn't think so, Greece and Spain were out for him, he couldn't enjoy himself when people were starving, but Adele went on about the islands anyway while Phil checked on the crowd behind him, recognizing, waving while he pretended to listen to Adele, watching Eugenia Sheppard, frail and powdered white in a beaded beige sheath, case the joint for *names* to highlight boldly in black, black print in her column, her eyes darting up and down, around at faces that were known to her as leaders of the fashion-social scene and others she might lead, if she felt like it, from the bottom to the top. And those islands, what color, Phil, what blue water. And of course Marvin couldn't be bothered traveling. He'd just as soon spend his life and every night traveling between Larchmont and the office. Didn't he look like an obelisk, really? Didn't he? "I warn you, Wilma," she took Wilma's arm, Marvin took Phil's and they joined the mainstream, "that if Phil won't go to Greece, won't take time off to go on trips anywhere, just anywhere, you should either get a divorce before you have any children or go away yourself, because you meet such interesting people anyway when you travel. You meet them, you get to know them, and then they're gone. It's marvelous. Nothing complicated . . ."

They passed the little statues of the young Greek boys with their pretty little pricks. The stream broke ranks, flanked the base of a massive column brought from an ancient temple to be placed before the entrance to the restaurant, a garden restaurant to come and rest in when Art was too much with you, where you could sit beneath the arch of palm fronds along the perimeter of a reflecting pool and eat and stare serenely at the statuary mirrored there, the Fountain of the Muses, the goddess Aganippe gushing water of inspiration for five other statues representing all the Arts. The five dripped magic water. The five were caught in fervent passage home, renewed, drunk with new songs to sing before the water trickled to a stop. A centaur and a faun looked on and watched enthralled, it seemed, as the Arts took wing and the champagne flowed freely from the makeshift bar in the corner of the restaurant. The food was light, party sandwiches. Help yourself. Help yourself to a table near the pool. Phil found one not too far from the bar.

Marvin managed the first round of champagne. Even he was drinking tonight. A special occasion. He'd be sorry, but he wasn't going to be a sour note. Wilma, Adele, and Marvin sipped. Phil gulped, went to get more, returned to stand, excited, surveying the circling mob, the knots of people near the bar, the women strutting, twirling, on display, like pop art, the men and half-men, half-women, like modern centaurs.

The air was spiked with piping sounds and shrieked phrases, what a pleasure to be here and see, be seen, how glorious it was to be a part of something truly grand, something that really mattered, and in a museum, in such a holy place, that was the only word for it, holy, it made a person feel such a strong sense of the past, like History and Art are alive again, living Art, as if everyone's a statue come alive, like Dionysus or someone, or Apollo, really, it's just too much, it takes the breath away, it does, it

379

really does.

The band began to play. Phil waved to some magazine girls, blew a kiss to Lovey Gray on the other side of the room. The band had to play louder. They played the new sound, the new beat, for the new winners who, bearing plaques, were mixing with the mixers, being kissed and patted. Wilma wanted to dance. She tugged at his sleeve. Marvin couldn't dance, he said, to that noise. He couldn't do those new dances. His daughters did them for him. Phil danced with Wilma and then he danced with Adele and then he bumped into Aram and brought Aram and his plaque over to the table to meet everyone, which was the thing for him to do and do quickly before he got drunk and defensive, because that was how he felt then, defensive, sliding back a little, he supposed, tonight, remembering Aram nostalgically, not the way it was, and those dumb years of Aram's friendship—he had to call it something. And it was a friendship of a kind that sprang from nothing but the neuter notion of himself as someone needing pushing, which was true in those days, which he hated to remember now as he introduced Aram to Marvin and Adele, and Aram kissed Wilma peckingly; he hated to remember how it was and what Aram made it mean; he hated Aram's winning anything because Aram's hand never fed him anything but hate, which fortunately, yes, fortunately he knew in time and bit it, bit it, the bastard. "Your clothes looked good, Aram. Very good." A chorus of confirmations and congratulations rose to join in greeting.

"Did you really think so? I thought the models were terrible. I tried to work with them before the show. They were so dull. . . . How do you enjoy being married, my dear? Is it *all* you thought it would be?" Aram grinned as his pear-shaped, buttoned body bent under the weight of his plaque. Adele reached out to handle and inspect it as if it were another precious work of art, another artifact to honor and adore. She passed it on to Marvin, who merely held it, felt it, his eyes occupied, his head cocked at a curious angle, watching Aram, then Phil, then Wilma, who waited patiently, between Marvin on one hand and Aram on the other.

"It's *all* I thought it would be, and more. Don't you think Wilma looks well?" Phil shouted, his voice cutting through the noise of the band, the squeals of laughter, the sliding, shuffling sounds of the dancers.

"As well as she always looks. A little fatter. I'm sure she's not pregnant. And you've gotten fatter too . . . Have you heard from Carl? I met him for drinks the other day. He wants me to do a line of gowns for him, to go back into some sort of business with. I'm tempted. He's gotten so terribly sad, you know. He misses you especially, still says you were the best thing in his life. The only one he ever really *cared* about."

Aram sought the eyes of everyone in turn, anticipating the effect his words would have. But Adele was staring off at a passing gown and Wilma, wounded—Phil saw that—seemed, nevertheless, as prepared for war as she always was. Only Marvin frowned openly. Aram's head swung back to him. He grinned, recognizing instantly something more than anger in that dark frown. Jealousy was there too, an instinct of protecting from invaders what was his.

Marvin stood up slowly, unwinding, toweringly big again, taller than anyone nearby. He stepped between Phil and Aram, touched, held onto Phil's shoulder, told him that what they needed was more champagne, that he and Phil should get it, as if he meant to save Phil that way, to be his bodyguard, to take care of Aram for insinuating himself where he wasn't wanted and wasn't needed, for souring this moment with words which Marvin didn't completely understand yet—that's what Phil read in those staring, sunken eyes—but which he knew could only mean bad news, news he would question Phil about later, don't worry about that, he would. By repeating his request for the champagne and saying that what they all needed was to get drunk, himself included, because this was a big night for Aram, and for Phil too, because in a few more years Phil would win one of those things if that's what he wanted, Marvin was trying to help. His lowered head close to Aram's now meant for Aram to move it, buster, to carry his shit and his plaque elsewhere, to scram, get lost, because he ate Aram's kind for breakfast, lunch, and dinner.

Phil took one giant step away from Aram, took two giant steps inside his head closer to Wilma, which she saw and understood. She smiled for his smile. She raised her empty glass to Aram—white teeth, white-on-white, radiant—screamed gladly, "Here's to you, Aram. I always knew you had it in you. You're a real artist—whatever that means. Carl can use *your* help, *tokah*. He needs a killer by his side."

"Thank you, Wilma, for your good wishes. Thank you one and all." Aram, unperturbed, retrieved his trophy, bowed, left for where he would be wanted, admired, respected, circled by sincere well-wishers on this night of nights.

His leaving left in its wake a swell of confusion, a silent moment, suspended out of time. No one moved. Phil felt as if all the secret parts of himself were suddenly surfacing, were going to ride the swell, out in the open now for everyone to see. He wasn't panicked. He wasn't humiliated.

His little life, what he knew of it, what he understood, was like a pebble floating and staying afloat on a great, rushing wave of certainty. Somehow he was going to make it to the shore safely. Wilma was still smiling at him. When he took hold of Marvin's arm then, a different kind of time began. "We'll get you ladies some more champagne."

On their way, Marvin stopped him. "Who's this Carl Kalb? What's he to you?" They were near the bar and being pushed and shoved. They were surrounded by a crush of bodies and tilting glasses.

"Come with me." Phil steered Marvin through channels lined with satin and chiffon gowns, out of the garden restaurant to the base of the Greek column at the entranceway.

Marvin leaned against the column, against the indifferent stone, just another person waiting for an honest answer.

"Carl Kalb and I had an affair years ago." No more parry and thrust. No more baiting and playing. Phil felt free, calm, the way he had felt that night with Paul when he announced he was getting married. "Carl Kalb was the one I mentioned at my first showing. Remember? The gray-haired man?"

"I remember." Marvin smiled, a real smile, not twisted to the side. Phil couldn't recall a smile like that on Marvin's face before. "So you finally got around to telling me."

"Telling you what? What didn't you know? You had to know, or at least you must have thought about it." Not all at once, not tonight, not here among the statues, tapestries and tombs where everyone was getting drunk on Art. No. In pieces. He would piece the story together in time, the honest story, the blood story, not his fairytale. Make believe wouldn't be necessary now, not with Wilma, not with Marvin. He would never have to live a Carl Kalb kind of life. Good old bitchy Aram. Another coincidence. Another manmade miracle. "Don't look so frightened, Marvin. Say something." But Marvin didn't seem to know what to say. He was relieved, but he was also embarrassed. He didn't want to stop being the leader, but his hands pressing against the column said he knew he was being led right now. He needed help too. He was a victim too, not a killer. And, Phil realized, whatever else Marvin was or wasn't, Marvin didn't wish him anything but well. He wasn't going to pick Phil apart with words or any other weapon anymore. He would just be trapped-in-his-own-shtik Marvin, working and wanting and waiting, rising above most people around him when he had to. Just as Phil would.

"You're the limit, Phil Hanssler, the top. And I love you like a . . . a brother. Does Wilma know about . . . that . . . part?"

"Don't stutter, Marvin. You're too big a man for that. She knows, but we've never talked about it, really. Now that it's a fact, we will. I won't have to lie to her. I can try to be as close as possible to the way I feel inside, the way I wanted to be before I met Carl."

"I'll tell you one thing, you're a lucky guy. If you can really talk to her, you're lucky."

"Can't you talk to Adele?"

"About what?"

"Come on, Marvin. This is no time to play games with me."

"It's not the same as with you. It's different. I'll tell you about it, but not now. Whatever it is, I can't talk to her about it. We live the way we live and I don't want that to change. Maybe I wouldn't have such bad ulcers though, if I could talk to someone."

"You can talk to me. You really can. I'll listen."

Marvin moved away from the column, his long arms coming to rest at his sides.

"You always tell me I'm a man of the world, Marvin. Well, I think I am, but I also think I'm learning tonight that my world is one step beyond your world. It's got new labels for the new ways people can live together. Wilma and I are going to be able to talk about what I do or don't do. My friend Howie used to say that it does help to talk about things to the right person, if you're lucky enough to find such a person. If not, you have to try and do it all by yourself, the way you've been doing. Now you're lucky. You found someone to talk to and someone who's making money for you. What could be better! A solid business and a friendship."

"It'll be the first time for me. And I'll promise you one thing. I'll never try to do anything to you that . . ."

"You don't have to promise, Marvin. I believe you, now that the air's been cleared." They stared at each other and then smiled. Marvin was decent. He could be trusted, not in the way Phil trusted Howie, but almost as much, and Phil felt good about that too. Together, they could shovel enough crap to the side of the road to keep on going. They could both win whatever there was to win. "Let's get the champagne or they'll begin to wonder what happened to us. Also, I'm hungry. And you better not drink anymore. Your stomach all right?"

"It's fine. Perfect."

Phil led the way back to the people and the party, to the noise and the smoke, to where the real battleground was, to where all honorable intentions were finally tested. The short leading the long for the moment, the little man and the big man, with differences that equalled, two stories with the same kind of ending, the same kind of ending that every story has, no matter how differently the people in them try to act them out.

Aram, still buttoned up, was twisting with Alo Astrid Hecke; their plaques, one on top of the other, rested on a nearby chair. Phil turned to Marvin. They stopped, watched, applauded, and moved on.

They carried champagne to their table, then they went for food. They drank and they ate and Marvin even asked Adele to dance, which made her choke on her chicken sandwich, but she got up and followed him to the dance floor. The five Arts gushed their magic waters of inspiration into the reflecting pool.

Liffey had been walked and now she slept, curled, content, on Wilma's pillow. Wilma's gown was hung on the back of the bedroom door. Phil's tuxedo, his dress shirt, bow tie, and black executive-length socks were piled on top of the swivel chair, whose back was toward them. Naked and above the cover, they lay in bed. The bed lamp was on. They weren't talking. All they did was look at each other, touch each other's faces and smile. Then Phil turned the light off. He kissed her. "I'm too tired to talk tonight. Tomorrow we will. I promise."

"I believe you. I'm too tired too." She kissed him. "Sleep well."

"You too. Pleasant dreams."

"Pleasant dreams to you, Mr. Jack by Phil Hanssler."

They laughed, kissed again, turned on their sides, their backs touching, and began the private, necessary business of falling asleep together.